Snowbound

Chris Phipps

Published by Eleven Jewels Publishing

This is a work of fiction. To create a sense of place, the upstate New York area is used as a backdrop. Other than public buildings and Belly's Mountain View Inn, the settings, characters, character names, and incidents are products of the author's imagination and experience or are used fictitiously.

Cover by Karen Phillips of Phillips Covers

ISBN 13: 978-0990914129
ISBN 10: 0990914127

This one is for Windy, Mark, and Christa

Who know what family is all about
and prove it, over and over again
each and every day

Acknowledgments

I'd like to thank the many people who helped bring this book to life:

Good friends and fellow writers Joli Roberts, Robin Rice, and Paddy Lawton, who read and critiqued the entire finished manuscript, ferreted out inconsistencies and errors and offered suggestions not only for fixing them, but for developing a better story;

Supportive fellow writers in my online Mystery Writers group, who caught any inconsistencies the other readers had missed and offered some great suggestions.

Christiana Bakarich, who did her usual great job of painstaking editing, and Winona Bakarich, who did the final read-through;

Karen Phillips for reading the manuscript of the first book in the series, *Love, Murder and a Good Bottle of Wine*, to get a feel for the characters, before offering suggestions for this cover, then working so hard to get it right.

Thanks to all of you, for making the book so much better than it might have been.

Chapter 1
Friday Morning

Sarah Wagner stood on tiptoe, her arms stretched as far overhead as they would reach, and silently swore. A line had formed behind her in the plane's aisle as she struggled to shove the bulky parka on top of the bags already crammed into the overhead compartment. This trip had been a miserable mistake.

"Here, let me."

Before she could turn to look, the man behind her reached over her head and pushed the dark blue parka into the bin.

"Thanks," Sarah said, as she slid into the window seat, and he moved on down the aisle. She had plenty of room, one of the few advantages of being small. She grabbed a pillow from the adjoining seat and stuffed it behind her back so her feet could touch the floor.

"Stealing my pillow?" A tall, wiry man dropped into the seat beside her. He had a deep, almost bass voice; dark, curly hair; and a matching, well-trimmed beard. His blue jeans were well worn, his cream-colored cable sweater a little newer.

"You don't look like you need it." Sarah motioned at his knees, jammed against the seat in front of him.

"And you do." He offered his hand. "Pete Bennett. And you're a tiny little thing."

She took the hand, which engulfed hers. "Sarah Wagner. And I'm not a thing."

His smile displayed a crooked front tooth. "My humble apologies, ma'am. You are most definitely not a thing."

He wasn't handsome; his face was too craggy and too large-featured, with a wide brow and thick black eyebrows above brown eyes. The grin, with the crooked tooth, was appealing, but what Sarah liked more was that, after a first glance, he'd kept his eyes on her face, not her chest. Some men seemed to have a problem doing that.

His attention wasn't on her now; he watched a couple with two little girls as they inched down the aisle. Not that there was much else to look at, other than the baggage handlers on the snow-slushed tarmac beneath her window, throwing bags onto the belt running into the luggage compartment. Had she wrapped enough clothing around the gift bottles of wine to avoid breakage? She'd packed only casual outfits—nothing dressy—but didn't want to wear merlot-stained jeans and sweaters all week.

If she stayed a week.

She turned away from the window. The man beside her still watched passengers, but not with the thoughtless glance of the casual observer. Eyes intense and assessing, he focused on each person for a minute or more, lingering just a fraction longer on the women. *Typical male.*

Right now, he was looking at a woman who was settling a little girl into a seat on the other side of the aisle, a few rows up. No, he wasn't watching the woman; he was studying the child. About six or seven, she had pale skin and long brown curls caught up in a ponytail. His gaze lingered, an odd, longing expression on his face. Sarah drew back into the corner of her seat until she was pressing against the window.

Perhaps sensing her observation, he turned toward her, and she almost flinched. But his eyes now showed nothing but mild curiosity.

"What takes you to Saranac Lake?"

"Oh." Her imagination was working overtime again. "A friend invited me to her vacation cabin for the week. Somewhere near Owl's Head, wherever that is."

"Kind of a girl's week out, hmmm? Just the two of you?"

Why was he asking? She'd already told him too much. But she couldn't let him believe she and Tracy would be alone in a remote cabin. He might know the area.

"No, Tracy's husband and children will be there, too."

One eyebrow raised, he asked, "What's his name?"

She hesitated, and he smiled. "I'm a native. Just thought I might know him."

"Greg." Better not give him their last name. She used the first one that came to mind. "Wheeler. Greg Wheeler."

Bennett looked at the ceiling for a few seconds. "I don't know any Wheelers." He turned back to her. "Where are you from?"

He smiled again, that open, friendly, crooked-tooth grin, and her own lips curved upward in response. She had to get over her distrust of men—something hard to do when the one you had loved and planned to spend the rest of your life with had betrayed you.

"Sacramento."

"You're a city girl then, not used to the kind of country you'll find up here. Heavily wooded, rough terrain. Cabins—a lot of them occupied only a few weeks of the year. Rented out to vacationers."

"I've never considered myself a city girl. Sacramento isn't San Francisco. It doesn't have much of a skyline. It sprawls, and there are still acres of farm land, vineyards and wineries around it." A surge of homesickness washed over her. But she couldn't go back. Not yet.

"Sounds nice." He tilted his head back and closed his eyes.

The plane had lifted off the runway, and Sarah turned back to the window. The sunlight glinted off the buildings below, its rays trying to find their way into Boston's bustling snow-lined streets, so different from those at home.

That's how Tracy had convinced her to make this trip: Sarah's homesickness and the chance to get out of the gray and bleak winter streets of New York City.

"It's wooded and green," she'd told Sarah. "The cabin is big, but it's fairly remote, so there's lots of room, both inside and outside."

Remote, indeed. If she'd known how long this trip would take, she wouldn't have come. An hour and eight minutes from New York to Boston, an hour and twenty minutes on the ground, and another hour and thirty-five minutes from Boston to Adirondack Airport. Four hours and three minutes, plus the drive to the cabin. She could have flown Jet Blue home to Sacramento in five hours and eight minutes. The lump in her throat swelled, and it hurt to swallow.

She'd almost turned down this invitation. She didn't know Tracy's husband or daughters—hadn't even known Tracy that long. If Sarah and the family didn't click, it would be a long week. But she had spent a miserable Thanksgiving and an even more miserable Christmas in New York, thinking about her friends and family back home. It was time to push herself to make new friends, and a week in the snow should be fun.

An announcement came from the pilot: they'd reached thirty-five thousand feet. There was now nothing outside the window but gray-tinged sky and clouds, so Sarah turned her attention back to the plane's interior. Bennett was again studying the little girl, that odd expression on his face, and a cold shiver crept up Sarah's spine.

The flight attendant would think she was crazy if she asked to change seats. She pulled the Kindle from her purse and tried to read, but even Jeremy Robinson's *SecondWorld* couldn't distract her. Well into the sixth page, she had no idea what she'd just read.

If she put it away, Bennett might be encouraged to renew the conversation, so she scrolled back to the first page, started over, and finally managed to immerse herself in the story.

A flight attendant pushed a cart down the aisle, offering drinks. Bennett ordered a beer and raised his eyebrows at Sarah. She shook her head and went back to her book.

Several chapters later, a sentence jumped out at her, bringing a memory of Dave Wheeler.

Why, of all the last names she could have given Bennett, had she chosen Dave's? While there had been a strong attraction between them, neither had ever acted on it, mostly—at least on her part—because she had still been staggering through those last weeks of her disastrous marriage to Scott.

She'd left all that behind in California. So why couldn't she let it go?

A bustle of activity in the cabin told her they'd be landing in a few minutes.

"You're deep in thought. Thinking about home?" Bennett asked.

She focused on the text displayed on the Kindle, ignoring him. Bennett repeated his question.

She let her head jerk a little, then looked up, widening her eyes. "What? I'm sorry, did you say something?"

"Yeah, you just seemed so deep in thought, I was wondering if you were thinking about home."

"Yes, I suppose I was." She put the Kindle in its case and slid it into her purse.

The flight attendant announced their arrival at Adirondack Regional Airport, and the seat belt sign dinged off. Sarah unfastened hers and reached for her purse, under the seat ahead. When she turned back toward Pete Bennett, he was holding out a small, folded piece of paper. "If you have any free time while you're here, I'd love to show you around. Maybe have a drink, or even dinner, at Belly's. It's a well-known restaurant in Mountain View, just a few miles from Owl's Head."

Sarah pushed his arm away. "No, I'm sorry, I'm not—"

"Maybe when you get back to the city, then?" He dropped the paper into the pocket of her loose-fitting navy blazer and rose to his feet. "Keep it for a while. You never know. You may get cabin fever, feel hemmed in, or just need to get out for a while."

They pushed into the aisle, along with the rest of the passengers. He pulled her parka from the overhead compartment and handed it to her. "Is somebody picking you up, or are you renting a car?"

"Renting." Tracy had offered to pick her up, but Sarah enjoyed driving and wanted her own transportation, especially for this trip, just in case she decided to cut her visit short.

"I'll walk with you," Bennett said. "I know the way."

"That's all right. I have to get my luggage—"

"Me, too. It's this way." He led her to the carousel.

His scuffed, sage-green duffel bag arrived first. Maybe he would take it and leave. No, he dropped it to his side and waited.

"Which one is yours?" He wasn't going away.

"The one with the tapestry-print, coming toward us."

He reached for the handle, but she stepped in front of him and grabbed it. She shoved the parka into the space between the suitcase top and handle and started walking, following the car rental signs. He fell into step alongside her, then waited in line behind her while she argued with the agent.

"I don't want an SUV. Don't you have anything smaller? With snow tires?"

The agent shrugged. "That's what most people around here want, and all we have left that isn't reserved. I've got a Highlander and a Subaru."

At least it wasn't a Ford Explorer; she never wanted to drive another of those. She would take the Highlander, just because it was a Toyota, and she had a yellow Corolla back in California, stored in a garage because she couldn't bear to part with it.

"Good choice," the agent said. "All-wheel drive, good in snow and ice and rough terrain. Get you where you want to go."

It took her a few minutes to program the navigation system and pull the seat all the way forward. Pete Bennett, reflected in the rear-view mirror, was standing beside a gray Subaru. He had just lifted his bag into the back and stood watching Sarah—observing, the same way he'd watched the women on the plane. Not quite as creepy as his observation of the little girl, but strange and unsettling. What was he thinking? *I probably don't want to know.*

Sarah sat back, flexing her shoulders to relieve the tension that had built in the last couple of hours, then finished adjusting the mirrors and fastened the seat belt. Pete Bennett still stood by the door of his rental, looking toward her. She punched the accelerator pedal. Tires squealed as the car shot out of the lot.

The unfamiliar vehicle and terrain demanded all her attention during the first part of the drive, but by the time she turned onto the Port Kent-Hopkinton Turnpike, she began to notice her surroundings. Nothing but white, as far as she could see through the falling snow.

She glanced in the rear-view mirror several times, half expecting to see the Subaru. But the light snow made visibility poor, and he wouldn't have followed right behind her.

She was getting paranoid. Why would he follow her? But his observation of the little girl and the way he'd behaved in the parking lot...She checked the mirror again.

Slushy snowflakes fell onto the windshield, prompting her to find the control for the wipers. She had little experience driving in conditions like this, other than a trip or two across the Sierra Nevadas several years ago, from Sacramento to Reno, when the snow removal crews couldn't keep up with the storm. But the turnpike had recently been plowed, and it wasn't far, once she reached her exit. *I just hope it doesn't snow like this all week.*

She fiddled with the radio, browsing for a weather station, and picked up a local news announcer with an ongoing story. A forty-two-year-old man serving a life sentence for murder had escaped the night before from Upstate Correctional Facility, a maximum-security prison in Malone, and had not yet been captured.

Malone? Wasn't that close to where she was going? Yes, that was the town Tracy had suggested she fly into, eleven miles from Owl's Head. A small airport, with only two asphalt runways, it had a charter service direct to New York City.

"It's the best way to get to the cabin," Tracy had told her. "It's just as comfortable as first class, and it's a direct flight, without all the hassle of baggage checking and security."

She'd almost done it—had her hand on the telephone to make the arrangements—but still reluctant to squander blood money, had instead booked the longer commercial flight in coach.

"It's not blood money," her cousin Laura had said, sounding exasperated, probably because she'd repeated it more than once. "It's an inheritance. Caro wanted us to have it."

"But we got it only because Caro was murdered, didn't we?"

Sadness had filled Laura's eyes. "Not spending the money isn't going to bring her back."

"I know that." Nothing was going to bring their young aunt back to her. And Sarah was using some of the money to pay her way until she could get her certification in graphic design and find a job. But she couldn't enjoy the money the way Caro had, traveling and entertaining. That would be stepping into Caro's shoes, living her life. Sarah couldn't even live in the house Caro had left her, much as she loved it. At least, not yet.

She glanced at the dashboard clock. One fifteen. The news announcer hadn't said what time the prisoner had escaped the night before, but, with the rough terrain and on foot, he could have easily traveled eleven miles by now. He might be somewhere in the surrounding area.

The car doors were locked, the gas tank full. There would be no reason to stop before she reached her destination. *I hope the cabin has good, strong locks.*

She turned right onto Pond Road, which had a thin coating of snow. At least it wasn't ice. A few miles farther, she was on Paquin Road, then Barnsville. More snow coated the pavement now. The lanes were becoming narrower, the turns sharper, the snow deeper, but she must be getting close to the cabin. And with this many roads, it wasn't that remote—not by northern California standards.

Despite the advance notice from the navigation system, visibility was so poor she almost missed the next turn—the one to the cabin. She braked, backed up a few feet, and turned into the narrow lane. The car bumped along, the road getting rougher, and Tracy's warning came back to her: "Your GPS may tell you to take the wrong road—the one just before ours. Don't take it. Ours has a sign with our name on it. The other one used to loop around into the back of our property, but it's a dead end now. The bridge has been out for a long time, and if you go that far, there's not enough room to turn around."

Sarah stopped. She sat still for a few minutes, staring out at the snow, falling faster and thicker now. She'd have to back out, following her own car tracks to make sure she stayed on the road. And she'd better do it quickly, before the tracks filled with snow.

Maneuvering in reverse was slow going, and as she inched along, the tracks became more indistinct. While applying slightly more pressure to the accelerator, she raised her body from the seat to get a better view out the back window.

The Highlander hit a bump. A little off balance, she pressed too hard on the gas pedal. The vehicle lurched toward the side of the road. She hit the brake, but the Highlander's right rear wheel had already dropped off the edge.

She shifted out of reverse and touched the accelerator with a light foot. The tire howled as it spun, but the vehicle didn't move. She switched to all-wheel-drive and tried again. It didn't help. Sighing, she turned off the ignition and lowered her head onto the steering wheel. *I hate SUVs.*

She sat still, peering into the trees closing in on both sides of the narrow road. Would they seem as ominous if she didn't know about the escaped convict? She checked the doors again to make sure they were locked and called Tracy's cell phone.

Nobody answered.

Chapter 2
Friday Afternoon

arah sat in the Highlander for more than half an hour, but Tracy never answered her phone or returned Sarah's messages. Where could she be? Sarah had sent her the flight number and arrival time. Maybe Tracy's phone was off, and she just wasn't aware.

Shivering, Sarah pulled the parka around her shoulders; the car's interior had cooled quickly. Starting the engine would warm it, but what was the point? She couldn't do that indefinitely, and nobody was going to come along this abandoned road—with the possible exception of the convict.

She called Tracy one more time. No answer.

Casting nervous glances toward the thick forest, Sarah climbed out, shrugged her arms into the parka, and knelt to brush snow away from the tire. It had settled into a deep rut. She looked around for something solid to lay in front of it, to keep it from digging deeper when she drove out. There was nothing visible.

The back of the Highlander's interior, pristine as a freshly-vacuumed hotel room, held only her suitcase. A search of the floor turned up a cubby, hidden under the carpet. She pulled out a lug wrench, assessing its potential as a weapon. It was solid enough to do some damage to an attacker if she got close enough. Not ideal, but probably better than one of the wine bottles. Not that she could discount them; she'd fought off an attacker once before with only a wine bottle as a weapon.

The cabin couldn't be more than a mile or two away, down the next turn. With the possibility of an escaped convict nearby, she couldn't stay in the Highlander. Leaving it wasn't a good option, either, but she had to get to safety. The vehicle would be an open invitation to a man needing transportation out of the area and, unlike her, he wouldn't be afraid to go into the forest to search for something to put under the tire.

She tried to ignore another unsettling fact. A hostage might be useful.

Best leave the bag for now. The wheels would probably dig into the snow, and she might have to run. Once she was safe, Tracy's husband could bring her back to get the car and suitcase.

If she could find the cabin before dark.

If she made it to the cabin.

But suppose the car was stolen? Her bag would be gone, too, leaving only the purse, with her wallet, tickets, and a small makeup kit. And the wine was in the suitcase. She had a feeling she was going to need that merlot. If she was going to abandon it, she'd just as well wait until she had no other choice. And maybe she wouldn't have to run.

Slinging her purse over one shoulder, she grabbed the suitcase and set off, the lug wrench gripped in the other hand. She'd gone only a few yards when the small wheels of the bag, designed for smoother surfaces, dug into the snow and jerked her to a stop. She tugged at the suitcase, trying to lift it free, but it was caught on something under the snow. Casting nervous glances at the trees, she set the lug wrench on the ground, lifted the bag and straightened its wheels, then grabbed the wrench and set off again.

A few yards farther along, the wheels caught again, and she had to put the wrench aside to straighten them. Fighting panic and fumbling fingers, she finally got it righted.

She reached the main road, and snow still fell, filling the tracks behind her. It was going to be a long mile and a slow one.

She should abandon the bag, but not just yet. It was pulling a little easier now. Maybe she had the hang of it.

The wheels caught again, jerking her to another stop.

She really, really had to leave it. But a wide space ahead suggested a road, possibly the way into the cabin. She slogged on.

Under different circumstances, she might have turned in a slow circle, taking in the Christmas-card scene: a white velvet cloak laid gently over the ground, soft folds draping over dead logs and uneven terrain; tree branches hung with icicles. But silence engulfed her, and the falling snow and gray skies hid whatever lay behind the deep shadows in the trees. With every branch that cracked from the weight of the snow, every animal movement that snapped a twig, her heart pumped a little faster, and her breath caught.

I have to take a break, have to rest. She ached with fatigue, and her legs felt like overcooked spaghetti. She brushed wet hair away from a cold cheek. If she could stop, maybe get the knit cap out of the suitcase, sit on the case for just a minute—No, the trees pressed too close.

These woods were exactly the kind of place where the convict might try to disappear. He would have studied maps, planned his escape. What had the man on the plane—Pete Bennett—said? Something about the number of empty cabins in the area. Perfect places to hide. The convict could be in the woods now, out of sight, waiting.

She pushed on, each step a little shorter, until finally, there was a sign on the right side of the road, snow piled across the top. She brushed it off with a gloved hand, exposing "Agerton," carved into the wood.

Thank you, God.

She turned, watching the bag to make sure it followed smoothly.

Only a few yards into the lane, a man's voice jolted her to a stop. Her arm jerked, yanking the suitcase sideways, before the sounds distilled into words:

"Come on, Gracie, hurry up!"

She'd found the cabin, and suddenly, her rubbery legs almost folded. But this was not the time to collapse. The cabin stood at the end of a long lane. She still had to get to it. She kept moving, taking one slow step after another, until a man and two little girls came into view, putting the finishing touches on a big snowman. She trudged toward them, details coming into focus as she came closer. The snowman was a little lopsided, with the bottom too big for the top, and was wearing a strange wooden hat with a square brim. It looked like it might be some kind of bird-feeding station with a ledge around it. She smiled. A snowman that fed birds. Clever.

The man took a red scarf from one of the girls. As he wound it around the snowman's thick neck, the child noticed Sarah dragging the suitcase toward them and tugged at the man's coat sleeve.

"Daddy."

Pushing a lock of dark-brown hair away from his face, he turned and stared at Sarah, then past her. She almost turned her head to look. Was the convict behind her?

The man's gaze shifted back, but he didn't speak until she was within a few feet of them.

"You're Sarah? Sarah Wagner?"

"Yes, I—"

Twin lines formed between his eyes as his focus shifted between her, the suitcase, and the lug wrench. "How did you get here?"

Heat rose up Sarah's neck. In hindsight, bringing the suitcase seemed ridiculous—pulling it through the snow when help was so close by. But hindsight was always wiser than its distant cousin, forethought. Too bad their order couldn't be reversed; it would save so much trouble and embarrassment.

"I...my car—"

"Where's Tracy?" His gaze again moved beyond her before coming back to settle on her face, the frown deepening.

"Tracy? I...isn't she here? I thought—"

"She went for a walk. To meet you on your way in." He took a few steps toward her. "I'm sorry. I've forgotten my manners." He held out a hand. "I'm Greg."

For some reason, Sarah had pictured Tracy Agerton, barely five feet tall, with a man nearer her own height. Greg was close to six feet.

Sarah released her grip on the suitcase and took his hand. "She went for a walk? They must have caught the guy, then?"

His expression suggested Sarah might be a little unhinged. He glanced at the suitcase and her makeshift weapon again, then back at her. "I'm sorry. What guy?"

The girls stared at her, the older one open-mouthed. Sarah hesitated, then nodded toward them before she responded. "Maybe we should talk somewhere else?"

The puzzled frown deepened as he followed her gaze. "Oh. Lottie, Gracie, go on inside, will you?" He watched while the older girl took the hand of the younger one and walked to the door, looking back over her shoulder. Greg turned to face Sarah. "What's this all about?"

"A convict. I heard about it on the radio on my way here. An escapee from the maximum-security prison at Malone. They said he might be anywhere in the area, and he's dangerous, serving a life sentence."

His eyes widened and his mouth dropped open.

"Good God! We didn't know. I hadn't heard. Tracy! You didn't see her on your way in?" He shook his head. "No, of course, you didn't, or she'd be with you. I thought it was taking her too long. I've got to call her." He grabbed the suitcase. "Come on, get in the house." He followed Sarah inside, dropped the bag on the floor, and locked the door.

"Stay here while I check the rest of the rooms—make sure everything is locked." Taking two treads at a time, he raced up the stairs.

How did he think the convict could get up to the second floor? Surely not with a ladder he carried around with him, and Sarah doubted the cabin had fire escapes. Maybe close-growing tree branches? No, Greg was just rattled, not thinking clearly. But maybe with good reason, if Tracy had crossed the path of a dangerous, hunted man.

"You have pretty hair."

Sarah looked down at the younger of the two girls. "Yours is, too. I like your braids. What's your name?"

"Her name is Gracie, and I'm Lottie," the other girl said and, as though marshaling all the information a visitor might need, added, "Gracie's six, and I'm ten. If we went to school, she'd be in first grade, and I'd be in fifth."

"You don't go to school?"

"Not now. Not regular school. Mom home schools us." Her bottom lip quivered. "I wish we still went, though, so I could see Emma. But Mom says we can have play dates when we get back home. After vacation."

They didn't look like sisters, and neither had inherited Tracy's small frame. Gracie's coloring—long, dark-brown hair and milk-chocolate eyes—was more like Greg's, while Lottie had her mother's cat-green eyes. The girl's hair was much lighter than Tracy's, though—straight, and that tow-head childhood color of natural blondes.

"Is Mom lost or something?" Lottie asked.

"It may just be taking her longer to get back than she expected. It's snowing pretty hard."

"But she said we could make cupcakes before dinner, and now it's gonna be too late."

"You got to make a snowman, though, a really big one. And maybe you can make cupcakes tomorrow."

"Daddy did most of it," Gracie said.

Of course, he did. That's what daddies do. At least, most of them. Sarah wouldn't know.

Or maybe she did. There was something behind that murky wall which hid every childhood memory of her father. She had warm memories of her mother from those years, so it was just her father she'd blocked out. The therapist she'd gone to in August didn't actually tell Sarah he suspected abuse. He didn't have to; his expression and follow-up questions said it all. But he was wrong. That wasn't it. She couldn't have told him how she knew her father hadn't abused her; she didn't even try, and left after a few sessions. He wasn't helping with the real problem, the reason she'd gone to him: nightmares that woke her, soaked in sweat, her hammering heart keeping rhythm with her strangled whimpers of fear.

She knew the source of the nightmares, had even known her attacker. She had seen his picture and had a brief prior encounter with him. But in her nightmares, the face was always that of her ex-husband Scott or her father.

She shivered, and Lottie asked, "Are you cold?"

"Um...yes, I guess I am," Sarah was also wet and tired, but with her worry over Tracy, none of that had registered once she was inside the cabin.

As she looked around the room now, her first impression was of darkness: knotty-pine ceilings and walls, the latter in a vertical pattern. The gloom was mitigated somewhat by banks of tall windows, but this late in the afternoon, with snow still falling, little daylight entered.

The downstairs portion was one huge room, at least forty-five by thirty, maybe bigger. A fireplace faced the front door, with the kitchen and dining area on the left, and the living room, stairs, and small bathroom on the right.

Greg bounded down the stairs and hurried toward her. "Everything is locked up. Tracy's not answering her phone. I'm going to call—" He glanced at the girls. "Why don't you two go up and get out of those wet clothes, and then maybe Sarah will make you some hot chocolate."

"We already had hot chocolate, Daddy, remember?" Gracie said. "When Mom called us in—"

"You're right, we did. I forgot. And that wasn't very long ago. Too soon to have chocolate again, isn't it?" His voice trailed off, his gaze drifting to the shadowed kitchen, then across to the tall windows facing the dining table and chairs, and finally, back to the phone gripped in his hand. "You still need to get those wet clothes off. Lottie, can you help Gracie with hers?"

He didn't speak again until the girls had reached the top of the stairs. "I'm calling the sheriff," he said, his voice low. Punching in numbers, he walked away from her, toward a small, bumped out laundry area beside the kitchen.

Sarah waited, looking around the room. Most of the living room was on one side of the stairs, with a small alcove on the other.

Greg's voice rose, drawing her attention back to the laundry room. He stood beside a washer or dryer, his free hand curled into a fist. Tension crept into Sarah's shoulders, and she rubbed the back of her neck. *Where are you, Tracy? And why aren't you answering your phone?*

Sarah pulled out her own phone. She could text Laura while she waited, let her cousin know she'd arrived safely. Laura would be waiting for the message. But before Sarah could use it, Greg was back. He stared at the phone. "What are you doing?"

"Texting my cousin, to let her know I got here okay." What was wrong with him? He still studied the phone, almost as though it were a loaded gun aimed at him.

"I'm sorry, I didn't mean to startle you. It's just...we keep ours locked up most of the time. Because of Lottie. We had to take hers away from her. She likes to play with phones, and we've had some mammoth bills—Hong Kong, Australia, Bali, you name it. And there's the danger. Not just in the calls, but in some of the sites she's visited. She doesn't understand, but it scares us, not knowing who she might connect with, and all the pedophiles out there." He motioned toward the phone. "So I'd appreciate it if you'd keep yours where she can't get her hands on it."

"Oh." Sarah slid the phone into her pocket. Just one more thing she didn't know about children and the dangers they might face. But at ten? That seemed so young.

Greg strode to one of the big windows in an alcove at the front of the cabin, his phone at his ear, and stared out into the darkness.

"She's still not answering. The sheriff says they haven't found the convict. The entire force is out looking for him, along with a lot of volunteers, including the fire department. He says they're already stretched thin, and we can't even be certain Tracy's missing."

"But if she was supposed to meet me, and she's nowhere between—"

"He says she hasn't been gone long enough. She might just be taking a longer walk than expected."

"I should think, with the danger—a convict on the loose—"

"He says he'll try to find somebody and send them out if she's still not back in a few hours."

"A few hours!"

"Yeah." He punched at his phone again. "Even without the convict..." He shook his head. "Even if we didn't have him to worry about, she could freeze before we find her."

He stared at the phone, probably willing Tracy to answer. "Something's happened to her, or she would answer her phone. She should have met up with you on the road. She never stays out this long—not on foot, with it snowing." He ran one hand through his dark hair and punched at the cell phone again.

"I might have missed her," Sarah said. "Not been on the road while she was there, I mean. I took a wrong turn on the one just before yours and got my car stuck."

He lowered the phone. "And you walked from there? How long—" His brow creased, and his eyes narrowed in concentration. "There's an old road we don't use any more down by the washed-out bridge, which leads back here. It's more like a footpath now."

"I didn't go that far. I realized I'd taken a wrong turn and backed out. At least, I tried. My car—"

"The footpath! She may be somewhere on it. Sometimes she goes that way, and she might have planned to walk to the bridge, then take the road on out to meet up with you. If she fell, twisted an ankle or something, nobody would ever find her on that abandoned road. I've got to go."

"But the convict...if he's out there, he's dangerous, and you'll be all alone."

"Which is why I have to find her." He patted a bulge in the right pocket of his heavy coat. "I have a gun, and I'll use it if I have to." He took several strides toward the back door. "Lock it when I leave, and—"

The closing door cut off his words, but there wasn't much more to hear. She would take care of the girls; she wouldn't open the door to anybody but him or the police. But it would be nice if she at least knew where to find her room; she needed to change her snow-soaked clothing.

Chapter 3
Friday Evening

T
he warmth radiated by burning logs, along with the faint scent of wood smoke, drew Sarah to the fireplace, a massive rock structure with a carved mantel of dark wood. She took off her parka and stretched her fingers toward the flames as she looked around.

The cabin was not the remote, rustic dwelling she'd envisioned, but an upscale vacation home. The alcove where Greg had stood was a seating area—two armchairs, separated by a small, round table—between the little bathroom and a bank of bookcases lining the entry wall.

The chairs faced a window overlooking a distant lake. A nice place to sip a glass of wine—especially if she had Laura with her. It was an intimate setting, with a lovely view. But tonight the windows were too big, too close. How hard would it be to break one of them and climb inside? Even if that weren't likely, if they were made of some kind of shatter-proof glass, they made her feel too exposed, vulnerable to whomever might be out there, watching.

She turned back toward the fire, whispering a little prayer for Tracy, and shivered again. She had to get out of her wet clothes.

Lugging her suitcase and the wrench, she climbed the stairs. Bringing the bag with her didn't seem quite as ridiculous now. Who knew when she'd get the Highlander out?

When she reached the landing, Lottie's and Gracie's voices drifted toward her, coming from the far end of the hallway. As she walked toward them, she passed a large room on the right with a pair of men's slippers on the braided rug by the bed. Opposite that room, on her left, was another, this one vacant, with a queen-size bed covered in a machine-made quilt and shams.

Assuming it was hers, Sarah rolled the suitcase inside, set the lug wrench on top of it, and walked down to the room the girls occupied, on the same side of the hall as hers.

They sat on a braided rug, pulling on woolen socks to match their sweaters, Lottie's purple, Gracie's pink. They looked up when Sarah paused at their door.

"Am I supposed to be in the first room, the one that's empty?" She tilted her head toward the stairs, "Or the one across the hall from you?"

Gracie giggled. "That's the junk room. Nobody sleeps in there."

"Yours is the first room," Lottie said, "by the top of the stairs. Mom put clean flannel sheets on the bed last night and hung some towels up for you in the bathroom." Her face turned solemn. "Did they find her yet?"

"Your dad just left a few minutes ago, so he hasn't had much time. But I'm sure he'll find her. He thinks he knows which direction she went."

Lottie studied Sarah with the frank appraisal of a child. "Are you and my mom best friends?"

Sarah considered the question. She and Tracy had just been classmates at first. Then, during their first real conversation, there had been a connection, perhaps a recognition of kindred souls.

"I hope we will be. We haven't known each other very long, but we sort of clicked right away. We decided two women as small as we are should stick together. I think that's why she invited me to come and meet all of you."

Lottie nodded, a quick little tip of her chin, like she under-stood how friends were made and that they should stick together.

Sarah glanced around the room. Each side contained a twin bed and dresser. A wide bookcase divided them. The furniture was white, the quilts red and white, and gauzy white curtains hung at the windows. The shelves held dozens of books, separated by stuffed animals. Drawing pads, puzzles, and boxes of crayons and colored pencils were stacked neatly at one end. She would have to examine the books. Everything else was so generic, she got little sense of the girls' individual interests.

Lottie and Gracie were close to the same ages as Eric and Jamie, her cousin's little boys, and Sarah always had fun with them, but girls might not be as eager to build forts or learn back flips. Besides, she'd never attempted gymnastics in the snow.

"What do you say I get out of these wet clothes, and we go down and start making those cupcakes? I think dinner's going to be late, and maybe we can have them for dessert."

Gracie uncrossed her legs and rose to her feet in one quick, fluid movement. Lottie sat still, with that same appraising look focused on Sarah, whose only credentials were a budding friendship with their mother, who hadn't been there to introduce them.

Sarah smiled at the girl and held out a hand. Lottie hesitated, before taking it.

"Okay. I'll go get the cupcake pans and stuff."

Sarah went to her room. It had an adjoining bathroom. Nice. She wouldn't have to share with the girls. They must have one, too.

She changed into jeans and a blue sweatshirt and looked around for a place to leave the phone. There were no drawers with locks, and the bedrooms were all close together. It would probably be safer to keep the phone with her. She slid it into her jeans pocket, put her purse in a drawer, and stashed the lug wrench on the shelf in the top of the closet.

She didn't have much to unpack. It could wait until later, when she came up to bed. Taking the wet pants and shirt, she went down to the laundry room.

The bumped-out area was well designed, with shelves above the granite counter for laundry supplies and tools. The opposite wall held a bench for boots and shoes, with pegs above holding an assortment of coats and jackets. A food freezer occupied the space beside it. Hooks on each side of the exit door held snowshoes and other outdoor equipment. A stack of firewood decorated the corner.

She stood for a moment at the door, looking out through the small pane. Trees with icy white trunks and limbs bordered a white expanse of back yard, with deeper, darker forest beyond. Was Tracy in there somewhere? In those dense trees, with all the snow? Lying hurt, unable to move, slowly freezing to death?

Maybe she wasn't cold at all, but in a warm cabin with a killer, gagged and shackled to a chair. Or worse.

Imagining the worst scenarios wasn't helping. *But how do I turn it off and think about something else?* Sarah sighed and turned back toward the big room.

The girls sat on stools at a granite counter facing the kitchen, with a mixing bowl and a box of cake mix in front of them.

"What kind of cupcakes are we making?" Sarah asked.

Gracie held up the box. "Chocolate. With chocolate frosting."

"To match your beautiful chocolate-colored eyes and hair? What about you, Lottie? Vanilla to match your hair, and chartreuse-colored frosting?"

"What's a chartreuse?" Gracie asked.

"It's almost the color of Lottie's eyes. A pretty yellow-tinted green. Almost like a cat's."

That finally got a smile from Lottie. Gracie said "yuk," and both girls giggled.

"Then we'll have to do strawberry-vanilla with gray frosting, to match your hair and eyes," Lottie said to Sarah, the corners of her eyes crinkling.

Gracie made a face. "Yuk. No gray frosting. Or cake, either."

By the time Greg returned, the kitchen counter held a tray of cupcakes, Sarah was taking another pan out of the oven, and the aroma of fresh-baked cake filled the room.

"Where's Mom?" Lottie asked, her voice rising a little as he closed the door behind him, shutting out the cold draft. He took off his coat and hung it on a hook before answering.

"I don't know, Lottie, but we're going to find her." He patted her shoulder as he sidled past, on his way to the coffee pot. "Why don't you take your sister upstairs for a few minutes, and let me talk to Sarah?"

"I don't want—"

"Charlotte."

Lottie lowered her head, tensing her jaw. "I want to know about Mom. It's cold out there, and if she's lost—" Tears slid down her cheeks. Greg reached toward her, but she pulled away.

His jaw clinched, and a twinge sparked deep in Sarah's memory, then died, smothered before it came to life. It wasn't a new sensation, but one she hadn't experienced recently, and she didn't welcome it.

Greg spoke softly. "I know, Lottie. I'm worried, too. But the best thing you can do right now is to do what Sarah asks and help take care of Gracie, so I can keep looking for Mom. Okay?"

Lottie nodded and wiped a hand across her cheek. "I just don't know why I have to go upstairs."

"And I don't know why you can't do what I ask without so many questions. I get it. You're worried, but I am, too, and I'm also very tired and frustrated. And sometimes, Lottie, grownups need to talk about things that aren't meant for small children to hear." He tilted his head toward Gracie. "So please take your sister upstairs, like I asked."

"Then can I come—"

"No. Not until I call you."

Lottie slid off her stool and waited for Gracie to clamber down from hers. Taking her little sister's hand, she flashed an angry look at Greg before leading Gracie away.

"Sorry about that," Greg said. "Lottie can be stubborn, and I don't have the patience to deal with her right now."

He poured a cup of coffee and took a sip. "Good. And I needed it. I'm about frozen."

He looked out the kitchen window. "I can't figure out why I can't find her. The snow might have filled in her tracks, but she couldn't have gone far. I thought she might hear me if I yelled loud enough, so I called until I was hoarse. Nothing. With her not answering her phone, the only thing I can think of is, she must have fallen, been knocked out. And if we don't find her, I don't know how long she can survive. Do you think..." His voice trailed off, and he looked into the depths of his cup. "Would you keep calling her, too? If she's unconscious, the sound of the phone ringing might bring her around." He shrugged. "I know it's a long shot, but it's about all I have, besides searching."

"Of course, I will. Anything I can do to help."

"Thanks." He tipped his chin toward the cupcakes. "Thanks for this, too. Taking care of the girls. I know it can't be easy. They're upset, and you don't know them, how to...handle them."

"And they don't know me. They need somebody they can turn to for comfort and reassurance, and I'm not it. Do you have family? Somebody who could come?"

He wore a dazed expression, as though he didn't understand, then shook his head. "Their grandparents, Tracy's parents. They're on a cruise. I don't know where. And I don't want to try to contact them yet. Not until..." His voice drifted off as he shifted his focus to the darkness outside the window.

"Okay, I'll do the best I can, as much as the girls will let me."

He studied her face. "Yes, I believe you will, but it's going to be difficult. Lottie is...troubled. Hard to reach. It's a lot to ask."

It wasn't like Sarah had a choice. None of them did, and it was nothing to be concerned about right now. Not with Tracy missing.

"I was just thinking about dinner," she said. "What did you guys have planned?"

"We were going to go out. Take you to Belly's. It's a restaurant in Mountain View."

"Then is it okay if I cook something?"

"God, yes. Whatever you can find. It may be a long night, and I need to be out there..." His voice wavered, and the hand holding the coffee mug trembled. "I called the sheriff again, but he won't listen. They're stretched too thin, and he insists Tracy hasn't been gone that long. She might have taken a longer walk than she planned, she could be back any time. I called some guys—people we know—and they're on the way."

"But it's almost sunset. How are you going to see?"

"Lanterns. Flashlights. We can't track her, unless she's still moving and we stumble over a fresh trail. But if we spread out a little, I'm hoping she'll hear one of our voices. Or we might find a makeshift shelter she's crawled into."

Did his words sound as devoid of hope in his own ears as they did in hers? Seconds ticked by, and he didn't say anything more. She shifted her weight, not sure what to do. Standing in that unfamiliar house, watching a man she'd just met agonizing over a wife she barely knew, she searched for the right words and found none.

He looked up again, his tobacco-brown eyes without expression, put on his coat and gloves, and left the cabin.

Sarah went up to check on the girls. They sat on the floor of their room, bent over thick drawing pads. Gracie's page held images of lopsided snowmen and stick-deer with too-short legs and too-long antlers.

Lottie's, more detailed and heavily shaded, depicted a woman standing between two little girls. A vague, pencil-darkened shape loomed over them. On the other side of the page, a man, his rough outline a little larger, ran toward the group.

When Sarah leaned in for a closer look, Lottie flipped to a fresh page. "Is he gone?"

"Your dad? Yes, he left a few minutes ago. He didn't mean to be impatient with you. He's just tired and worried."

"Is it all right if we go back downstairs?"

"Yes, of course. Are you and Gracie getting hungry?"

Gracie put her pad aside and rose to her feet. "I'm really hungry for a cupcake."

"After dinner. Let's go down and see what we can find, okay?"

Sarah stood at the kitchen window for a few minutes, looking out at the woods behind the house. Strange that a landscape so beautiful could hold menace so strong it almost vibrated through the glass. She hugged herself and turned to face the girls, sitting at the kitchen counter.

"Any suggestions? Things you really like? Or, more important, things you don't?"

"We could have peanut butter and jelly," Gracie said. "Strawberry."

"That might be better for lunch tomorrow, don't you think? Wouldn't you like something hot?"

Sarah opened a nearby cabinet: boxed macaroni and cheese, baked beans, pasta sauce, couscous, canned vegetables. The one next to it held breakfast cereal. Another held baking supplies.

"Grilled cheese and hot chocolate," Lottie said.

"Grilled peanut butter and jelly." Gracie giggled, hands over her mouth.

"Grilled lettuce." Lottie giggled now, too, their hilarity escalating as they fired off more silly suggestions for grilling.

"Candy bars."

"No, peanuts."

"Ice cream."

"Jell-O."

Sarah opened another cabinet. "Soup."

When they laughed, she reached for a can of bean with bacon and held it up. "Grilled cheese and soup."

"Chicken noodle," Gracie said.

Lottie scrambled down from the stool. "We used up all the bread this morning making toast, but there's more in the freezer. Come on. I'll show you."

Sarah smiled. "Okay. Lead the way."

Lottie opened the freezer and pulled out a loaf of bread. But Sarah spotted a bag of frozen meatballs. One of the kitchen cabinets held several jars of marinara sauce, and in another, there'd been some angel-hair pasta. If she added a few spices, they'd have a good, hot meal, one it wouldn't take long to put together. Adding a salad would make it healthier than the soup and sandwiches. She dug a little deeper, searching for some sourdough or frozen garlic bread.

"I've already got the bread," Lottie said.

"I'm looking for something I can use to make garlic bread, sweetie. I think I'll make spaghetti."

Lottie yelled, and the impact of her words hit Sarah about the same time the frozen loaf connected with her shoulder and bounced to the floor.

"No! No spaghetti! You can't just change stuff like that. You said we could make grilled cheese." She collapsed onto the floor in a sobbing little curled-up ball.

Kneeling, Sarah reached toward the child's shoulder, but Lottie batted at it. "Go away. I don't like you. You're mean."

Sarah withdrew her hand but still knelt beside the crying child. "Honey, I'm sorry. I didn't know—I thought we were still deciding what we were going to eat."

"I was...I was going to help." Lottie hiccuped. "Mom lets me put the cheese on the bread. And now I can't. Not if you make spaghetti."

"Well, of course, you can help." Sarah mentally scrolled through the process, trying to think of something a child could do. "You could butter the bread."

Rubbing her eyes, still crying, Lottie shook her head. "It's not the same. I have to get the cheese exactly in the middle, so it spreads out right. It doesn't matter how the butter goes on."

"You can tear up lettuce for the salad. It has to be in bite-sized pieces. Not too big, and not too little. You do like to tear things up, don't you?"

Lottie peeked through fingers covering her face. "Can I really tear it up? You won't change your mind?"

"Nope. No mind changing allowed this time. Unless somebody already ate all the lettuce. You don't have any pet rabbits running around in here, do you?"

"No, 'course not. And even if we did, they couldn't get in the crisper."

"I'll bet Bugs Bunny could. Especially if he smelled carrots inside."

Lottie rolled her eyes, but she allowed Sarah to help her up. Then she dropped Sarah's hand and went back into the kitchen, her small back rigid.

Gracie still sat at the kitchen counter, her face showing no emotion as Lottie marched toward her.

Chapter 4
Friday Night

L ater that evening, after the girls were finally asleep, Sarah sat in a chair facing the front yard and the lane leading to the road. She poured a glass of merlot from one of the bottles she'd brought as a hostess gift. A search of the cabinets had turned up nothing but hard liquor, which she rarely drank. As soon as she got the Highlander out of the ditch, she could buy another bottle to replace the one she'd opened.

The snow still fell, and the muffled silence of the woods around the house crept into the cabin, infiltrating the shadowy corners. She'd toyed with the idea of staying in the bedroom with the girls or putting them to sleep on the sofa, so she could keep a more watchful eye on them. *And, admit it, Sarah, to keep you company.* But their routine had to stay as normal as possible—despite having their mother lost in a snowstorm, their father searching for her, and a strange woman caring for them.

She dialed Tracy's number again. There was no answer, but she hadn't expected one. *Where are you, Tracy?*

An image came to her of an evening when they'd worked together on an assignment. At least that had been the intention. But they had ended up sitting cross-legged on Sarah's bed, drinking merlot and talking about old movies and long-dead authors, both of them a little excited and surprised that they'd found another person with the same tastes. Sarah had acquired hers in

Caro's well-stocked library. Tracy said she got hers from the floor-to-ceiling shelves in her grandfather's study.

"I used to spend hours in there every summer, curled up in a chair, lost in some other world, not knowing those would be the best years of my life," she'd said, and Sarah had glimpsed a sadness, something unspoken that Tracy wasn't ready to share.

They'd talked about James Hilton's *Lost Horizon*, Herman Wouk's *The Winds of War,* and several of Michener's books, making Sarah think of Dave Wheeler, who also liked Michener. He had brought *The Source* to her in the hospital the year before, after she'd been attacked by the man who killed Caro.

Don't think about that. Not now, with Tracy missing. You'll bring on the nightmares.

She thought instead of Dave Wheeler: his baritone voice, those amber-ringed brown eyes, and the sensual lips. Why couldn't she get him out of her head? He was thousands of miles away, in California. So was her family, all the people she loved. There weren't many, but they were all she had left.

She should call her grandmother; it had been too long. She pulled out her phone, then hesitated. Much as she loved Nan, she couldn't handle the woman's disapproval tonight, nor could she do anything about it. Nan blamed Sarah for the family rift, and Sarah couldn't tell her the truth without causing even more pain.

Tonight, Sarah needed support, not reproach. She called Laura, who picked up on the first ring.

"Is it too early?" Sarah asked. "I know it's about dinnertime there."

"No, we're all through. Sam just left a few minutes ago."

Sam was Laura's ex-husband. They were trying to work their way back from a divorce neither of them had ever really wanted.

"How's he doing?" Sarah asked.

"Great. He's still going to A.A. meetings every day. He's going to make it this time, Sarah."

"I'm glad." And she was. Not just for Laura and the boys, but for Sam. He was a good man who needed his family, and they needed him.

After Sarah told her cousin about the day's events, Laura asked, "What is it with you and SUVs? That night you spent out at the casino in the Ford Explorer, holding a dull camping knife to fend off that creep—"

Sarah laughed. "I've been thinking about that all day. He was probably just a drunken pervert, but that was one of the most frightening nights of my life. Today was almost as bad. I've made myself a solemn promise that I'll never drive another."

"I suspect it's not the SUV. You just seem to find trouble."

"It's my magnetic personality. It draws bad men and troublesome cars." Probably best not to add traumatic events and terror to that list.

"If you say so. Dave Wheeler was asking about you the other day, and he's not a bad man."

"How do you know? You haven't lived with him. And you never really know until then, do you?"

"You have a point. But he seems to be a nice guy, and I think he'll be glad to see you when you come back home."

I don't want another man in my life. "Tell him 'Hi' for me. Dee, too. They're my favorite detectives."

"Really? Not Matt Coleman? I thought you had a thing for him."

"If you mean an urge to murder, yes, I have a thing for him. He was so sure one of us killed Caro, and he put you in jail!"

It had been nine months since Caro died, killed by a burglar in her upscale Sacramento home, but Sarah still had to fight tears every time she thought of the young aunt who had taken her in after her mother died. Sometimes she despaired of ever getting past her grief. Maybe it was because she'd lost so many: her little brother, her mother, Caro.

Laura was somewhat psychic, but Sarah knew that wasn't the reason she picked up on Sarah's sorrow.

"It'll get better with time," she said. "I'll be so glad when you're home again, close to everybody who loves you. I miss you.

The boys do, too. The holidays just weren't the same, and you've always been here for their birthdays."

"Give them a hug for me. Sam, too, the next time you see him."

"I'll do that. In the meantime, be careful. You and those two little girls alone, with a dangerous convict loose—that worries me."

Sarah glanced at the darkness outside the windows. She didn't need reminding. "It's okay. There are plenty of people around. I just...I wish you were here to help me with Lottie and Gracie. You'd know what to say to them."

"You don't have any problem talking to kids, Sarah. Eric and Jamie always have a great time with you."

"I know, but this is different. Their mother is missing, and I don't know what to say to them...and there's something strange about Lottie."

Sarah told Laura about the incident at the freezer. "And both of them were sitting on their bedroom floor, drawing, before dinner. Gracie left her pad and pencil on the floor, but Lottie put hers on top of the bookcase, the pad squared perfectly with the edge, and the pencil in a straight line beside it. Later tonight, when I started to put away the book I'd been reading to them, she grabbed it from the shelf and put it in another spot. She said it 'went' there. I noticed that her side of the room was in perfect order. Isn't that unusual for a ten-year-old?"

"Well, it certainly is for a nine-year-old boy. I don't know about girls. But I don't remember being very orderly when I was a kid, and I don't think you were either."

Sarah shifted the phone, so she could take a sip of wine, and darted another glance through the window. Nothing stirred outside the house, other than falling snow.

"There was something odd about Lottie's drawing, too," she said, "but I can't put my finger on it. She drew a woman, holding hands with two girls, but something big and dark loomed behind them. It was indistinct, just a dark blob shaded in with pencil.

And the man—I guess that was Greg—was a little larger, and he was running toward them."

"That is a little odd. I could talk with the therapist who worked with Jamie if you like. Ask her about it."

"Would you mind? It might help me handle things better."

"You haven't had a chance to talk to their father yet? I'm sure, once you do, you'll figure it out."

"The only thing he's told me is to keep my cell phone away from her. Apparently, she was making long distance calls and possibly visiting some questionable sites. They're worried about pedophiles."

"Oh, wow, that's scary."

"I wish you were here to share this bottle of wine with me."

"To help you figure it out?"

"That...and it's hard to think of witty things to say to myself."

"Wine-induced wit? Just as I suspected. Why else would you be so fond of merlot? How long are you going to stay there?"

Sarah glanced at the snow piling up at the bottom edges of the window sill. "I don't know. With Tracy missing, a convict out there, and my car stuck in a ditch—"

"You don't have any way to leave." Laura's voice rose a little on the last word. "Sarah, ask some of those people, those searchers, to help you get your car out."

"Maybe later, in the daytime, when it's not snowing. It's not a high priority right now. There are not enough searchers, and I don't want to take up their time with my car."

"Well, can't you call road service or a garage or something?"

"I'd have to be there, by the car, and I can't leave the girls alone in the cabin. Not with a convict out there somewhere. There's nobody else to take care of them while their dad is out looking for their mother."

After a moment of silence, Laura said, "I wouldn't want you out there either. But I'm going to call you at least once every day, to make sure you're all right. And you have to promise me. Get out of there as soon as you can."

"I will. Believe me, I will. Tell Eric and Jamie I love them." Sarah tried to swallow the lump in her throat as she said a quick goodbye and ended the call. This was no time to wallow in homesickness. She'd go up to check on the girls.

The back door opened and she jerked, almost upsetting the wine glass.

Greg led several men into the laundry room, where they started shedding their heavy coats.

"Everything okay here?" he called, his gaze sweeping the big room.

"Fine. The girls had dinner and their baths. Gracie is asleep, but I'm not sure about Lottie. They both had a difficult time settling down."

"Thank you. Is there any hot coffee? We're about frozen."

Sarah jumped to her feet. "I'll make a fresh pot. There's leftover spaghetti, too, but probably not enough. I think you have enough cheese for some grilled-cheese sandwiches, if you want, and I can open some soup. You must be hungry."

Greg nodded. "Thanks." He went to the fireplace and added another log to those already burning. The other men tipped their heads toward her and joined Greg, jockeying for position in front of the fire, their movements slow and heavy-footed.

Greg trudged toward the stairs. "I'll check on the girls and see if I can get Lottie calmed down a little."

Sarah started the coffeemaker and rummaged in the cabinet drawers for a cheese slicer. The aroma of fresh-brewed coffee, mixed with the faint smell of wood smoke, made the room feel warmer than it had a few moments before, when she'd sat in the alcove alone.

While she worked, she studied the five men. Two appeared to be father and son, one in his early twenties, the other in his midforties, both with the same light-brown hair, ruddy skin, cleft chin, and stocky, muscular build. The son, who darted frequent glances at Sarah, had at least an inch, maybe two, on his father, who was five eight or nine.

The man on their right looked as though he might have some American Indian ancestry, with a lean, wiry build; high cheekbones; dark skin; and raven-black hair.

On their left, a slightly stooped man, a little shorter than the others, with thinning gray hair, wore gold-rimmed glasses and a grizzled beard.

The last man, the tallest, had dark, almost sable-brown hair, with a matching beard and mustache, much better trimmed than the older man's.

"Coffee's ready," Sarah called, just as Greg came back downstairs.

He put mugs on the counter. "Gracie was asleep, but I had to give Lottie a sedative. I'll check on her again after I eat."

"Is it okay to give sedatives to children?" Sarah asked.

He stared at her, a frown forming between his eyes, not saying anything.

She shrugged. "Sorry. I don't have kids, and you do. I guess it makes sense, with her so distraught."

The men shuffled over to the kitchen stools, where Greg introduced them: Tim and Robert Grayson, the father and son; Bill Ayers, the Indian-looking man; Jake Nichols, the tall man with the dark beard and mustache; and Paul Jackson, the older man with the gray hair and beard.

Tim reached for the mug of coffee Sarah handed him and took a tentative taste before nodding his thanks. "Weatherman on TV this morning said the snow's not letting up much. It's going to be rough going tomorrow."

Paul nodded. "It's piling up pretty good out there."

Greg ran his hands through his hair. "Tomorrow may be too late, anyway. If she's out in the open—if she hasn't found cover—she'll freeze."

"Tracy's smart." Jake put a large hand on Greg's arm. "She walks in these woods all the time. She'll know where to find shelter, even if she has to cobble something together."

"But if she's hurt, not able to move—"

A heavy silence settled over the room. Tim watched Sarah cut slices of cheese, but she suspected his mind was probably elsewhere. His son's wasn't. Robert's gaze followed her as she moved around the kitchen, often drifting down to her breasts and hips. Best let it go. He was young, hadn't learned to be discreet with his glances, but this wasn't the time—and definitely not the place—to teach him.

Jake reached for a lined tablet and pencil Gracie had left on the counter and pulled it toward him. "Instead of just heading out, taking whatever path seems best at the time, I think we need a plan. A search method, to make us more efficient. Let's map it out. We found the scarf here." He marked an "x" on the paper, drew a short line, made another "x," and pointed the pencil tip at it. "And the cell phone here. So we know which direction she was going."

Sarah stood still. "You found her phone?"

"Only because Greg was smart enough to keep calling her number," Tim said. "We could hear it ringing, all muffled like. We'd already found her scarf. Just an edge of it was sticking out from the snow, and we were honing in on that area, our noses practically on the ground. They were just a few yards apart—the scarf and the phone—but it was enough to give us an idea which direction she was going."

Paul rubbed his knee, winced, straightened it, then lowered it to the floor and rubbed again. "Lucky we found it," he said. "Probably wouldn't have, with the flashlight, if it hadn't been such a bright blue color."

A chill ran up Sarah's back. Every call she'd made to Tracy's phone had rang into the emptiness of the snowbound forest, with nobody to hear it. When Sarah had sat in the disabled Highlander, calling her friend, afraid to get out of her car because of the convict, he might have already had Tracy.

Greg looked up at her, his eyes bleak. "She was going the wrong direction—not the way she'd have to go to meet up with you. If I hadn't been so sure...if I'd gone the other way when I first went out, I might have found her before she got too far away."

Jake's frown formed creases at the corners of his eyes. "She knew what time Sarah would be coming along that road?"

Both Sarah and Greg nodded. "Pretty close," Greg said.

"Then why in hell would she go the other direction? That doesn't make any sense."

Paul stroked his grizzled beard as he looked down at the rough map. "Maybe somebody grabbed her on the way to meet Sarah, and took her back the other way for some reason." He rubbed his knee again, pushing in with the fingertips.

Bending his head over the pad again, Jake drew more lines. "That old, two-track road is over here, not too far from where we found the phone. It leads back to one of those abandoned coal mines."

Greg glanced up from the coffee he'd been studying. "Tracy wouldn't go near that mine. It's too dangerous." His voice cracked. "But if somebody has her—" He set the mug down a little too hard, sloshing coffee onto the counter.

"I was thinking more about that road," Jake said. "If somebody drove in there—" He jammed the paper so hard, the pencil lead broke. "When is Sheriff Maynor going to get some people out here? The area's too damned big for us."

"Aren't they coming?" Sarah asked. "The things you found—don't they prove the convict has her?"

"That's just the problem," Greg said. "The Feds and state people don't believe he's in this area now. They have a sighting at a cabin several miles north of here. They think he's trying to get to Canada. The border is only eleven miles from Malone."

"Then I don't get it," Sarah said. "Why would he come this way to begin with? If the correctional facility is so near Malone, why didn't he just head north, over the border?"

"Apparently, they picked up his trail, and once they knew he was coming this way, they checked for family and friends in the area and found a couple of old Army buddies. He probably knew there would be a massive manhunt between Malone and the border and figured it was safer to come this way. With the help of his buddies and a vehicle, it wouldn't take long to get into another state and up to the border from there."

"But the friends—they could go to prison, too, for helping him."

Greg shrugged. "Lots of stupid people in the world. They might not have helped him, anyway. He never got a chance to find out. The cops had the places staked out, waiting for him. Once he realized that, he probably backtracked."

"Maybe he never had any contact with Tracy,"Sarah said. "He might have headed back north before she went for her walk."

"That's what Maynor said. He figures, if she was taken, it has to be somebody else," Greg said. "Maybe for ransom—one of the fringe benefits of having money, I guess. Being kidnapped."

He rose from the stool and paced back and forth. "So, under the assumption somebody has taken her, our esteemed Sheriff Maynor expects the kidnappers to call me. He says there's not much he can do until then. He's put a BOLO out on her, hoping somebody will spot her, and is trying to round up more people to help us search."

"Maynor is an idiot," Paul said. "We'll round up everybody we can and do our own search."

Bill had remained silent, his face betraying no emotion as his intent gaze settled on each speaker in turn. Sarah looked up to find that scrutiny aimed at her. She shifted her focus to Greg who still sat, elbows on the counter, head cradled in his hands. Jake met Sarah's gaze, sorrow in his gray-blue eyes.

She turned back to the griddle, mindlessly flipping grilled cheese sandwiches. Tracy was in serious trouble—if she was still alive—and Sarah would do anything she could to help. But if they didn't find her tonight, what was she going to tell Gracie and Lottie when they woke up the next morning?

Chapter 5
Saturday Morning

The searchers arrived just after dawn on the same road Sarah had taken to reach the cabin. They parked in the front yard but didn't come inside. Their voices, muffled by the snow, were indistinct as they called to each other, first from around the cabin, then from the back. The sounds gradually faded as they moved farther into the woods.

Sarah sat in the alcove with her Kindle, waiting for news, the minutes dragging by so slowly she could have sworn the clock was broken. Had Tracy survived the night, out there in the cold? Sarah could only hope Jake was right, that her friend had found shelter. It was impossible to imagine what it would be like alone in that frozen forest, cold and hungry and probably in pain, not knowing if anybody would find her.

Snow still fell, adding to big drifts alongside the lane. A track had been broken through it, probably with a heavy vehicle. Part of the front road was blocked from view by patches of trees so white they blended into the drifts around them. The abandoned road she had driven down yesterday would probably be impassible today, and snow would be piling up around the Highlander.

She was tired, having spent a restless night in an unfamiliar bed. Worry and fear had tugged at the back of her mind, complicating even the simplest of tasks. Conversation with Greg had been impossible, even if she'd known him well. He didn't sit still long enough. His cell phone rarely left his hands. Every few minutes, he rose from his chair and either paced the length of the cabin or walked around outside. And it had seemed awkward, being in the cabin with another woman's husband.

She'd asked him again about the girls' grandparents, and he'd admitted he had no idea where they were, or which cruise line they had taken—only a vague memory of Tracy mentioning it, on their way to the cabin.

"I'll dig through some of her stuff, see if I can find something," he said.

"Maybe in her phone calls?"

"Yeah. Good idea." He'd looked so distracted, she wasn't sure he'd remember to do that. She'd have to remind him again when he came back.

"Sarah?"

With her back to the stairs, she hadn't noticed the girls' quiet descent. Even Lottie's voice, from directly behind her, was low.

"Is Mom sleeping?"

The master bedroom door was closed, so they had no way of knowing their mother hadn't come home during the night. Sarah closed her eyes for a moment, trying to think. She shouldn't be the one to tell them; they needed someone closer. It would have helped if Greg had stuck around until they woke up, but he was frantic to find Tracy.

Sarah turned to face them. "Lottie, honey, your—"

But she had waited too long to respond. That, or the girl had sensed the answer. Lottie's eyes brimmed with tears. "They didn't find her, did they?" Her voice rose on the last two words, and tears leaked from her eyes. Sarah reached out, but Lottie ignored the outstretched hand. "She's lost and they can't find her and it's going to snow some more and she's cold and maybe hurt and maybe even scared." Tears streamed down the girl's face now, dripping off her chin, and Gracie, watching her sister, let out a loud wail.

Sarah rose and put her arms around both of them, pulling them close. "You have to remember, it was dark last night—hard to see. And your dad had only four people to help him. If your mom was asleep in some kind of shelter, she might not have heard them. They started searching just as soon as the sun came up this morning, and they have more people coming to help."

Lottie looked up with anxious eyes. "Do you think they'll find her today?"

How do I answer that? "They've got a lot better chance than they did last night, in the dark."

Lottie swiped at her eyes with the heels of her hands. "I wish I could go and look. Mom takes walks all the time, and I know the places she likes a lot better than anybody else does. We went together. Just me and her, and Gracie. Lots of times."

"Maybe you can tell your dad about them. I know you'd like to help search. Me, too. But it's easier for your dad if he knows you and Gracie are safe. If one of you got lost, he'd have to look for you, too, and they'd have less time to find your mom. I think the best thing we can do is make sure there's hot food for the searchers when they need it."

After a brief silence, Lottie nodded. "I can help. Mom was teaching me how to do some stuff in the kitchen."

"That's great. I'm going to make stew for lunch and thaw out some sourdough bread. Can you peel carrots?"

Lottie's head bobbed. "I know how. Potatoes, too. I'll get the peeler."

"Let's fix you and Gracie some breakfast first."

The girls ate cereal at the counter and watched while Sarah braised the bite-sized pieces of beef. Gracie's hair was down today, forming a soft frame of brown curls around her face. She was a beautiful child, with perfectly proportioned features—much prettier than her sister, but Sarah suspected Lottie would be striking, with those eyes, if her hair darkened to the same shade as Tracy's.

These sisters didn't bicker with each other. Not like Eric and Jamie. Was it because they were girls? Sarah's cousin Laura was the closest thing to a sister she'd ever had, and she couldn't remember any friction between them as children. But they hadn't lived together, either.

The relationship between these children was more like mother and child than sisters. Lottie took care of Gracie, and Gracie looked to her big sister for help.

Gracie was the more outgoing of the two and the most even-tempered, but Sarah suspected Lottie's tantrums might be stress-related. Still, once they had the stew started, and Sarah suggested cookie-making, she was careful to ask Lottie how Tracy went about the process.

Sarah glanced at the clock when they finished. Only a quarter to eleven. Lottie had pulled out a pair of video game controllers and started some sort of racing game. She seemed lethargic, probably a combination of anxiety, too little sleep and the sedative Greg had given her.

Grateful for anything that might provide some distraction for them, but with nothing to occupy her own time, Sarah surveyed the room. A dark print covered the sofa the girls sat on. The box for their video game rested on a matching ottoman. A couple of rustic-design wooden end tables flanked the sofa. Two rocking chairs completed the furnishings.

The girls soon abandoned the video game and went upstairs. When Sarah looked in on them later, both their heads were bent over coloring books. Apparently, she was working too hard at providing entertainment; they were used to managing on their own, and it appeared they'd been doing it for a long time. *And they're better at it than I am.*

She called Laura. "Did you ever give sedatives to Eric and Jamie?"

"Sedatives? What kind of—no, never. Are you talking about the stuff children's dentists use sometimes?"

"No. Lottie had a hard time going to sleep last night. Not surprising with her mother missing and a complete stranger taking care of her. When Greg got home, pretty late, he went up to see the girls and told me he gave Lottie a sedative."

After several seconds of silence, Laura spoke haltingly. "I don't know. I mean, I've never dealt with anything like that. But I think I would have called the kids' pediatrician."

"I doubt they have one here. It's a vacation cabin. But it's a thought. Maybe he or Tracy did, earlier, back in New York, and it's an ongoing prescription. She's obviously got some problems."

"That could be. Do you know what he gave her?"

"He didn't say. What about Jamie? He had trouble sleeping for a while, didn't he?"

"Not for that long. Kids—at least those as well adjusted as Jamie—bounce back pretty fast."

Sarah's throat tightened. "I miss him and Eric so much."

"They miss you, too. We all do. Next time you get a week off, come home, okay?"

That was a promise Sarah had no trouble making.

She ended the call and searched online for sedatives for children, but found nothing, other than references to dentistry and test procedures.

The girls had left the television on. She picked up the remote to switch it off, but hesitated. Maybe she could find a good talk show, something to get her mind off Tracy and the search. She changed the input from video game to the television channel and caught the weather report at the end of a news report. The prediction was for continuing intermittent snow, with another big storm on the way, arriving sometime late in the week.

"What are you doing?" Lottie asked, from behind her.

"Oh, you startled me!" Sarah grabbed the remote she'd almost dropped. "You move like a cat in those socks! I was changing the channel." A glance at Lottie's pinched mouth prompted Sarah to add, "Unless you wanted to play your game? I thought, when you went upstairs, you were through with it."

"I don't want to play it now, but...Gracie fell asleep. She was crying. She wanted Mom and I couldn't...I couldn't make her stop crying." Lottie used a balled-up fist to swipe at her own cheek. "I tried everything I could think of. I covered her up with that soft blanket she likes, and put Lucy—that's her favorite doll—on one side of her, and Rudy—he's her best stuffed dog—on the other side, and I tried to hug her, but I...I couldn't get her to stop."

"Do you need a hug?" Sarah asked, opening her arms. She couldn't pull the girl in; she had to let Lottie decide.

Lottie took a tentative step toward Sarah, then stopped, her gaze searching Sarah's face before she came the rest of the way. But she didn't lean into the hug, didn't snuggle, and her shoulder and back muscles were tense. Sarah rubbed at them.

"Let's just sit here for a minute." She pulled Lottie to the sofa and sat down. "We can talk if you want, but it's okay if you don't. Maybe if we both think about it, we can figure out a way to make Gracie feel better."

Lottie nodded and pushed a little closer to Sarah. Sarah welcomed the warmth of the small body. It had been too long since she'd had any human contact. She resisted the urge to pull Lottie closer.

"I just...I think she's scared Mom isn't coming back," Lottie whispered.

And so are you. "I think you may be right, and that's hard. Maybe it would be a good idea if she talked to your dad about it."

"I don't know," the girl said. "He's always tired, and I don't know what to say to Gracie. I mean, if they don't find Mom pretty soon."

The little girl's body shook, and Sarah pulled her closer, her mind flooded with images of the night her own mother had died. She had been almost sixteen, older than these little girls, and she'd never found a way to fill that aching void, even after Caro took her in. The sorrow deep inside never quite healed, pulled open anew by every major event that her mother had missed: Sarah's wedding, graduations, proms, and perhaps some day the birth of Sarah's children.

Lottie pulled away, so she could see Sarah's face when she asked, "Do you think they're going to find her?"

Sarah groped for words. She couldn't tell the child that a kidnapper might have her mother. "All we can do, Lottie, is hope and pray they do. Your dad has a lot of people out there looking for her. And your mom is smart. She'll—"

But the girl had pulled free and raced toward the stairs. Sarah sighed. She should have handled it better.

A noise drew her attention to the laundry room. Greg stood just inside it, looking at her, with a group of men behind him.

Tim took a piece of bread from the basket Sarah handed him and passed it on to his son. "I don't know where to go next, Greg. There's a lot of forest out there and not much daylight left. I keep thinking about all those cabins, a bunch of them empty. I figure whoever has her might be holed up in one of them. Maybe one we don't even know about."

"I don't think so," Jake said. "If a kidnapper took her, why stay around close to get caught? There's that old road back there he could have got into with a four-wheel drive. Once he grabbed her, wouldn't he get as far away as he could before anybody knew she was missing?"

"Could be," Paul said. "But, what I can't figure is, if he was after Tracy because she has money, how did he know she was going to be in that spot at that particular time?"

Robert slathered butter on his bread. "I heard a couple of guys talking about it today. They were wondering if she maybe set it up ahead of time and knew where she was going. She wasn't even headed in the right direction to meet up with her." He inclined his head toward Sarah. "They figured maybe she just took off. Had some guy waiting."

Jake glanced at Greg's clenched jaw, then clamped white knuckles around his own cup.

Tim glared at his son. "For the love of God, Bobby, won't you never learn not to rattle your gums 'til after you get your brain warmed up?"

Robert paused in mid-chew and stared at his father. "What? What did I say?"

Tim shook his head, and the others sat in strained silence.

Jake stood and helped himself to another piece of bread. "Doesn't add up. If she was meeting somebody, why would he grab her? If she'd gone willingly, her scarf and phone wouldn't have been out there in the snow. And why now, when she was expecting Sarah?" He shook his head. "None of it makes any sense. Damn it, we need Maynor." He put a hand on Greg's shoulder. "We can't do this by ourselves, Greg. I know we've got to keep searching. We don't have any choice. But there's too much terrain, and with all this weather, it's slow going. Besides, we can't check inside those cabins. That takes authority we don't have."

"This is our own beloved sheriff you're talking about, right?" Paul said. "Fat chance. He's so stupid, he'll hang on to his kidnaping theory until—"

"Maybe not, if you handle it the right way," Bill Ayers said. It was the first time he'd spoken in Sarah's presence, and his voice was so melodious, the cadence so lyrical, it took a few moments for Sarah's brain to get past the sound, to the content.

"He's ambitious, and there's an election coming up. Right now, his deputy is looking pretty good for the job, and Maynor is running scared. Draw him a picture—how stupid he's going to look if there's no kidnapper. And the publicity he's going to get—good or bad, depending on how he handles this."

Jake said, "I take it all back." He slapped Bill on the shoulder. "All those times I've said you don't talk because you don't know anything—"

"Jake, everybody knows—ever since we sang *Happy Birthday* to Mindy Stevens in second grade—you've been jealous because I can sing and you can't. You had that pitiful crush on her, but after she heard that squawking, off-key noise you make, she just couldn't help but like me best." Shaking his head, he placed a hand over the left side of his chest. "I decided, since my voice causes you pain, I'd try to stay quiet around you."

Jake spewed coffee on Greg's back. Laughing, he set the cup on the counter. The rest of the men joined in, relieving much of the tension in the room. Even Greg smiled, the first one Sarah had seen, displaying a small dimple in his left cheek. Then his expression sobered.

"That's the best idea I've heard all day. Let's go talk to Maynor."

Chapter 6
Saturday Afternoon

L ottie looked over the stair railing at Sarah. "Is he gone?" Gracie stood beside her, cradling the doll. What was its name? Lucy.

"Your dad and the others? Yes, they went to search. But he'll be back sometime tonight and, if it's not too late, maybe you can talk to him. He could even wake you up, if you want."

"I don't want to talk to him. He would just tell me a bunch of lies. Like he always does."

She knows nothing about real lies and deceit from a father, and I hope to God she never does. Lottie was upset and worried about her mother and was too young to understand that her father was too stressed to deal with her right now.

"I'm sure he doesn't mean to lie," Sarah said. "It's hard for him, too. And it can be difficult to find the right words."

"You just don't know." The girl gripped the rail with a white-knuckled hand. "You don't know anything!" She flounced past Sarah and settled onto one of the kitchen counter stools, arms folded across her waist. Gracie hesitated, her lower lip trembling. Clutching Lucy to her chest, she followed Lottie with slow steps, glancing back at Sarah before she climbed onto her stool.

Now what? Try to talk to Lottie or leave her alone for a while? And what about Gracie? She was giving every indication she wanted something from Sarah. Probably best to let them alone

for now, allow Lottie to settle down a bit. Sarah didn't know what
to say to the girl, anyway.

She stood at the window for a few minutes, looking out at the
snowflakes drifting past the window. She'd gained at least one
thing from this trip. She now fully understood the term "cabin
fever." How could people stand day after day of this?

She went back to the kitchen, edging around to the other side
of the counter so she could talk to the girls. Lottie jerked a hand
away from Sarah's phone, beside the sugar bowl. Sarah had
forgotten Greg's warning not to leave it out.

"Lottie, were you using my phone?"

The girl kept her eyes downcast. Sarah studied her flushed
face, then Gracie's. She wouldn't look at Sarah, either.

What now? She couldn't insist on an answer. The girls were
emotionally fragile, and she was a stranger to them. Best let it go,
make sure she kept the phone in her pocket, and let them know
she was there to help. She could look at the call log later.

"Lottie, Gracie, I'm so sorry your mother isn't here. If I could
bring her back, I would. But I can't do that. All I can do is stay
with you until your grandparents get here and hope somebody
finds your mom soon. If you want to talk, I'll listen. But you don't
have to if you don't feel like it. And I really, really like hugs, if you
ever need one of those."

Gracie smiled and glanced at Lottie, who looked into Sarah's
eyes, her own filled with tears. "Okay. Can we watch *Frozen*?"

"What?"

"Can we watch *Frozen*?"

"Uh. What is *Frozen*?"

Gracie giggled. "The movie. About Princess Elsa and Princess
Anna. They're sisters, but Elsa can make everything cold. Snow
and ice. And she has to go and hide and Anna has to go find her."

"That's because Anna has to save the kingdom," Lottie explained. "Elsa has secret powers, but she got in trouble because
she used them too much. So she has to run away and hide, and
Anna has to find her. And save the kingdom."

"Okay." They obviously didn't need her.

Gracie ran to get the movie. Lottie set it up on the game controller, and the two girls nestled together on one end of the sofa. Gracie had wrapped herself in a small, fleecy blanket, and as the movie progressed, snuggled closer to Lottie. *Probably because the film is so full of ice and snow.* Why did they want to watch this, when there was so much of it outside? Sarah shivered and turned back to the window. The snowfall had stopped, rays of pale sunlight casting a faint glow against the panes.

She had to get outside; had to breathe some fresh air while the sun was out. It should be safe enough. Safer than staying inside and ending up in a straightjacket. After all, the men had already searched the area around the cabin. The girls wouldn't miss her for a few minutes; they'd withdrawn from her, keeping to themselves most of the time. And she needn't go far: just around the cabin a few times to get some fresh air and exercise.

Shrugging into her parka, she stepped out the back door and lifted her face to the sun. How long had it been since she'd felt its warmth on her skin? Winter vacations were overrated. She'd take a California beach anytime. Even better, Maui. She closed her eyes, picturing the huge banyan tree at Lahaina.

A sharp crack startled her eyes open. Just a branch, breaking from the weight of the ice.

Greg had hustled her inside so fast when she first arrived, this was her first good look at the cabin's weathered-log exterior. The roof was some kind of metal, probably so the snow melt could slide off easily.

The landscape didn't look as picture-perfect as it had through the windows. From that viewpoint, she hadn't seen the foot-churned areas near the cabin, turned to a brown-tinged slush, then re-frozen. A few yards ahead, to her left, a cleared path led to a shed with a wide door. It had the same type of roof as the cabin, though much steeper, and the siding was older, more weathered.

Snow crunched under her boots as she moved out a few yards beyond the trampled and frozen footsteps, angling right to make her trek around the house. At the corner, the snowman came into view, up close to the wall near the front of the cabin, much of the base buried under a mound of snow. Parked beyond it were three vehicles: a black Jeep and two pickups—one a gray Chevy Silverado, the other a dark green Dodge Ram. Beyond them in the distance was the main road.

To her left, a long white expanse wound through the trees, noticeable only because of its smoothness—the lack of vegetation. It had to be the back road, the footpath leading to the washed-out bridge and her abandoned car.

Her steps faltered. The shed might contain a plank or, if not that, at least something she could place under the Highlander's tire. But she couldn't go out there now; it would have to wait.

A blur of motion brought her to a stop, and she peered deep into the woods to the right of the footpath. Nothing moved. Just as she shifted her view, it came again, in her peripheral vision. Probably a deer. She stood still, squinting. Nothing. She took another step. A glimpse of sunlight reflected off metal. Her heart thumped. A gun? Seconds ticked by and the silence remained unbroken. She focused deeper into the trees. There! Another flash of metal. Something gray. Definitely not a gun. Much bigger than that—gray outlines in gaps between the trees. A car on the old road—the wrong one she'd started down yesterday.

Maybe it belonged to one of the searchers. She took a step, then halted. Why wouldn't he park in the yard with the other cars, rather than on a dead-end road? She edged back toward the door and the binoculars she'd spotted earlier, hanging above the snowshoes in the laundry room. It took a few minutes to get them adjusted to her eyes and a few more to pinpoint the position of the object again: a gray car, too far away to determine the make.

She searched for the Highlander, but it was out of range, closer to the main road. She probed the trees. Nothing moved. At least, nothing she could see. Maybe from a higher elevation? She turned and studied the cabin's upper story. Four windows looked out onto the back yard: hers, Lottie's and Gracie's, and the small ones in each of their bathrooms. Her room looked out onto the shed and part of the woods. Lottie's and Gracie's room would provide the best view of the footpath and the abandoned road, but they would also be visible from the more isolated "junk" room—whatever that meant. She went inside, past the living area where the girls still watched the movie, and climbed the stairs.

The name was apt. The room contained the usual household discards, the sort of things one might find in an attic or garage: odd pieces of furniture, labeled cardboard boxes, a battered foot locker, and outgrown toys. A crib, rocking chair, and pink-and-white-striped chintz curtains told her the room had probably last served as Gracie's nursery before she had abandoned it to move in with her sister.

Sarah pulled an edge of the curtain away from the wall and peeked out. The view over the tops of the trees was better from the higher elevation, but not as well lit. The sun was behind the house now, below the roof line.

She worked the rocking chair free from a pile of toys in the corner, pulled it to the window, and leaned forward with the binoculars. The roof of the gray vehicle came into focus. She panned the area, but saw nothing else. Yes, there. A darker blur, a slight movement...She moved the glasses back to it. Nothing but shadows. Slowly, a dark shape emerged—the upper body of a man. The earlier glint had probably come from the binoculars he held in his own hands.

He was watching the house.

She gasped, fumbled with the binoculars, took a firmer grip, and shifted, trying to get a better image. He was gone, perhaps warned by a flash of sunlight from her own position. No, the sun was behind the house; there would have been no glint. Something else then?

She scanned the area where he'd disappeared but the motion, when it came, was from the other side of the vehicle. He'd opened the driver's door on the far side, only his shoulders and the top of his head visible. So he'd backed in; he knew the road, knew it was a dead-end, knew it well enough to get around her disabled vehicle without slipping off into the deep rut.

He slid into the seat, becoming a dark smudge in the dim interior. The car edged forward. He might pass a clearing where she could get a better view of the interior, so she kept the glasses trained on the car window. But the inside remained dark until he was out of range.

Letting the curtain fall, she sat back in the chair and closed her eyes, picturing him again, slightly bent, opening the car door. Dark hair had covered the top of his head and, judging by the height of the car, he was about six feet tall.

Bill Ayers had black hair, and he was tall enough. But so were Jake Nichols and Greg Agerton, and they all had dark hair. The man she'd seen couldn't be one of them; they were all together, searching for Tracy. *I'm becoming paranoid.* But maybe with good reason. Why would anybody be watching the cabin?

The sun was lower now, dusk fast approaching. Was that why he'd left? Because the searchers would soon return? If so, this wasn't the first time he'd watched—he knew their routine. She had to call somebody, let them know.

As she rose from the chair, a sudden movement on her right sent her scrambling to the floor. From behind the chair, she peered into the shadows at her own terrified face.

A mirror.

She had glimpsed her reflection in an old-fashioned, stand-alone mirror, the kind she'd only read about, never actually seen. The musty bedspread covering it had been jerked aside, caught on one of the rocking chair's runners.

Get a grip, Sarah, before you scare the girls out of their minds! But she couldn't stop the thump of her heart, trying to pound its way out of her chest. She righted the chair and went down to the laundry room to put the binoculars away.

As she reached to loop the cord over the hook, a blast of cold air hit the back of her neck. Somebody had opened the door behind her. Had she locked it after the men left?

Stifling a scream, she whirled. Greg stood in the open doorway.

"Oh, my God!" She gasped as her hand slammed onto her chest. "You scared the crap out of me!"

"What are you doing with the binoculars?"

"I was just going to call you. There's a man...there was a man. Out on that old road, at the end of the footpath."

Greg leaned his head back out the door. "Jake! Hold on a second, you guys." He turned back to her. "When?"

"Just a while ago...maybe five or ten minutes—"

He ran to the blue Chevy Tahoe they'd apparently just arrived in and climbed into the driver's seat. The others piled in while Greg barked a few words, pointing toward the footpath. He turned the vehicle and accelerated down the lane. The tires slipped on the icy track, almost sending the car into a spin. Greg slowed and corrected, then picked up speed again.

Lottie had turned off the movie and taken Gracie upstairs. Odd. When Sarah was a child, she would have tried to eavesdrop, to find out what was going on.

◆◆◆

The men were back within forty-five minutes, and Greg told her what they'd found: tracks in the fresh snow—tires and boots—the footprints leading into and out of the woods at the back of the cabin. Another set led a few yards down the wooded edge of the footpath, toward the house.

"We called Sheriff Maynor. He'll go out there in the morning. Track the prints, see if the man went deeper into the trees, try to find out where he went. Did you get a good look at him?"

"Not really. All I saw was his upper body. I'd say he was about six feet tall and had dark hair."

"What about the car?"

"I couldn't see much of it between the gaps in the trees. Just the outline and the gray color." She frowned. "I thought that road would be impassable, with all the snow. It's abandoned, so they don't plow it, do they?"

"No, but he—or somebody—has been in and out on a regular basis, enough to keep a track broken."

"He was watching the house. With binoculars."

The men stared at her, their motions frozen for an instant—a cup stopped halfway to a mouth; a spoon halted at the edge of a sugar bowl.

"With binoculars? You're sure?"

"I'm sure."

Jake glanced at Greg. "Then he wasn't just watching the house. He was looking for the people around it. Or in it."

Tim slammed a hand down on the counter. "It's one of them damned reporters. Somehow, he's got the scent of a story. They'll be all over the place now, crawling around like pissants in a pantry."

"I don't think so." Jake shook his head. "It's got to have something to do with Tracy. If the convict's been spotted in a different area, Maynor could be right—it's a kidnapper. Do you think this guy might be trying to make contact? It's not likely he has your cell phone number."

"Wouldn't that be risky?" Sarah asked. "Approaching the cabin? Wouldn't it be safer for him to make contact through a third party, like the newspaper?"

"No." Paul massaged his knee. "In a town as small as this, a stranger would be noticed. Especially in the newspaper office. Even a local would be remembered."

"And if he sent a ransom letter," Jake said, "it wouldn't even be picked up until Saturday, so the newspaper office wouldn't get it until at least Tuesday."

Paul took off his gold-rimmed glasses and blew moist air on them. "Well, if this guy is the perp, the last thing we want to do is scare him off." He dried his glasses with a napkin. "He may be trying to find out whether it's safe to leave a note on the door or one of the vehicles. And the cabin looks pretty deserted all day, with Sarah and the girls staying inside."

"You're not suggesting they go out?" Greg asked. "That could be dangerous. We don't know for sure who this guy is or what he has in mind."

"Can't we call the FBI?" Robert asked. "Don't they investigate kidnappings?"

"They might if we had anything solid," his father said. "But we don't have much. Maynor's theory, for what that's worth, and Sarah spotting the guy. There hasn't been any contact."

Bill studied the room, his gaze settling on the end divided by the stairs. The big-screen TV took the living room wall, and the bathroom occupied most of the other. Neither side had a window. His penetrating gaze shifted to Sarah.

He's wondering how I saw the car. She glanced at Greg. How would he react if he knew she went outside? Best leave that alone.

"I don't think he saw me watching. I didn't pull back the curtain on the window upstairs—just lifted an edge enough to see with the binoculars." Bill wouldn't know how the rooms were laid out upstairs.

His lip quirked, and he gave her a slight nod, so she continued. "If it is a kidnapper trying to make contact, he'll come back. I can keep watching and, if I see him, call the sheriff."

"Good idea," Jake said. "And we could stay closer to the cabin tomorrow, maybe spread apart a little—help Maynor cover the area better."

Greg hesitated for a few moments before he nodded. "Okay." He turned to Sarah. "But I don't like this—somebody so close to the cabin. Make sure you keep the doors locked and the girls inside until we find out what's going on."

Bill Ayers still watched Sarah, his eyes assessing, his expression now a little quizzical.

Chapter 7
Sunday Morning

Noise jolted Sarah awake: car engines, dogs barking in the distance, men yelling, and the chattering of a helicopter's rotors, so close she could have sworn it must be landing in the yard—or on the roof. She rolled out of bed, pulled on the same jeans and sweatshirt she'd worn the day before, and ran downstairs, twisting her long hair into a ponytail.

The men were at the kitchen counter, much as she'd left them the night before.

"What happened? Did they find Tracy?"

Greg looked at Sarah with bleak eyes. "Sheriff Maynor happened."

Jake gestured toward the front windows. "Our esteemed sheriff, ever mindful of the pending election, decided this occasion called for a press conference."

The sun was breaking out from heavy, dark clouds, and the snow had stopped again. Vehicles filled the yard, parked at odd angles, men and women clustered around them. Several people, some with microphones, others with cameras, had converged around the sheriff, who stood with his back to the cabin.

"But that'll scare the kidnapper off," Sarah said.

Jake cocked his head. "I'd ask if you want to run for sheriff, Sarah, since you're obviously much smarter than the one we have.

But, then, so is everybody else in town. Including the stray cats and dogs, and even the birds, with their tiny little brains."

"What are you going to do?" Sarah asked Greg.

He dropped onto one of the kitchen stools, elbows on the counter, his hands clenched into fists. "I don't know. I should never have called him. He won't come out and help us hunt so we can get inside those empty cabins, and now he blows our only chance of catching the kidnapper."

"And you're going to have reporters camping out all over the place," Tim said.

Greg's head jerked up. "No. I can't have them around here. They're just going to be in the way, and the girls—"

"Well, I suppose you could call the sheriff's office and have him remove them. They're on private property," Jake said. "Oh, wait, that won't work. The sheriff invited them, didn't he?"

"Use them," Sarah said. "The sheriff, too."

Bill narrowed his eyes, unnerving her. "Go on."

"I just...I think, if you go out there, Greg, and talk to the reporters, you can tell them you appreciate the sheriff coming to join the search. It's something you've needed so you can get access to those vacant cabins. You're grateful he's committing so many resources to search for your missing wife."

Paul smiled. "I like it."

"That's not all," she continued. "Finish up with an emotional pitch to the reporters. Tell them the girls are scared their mother isn't coming back."

Jake finished for her. "And when you have the reporters' sympathy, ask them to respect your privacy—especially that of your little girls—to please move out of the yard, back to the main road."

"Sarah, you're...I don't know what to say." Greg headed toward the front door. "Thank you."

"Maybe," Jake said, grinning, "you could even hint that the sheriff is reaching out to state and federal forces...committing all his own resources..."

Greg gave him a thumbs up and went out to join the sheriff. The rest of them moved a little closer to the windows so they could watch. Greg's face wasn't visible from Sarah's position, so she tried to read the expressions of others. The sheriff's shifted rapidly—surprise, preening gratification, irritation—the latter masked with a wide smile as the camera came back to him. The change on the reporters' faces, from curiosity to sympathy, told her Greg's appeal was working.

"You know you've done a disservice to this entire community," Jake whispered from beside her. "Your suggestion is making the sheriff look fairly competent."

"Then I'd better get out of town fast."

He smiled, obviously under the mistaken impression she was joking. "Sarah, I've been meaning to tell you how much it means to all of us, what you're doing for Greg. I talked to some of the women in town, and you may be getting some help out here—"

A flash of white drew Sarah's attention to the stairs. Lottie and Gracie had just reached the bottom. Gracie wore pink pajamas. Lottie had on a long, white flannel nightgown with a tiny red bow at the neck. Their hair was still tangled from sleep.

Lottie took a step back toward the stairs when she saw the men and stopped. She pointed at the window.

"What are those people doing in our yard? Did they come to help?"

Sarah moved toward her. "No, honey. They're reporters. They're talking to your dad about...about finding your mother."

Lottie took several more steps toward the window, pulling Gracie with her. Sarah followed. "Stand back a little, so they can't see you. Your dad doesn't want—"

"Sheriff Maynor is out there too, and he looks kind of mad. I have to talk to him."

She whirled and ran toward the door and Sarah, caught by surprise, was too slow to catch her. Lottie had her hand on the knob when Greg opened it, throwing the child a little off balance.

"Whoa!" He wrapped an arm around her. "Are you okay? I didn't know you were there. Did the door hit you?"

Lottie glared at him and pulled away. "I wanted to talk to Sheriff Maynor. Did something bad happen? Is it...is he here about Mom?"

Greg reached out to touch Lottie, but the girl's rigid shoulders discouraged contact. He let his arm drop. "No. He's going to help with the search."

Lottie turned to face Sarah, one small fist gripping the front of her nightgown. "Are they going to be on the television news and talk about my mom?"

"Yes. Your dad was telling them—"

"That's good, isn't it?" The girl's eyes were so beseeching, tears welled in Sarah's. "If everybody knows she's lost, lots of them might come and look for her. Right?"

"Yes, I think you're right." Sarah blinked away tears, not just for Lottie and her anguish, but for Greg. Why did the child continually push him away? What was her problem?

Lottie's relationship with her father reminded Sarah of her own. But, unlike Lottie, Sarah had good reason for her anger. Lottie's seemed to be a coping mechanism, somehow transferring the anger and fear over her mother's disappearance onto Greg—pushing him away, rather than clinging to him.

The reporters, heeding Greg's request, moved out to the main road, where they milled around outside their vehicles, stamping their feet to keep them warm. They stepped dangerously close to passing traffic, thrusting microphones at the windows of potential searchers.

After cautioning her again—for the second or third time—to keep the doors locked, Greg left with the men.

"Keep watching," Jake said, just before he went out the door. "There's still a chance the guy will come back after everybody clears out."

After everybody left, Lottie and Gracie went back to their video game, but it couldn't compete with the novelty of the reporters. They got a small voice recorder from the bookcase and, using a hairbrush for a microphone, busied themselves interviewing each other, then playing it back. They kept their voices to a low murmur so Sarah couldn't hear their questions and responses.

She went back to the junk room and the binoculars to search among the reporters' vehicles for a gray car. Up close, most of the journalists looked bored. They might not stay long if they had nobody to question and there was nothing going on around the house. Sarah crossed to the other window and checked the back road. No car. The man she'd seen the day before was probably gone for good, scared off by the sheriff.

She went back to the first window and the reporters again. A white king cab pickup turned into the lane, followed by a smaller red one. More reporters? She hurried down to head them off.

By the time she yanked the front door open, the vehicles had stopped in the yard. Three women got out, all of them in their mid-thirties to early forties. One of them, her boyish shape clad in jeans and a green sweater, clambered into the bed of the red pickup. A green and white knit cap topped her shoulder-length hair, which glowed carrot-orange against the red cab.

The other two women approached Sarah. One wore pressed navy slacks and a powder-blue turtleneck sweater. She held out a well-manicured hand. "I'm Ellen Tisdale, and this is Roberta Adrickson." Roberta had dark, curly hair, and wore a gray sweat shirt. "And that's Julie Osborne." She gestured toward the skinny woman in the pickup, then turned back to Sarah.

"Jake Nichols says you've got quite a few searchers out here, and we've come to help you feed them."

Julie pushed boxes toward the end of the pickup bed, using her booted feet and gloved hands. Roberta picked up one of the boxes and turned toward the cabin. Sarah opened the door wider.

"I'm Sarah Wagner, a friend of Tracy's, visiting for the week. Here, let me help you." She took the box from Roberta and led them inside.

Julie jumped down from the pickup and followed. She surveyed the room, then pointed, displaying crimson polish on short fingernails.

"Maybe we can set up some tables in the middle. One down between the kitchen stools and the dining room table, and another one, at the end of it. On the other side—"

"We'll bring in the folding tables." Roberta smiled at Sarah, an expression that looked as though it might be more or less permanent, in a round, rosy-cheeked face. Short and sturdy, she looked fully capable of carrying a table by herself, but Sarah asked if she needed help.

"Thanks. They're not that heavy, but they're bulky."

"Go ahead and bring them in," Julie said. "The roll of paper, too."

"I think we know what to do," Roberta said. "Exactly when were you appointed foreman?"

A red stain crept up Julie's neck, erasing the freckles. "Sorry," she muttered. Guess I'm too used to ordering kids around." She grinned at Sarah. "Teacher. Fourth grade."

Ellen, a tall, slender woman with blue eyes and short, well-styled brown hair, placed a paper grocery bag on the counter. "How much room do you have in the refrigerator?"

Sarah opened it. "Plenty. I'm running low on fresh supplies, and wasn't sure what I'd fix for dinner tonight." She glanced at the clock. "What time are you expecting the searchers? It's already a quarter after ten."

"Noon, and we have plenty of time." Julie plugged a roaster into a socket above the counter top. "Turkey, almost done. It'll go a long way, along with some mashed potatoes and gravy and green beans, and it's not going to take long to do those. But the searchers will come in two shifts, and we have to allow for that."

Roberta unpacked a commercial-size coffee percolator while Sarah rearranged several containers in the refrigerator to make more space. "You've obviously done this before."

"Well, not this exactly," Roberta said, "but enough church and school and community events to get the routine down."

"Then I'll try to help without getting in your way."

Gracie had fallen asleep on the sofa. Lottie sat beside her, playing a video game while she studied the new arrivals.

Sarah worked alongside the women, enjoying the company and the warmth they brought to the cabin. They said they were local, year-around residents and knew little about most of the visitors who periodically occupied the cabins. Greg was an exception.

"We've known him since kindergarten," Ellen said. "He grew up here. But he went away to college and never came back to live. Just vacations and long weekends."

"For a long time, he didn't come at all," Roberta added. "The cabin was rented out a lot. The last couple of years, he started showing up again, with Tracy and the girls. Not that we saw much of them. They flew in, stayed a week or two, and flew out again. Greg usually managed to make some time for the old friends he grew up with, but Tracy didn't know anybody and didn't seem to be interested in socializing with the locals."

"It was odd," Ellen added. "We'd known Greg for so long, but weren't even aware until he showed up with Tracy and the girls that first time, that he'd married—"

"More work and less gossip, please." Julie slashed at the potatoes. Thick strips of potato skin fell atop the thinner ones coiled in the sink.

Ellen eyed the peelings. "The thing we're going to have less of is potatoes, if you keep that up. Want me to take over for a while?"

Julie dried her hands on a paper towel. "Help yourself. I seem to be all thumbs today. Nerves, I guess." She headed for the stairs. "I need a bathroom break, anyway."

Sarah opened her mouth to tell Julie there was a half-bath downstairs, but the woman was halfway down the length of the room.

Ellen and Roberta shared a glance, then Roberta said, "She still has a thing for Greg. They went together most of their last two years of high school, and everybody thought they'd get married. I guess Greg had other ideas."

"I don't think she ever got over it," Ellen said. "Apparently Greg never took the relationship as seriously as she did, and she felt betrayed."

Sarah nodded. Betrayal, especially by the man you love—the one you think loves you—is a hard thing to put behind you.

They worked silently after that, each engrossed with their own thoughts. *I hope Julie's not like me—that she won't find it hard ever to trust again.*

◆◆◆

Julie came back downstairs with her hair neatly combed and wearing fresh lipstick. The sweater was gone, and the long-sleeved shirt she wore underneath had two buttons unfastened at the neck, displaying more freckles than cleavage.

Ellen poked a piece of potato with a fork. "These are about ready to mash. Gussying up for the men, Julie? I think they're going to be too tired to notice."

Roberta smiled at Sarah. "Not many eligible men around, especially our age, so when there's a bunch of them in one place—"

"They're here," Roberta said. "Sarah, if you want to pour coffee, we'll get the potatoes and gravy finished up and slice the turkey."

The searchers crowded into the room while Sarah pulled Styrofoam cups from a plastic sleeve. Some of the men went to the fireplace, where they rotated their bodies every few minutes to warm both front and back. Others settled at the kitchen counter or the makeshift tables. Greg went back to the laundry room for logs and added one to the fire. Sarah, already too warm from working in the kitchen, pulled her hair away from her neck. If the men didn't thaw out soon, the overcrowded room was going to get stuffy.

She glanced around, looking for the girls. Gracie, her face animated, chatted with Paul, who bent his head toward the child. Lottie wasn't listening to whatever her sister was telling him. Her attention was on Greg and the other men who had been coming to the cabin after searching for her mother.

Sarah drew two cups of coffee from the percolator but, before she could carry them to the counter, Julie grabbed them. She took one to Jake and the other to Greg, both standing by the fireplace, then stayed between them, chatting.

"Spends more time flirting than working," Ellen muttered. "Seems like she'd have a little common decency at a time like this, and leave Greg alone..." She blushed when she realized Sarah had overheard. "Sorry. Don't pay me any mind. I'm just tired and cranky."

Sarah stole a glance at Greg, to see how he was reacting to Julie's flirting. But Julie had edged closer to Jake, whispering something in his ear. Was she trying to make Greg jealous?

Snatches of conversation came to Sarah as she worked her way around the tables, serving food.

"...can't figure out why we're just getting out here...how long has she been missing?"

"...search those mine shafts...need people experienced with that...glad I'm not the one going down into them..."

"...had more than his share of bad luck...damned shame, though..."

"...hear she's loaded...may be a kidnapper, instead of the convict...but you'd think they'd have made contact by now..."

The girls shouldn't be here, shouldn't hear any of this. Sarah hurried toward the dining room table, but Greg already leaned over Lottie, his mouth close to her ear. She nodded, took Gracie's hand, and pulled the reluctant little girl away from Paul.

When they reached the bottom of the stairs, Lottie looked back at Jake. He was seated at one of the folding tables, Julie leaning over him. She held a coffee carafe in one hand. The other rested on Jake's back.

From the chair beside him, Bill surveyed the room, his gaze settling on each occupant for a minute or more—sometimes several more—before moving on. At the moment, his attention was on a man across the room, one Sarah didn't know. The man was watching Greg and, for an instant so brief it barely registered, a look of pure hatred flashed across his face. Who was he?

Stunned, Sarah looked back at Bill. His gaze locked with hers, his dark eyes intense, his face void of expression.

Chapter 8
Sunday Afternoon

Sarah had little time to think about either Bill Ayers or the man who had displayed so much hatred toward Greg. The temporary lull had subsided, the women preparing for the next group of searchers.

They came in small clusters of two or three, mixing with the few stragglers left from the first shift. Sarah worked around them, dumping paper plates and plastic cutlery into a black garbage bag. Julie followed, wiping down tables.

Loud voices drew her attention to the front door. A portly man stood just inside, a holstered gun hanging from his belt, and a star-shaped badge pinned to his shirt. Sheriff Maynor. The belt cradled a hefty paunch, and the shirt buttons strained against the edges of their holes. His sausage-like fingers didn't look like they would fit into the gun's trigger guard. How long, in an emergency, would it take for him to fire it?

He glared at Greg, who, along with Jake, had followed the sheriff inside.

"Those dogs can't find what's not there. If you guys hadn't mucked up the trail so much—"

Greg, fists curled into tight knots, took a step forward. Jake put a hand on his shoulder.

"Sheriff, we didn't have a hell of a lot of choices," he said. "Nobody else was looking for her."

Maynor shook his head. "All you did was mess up any scent trail. The dogs could have followed the scent on that scarf from where she dropped it in the snow. Now that's all gone."

"Maybe there's no scent because somebody shoved her into an off-road vehicle of some kind," another man said. "That old two-track's close to where they found her stuff. It's overgrown, but passable. At least, it would have been Friday afternoon, before it snowed so much."

Sarah drew in a sharp breath. If Tracy had left the area in somebody's vehicle, the searchers might never find her.

"You could be onto something," the sheriff said. "The scarf and phone led toward that old road. In fact, they weren't far from it. Maybe she went out there to meet up with somebody." He squinted at Greg. "Didn't you say she was going the wrong direction?"

Greg's face reddened. "She wouldn't do that. She's not that kind of person, and she'd never leave the girls." He turned, his gaze drifting toward the stairs. Gracie stood on a tread about half-way down, holding her doll by one arm, looking over the railing.

Irritation flitted across Greg's features. "Where's Lottie? Did she bring you back down, after I told her to stay up there?"

Gracie's arm jerked, and she dropped the doll. Was she afraid of him? "I...I was looking for her. I can't find her anywhere."

"Isn't she in your room?"

Gracie shook her head and bent to retrieve the doll. "And not in the bathroom, either."

"What about the junk room?" Sarah asked. "She's probably in there, hiding from you."

"No, she's not. I looked everywhere. She's not here."

Would Lottie have sneaked back down after Greg sent the girls upstairs? No, one of them would have seen her. Something was wrong. Sarah raced to the stairs, Greg close behind.

"You take the left side," he said. "I'll go right."

Sarah headed for her room. It was undisturbed, everything in place, and there were few places to look. She opened the closet door and flicked on the light.

"Lottie, are you in there?"

The few garments Sarah had brought with her occupied little space, and the bottom held only her suitcase. She eyed it for a second. Not big enough. Bending, she peered into the dark space under the bed, then moved on to the bathroom, checking behind the door and the shower curtain. Lottie wasn't there.

"Lottie, where are you? Are you hiding from us?"

Sarah ran down the hall to the girls' room. It, too, was neat, Lottie's side in its usual perfect order. Sarah searched under the beds and in the closet, her chest tightening with fear. *Don't panic. She's got to be here, somewhere.*

She wasn't in this bathroom, either. Maybe the junk room. Lots of hiding spaces there.

Greg was already in the room, calling for Lottie, pushing through the jumble of cast-off furnishings, toys, and boxes, shoving them aside as he worked toward the back.

A flicker of motion drew Sarah's attention to the right.

Just the mirror. Fear clutched at her throat. Lottie had to be downstairs, hidden away somewhere. Maybe in the small bathroom or—where? There weren't many places to hide in that big room, especially with so many people in it.

Greg ran downstairs, yelling, "She's not up there. She's got to be— "

"Not here, either, Jake said. "We've looked everywhere."

"The bathroom?" Sarah called.

"She's not there," Jake said. "Fan out, everybody, and start looking. She can't have gotten far."

Sarah ran to the laundry room for her parka. Which direction would Lottie go? Not toward the main road. It was too open; she'd be too visible. The footpath would be out, too, for the same reason, unless she used the tree-lined edge for cover.

Okay, Sarah, calm down and think. If the child was looking for her mother—and Sarah could think of no other reason why she'd venture out—she would choose the same route Tracy had taken. Would that be toward the washed out bridge? Did Lottie even know her mother hadn't gone that way? And the child had said something about knowing where to look—the places where her mother liked to walk.

Before Sarah could put an arm into the parka sleeve, the sheriff held up a pudgy hand. "Hold it, everybody. We don't want these tracks messed up, too. It's snowed since the last search of those woods right behind the cabin, so there shouldn't be many footprints out there. Hers will be small—easy to spot. I should be able to pick up her trail easy enough. So everybody just stay put, while my team conducts a professional search."

Greg pushed past him. "Can it, Maynor. That's my little girl out there, and I'm going to find her."

Paul grabbed his arm. "Greg, wait. The sheriff has a point. Lottie will leave tracks. If everybody goes out there looking, somebody is going to walk all over them. Let the sheriff and his men try first."

"I'm not saying everybody. Just me. I can keep back, away—"

The sheriff sighed. "Mr. Agerton, I'm doing my best to work with you here. I know you're distraught. But the longer we argue, the farther away your little girl is getting. And I can order you to stay here if that's what you want. Arrest you if you get in my way."

Greg stared at him. "You...you wouldn't—"

Jake stepped between them. "Okay, Sheriff, you've made your point. You've got thirty minutes. Make good use of it. Keep in mind that there may be a kidnapper out there, waiting to grab her."

Sarah shoved one of Lottie's mittens into Maynor's hand. Dropping the parka, she sank onto the boot bench, wrapping both hands across the knot in her stomach. Once again, she could do nothing but stay in the cabin and wait for news. But this time it was a little girl out there in the woods, a troubled child who just wanted to find her mother.

Lottie probably thought the woods near the house were safe; they'd been searched Friday night and all day Saturday. She didn't know a kidnapper might be lurking there, watching the cabin. In trying to protect her by withholding that information, they might have put her at greater risk.

Footsteps approached, and Sarah raised her head, her gaze moving from the gnarled hand offering her a napkin to the soft eyes behind gold-rimmed glasses. She hadn't realized until then her cheeks were wet.

"We'll find her," Paul said. "She can't move fast in the snow, and she doesn't have much of a head start. The sorriest mutt in the world should be able to track her in just a few minutes."

Swiping boots off the end of the bench, he lowered himself to sit beside Sarah. Arms around her, he patted her back while she cried silent tears. Just for a moment, she relaxed against him, welcoming the comfort of his arms—something she'd missed for too long. He smelled of the outdoors, a clean, woody scent she couldn't define, and something else that drew her closer, back into the past and another man's arms. In them, she had been safe, secure, loved. She closed her eyes and nestled closer, drawing in the scent. Aqua Velva, her father's shaving lotion. She pulled away, scrambling to her feet.

Paul hesitated, then rose, too, the look in his eyes puzzled, with perhaps a hint of hurt.

Embarrassed, she patted his hand. "Thanks, Paul. I just...I forgot all about Gracie, what she must be feeling, with Lottie gone."

Sarah looked around the room. Roberta Adrickson gave her a little half-wave. Gracie sat on the woman's lap, eating a cookie. Roberta leaned down, murmuring something to the child as she brushed hair away from Gracie's cheek. The girl smiled up at her. Gracie was all right.

Sarah followed Paul toward the alcove, where Greg and Jake sat. Bill leaned against the bookcase, watching as she approached. Jake rose and offered his chair, while Paul retrieved two more. The room's other occupants stayed near the kitchen, talking among themselves in low tones, while Julie and Ellen moved among them, serving food and coffee.

Greg sat, elbows on the table, his hands cupping his face.

"I don't understand. I've told her over and over again that she has to stay inside, that it's not safe out there. Why would she sneak out like that?"

"To look for her mother," Sarah said. "She's ten years old and I doubt she really understands the danger."

He raised his head. "But she knows we're spending hours out there searching. What does she think she can do that we can't?"

"She believes she knows, better than anybody, where to find Tracy. They went on walks together..." Sarah looked deep into his eyes. "And those hours you've spent searching? She's been where you are right now, waiting. You've had less than fifteen minutes of it. She's had two days. How does it feel?" Sarah waited, but he said nothing. "And you get to the point where you have to do *something*. I think that's where Lottie is right now."

"I'm sorry. I didn't think. I guess I didn't realize..."

An uneasy silence enveloped them as the minutes ticked away, more noticeable because of the low buzz of voices at the other end of the room and the dull clatter from the kitchen.

Jake shifted in his chair. "She'll be okay, Greg. Maynor will find her. Even he can follow fresh tracks."

"What if he doesn't? If the kidnapper is out there, watching and waiting?"

Bill Ayers, still leaning against the bookcase, looked up from his cell phone.

"Maynor will find her. If he doesn't, we will. And if we don't find her right away, well—we have to do it right. Bring in some real search dogs, some that have been trained for tracking. I've been doing a little research—found some sites. They say you should call them as soon as possible after somebody goes missing." He raised a questioning eyebrow at Greg. "Maybe we should think about that. To find Tracy."

That was the longest sentence he'd uttered in Sarah's presence, and she let the melody of his words play over her, soothing her.

"We don't have to go through the sheriff?" Greg asked.

"I don't think so. It just says to call them as soon as you can after the person goes missing. Doesn't say anything about law enforcement."

"I don't know. Maybe we should—"

The low hum of voices at the other end of the room had escalated. Sarah looked out the window. The sheriff came around the corner of the cabin, leading Lottie toward the front door.

"Oh, thank you, God." Sarah rose and took quick steps toward the door, but Greg pushed past her.

Stop, Sarah. She's his daughter, not yours.

The sheriff, preening for the room full of people and wearing a smug smile, brought Lottie into the cabin. She ran past Greg, straight into Sarah's arms.

Sarah held her tight. "Oh, Lottie, honey, I was so worried. Are you all right? Why—"

"Charlotte."

The girl stiffened at the sound of Greg's voice. He had her arm, pulling her away. She clung to Sarah, then let go as Greg turned her toward the stairs.

Couldn't he have given the child just a moment to feel safe in somebody's arms before he jerked her away? He was upset and probably over-reacting because he was scared. But Sarah had to fight the urge to go upstairs, to make sure Lottie was all right.

The men sat in awkward silence, not looking at each other or at Sarah.

I hope Greg handles this gently. Lottie was so fragile, this wasn't the time to punish her. Yet, they had to make sure she never went out there again. If she hadn't been missed so quickly, and if the man who took Tracy still lurked near the cabin, the searchers might be looking for both mother and daughter. A chill crept up Sarah's arms as she looked out at the snow-covered trees and the deeper, darker forest beyond. She would try to talk to Lottie later and explain the danger.

A reflection of afternoon sun off metal drew her attention to the road. A dark blue SUV approached, followed by two more cars. They came to a stop in the yard. Beyond them, just turning into the lane, three more vehicles appeared. More searchers to feed?

She started toward the door, but Sheriff Maynor cut in front of her. The occupants of the first cars were already getting out, carrying microphones and cameras. The sheriff straightened his tie, hoisted his belt a little higher around his waist, and opened the door. Holding up both palms, he walked toward them.

Greg bounded down the last two stairs and strode across the room. "That pompous jerk! He's called the damned reporters. Had to have called them as soon as he found her, for them to get here that fast. Now he'll tell them all about how he tracked a missing little girl through the snow and found her in the woods."

The instant he stepped out the door, the reporters turned from the sheriff, who was just beginning to speak, and converged on Greg. He batted a hand at the microphone thrust toward his face. A photographer aimed his camera at the confrontation. Others milled around them, trying to get closer. A woman with short-cropped blonde hair thrust a microphone toward Greg.

"What can you tell us about the search, Mr. Agerton?"

Before he could respond, another asked, "Is your little girl all right?"

Greg backed toward the cabin door. "She's fine. She just wandered off, wasn't gone for more than half an hour." He glared at the sheriff. "I'm sorry you were called out here, because there's no news, other than the sheriff failing to find any trace of my wife. I gave you a statement this morning, including an appeal for Tracy's return. I don't know what more I can tell you."

The blonde pushed closer. "We want to know how you feel—"

"How I feel? How do you think I feel?" His voice rose. "What you really want is to arouse emotion you can capture on camera. I guess it plays well on TV. You probably hoped my daughter was lost, so you'd have a bigger story. You'd just love to get a picture of one of our little girls crying, wouldn't you? Well, I've got news for you. You're on private property. I'll give you fifteen minutes to get out, or I'm asking the sheriff to remove you."

"But it was the sheriff—"

"I don't give a damn. He can schedule his press conferences somewhere else. So the next time he calls you, arrange a different meeting place."

He turned and went back into the cabin, slamming the door behind him.

Jake applauded, three slow claps. "Nice speech. But are you sure you want to make an enemy of the sheriff?"

"Not to mention the reporters," Paul added.

"I don't think I could hurt my relationship with Maynor much more than I already did this morning." Greg shrugged. "I doubt he's going to be the sheriff, anyway, after this next election. By the time I come back up here, Deputy Martin is probably going to fill that spot. As for the reporters—yeah, I guess I went a little overboard. I'll apologize tomorrow. But they have to stay away from here."

As soon as everybody left the cabin that afternoon, Sarah went back to the junk room, now strewn with the boxes and discarded toys Greg had dug through in his search for Lottie. Shoving them aside, Sarah worked her way to the window. She didn't see anything, but hadn't expected to. There had been too much activity around the cabin. The kidnapper would keep his distance.

Leaving the binoculars, she went back into the hall, passing the girls' open door. Lottie lay on her bed, looking out the window into the woods behind the house.

"Lottie, are you okay?"

The girl nodded but kept her focus on the outside view.

Sarah sat on the edge of the bed. "You scared everybody when you went out there. We were afraid something bad might happen to you."

Lottie turned to look at her. "Nothing happened. Besides, they already searched out there, around the cabin. I don't see why we have to stay inside all the time."

Maybe Greg should tell the girls about the man watching the house. It might scare them, but better frightened than kidnapped.

"Honey, I'm not scolding you. I just want to keep you safe. I know you want to help look for your mother—"

Lottie shook her head, quick little shakes. "I didn't..." Her gaze slid away from Sarah's, back toward the window. The girl didn't—what? If she hadn't been looking for her mother, what was she doing? Running away? Sarah waited, but Lottie didn't say anything more.

"Okay. If you need to talk, just let me know." No response.

What had happened to the little girl who ran into Sarah's arms earlier? Something had changed. What had Greg done?

Chapter 9
Sunday Evening

That evening, after the search had ended for the day, Jake, the Graysons, Paul and Bill returned to the cabin with Greg, all of them tired and discouraged. It had started snowing again, big flakes adding to the drifts under the windows.

Greg poured coffee, then pulled out a bottle of Knob Creek bourbon and added a splash to their mugs. Sarah put a hand over her cup; the smell of whiskey brought back too many unpleasant memories of her failed marriage.

Strangely, the strongest ones were no longer those of Scott finally coming home after the bars closed, the foolish grin on his face sending a message that it was all just good fun—unless she made an issue of it.

Now the memories that most often resurfaced were of the hours she'd waited alone, many of them at the window facing the street, watching headlights as cars turned the corner, then drove on past the house. And, finally, the night she'd found herself hoping something would happen to him, that he would never come home again, followed by the bitter thought that he probably wouldn't die—he'd just do enough damage that she'd have to take care of him the rest of her life.

She looked up, raising her hand from the cup. They'd finished pouring the whiskey, and somebody was speaking to her.

"The sheriff is getting some dog teams out here," Robert said. "Some air scenters."

"What is an air scenter?"

"I guess there are different kinds of search dogs," Jake said, "depending on the circumstances. There are trackers, that mostly just follow a scent trail, usually from something the person wore. But if somebody else crosses that trail, the dog may get distracted and follow the new scent.

"Then there are trailers. They track, too, but they also have some air-scenting training. If they lose the track, they can some-times smell the person they're following and pick it up again. Last are air scenters. They don't track. They just hone in on whatever human scent is in the air."

"Not just Tracy's?"

"No. Anybody in the area. But that might not be a bad thing. The dog could search for both the kidnapper and Tracy at the same time. The disadvantage is, the dog can't discriminate between the targets and other people who may be in the area, so the searchers would have to pull back."

"What kind are the ones the sheriff used?" Robert asked.

Bill studied him with the same intent gaze that had so often unnerved Sarah. "Probably none of them. All dogs have innate abilities, but search dogs need to be trained. So do their teams of handlers. Maynor's dogs aren't worthless, Robert. The sheriff just expected more than he or the dogs were capable of doing. I'm glad he realized that and brought in the professionals."

"I suspect Jody Martin had something to do with that decision," Bill said. "That deputy is smarter than Maynor, and he knows it."

"Which is probably why he's worried about the election," Jake said. "Anyway, if they use one of the air scenters, everybody will have to pull out except the dog teams. Maybe we can search over to the east, beyond the old bridge, while they're doing that. We don't think she's there, but—" He shrugged, and Sarah nodded.

They can't stand by and do nothing.

"Greg," she said, "if you can't join the search, do you suppose we could get the Highlander out of the ditch? We're low on supplies. If I had the car, I could take the girls with me to do some shopping." A trip to the grocery store had never seemed so enticing.

Robert shook his head. "No way you're gonna get that car out. The road back there is snowed in. They don't plow it, you know?"

Greg avoided her eyes. "I was going to talk to you about that. I think everybody's agreed, after what happened today, we're moving the search base somewhere else so the girls won't be exposed to all the talk, and we can keep a closer eye on them. So we won't be needing so many supplies."

He meant she could keep a closer eye on them; he wouldn't be around. "So the women won't be coming? They'll do all that somewhere else?"

He nodded. "Less work for you."

Less contact with other people, too. No break in the stifling boredom of the cabin. And if she had to keep the girls in a confined area, away from the windows because of the reporters, she might end up crawling under her quilt and pulling it over her head.

"We'll still come by at night for coffee," Jake said, "catch you up on what's going on. If you don't mind, that is."

Greg shifted and looked toward the big windows. "Look, I know that's going to make it tough for you, being cooped up in here all the time. But it should only be for another day or two, at most. Give me a list of the groceries we need for the four of us, and maybe something for the rest of these guys once in a while. I'll get somebody to bring them out."

She bit her lip to ward off tears. She should go up and check on the girls—get her emotions under control. She'd heard a noise earlier in the hallway, maybe Lottie or Gracie looking for her, then realizing the men were still there.

Jake was studying her face, his gaze lingering on her eyes. Were her eyelashes damp?

"Sarah," he said, there's something you could do while you're cooped up in here. We can't be sure the kidnapper's in the search area. By now, he'll be getting desperate to make contact. If you kept watch with the binoculars, and we positioned ourselves to move in fast when you called us, we might have a chance at catching him."

"He'll come at night," Tim protested. "She can't stay up all night and still take care of the girls during the day."

"She won't have to," Jake said. "The rest of us can do night shifts. We won't be out searching during the day for a while, and he's going to make contact soon. He has to."

"If he's watching the cabin, he'd see you coming and going during the night," Greg said.

"We don't have to watch from here. Sarah can probably manage the early evening, then you can take a big chunk in the middle of the night. The rest of us can alternate, from someplace else. Maybe our cars."

"I don't know about that," Greg said. "The girls will be scared if they know a man may be trying to sneak up to the cabin, and I'm not sure we can keep watch without them suspecting anything."

Sarah needed this. It would keep her busy, occupy her mind. "I think we can if you spend more time with them at night." That's something he should be doing anyway. "During the day, they pretty much entertain themselves, so I should be able to get away every so often without them noticing."

Greg shook his head. "You can't stand in front of the kitchen window or the pane in the laundry room door without alerting the girls. You'd have to go upstairs to see the back. You'd have to spend too much time up there. The girls would wonder what was going on."

Jake nodded. "He's not going to come to the front. He'd be in full view of the road, and any cars that might be passing by. He'll come through the woods at the back, where he's got some cover, or from one of the sides."

"I'm telling you, the girls don't pay that much attention," Sarah said.

"No. There's no way we can make it work..." Greg's voice trailed off for a moment when he glanced at Bill, whose unblinking gaze was locked onto Greg's face. Greg shrugged. "Okay, let's say she's right, and we do this. How can we stay out of sight, especially during the day, and still be close enough to catch him?"

Paul rubbed his glasses with a napkin and held them up to the light, peering through one lens. "I've been thinking about that. If he doesn't come through the search area, he's got to use a vehicle to get close enough. There's only the main road, the old road to the bridge, and the overgrown two-track in the woods. I'd say, if we can watch all those roads, there's no way he can escape, once Sarah calls us. Even if she misses him, we'd still have a good chance of spotting him."

"But he'll see our cars," Greg protested.

"Several pull-outs with good cover we can use. They're a distance from the cabin, but it doesn't matter. We'll still be able to cut him off before he can get to his rig. And if he should get past us, we'll see him, get a license number or something."

Jake drummed his fingers on the counter. "It's slim, but it might work. He's got to make contact to have any chance of collecting the ransom, and this may be his best chance."

Tim slid off his stool. "Well, we don't have anything else going on. You think we should talk to the sheriff about it? Maybe get some help?" Before anybody could respond, he shook his head. "Nah, we don't want Maynor anywhere close to this."

Jake slapped his hand on the counter as he rose. "Okay, let's do it. Sarah until about nine tonight, then Greg until what? Midnight? I can take it from then until three if the rest of you guys can cover it until seven. That gives everybody a short shift and time to rest before we come back to our daytime positions."

"Sounds good," Tim said, "I'll take the three to five shift. Give the old man here a good night's sleep. He's up at five, anyway." He gave Paul's shoulder a light tap.

"Sarah," Jake said, "I doubt he'll show himself during the day, but if he does, just call one of us as soon as you spot him. I think he'll come tonight. Tomorrow night at the latest."

Finally, there was something useful she could do to help with the search and, as a bonus, it would keep her occupied.

The others nodded their approval, saying nothing more as they took their leave. Just before Jake joined them at the door, he touched her arm. "I'll help you get your car out if you can wait a day or two."

She squeezed his hand and nodded, afraid her voice might tremble if she spoke. Then Greg clasped Jake's shoulder and walked him out to his vehicle.

Echoes of their voices filtered into the cabin as they headed for their cars, followed by the sound of the engines starting up, one by one. Sarah waited, but Greg didn't come back inside. The kitchen window gave her a clear view out the back, and the big windows across the room looked out on the front. Nothing moved.

She went upstairs, got the girls to bed, and came back down to the laundry room window. Giving her eyes time to adjust, she peered out into the darkness. Seeing nothing, she crossed to one of the big windows. There was no movement. Where was Greg? What did he do out there at night?

Was he keeping watch, or trying to avoid an awkward conversation about Lottie? Or another question from Sarah about the grandparents' arrival?

If he didn't want to talk, she couldn't force a conversation, but she needed to leave as soon as she could get the Highlander out. *I wonder if I could hire somebody to plow the road?* Probably not, but it was worth checking out.

She went up to the junk room to start her shift. A scan from the east-facing window showed her nothing but darkness. Through the other, front-facing window, distant lights moved, so dim they probably came from a road beyond the one leading to the cabin. Time to go to her room and check the west side.

On the way, she glanced through the girls' open bedroom door. They slept, Lottie's face buried in her pillow, Gracie's foot sticking out from under the quilt. Sarah tucked the foot in and went to her own room. She pulled her phone out of the drawer and checked for messages. Laura had called three times.

"I've been worried," she said, "and you had your phone turned off."

"I'm sorry. It was in my room. After Lottie got her hands on it, I thought it would be safer—"

Laura interrupted. "It's all over the national news. They're saying now they're not sure the convict was ever spotted up there closer to the border. The woman who reported it was on edge, and, from what her neighbors say, jumping at shadows ever since the convict escaped. When the cops talked to her again, the description didn't really fit."

Sarah stood at the window, looking out with the binoculars. "Great. That's all I needed to hear—that he may be down here, after all."

But it might mean the federal and state authorities would look closer at Tracy's disappearance and finally get involved in the search. It might also mean Tracy was in the hands of the convict, not a kidnapper. Which would be worse? And if no kidnapper had ever, existed, who was the man watching the house?

"Are you still there?" Laura asked.

Sarah lowered the binoculars and moved to the other window. "Oh. Yeah. Just thinking. I hadn't heard. But the area around the cabin has been thoroughly searched, and I keep the doors locked all the time. I'm concerned, though, about Lottie. She ran away today." Sarah told Laura about the rest of the day's events.

Laura was silent for so long Sarah prompted "Laura?"

"I...I don't know what to say, except...you have to get out of there as soon as you can. When are the children's grandparents supposed to get there?"

"I don't know. To be honest, I'm not sure they're even on the way. Greg doesn't seem to be sure how to find them—said something about a cruise."

"What kind of people are these? Some of them sound so creepy...everything happening so strange."

On a par with your dreams, cuz. Sarah smiled. "I was hoping you could explain some of it to me. Are you telling me you haven't had any dreams?"

"Don't even joke about that." Laura's voice sounded thick. "I only dream when somebody I love is in danger. You know that."

"Then everything must be okay, right?"

Laura's voice sounded even more strangled. "No, it's not. By the time I dream, it will be too late. You'll already be in trouble." Was she crying?

"I'm sorry, Laura. I didn't mean to upset you. I was just trying to lighten things up a little, maybe make you laugh."

"I'll laugh when I hear you're on a plane, on your way home. Sarah, seriously, those people are just weird, and all the stuff going on—"

"I'll admit I'm not sleeping well. I can't figure Bill Ayers out. He and Greg must be good friends. They were in second grade together, and he came that first night when Greg had trouble getting anybody to help him look for Tracy. But he rarely speaks. He just watches—no, studies—everybody else. And his look is so penetrating, it's like he's looking right into your soul. Maybe that's just because he's so quiet, and he has those dark eyes and almost jet-black hair. Then he speaks, and his voice—it's like angels singing, and you forget all the rest of it."

"You do have a rather vivid imagination."

"I'm not imagining the guy who was looking at Greg with so much hatred. And Lottie. Why would she leave the cabin? The way she ran right past Greg when she came back, straight to me...I don't think I've ever seen that child show any affection for her father."

"You don't think there's anything going on there? Molestation? The way she behaves and that drawing...she's obviously troubled."

"Oh, God, I don't even want to go there. Things are bad enough already, without thinking—"

"You're right. But if something like that _is_ going on, what is that little girl going to do? Her grandparents may or may not be coming, and it doesn't seem likely her mother will be found. If you leave, she's going to be even more vulnerable."

"I thought you wanted me to leave."

"I do, but...is there any way you can find help for her first? See that she and her little sister are safe?"

"I can't do anything without her father's approval, unless there's actually some kind of abuse going on, and I don't know how I'd find out what's troubling her. Whatever it is, she's keeping to herself. I thought, the way she ran to me, I was finally getting close to her, but apparently not."

"I guess you just keep an eye on things and decide what to do when the time comes. Maybe you'll know more by then."

"Okay. I guess that's the best I can do. Give everybody my love."

She ended the call and turned back to the first window. Nothing was stirring in the yard. Not on this side, at least. She went back to the junk room and settled into the rocking chair. It took a few minutes for her eyes to adjust so she could discern a difference in the shades of darkness. The next time she went to her room, she'd leave the lights off.

There, a flicker of motion. Could it be him? She intensified her focus. A deer, standing at the edge of the woods. She inched the binoculars along at the same level but saw nothing else. Two more sweeps of the entire area showed her nothing more.

She yawned, waited a few minutes, and made another sweep. Still nothing, and it was after ten. Past time for Greg to take up the watch. She rose and headed back toward her room.

A glance at the girls as she passed their room told her Gracie's foot was still under the covers. And Lottie—

Lottie wasn't there. Her bed was empty. She wasn't in the room.

The bathroom door stood open, and nobody was inside. A little panicky, Sarah rushed down the hall, past Greg's open door. Nobody was there. This time, she didn't call out to Lottie, for fear of waking Gracie and scaring her.

Sarah ran down the stairs. The big room was dark. Would a child venture down there and not turn on the lights?

Flicking them on, Sarah stood and listened. Nothing but the hum of the refrigerator.

Fear pushing up into her throat, she searched the room. It didn't take long. There weren't many places big enough to conceal the girl.

What was going on? The mother disappearing, and now the child? Had Lottie run away again? Sarah shook her head. No ten-year-old ran away in the dark. That meant somebody had taken her. But how? Sarah had checked the locks before she went upstairs, and she'd been right across the hall, with both doors open. That meant Lottie had sneaked downstairs and outside. But Greg was out there somewhere. He would have seen if anybody approached or left the house, and Sarah had been watching. *The back. I was watching the back, not the front.* Greg undoubtedly was doing the same thing.

You're wasting time. The fastest way to contact Greg would be by phone. She ran up the stairs. She'd call him, then 9-1-1.

Panting for breath, she flung the door open and ran for the phone. Out of the corner of her eye, she glimpsed movement and whirled.

Lottie sat in the dark corner beyond the bed, the phone held to her ear. She looked up at Sarah, her eyes wide.

"Don't tell," she pleaded. "I had to. Please don't tell."

Chapter 10
Monday

Still tired, Sarah lay under the warm quilt, reluctant to get up. Two shifts of meal preparation, along with Lottie running away, then staying up late to keep watch, had all taken their toll. Now she had a new problem—what to do about finding Lottie with the cell phone.

The obvious answer would be to tell Greg, but there was something about the girl's frightened eyes, her pleading "Don't tell. I had to," that made Sarah hesitant. She needed to know more, especially after the questions raised by Laura in last night's telephone conversation. There was something off about the relationship between this father and daughter.

The number Sarah had found in her cell phone log was not a local area code, and it was the same number Lottie had called the day before, when Sarah had suspected her of using the phone. So the girl wasn't making random calls, as Greg had suggested, nor was she calling exotic locales. Who had the child been talking to, and what could be so important to her that she would risk sneaking into Sarah's room to use her phone? Sarah would have to put a pass code on it.

She could call the number in the call log and find out who was on the other end but, until she knew more about what she was dealing with, she had to be cautious. Best try to find out who the number belonged to first, maybe through a reverse phone directory.

She'd also like to know more about the man whose face had displayed so much hatred toward Greg. It was difficult to ask about him because she didn't know his name, and couldn't have provided much of a description: average height and build, hair probably dark brown or black, smooth-shaven, even features.

Finally, she threw the covers back. She didn't understand any of it. So many of these people just seemed strange. She got dressed, ate breakfast, and went to make her first sweep with the binoculars, even though she suspected the kidnapper would not approach during the day. Apparently, he hadn't come during the night, either. If he'd made contact, left any kind of message, Greg would have let her know.

She couldn't see much through the falling snow. Judging from the height of the drifts alongside the lane, it must have fallen all night. No cars lined the road, and no sound penetrated the windows of the cabin.

She let out a little sigh of relief. She wouldn't have to worry about keeping the girls away from the windows and the reporters today.

She needed to be more understanding. They were just trying to earn a living. It was a small community, and this was undoubtedly the biggest story they'd had in years. But their presence had made a difficult task even harder and had probably kept the kidnapper away.

The kidnapper! What better time to approach than under cover of the snowstorm? And they hadn't foreseen this, hadn't planned for a daytime watch.

She grabbed her phone and called Greg. He assured her they were aware of the changed situation and were depending on her to alert them if the kidnapper came near the cabin.

"We're watching, too," he said, "so even if you miss him, one of us should pick him up with the binoculars. He can't get in close by car. All the back roads are pretty deep in snow. He'll have to come in on the main one—the one out front—and hike from there. Probably not straight in. He'll angle off into the woods and come from the back or side, to stay out of sight." He paused. "But, then again, if the snow keeps coming down like this, he may figure that gives him enough cover. Just do the best you can. We're spread out close enough to come in quick."

She put the phone down and pushed one of the boxes aside with her foot to make more room around the window. She wouldn't be able to get the Highlander out for a while; she was trapped.

"What are you doing?" Lottie again, in her silent sock feet.

"Cleaning up." Sarah pushed the box toward the corner. "Your dad threw some of this stuff around yesterday, looking for you." She shoved the carton against two others, still stacked along the wall. The girl watched, solemn-faced, not moving.

"Did you...are you going to tell him?"

"Tell? Oh, the phone. I don't know, Lottie. He's your father, and he should know about it. But I think you should tell him, not me."

"I can't." Lottie looked down at the floor.

"Is there something you need to talk about? Tell somebody? Because if you do, I'm a pretty good listener. And maybe I can help."

"I...I can't. But please don't tell. I won't do it again. I promise."

Sarah's nod was instinctive, unplanned. It might not be the right thing to do, but it felt right, and she wouldn't have to put a password on her phone. If there were consequences later, she'd just have to deal with them. But she couldn't help wondering if her strained relationship with her own father was skewing her judgment.

"Thanks," Lottie whispered before she turned and ran down the stairs.

Sarah sat in the rocking chair, staring at the doorway, long after Lottie ran through it. How could she help the girl if she couldn't figure out what was going on, and Lottie wouldn't talk to her?

Had it been like that with her own father? No. Nothing like this. Whatever was back there in her childhood, it didn't feel threatening. It was just a void, a dark emptiness—until the night her mother died. Sarah sighed and went back to the window.

In between sweeps of the area with the binoculars, she checked the news bulletins. The convict was still on the loose, despite the massive manhunt, and there was speculation he might have slipped past the searchers, over the border and into Canada.

The day wore on, with nothing disturbing the stillness. Snow still fell, piling ever higher in the lane. Would the men be able to get their vehicles back in? They hadn't called, but they must be aware.

Back at the front-facing window late in the afternoon, Sarah surveyed the empty road. A vehicle approached in the distance, coming from town. One of the searchers, on his way back to the area around the mine? No, it was Greg's blue Chevy Tahoe, slowing for the turn into the snowy lane. Why was he back so early?

"I went to town for some groceries," he said, putting two paper bags on the counter. "Something smells good."

"Lasagna, with what's left of the sourdough. I'm glad to see you brought some stuff for salad." She pulled a bundle of lettuce from the bag. "You're back earlier than I expected."

"Maynor called me into his office, and I thought as long as I was there, I might as well pick up the groceries."

"What about the others? Jake and Paul and Tim?"

"I just called them. They haven't seen anything all day." He shook his head. "The dogs didn't find anything. Nothing but a kid out there, snowshoeing. Guess he didn't get the word. Anyway, no sign of Tracy, or anybody else. Not even a scrap of clothing. And these were trained dogs. Air scenters."

He pulled groceries out of the bags and put them away. "Maynor says the kidnapper must have taken her that first night, loaded her in a vehicle, and is holding her somewhere."

Greg paused, a package of frozen broccoli in his hand, looking around as though he didn't know where to put it. Sarah took it from him.

"So what does the sheriff plan to do?"

"He figures the ransom demand has got to be in the mail. Nothing else makes any sense. I tend to agree with him. The kidnapper wouldn't have had my cell phone number, and if he was trying to make contact here, he had all of last night and today, with nobody around."

"So we just wait?"

He nodded and stood, motionless. "I can't help thinking...if Maynor had come out here the first night, like I'd asked, we might have caught the guy." He pulled a can of coffee out of the bag. "No, I guess not. I think Tracy was gone before I even went out to look for her. Probably before you got here."

A cold prickle inched its way up Sarah's spine at the suggestion that the man might have been out there during her frantic but slow trek to the cabin.

"They finished searching the mine today." Greg was silent for a few seconds as he put more groceries away. "Nothing there, either. I think they plan to move on to the lake."

Dragging it for Tracy's body, if no ransom note surfaced? Picturing the cold depths of that lake, Sarah shuddered. Would any of them ever be able to sit in the alcove and enjoy the view of the lake again?

"A lot of people are leaving. The sheriff had brought in some teams—dog handlers, and experts in searching mines. They left this afternoon. Some of the local guys are about done, too. I can't blame them. Unlike the sheriff's crew, they have jobs, things they need to take care of, and I can't expect them to do this forever. And we've covered everything close."

He was talking as much to himself as he was to her. Pulling groceries out of the bags, putting them away, talking—just to be doing something. And when he didn't have that to occupy him, would he crash?

"I wish we'd had more time in the woods east of here," he said. "That's the way Tracy should have been going, and I keep thinking about that. We're going to try to get out there tomorrow—just me and the guys."

So that's what Greg would do to keep going, to avoid crashing: find another area to search. But Sarah wasn't sure she could endure even one more day in the cabin, especially with snow obscuring her vision of the outside world. How long would he and the girls stay at the cabin if they didn't find Tracy? How long before he ran out of things to do, places to search?

"Greg, I should be leaving, too. Have you had any success finding Tracy's parents?"

"Maybe. In one of Tracy's texts to them, she mentioned Jamaica. So I'm trying to check out all the cruise lines going there. I also found the number for a couple they spend a lot of time with and left a message, asking if they can help. Do you think you could manage to stay for another day or two until I can find them?"

She nodded. She couldn't leave until she knew the girls would be safe. Maybe another few days would give her a chance to find out what was going on between Lottie and Greg.

Pulling a six-pack cardboard wine tote out of a bag, Greg said, "I hope I got the right brand. I saw you'd marked it off your list when you found out you wouldn't be doing the shopping, and I realized we don't have any wine in the house. You've done so much since you've been here, I wanted to show my appreciation."

"That does it very nicely. Thanks. It was thoughtful of you." She would have to ask about the Highlander later. She put the bottles away. "Dinner is almost ready. If you'll get the girls, I'll finish this up and set the table."

As he headed for the stairs, he said, "Those bottles look a little lonely. I'll pick up some more the next time I'm in town."

Wine wasn't going to help if she had to stay in the cabin much longer. *And if it did he couldn't buy enough and I'd end up taking a lead role at AA meetings.* Three days and one night of intense searching had turned up no trace of his missing wife, but even if the others quit, Greg wouldn't stop looking. Sarah had to find out what was going on with Lottie so she could leave.

"Greg, while you're out there, searching that area, could you guys shovel my car out? I have to get back to New York."

"Yeah," he said. "Of course. I should have thought of that. You've done enough. I keep forgetting you have a life you need to get back to."

"Mom lets us eat at the counter." Lottie stared at the table, her lower lip quivering.

"Charlotte." Greg's voice was low and even, but Lottie's head jerked upright. Was she afraid of him?

"I'm sorry," Sarah said. "I didn't know. I thought, with everybody gone, when it was just family...would you like to help me move everything? If you take the silverware and napkins, I can get the plates and glasses."

Lottie glanced at Greg, then back at Sarah. "No, this is okay." She slid into a chair.

Greg looked on, a frown clouding his face. Sarah would have to talk to him later, try to find out more about the girl's strong reaction to change or disorder. And possibly some insight into their strange relationship.

"I have to apologize for my daughter's rudeness," Greg said, as he took his seat.

He was looking at Sarah and didn't see the anger flash across Lottie's face before she ducked her head. No, it was stronger than anger, but Sarah couldn't quite put her finger on the emotion, it had been so fleeting.

"I'm sorry, too, for the way we've all had to impose on you. Instead of the week of fun my wife had planned, you've been shut up in here, babysitting and cooking and cleaning. I appreciate it more than I can say. Tracy is lucky to have a friend like you."

"I'm glad I could help." The feeble response was all she could manage, and the silence that followed, broken only by the clatter of cutlery on plates, grew heavy. He'd caught her off-balance, spoken more words to her in the last half hour than he'd uttered in the preceding three days.

"Tracy tells me you're from California, that you're going to the design school where she's been taking a class," Greg finally said, in an obvious attempt to break the silence.

"Yes. Commercial design. When I finish, I'll go back home and look for a job."

"You're not working now?"

"No, my aunt left me some money to live on while I go to school."

"It must be hard to be away from home, but I suppose you have a circle of friends in New York?"

"A few." She didn't, really, other than Tracy. Some acquaintances who might become friends, if she put more effort into it. But she had little time to spare. The courses were intense, and she spent long hours after class working on assignments. She'd been in the city for almost nine months and still hadn't found time to explore it the way she wanted. Mostly, it had been the usual tourist attractions: Ellis Island and the Statue of Liberty, the World Trade Center memorial, and Times Square. She'd also taken in a few Broadway productions but still felt more like a tourist than a resident.

"Tell us about your family," Greg prompted.

Heat crept up her neck. He was working hard at conversation, and she wasn't holding up her end. "I don't have a lot. My aunt...the woman who took me in after my mother died, was killed last year. Now there's just my cousin and her husband and their two little boys."

"How old are they?" Lottie asked, interested now.

"Close to the same ages as you and Gracie. Eric is nine, and Jamie is seven. They just had their birthdays, this past August and December."

"What are they like?"

"Eric is a little like you, Lottie. He takes care of his little brother. And Jamie can sometimes be stubborn. Once, about a year ago, his mother got a call. She needed to go to the school because Jamie had passed out."

Lottie's eyes widened. "Passed out? You mean he fainted?"

"Yep. You know why?"

Both girls shook their heads.

"Because he had bet another little boy he could hold his breath the longest."

Greg laughed, the first Sarah had heard from him. Lottie smiled, and Gracie giggled and asked, "What do they like to do?"

Sarah hesitated, reluctant to talk about the gymnastics she'd tried to teach the boys. "Lots of things. They like the River Cats and the Kings. Jamie has a cap with the River Cats logo he wears almost all the time."

Gracie screwed her face into a scowl. "I don't like cats. They scratch."

Greg had risen from his chair and gone into the laundry room. He came back empty-handed, just as Lottie squinted her eyes at Sarah.

"I never heard of a river cat. Are they wild? And we don't have kings in this country. Are you making up stories?"

Sarah laughed. "No, I wouldn't do that. Not unless I told you it was a story. The River Cats is the name of our baseball team. Like the Dodgers or the Giants. And the Kings are...well, they're really the Sacramento Kings, our basketball team. Like the New York Jets."

"Oh." Lottie looked a little disappointed. "What else do they do?"

"Build forts or castles and pretend they're pioneers or cowboys or knights fighting dragons."

"Do they rescue princesses?" Gracie asked.

Sarah laughed again. "I don't know about that. They're boys, after all, and I doubt they think much about girls."

Lottie nodded. Apparently, Sarah had confirmed her own conclusions. But Gracie had more questions.

"Do they like *The Land of Stories*, too? 'Cause it has dragons and castles."

Sarah had downloaded the first book of the series and started reading it to the girls at bedtime.

"I don't know. I haven't seen them for almost a year. But I suspect they do. They like to read."

"Can you read some more to us? After we get ready for bed?"

Sarah glanced at Greg. This was the first night he had been home in time to have dinner with his daughters. "Would you rather do it?" she asked.

"What?"

"Read to the girls before they go to bed. We've been exploring one of the *Land of Stories* books. It's about—"

"A brother and sister who go to an island looking for their father. He's lost," Gracie explained. "Like Mom. And they see dragons and castles and animals that talk."

Greg didn't respond, and Gracie said, "I think maybe Mom is somewhere like that."

Greg stood. "You go ahead." His voice was hoarse. "I'm going out for a walk."

Chapter 11
Monday Night

Sarah's father called while the girls were getting into their nightgowns. Sarah pulled the phone from her pocket, glanced at the display, then hurried from their room before she answered. She walked down the hall toward her own room, keeping her voice low until she could get inside and shut the door.

"What do you want?" she asked.

After a moment of silence, he said, "I want to talk to you, to know what's going on, why you don't answer my calls."

"You know why. Anna."

"Sarah, she's trying her best. I know you two got off to a bad start, but..."

"Oh, is that what she calls it? Getting off to a bad start? When she took my mother's things—jewelry that was supposed to be handed down to me, said hateful things to me about Mom, and drove me out of the house? That was getting off to a bad start?"

"You're blowing it out of proportion. She didn't really—"

"No, you just choose to believe whatever she tells you. And that's fine with me. Just don't expect me to have anything to do with her. Or you."

"Sarah, wait. If you won't do it for me, will you do it for your grandmother? She doesn't understand."

"Because nobody has told her the truth. About Anna, about the night Mom died."

Sarah fought back tears. It was time to end the call. But before she could push the button, he spoke again.

"I'm sorry I wasn't with her that night, Sarah. I wish I'd been there. If I'd known, when I stepped outside the hospital for a breath of fresh air—"

"But that wasn't all you stepped out for that night, was it, Dad?"

"A smoke. My pipe." He hesitated. "You... how did you know I went out to smoke?"

She closed her eyes. She could almost smell the tobacco he used and his Aqua Velva shaving lotion, the scents that had led her to him in the parking lot.

"I saw you," she said, her voice slow and even. "The doctor said there wasn't much time, and I was frantic, dodging around cars, trying to find you. And there you were. You and Anna, in a lip lock so deep you didn't even see me. As far as I know, you were still in it when Mom died."

"Sarah, no—" His voice was strangled now.

"So there I was, fifteen years old, alone, holding my mother's hand while she died."

"You were there? You were in the room?"

"Somebody had to be, and I wasn't going to let her die alone." Sarah ended the call.

When she came back downstairs after reading to the girls, Greg was opening a bottle of wine. "Sorry about earlier. I had to get outside—get some fresh air."

"I had no idea Gracie would identify so much with the book and make a connection between the missing father—"

"—and her mother. Grasping at anything that gives her hope. Just like the rest of us." He poured the wine and carried two glasses to the alcove. "Come and relax for a few minutes. I'd like to know more about your life in Sacramento."

Why was he suddenly so friendly, so interested in her life? Even his interaction with the girls at dinner had been out of character. *You don't know that, Sarah.* Maybe this was his real personality, when he wasn't under so much stress. *And you have trust issues.*

She sank into one of the two armchairs. "There's not much more to tell. Laura is more like a sister to me than a cousin, and I'm fond of her husband Sam. We spend a lot of time together, and I often look after Eric and Jamie."

"What's life in Sacramento like?"

"Wow, that's a broad question. Lots of trees. We rarely get snow, but usually a lot of rain in the winter and hot days in the summer. We have two rivers, so we get fog during the winter, sometimes so thick you can't see to drive."

"You must have lots of water sports, then."

"Skiing, fishing, white-water rafting. And the Sierra Nevadas are close enough for day trips to go skiing or snowboarding, or up to Lake Tahoe. And there's a salmon run."

"And if you're not the athletic type?"

"San Francisco is a couple of hours away, and Napa Valley. We often go wine-tasting, and in the fall, up to Apple Hill. Or Daffodil Hill in the springtime. Then there's the community theater, the Music Circus—one of the few theaters left with a round stage—and the annual music festival in Old Sac."

She took a sip of wine to ease the lump in her throat. "I'm sorry. I didn't mean to give you a travelogue. Like I said, it's a broad question. And it's home."

He was silent for a few minutes. "It sounds nice. I'd like to visit sometime. You've never married?"

"Yes, but it ended last year." *A subject I don't want to get into.* "Enough about my life. Tell me, how did you and Tracy meet."

"A matchmaking friend introduced us. I wasn't ready for another relationship, but Tracy—well, she was something else. We hit it off right away and were married six months later."

"I haven't got to know her very well," Sarah confessed. "We just kind of clicked when we met. We share a love of wine, old movies, and good books, but I don't know much else. What's she like?"

"Tracy? She's...well, how do you describe your wife?" He cupped the globe of his empty wine glass with both palms. "She's fun, likes sports. She's a great skier. But she's smart, too. Probably smarter than I am." He turned to look out the window. "It's stopped snowing." His voice sounded odd, almost like he was disappointed. Then he shook his head and refilled their glasses, dividing up the last of the bottle's contents.

He hadn't said anything about Tracy's role as a mother. "You said you weren't ready for another relationship. Why not?"

"Oh, I..." He took a big gulp of wine. "I'd just lost my wife, and I wasn't looking for another."

"Lost? Like Tracy?" Sarah sat up straighter.

"No. She died. An accident. We were having a pool party at our beach house and she drowned."

"How? At a party with other people around?"

"She didn't drown in the pool. She went upstairs and didn't come back, so we finally went looking for her. She wasn't there. She'd gone into the ocean. I don't know why because she wasn't a strong swimmer."

"My God, how awful! And now Tracy..."

"Yes. And now Tracy. I don't think I can handle it if I've lost her, too." He looked out the window again, drained the last of his wine, and rose to his feet. "Do you mind if I turn the television on? I'd like to check the local news."

Sarah rose. "Of course, not. I'd like to see it, too. Then I need to go to bed. I didn't sleep well last night."

"Is the bed okay? Do you need—"

"The bed's fine. It's just not mine, and I'm not getting enough exercise to make me tired. But the wine has made me sleepy, so maybe I'll do better tonight."

She didn't really believe that. Her father's call and talking about her past had pulled her back to everything she'd tried to leave behind and stirred up too many memories: Caro's death; Scott's betrayal; the man who had attacked her.

You're inviting the nightmare by thinking about all this. She would have to read late into the night, bury the memories before she could sleep. Sometimes it worked.

She picked up her partially-filled wine glass and his empty one and carried them to the kitchen. But before she could open the dishwasher, the news anchor's perfectly-groomed head appeared on the screen, and his well-modulated voice announced breaking news. The convict had been captured in a remote Canadian cabin just over the border. He was alone and claimed no knowledge of the missing New York woman. The news team would have more details at eleven.

Greg sat motionless, staring at the commercial that followed the news flash. Sarah lifted her wine glass. It was empty. She rarely drank more than two glasses, but tonight she needed another. She reached for a bottle but pushed it back. It wasn't wine she needed. She had to get out of that snowbound cabin.

◆◆◆

Somewhere, deep in her subconscious, she knew she was dreaming, but that didn't lessen the terror.

Scott chased her through the snow, one of his long strides covering as much distance as two of hers. Narrow gaps in the trees beckoned, too small for him to enter, offering paths for her through the underbrush. But she couldn't go there, either—not with the cast on her leg and the crutches.

She tried to plant the tip of the crutch as far ahead as she could, swinging her body in a long arc. But the cast was too heavy; it caught and dragged in the snow. He was gaining on her, so close his wheezing breath rasped in her ears.

Light glinted off the broken edges of the wine bottle as he raised it high overhead, and she saw his face. Her father, not Scott. She dodged to the right and fell. His hand, holding the jagged bottle, was outlined briefly against the sun before it plunged down, toward her face. She twisted and felt an abyss beneath her. Reaching out, she clutched at anything she could grab.

She bolted upright, still grasping the quilt, and pushed damp hair away from her face. The sheets were tangled around her legs. Had she heard a noise? Is that what woke her? She threw back the covers and padded to the window. It was too dark to see anything.

She went back to the junk room for the binoculars and scanned the yard, letting her eyes adjust to the darkness. She could see nothing moving, and cold air was seeping through the windowpane, chilling her. The house was quiet, cocooned in the silence of sleep. She must have imagined the noise.

She crawled back under the covers and pulled them up to her chin, rubbing her feet against each other to warm them. Still shivering, she pulled her knees up, tucking herself into a tight ball. Finally, she got warm. But not drowsy. The cold wasn't the problem; she was afraid to fall asleep, terrified of the nightmare.

The sound came again, muffled this time, too faint to identify. A door creaking? No, something else. Muffled footsteps or clothing brushing against a wall? Probably somebody up to use the bathroom.

No. Those sounds would be distinct: footsteps, closing doors, flushing toilet, water running. This was quieter. Stealthy. Could somebody be inside the house?

Calm down, Sarah. It's probably just a mouse. But if it is, it's a freaking big one.

She got out of bed, put on her robe and slippers, and went to the window. Cold darkness pressed in through the glass. Somehow, it felt ominous, and cold prickles of fear crept up her neck. Something—or somebody—was out there, watching the house.

She was being foolish, irrational. *It doesn't matter. I don't want to be here. I want to be back in the city, in my apartment, away from all this fear and grief. No, I want to be home, in California.*

She shook her head. She was just tired. Afraid to go back to sleep, she sat in the rocking chair by the window. A dim light flashed through the trees and went out. *Did I imagine that, too?* It came again, a little closer. A flashlight? The kidnapper, finally making his approach? Then what was the sound she had heard earlier?

A soft thud from the other end of the hall pulled her away from the window, toward the door. She went back to her bureau and got her phone. Once she knew somebody was out there, she could text an alert to Greg.

She slipped down the hall in the darkness, past his room, toward the junk room and the binoculars. The girls' room was faintly lit by a nightlight. She took another stealthy step toward the open junk room door on the other side. But just before she turned, something fluttered in her peripheral vision. Had Lottie left a window open? Was that why the house felt so cold? No, the girl stood at the back-facing window, her long nightgown a blur of white in the faint light. She, too, was watching the on-again-off-again flicker filtering through the trees.

Sarah stood still, studying the girl. Had a sound awakened her, too? Lottie's posture indicated more curiosity than fear. Her body looked relaxed as she moved her head closer to the window for a better view, then put her palm on the pane.

For a moment, fragments of every horror movie Sarah had ever seen coalesced in her mind. The pale light, the fluttering white gown, the girl's stillness—all the props were in place to generate a creepy setting.

Sarah took a step forward, then hesitated. Could the child be sleepwalking? Was that why she showed no fear or even curiosity? Best not wake her.

With slow, careful steps, Sarah moved backward until she was out of Lottie's line of sight, should the girl glance toward the hallway. If Greg came up behind her and she didn't hear him...She shuddered, turned to face the stairs, and crept back to her room, ignoring her brain's commands to hurry. Hurry and lock the door behind you. All the while, for some undefinable reason, images of Jack Nicholson from *The Shining* flooded her brain. She had to stop watching those old movies.

What was she so afraid of? Lottie? No, she'd been more afraid of startling the child. There definitely was something strange about a ten-year-old standing at a window in the middle of the night, staring into the darkness.

Sarah went to her own window again so she could see whatever Lottie was observing. But there were no more flashes of light and no movement. If it was the kidnapper finally making his approach, they'd missed their chance to catch him.

She crossed the hall and tapped on Greg's door. No response. Was he a heavy sleeper? She hesitated, not wanting to startle Lottie, then turned back to her own room. It would take too long for Greg to wake and get dressed. The intruder would be gone, if he wasn't already. And if Greg hadn't come upstairs, if he roamed around outside the cabin, he would have seen the flashes of light. He would be trying to find the source, or any message the kidnapper might have left.

The dark seemed ominous even now, threatening, and she had an unreasonable urge to barricade her door.

Despite her misgivings, she had no real basis for fear. It was just the uncertainty, not knowing who was out there, that troubled her—that, coupled with the nightmare, Greg's dark despair, and Lottie's odd behavior.

What I could really use is another glass of merlot. But even that couldn't tempt her down the stairs, not even for an entire bottle. Maybe she'd bring one up tomorrow and stash it in her bedroom. She shook her head, startled at the thought. She didn't need wine; she needed to get out of that cabin.

Chapter 12
Tuesday

Gracie stood beside the bed, her hand on Sarah's shoulder. "Sarah? Sarah, are you awake?"

"I am now." Sarah sat up, brushing hair out of gummy, itchy eyes. Yawning, she glanced at the clock: seven thirty. She'd had only four hours of sleep. "Where's Lottie?"

As soon as she asked, an image came back to her of the girl standing at the window, dim light reflecting off her white nightgown.

"She's still asleep and Dad's gone and I'm hungry. Can we have waffles?"

"May we have waffles."

Gracie frowned. "That's what I said. Can we have waffles?"

Lottie might sleep for several hours yet if she were as tired as Sarah. "Why don't we save waffles until Lottie's awake, too, so she won't miss them?"

"Can I have pancakes, then?"

Sarah sighed. "Let's get dressed, then see what we can find in the kitchen."

What she found was a note from Greg: *Will be with the sheriff at the lake most of the day. Still hoping for word from his office or the newspaper about the mail. Kidnapper must be out of the area. Thought he tried last night, but it was an out-of-state hiker, lost in the woods. Call if you get anything.*

Sarah tried to read between the lines. Nobody had tried to approach the cabin or contact Greg or the sheriff. Their last thin hope, that a ransom note might come in the mail, was fading, along with the premise that Tracy had been kidnapped. If she hadn't been taken by the convict as a hostage, or by a kidnapper for ransom, what had happened to her? She wouldn't have run away and left two children, and the things they'd found in the snow indicated somebody had grabbed her, likely a man who had stumbled across a lone woman in the woods. He had left the area quickly or the search teams, along with the trained dogs, would have found some trace of him.

The searchers might be hoping for a ransom note, but they were also looking for a body, first in the mine shafts, and now at the bottom of the lake. Why would Greg want to be there for that? But, in all fairness, what else would he do?

Maybe spend a few hours with his girls, trying to prepare them for the loss of their mother? *Easy to judge, Sarah, when you're not the one suffering.*

She had two messages on her phone, one from Laura, the other from her father. She called Laura.

"Did you find out why Lottie left the cabin?" she asked.

"No, and I didn't want to press her too hard. She's got enough to deal with. But I'm not sure I did the right thing, not telling Greg about her using my phone."

"I talked to Jamie's therapist today. She says the drawing is troubling—the dark shading you described. The girl obviously feels something is threatening her, and probably her mother and sister, too. Margaret—that's the therapist's name—is not sure what the running man means, but his size is significant. He's important. She thinks Lottie may be suffering from PTSD or OCD."

"I didn't know kids could have PTSD. I guess I always associated that with wounded soldiers, or other adults suffering from massive injuries."

"She says both can be caused by trauma—physical or mental—and can happen to very young children. And that would fit if the girl is being molested. Have you talked to Greg? Tried to find out?"

"No. I should have done that last night, but things got kind of weird."

She told Laura about the evening. "I'm wondering...do PTSD or OCD cause sleepwalking?"

Laura was silent for a few seconds. "I don't know. I guess I can do a little research. Maybe about Greg's story, too. The one about his first wife's death."

"Okay, if you have the time. Or I can do it. I have nothing but time."

"How soon can you get out of there?"

"I'm hoping they can get my car shoveled out today. Greg said they would. As soon as I get it, I'm on my way. I can't stay indefinitely, just to try to find out what's going on with Lottie. Maybe I can stay in touch, try to help her through an agency that investigates this sort of thing. Anyway, I'll call you as soon as I know."

She ended the call and slid the phone into her pocket. Arms wrapped around her waist, she stood, looking at the big room, the vacation home Tracy wouldn't be coming back to. Despite Sarah's dark thoughts, the cabin had again changed personalities, the hard edge of last night's darkness giving way to soft sunlight streaming through the windows.

Gracie pressed her nose against one of them. "Can we go outside and play? It's not snowing."

"May we go out. And yes." Yes! Of course, they could. The convict had been found, the area around the cabin had been searched multiple times, and the kidnapper, if he'd ever been there, was gone. It wasn't likely he would have approached while all of them were in the yard, anyway.

"Why are you humming?" Lottie asked, from behind her.

"Because I can't sing." Sarah took a firmer grip on the bowl she was holding and looked down at Lottie's sock-clad feet. "And I wish you'd quit sneaking up on me like that."

"Can we really go outside?"

"May we go out."

Lottie sighed. "May we go outside?"

"After breakfast, if both of you bundle up. Maybe we can take a walk in the woods or make another snowman." It would keep them entertained until some news came. And Sarah could be wrong. There was a chance Tracy might still be alive, trying to get back home.

The girls hurried through breakfast and raced upstairs to get dressed. Sarah's phone buzzed. Her father. She ignored the call and jammed the phone deep into her pocket.

Fifteen minutes later, she was outside, reveling in the warmth of the sun. Lottie and Gracie, having the freedom to run for the first time in days, whooped and yelled as they chased each other around the cabin. When they tired of that, they pelted each other with snowballs. Sarah smiled. This was a different Lottie than the one she'd known thus far.

While she watched them, she kept an eye on the woods. She wasn't sure why. Probably habit, she'd been doing it for so long. But something about Greg's account of a lost out-of-state hiker bothered her. Why would a hiker be out there in the middle of the night, especially if he didn't know the area?

Lottie threw a snowball and Sarah ducked, scooped up a handful of snow, packed it, and tossed it back.

Lottie laughed, sending a warm glow through Sarah. "Can you show us how to build a fort?" the girl asked. "You know, like those boys—Eric and Jamie—did? It would be fun to make two. We could have sides for a snowball fight. Me and Gracie against you."

"Planning to gang up on me, are you? Okay, come on. We'll build some forts. A really big one for me."

Lottie laughed again and grabbed Sarah's hand, pulling her toward a big snow drift. But fort-building was cold work. Within a half hour, Sarah's face felt numb, and her fingers were tingling, even through the mittens. Gracie's nose was red; so was Lottie's.

"Let's go in for a while. It's almost lunchtime, anyway, and some hot soup would warm us up. We can come out again later."

The girls readily agreed and drifted back to the sofa and the television screen after they ate. That was all right with Sarah. She'd had enough fort building for a while. But she'd like to venture into the edge of the woods near the back of the house and look for tracks from the night before. She couldn't leave the children alone, though, even for a half hour.

"Want to take a walk?"

Lottie looked up. "Where?"

"I thought...maybe through the woods?"

Lottie slid off the sofa. "I'll get our coats and boots."

Gracie shook her head. "I don't want to take a walk. I want to build my fort."

Sarah knelt beside her. "How about we compromise? We'll go for a short walk, and when we come back, we'll have some hot chocolate before we go out to finish the fort?"

The little girl shook her head, shifting her gaze to her big sister. But Lottie surprised Sarah. She didn't give in.

"It'll just be a short walk, Gracie, and we'll play in the snow as long as you want. I promise."

Sarah winced. That snow was numbing cold. But Gracie, no longer resisting, let Lottie lead her to the laundry room and their coats.

They'd gone only about a hundred yards into the woods when the first tracks came into view—going both to and from the cabin. In several places, they overlapped.

If she could get down closer, she might determine their sequence—whether Greg had made them going into the woods, then overlapped some of them coming back, or whether an intruder had reversed that pattern. But the girls would notice if she showed too much interest. She might be able to come back for a closer look later, but she'd have to do it before it started snowing again, filling in the tracks.

To keep her gaze from lingering on the boot prints too long, she raised her head and caught a glimpse of another pattern, just a few yards ahead, one from the nightmare. The footprints zigged through the woods, finding the paths with little or no vegetation. Why would a lost hiker do that? Avoid breaking twigs, making noise?

Lottie knelt and examined the tracks, nodded, and rose to her feet, brushing the snow from her knees. She said nothing, but an odd little half-smile lingered around her lips. Other than that, her face betrayed no emotion, and unease crept up Sarah's spine—the same sensation she'd experienced the night before when Lottie had stood at the window, looking out into the dark.

Gracie tugged at Sarah's hand. "I'm tired of walking. I want to go build the fort."

"Okay. We've probably gone as far as we should. Let's head back."

Within a few steps of the snow structures, a clump of snow hit Sarah's back. She whirled just as Lottie picked up another snowball. The girl had dropped behind and now stood by the shed, taking aim at her little sister. Gracie laughed and ran around the corner of the house with Lottie close behind.

Sarah went the other direction. She would circle the cabin and pelt them from the front corner. She got there just as Gracie took refuge behind the snowman. Sarah bent to scoop up a handful of snow, but before she could throw it at Gracie, Lottie lobbed a snowball at Sarah.

Gracie peeked out from behind the snowman. Sarah had plenty of time to attack her before she could get back to the fort, so she drew back her arm to throw the snowball at Lottie. The girl turned and ran, and Sarah chased her back toward the forts.

The sound of a motor drew her attention back toward the front. Greg had pulled his car into the yard. He jumped out and ran toward Gracie, yelling, "What the hell are you doing?"

He jerked the little girl's arm, and she cried out. Holding her, he glowered at Sarah. "I thought I could trust you to keep them inside."

Lottie ran toward her sister, and the old, familiar rage surged through Sarah, the temper she'd always fought so hard to keep in check. "You can't trust me to do a damned thing. You don't even know me. But I sure as hell wouldn't hurt a child!"

His mouth fell open, and he looked down at his hand, grasping Gracie's arm. He released it and wiped a hand across his forehead. "I'm sorry. I—"

But Sarah's attention was on Lottie, who stood with her arms around Gracie, a little smile curving her lips as her gaze caught Sarah's.

Greg knelt in front of them. "Lottie, Gracie, I'm so sorry. I didn't mean to hurt you. I was just scared..." He rose to his feet and turned to Sarah. "I don't want them outside. I want them in the house, where they'll be safe."

"But they caught the convict, and—"

"I know that. But I found tracks...moose tracks. I want the girls kept inside."

"Then you're going to have to find somebody else to do it because I'm tired of being cooped up in there. I'm going back to the city."

She whirled and stomped toward the cabin, catching just a glimpse of Lottie's stricken face.

The girls retreated to their room, and Sarah followed them upstairs. With Greg's return, the cabin had shrunk even more. It was snowing again. Big flakes drifted past the window.

Had they got the Highlander out or was the vehicle being buried in more snow? If she had to, she'd leave it, let the rental agency handle it. One of the men would probably drive her to the airport. Greg could take care of his girls, instead of skulking around the cabin and the woods.

She called the airline. Flights were backed up because of the heavy snowstorms, with long waiting lists. They could put her on standby. Otherwise, she'd have to wait until her scheduled flight Sunday morning and hope it left on time.

Okay, she'd find a hotel room, wait it out there. And do what? Worry about what was happening to the girls? No, Greg was too volatile. As long as she was stuck, she'd stay with them, keep them as safe as she could, try to buffer them from his outbursts.

When she went to the kitchen to start dinner, he was no longer there, nor was he in his room; she'd have heard him climb the stairs. No, he was outside again, prowling around the house. She shivered and rubbed her arms. He was worried and grieving, but his restless wandering of the property and the woods was creepy.

She glanced through the big dining room window. New snow already covered the ground, like a fresh white sheet laid over an unmade bed, the flakes coming straight down. She turned on the lights, glancing out at the snow as she worked. Maybe it would stop before morning.

Greg came inside, shaking snow off his boots, just as the girls sat down for dinner. "Are you okay, Gracie?" He looked at her arm, encased in a heavy sweater. Gracie nodded and slid into her chair, her head down. Lottie, too, kept her gaze on her plate. Sarah would check for bruises later, when the girls got ready for bed.

"I feel bad if I hurt you, Gracie, and I'm sorry I yelled. I shouldn't have done that. But I was scared when I saw the two of you outside. I saw moose tracks this morning, and I have to keep you safe until I'm sure it's not hanging around."

"Moose are dangerous?" Sarah asked.

"Mostly because of their size," Greg said. "And they can be unpredictable. You don't want to get too close to one."

Gracie's eyes widened. "Do you think a moose got Mom?"

Sarah gritted her teeth. *Nice job, Dad. Grab her, yell at her, and scare her so much she'll probably have nightmares.*

Lottie looked up, flashing a quick glance at Greg, then Sarah. She couldn't read the child's expression but suspected Lottie was thinking the same thing Sarah was: the tracks they'd seen in the woods weren't made by moose.

"No, Gracie," Greg said. "This moose never came around the cabin before last night."

Nobody responded and finally, to alleviate the tension, Sarah said, "I made chicken and brown rice for dinner. I hope everybody likes it."

Gracie nodded, a quick little tilt of her head. "Chicken's my favorite."

While she dished up the food and carried it to the table, Sarah tried to decipher that glance Lottie had cast at Greg. Anger? No, it was more like dislike. Or disgust. Or contempt. *I must have misinterpreted.* Lottie could be sullen and belligerent, and she was over-protective of Gracie. That first night, Lottie had screamed "I don't like you; you're mean," over a simple change of dinner menu. How might she have reacted if she'd thought Sarah had harmed Gracie? She couldn't scream at her father, though; she could only cast quick, baleful looks.

"Everything looks great," Greg said, reaching for a dinner roll. "Doesn't it, girls?"

Again, they nodded.

Apparently realizing they weren't going to talk to him, he told Sarah, "I have to apologize to you, too. I was way out of line. It looks like the three of you were having fun out there. That's quite a fort you built. Or forts. Did you stock them with snowballs?"

"Not yet. We were going to do that—"

"Later," Lottie said. "We were going to do it later so we could have a snowball fight." She rubbed at her eye with the back of her hand. "Me and Gracie against Sarah."

"I'm sorry I spoiled your fun. Would it help if I joined you tomorrow? I could keep an eye out for the moose while you guys play in the snow."

Gracie looked at her sister. "Can we, Lottie? 'Cause I didn't get to throw a single snowball. Even after you threw one at me."

"I suppose so if Sarah still wants to."

Sarah hesitated, trying to read Lottie's expression. *What does she want me to say?* Finally, Sarah nodded, and Lottie's tense mouth relaxed into a half-smile.

Gracie asked Greg, "You promise? You won't change your mind?"

He held up a hand. "Scout's honor."

He'd broken their icy silence. Gracie chattered about their fort-building and Lottie eventually joined in, laughing about her surprise attack on Sarah.

"I got you good, right in the back."

Sarah smiled. "That was sneaky, but tomorrow is get-even time. I think I'll wake up early and make a whole pile of snowballs."

Lottie squealed. "That's not fair."

"Sure it is. You can get up early, too, and there are two of you, so you can make lots more than I can."

Lottie frowned, and Sarah pictured the girls out in the yard at midnight, building a stockpile of ammunition. "How about a rule? No snowball making until after breakfast?"

Lottie looked suspicious. "Are you going to wait for us to get up before you eat?"

"Sure. I can do that."

"Okay. It's a deal."

"Greg," Sarah said, "were you guys able to dig the Highlander out?"

"Oh, yeah. I forgot to tell you. We got it shoveled out okay but didn't have anything with us to put under the tire, so it's still in that deep rut. We planned to get it out today. But now, with the snow, I don't know." He glanced at the window, then back at her. "Don't worry. We'll get it out."

He was in a better mood tonight. She supposed she could make it through one more day. Not that she had a choice.

They lingered over the meal a little longer than usual and when Sarah rose to clear the table, Greg stood, too.

"How about we all pitch in? Then, while you girls are taking your baths and getting into your pajamas, I can make some hot chocolate with those little marshmallows. I'll bring in a couple of logs, and we can drink it by the fireplace. Maybe Sarah will even read one of those stories you like."

They did a quick job of the baths and came back downstairs a half hour later, Gracie clasping a stuffed brown dog against her pink pajamas. Sarah went up to get her Kindle while Greg settled the girls on pillows in front of the fire. Sarah sank into one of the rocking chairs.

"Here," Greg said, handing her a glass of merlot. "I figured you'd rather have this than hot chocolate."

She didn't want to drink wine with him, but couldn't come up with a way to decline gracefully. She'd have one glass, while she read, and when the girls went upstairs, she'd tell him she was tired, that she wanted to go to bed, too.

She took a sip and started to read.

She awoke in the darkness, disoriented. She lay still, but no sound reached her ears—only a feeling of space. Something soft touched her neck and arms. A blanket? She was still dressed. Sliding one hand down the surface under her, she touched nubby cloth, then a seam—a welted cushion. Turning, she felt the other side, made of the same material, curving upward. With her head tilted, her peripheral vision caught a hint of glowing red. The burned-down embers in the fireplace. She was on the living room sofa, fully dressed, covered with a throw, a little queasy, a little headachy, like she had a hangover. *But I didn't drink that much. Did I?*

She couldn't remember. She'd been by the fire, reading to the girls, and Greg had brought her a glass of merlot. She'd been angry with him, didn't want the wine, but couldn't make a scene in front of the girls.

She'd read the story—all about a boy and a dragon, but it hadn't been long before the girls got sleepy. Greg had carried Gracie upstairs. Sarah had helped her get ready for bed and tucked both girls in, then went back downstairs to get her Kindle. Everything after that was a blank. Nothing Greg Agerton had said would have kept her there, drinking wine with him. Unless—she had planned to talk to him about Lottie. Had she done that, and drunk more to ease a difficult conversation? She shook her head, but stopped when pain shot up her temple. Rising slowly, she wobbled to the kitchen for aspirin and a big glass of water. A glance at the kitchen clock told her it was only a little after one o'clock. She climbed the stairs to her room, undressed and got into bed, pulled the covers over her head and went back to sleep.

Chapter 13
Wednesday Morning

When she woke the next time, to a room that was not yet light, it was almost eight o'clock and still snowing. The house was quiet. She showered and dressed and went down the hall to peek in on the girls. Neither stirred when she opened the door. There was no reason for them to get up; another long day stretched ahead with little to do.

The big room downstairs was empty, ashes gray now in the fireplace. Pillows lay on the floor in front of it, Gracie's stuffed dog on one, the Kindle beside another, along with sticky hot chocolate cups. Two wine glasses and an empty bottle occupied the table between the chairs in the alcove. Had she sat there? She shook her head, trying to clear it of whatever blocked her memory.

She picked up the cushions and put them back on the sofa, along with the stuffed dog. *You're being irrational, Sarah. Whatever happened last night, you can't erase it by cleaning up.* But she still cleaned and polished, threw the bottle away, picked up the Kindle, and loaded the cups and glasses into the dishwasher.

Greg's coat still hung on its peg in the laundry room. He was in his bedroom, then. She could go out and stay as long as she wanted, without feeling responsible for the girls—maybe find something she could use later to get the Highlander out. Slinging the binoculars around her neck, she went outside.

Yesterday's tracks were gone. An unbroken white expanse filled the spaces between the buildings and trees, curving around them, so beautiful in its flowing symmetry, she hesitated, reluctant to disturb it. She drew the cold air into her lungs and let it out, then stood still, a little afraid of taking that first step. What if she couldn't force herself to turn around and come back?

She shook her head and stepped off into the fresh snow. A few yards took her within view of the footpath and back road. Snow fell more gently now, and sporadically, making visibility better. The binoculars showed her nothing but dark branches, covered in white, some of them, those closest, dripping crystal-clear drops. She swung the glasses toward the front road.

The nearest snow fort was broken, uneven gaps torn through the walls, softened by the new layer of white. The snowman was down, too, nothing but loose, uneven lumps scattered around the bird feeder on its sturdy metal pole. The moose?

Sarah bent to pick up the snowman's red scarf, shook it out, and shoved it into the right pocket of her parka.

She broke a path to the shed, a weathered structure between the cabin and the woods. There was no lock. Lifting the end of a metal bar from its slot on the door frame, she it into a makeshift rope loop nailed to the door itself. When she pulled the door open, it creaked.

An overhead bulb and one small window, high over the end opposite the door, provided the only light. A wood beam ran the length of the high, peaked roof, and from it, a rowboat hung, anchored by lengths of chain. Underneath, a wooden cradle-like structure seemed designed to hold the boat—or at least, some boat. Right now, it held nothing but a thick layer of dust.

Worn shelves ran along the back wall and part of the sides, holding cans and bottles of various sizes, some fairly new, some rusted with undecipherable labels. Between them nestled coils of wire and rope, rolls of duct tape and masking tape, and cardboard cartons.

Along the side walls, or hanging on them, was an assortment of snow gear: skis, snowshoes, and other objects she couldn't identify. Mounds of canvas-covered material occupied both front corners, one of them partially obscured by a shiny blue sled.

She searched under the tarps but found nothing wide enough or sturdy enough to use under the Highlander's tire. The ditch was too deep. Snow would be piled around it, anyway, so it was pointless to hike out there.

She didn't want to return to the cabin. She would go into the edge of the woods—to the place where she and the girls had found the tracks. It should be safe, if she used the binoculars to scan the area ahead of her. The snow had stopped, the sun shining—at least for a few minutes. Maybe the fresh air would clear out some of the soot clogging her memory.

She tried to stay on the same zig-zag path she'd noticed the day before, weaving her way between the trees, watching for tracks. All she found were those of deer and small animals, probably rabbits. No moose. *I don't even know what a moose track looks like, but it has to be big.*

A few yards ahead, a glow of sunlight on metal drew her attention to a low shrub. Caught on one of its branches was a gold charm, the rest of the bracelet covered in snow. Kneeling, she pulled it loose and dried it on her sleeve. The gold chain held eight charms, two of them heart-shaped, and even before she looked, she knew what she'd find: the names of Lottie and Gracie, one engraved on each charm, with their birth dates.

When had Tracy last stood here, and had she lost the bracelet then, or sometime earlier? It was a fluke that Sarah had found it. She'd been scanning the ground when the sun happened to be positioned to reflect off the tiny piece of gold. The bracelet could have hung there for days or weeks, held aloft by the bush, its bulk covered with snow.

The cool feel of it in her hand brought back a vivid memory of Tracy, her wrist thrust toward Sarah so she could inspect each little gold charm. Tracy's face had glowed when she spoke of her daughters.

"I can't wait for you to meet them. You're going to fall in love, and I know they're going to like you."

They'd been talking about Irving Stone's *The Agony and the Ecstacy* just before that, telling each other they'd take a trip to Florence and Rome someday to see Michelangelo's work. They'd have to wait, though, until Lottie and Gracie were old enough to appreciate his sculptures. It was an unspoken promise of a long friendship to come.

Sarah's eyes welled with tears as she pushed the parka aside and shoved the bracelet into the left pocket of her jeans.

When was that conversation? Sarah couldn't remember, but certainly after they'd finished the class project, not long before the invitation to the cabin. It was unlikely the family had come here between then and this trip. So Tracy had lost the bracelet recently.

Sarah moved on, searching one side of the path for about half a mile before turning and searching the other side. She found nothing but a few broken branches, most of them low to the ground.

She trudged back to the cabin, her hand still grasping the bracelet in her pocket.

Greg came downstairs a little later, brushing hair out of his eyes as he passed the chair by the fireplace where she sat, reading. "The girls still asleep?"

She nodded, but he didn't seem to notice, probably didn't even remember the question he'd asked, as he headed toward the kitchen. Sarah rose, reaching into her jeans pocket for the bracelet. Best to give it to him now, without Lottie and Gracie around. But before she reached him, the girls' voices floated to her from the top of the stairs. She pushed the bracelet back into her pocket.

The laughing, mischievous Lottie of the day before had disappeared, replaced by a quiet, thoughtful child who showed no interest in going outside for the promised snowball fight. Her lack of enthusiasm infected Gracie, and they sprawled in front of the television screen, watching an animated movie—*Pinocchio* this time.

Greg pulled a steel thermos from the cabinet and filled it with coffee. "I finally reached Tracy's parents. Or rather, the Coast Guard did, by shipboard radio. They'll get off at the next port of call, early tomorrow morning, and fly back." He glanced at Sarah. "I've got to go. I don't know when I'll be back, so don't worry about dinner."

Sarah bit her lip, fighting back a sudden surge of anger at his assumption that she was there to do his bidding. She closed her fingers around the bracelet and turned away.

"You do what you have to do. I'll take care of the girls." She started to add more—to tell him how thoughtless and unreasonable he was—but a glimpse of Lottie's strained face stopped her.

The Tahoe was barely out of the yard when Lottie asked, "Can you help me do something? I can't..." She looked at Gracie and flushed.

"Of course, I'll help you if I can. What do you need?"

Lottie glanced at Gracie again, but the little girl kept her eyes focused on the screen. Lottie got up and grabbed Sarah's hand.

"Come on. I'll show you."

Sarah hung back a little, waiting for Gracie to join them; she usually followed wherever her sister led. Not this time. She stayed on the sofa, watching the movie.

Lottie led Sarah up to the girls' bedroom. The blankets and sheets had been pulled back from Gracie's wet mattress.

"She wet the bed, and I don't know how to fix it. It was an accident. She always wakes up at night and goes, but she didn't last night. She couldn't help it. Please don't tell—"

Sarah crossed to the bed and picked up the blankets. "Of course, it was an accident. It happens sometimes. Don't worry. We'll fix it." Why was Lottie so worried about Greg finding out?

Sarah wasn't sure what to do, never having dealt with a wet bed before. She carried the blankets and sheets down to the washing machine and started a load before she went back to the bedroom and opened one of the windows a few inches.

"How about this? I'll wash all the blankets and sheets, but we'll have to dry out the mattress before we make the bed. If it's still damp tonight, do you think you and Gracie could sleep together?"

Lottie let out a sigh of relief. "And you won't tell?"

"Of course not. But it's nothing for Gracie to be ashamed of. She's just a little girl."

"I know that! But...well, she doesn't want Dad to know."

Sarah's supply of clean clothes was getting low. She might as well do her laundry and that of the girls while she was washing the bedding. It would give her something to do. She shook her head. This was a new low, looking forward to laundry because she needed something—anything—to keep her occupied. Never again would she complain about long hours in class or doing assignments.

She sent the girls upstairs to gather their soiled clothing and brought down her own. She'd started back to the stairs when somebody tapped on the front door. She hurried to open it, hoping it might be Ellen or Roberta. Or even Julie.

A man stood in the doorway. Sarah had to tilt her head to see his face. Jake Nichols smiled down at her.

"Morning, Sarah. I just stopped by to see if you'd got your car out yet. If you haven't—"

"I haven't. Come on in. I've got some fresh coffee if you want a cup."

He took off his coat and hung it over the back of a chair. "Coffee sounds good. I brought some two-by-twelves with me, out in the truck." He motioned with his head toward the front yard. "I think one of them will do the trick."

"Bless you!" Sarah poured coffee and handed him a mug. "That's really thoughtful."

He grinned and took a sip of coffee. "Hits the spot. And it's the least I can do, after the coffee and meals you've made for me. Is Greg around? I wanted to ask him—"

Lottie and Gracie clattered down the stairs, Gracie jumping from one tread to the next with both feet. Lottie carried a laundry basket.

"Sarah, can we go—" They stopped, staring at Jake.

"Greg's gone..." Sarah glanced at the girls, and back to Jake. "Gone to help search, I guess."

Jake nodded, still watching Lottie and Gracie. "Maybe it would be better if you gave me your keys? I can drive over there in the Silverado, get your car out and drive it back here, then hike back to my rig."

"That'll work. Or I can take you. It would get us out of the cabin for a little while." Greg couldn't complain about that. The girls would be safe inside the car with the doors locked.

"Can we have the snowball fight when we get back?" Gracie asked.

Greg wouldn't like it, but they had to get outside, breathe some fresh air, and she had seen no large tracks near the cabin. "I don't see why not, if you really want to be bombarded."

Gracie giggled and Jake grinned. "Sounds like a plan to me."

"Clobbering them with snowballs?"

"No, getting your car out. But it'll probably be faster if I go by myself." He lowered his voice. "They don't know—?"

"There's really nothing to tell yet. That's what makes it so hard. I think Lottie suspects. Gracie...Gracie misses her mother and knows she's lost, but doesn't seem to be worried about it. Kids always just assume everything will be okay, don't they?"

Jake nodded. "I suppose. Never had any, so I don't know much about kids. You seem to get along pretty well with them."

Gracie, maybe. Sarah wasn't sure about Lottie. Although she was warming up.

Jake ran a hand down his beard, smoothing it. "I wanted to ask you...I'd like to pay you back for those meals you cooked. Would you like to go out for dinner? I thought we could go to Belly's—"

"Yes. Yes!" *Boy do I sound over-eager.* "I've been cooped up in this cabin so long, there's nothing that sounds better."

He had a nice smile. "That was my plan. Wait until you had cabin fever so bad you couldn't resist the invitation. Is it okay if I pick you up around seven?"

"Oh, I can't. I mean, I don't know what time Greg will be back, and I'll have the girls."

"How about tomorrow night? It'll be Fiesta Thursday, and they have pretty good Mexican food. Lots of folks come in for it."

"Sounds nice. But I can drive in if you get my car out. Let me get the keys."

When she came back downstairs with them, the girls were pulling on their boots.

"Don't go until I check it out. I'll just be a minute." She handed the keys to Jake.

"But we have to make snowballs," Gracie protested.

"That's okay. I'll give you a head start." She turned back to Jake. "I hope you don't have any trouble getting it out of the rut."

"Don't expect to." He hesitated for a moment, then nodded at the girls and went out. Sarah stood at the open door watching while he climbed into a gray Chevy Silverado. He waved and backed out of the yard.

She closed the door. "Now, I'll give you five minutes to build a stack of snowballs. After that, you better watch out."

Squealing with laughter, the girls tumbled out the laundry room door. Sarah poured another cup of coffee and stood at the window watching them make snowballs, ready to pelt her as soon as she stepped out the door. Not that they'd have much impact. Rushing to get a stockpile built, they weren't packing the mounds of snow; they'd be slushy. Sarah would have to teach them how to make good snowballs.

But now it was time to attack. She set the cup on the counter, opened the door, and ran for her fort.

She kept an eye on the woods and the open expanses around the house as they played, but saw nothing other than a couple of deer pawing at the snow.

"Why are they doing that?" Gracie asked. "Are they playing in the snow, too?"

"I think they're looking for food, Gracie. With all the snow, they're probably having a hard time finding something to eat. Maybe that's why they tore down the walls of the fort."

"That's Mom's!" Lottie said, pulling the red scarf that had worked part of the way out of Sarah's pocket. "Can I keep it?" Her voice quavered. "It's the one she used to wear."

"Yes. Yes, of course. If it's okay with your dad."

Gracie brushed her fingers down the length of the scarf and sniffled. Time to take them inside.

Chapter 14
Wednesday Afternoon

Sarah locked the door behind them, and by the time Lottie and Gracie got out of their boots and coats, put them away, and climbed onto the kitchen stools, she had chicken noodle soup heated and ready to pour into their bowls.

"Can we have hot chocolate?" Lottie asked. "Mom always made it for us when we got through playing in the snow."

Gracie bobbed her head. "With marshmallows."

"Okay. After you eat your soup."

She made the hot chocolate while they ate, then put the soup bowls in the dishwasher while Lottie got the marshmallows.

"Four for you"—she dropped them in Gracie's cup—"and four for me." She put her hand in the bag again. "And four for—"

Sarah pulled her cup away. "Not for me. But thanks, Lottie."

Lottie nodded. "Mom didn't like them much, either." She set the bag aside and, still wearing the snowman's scarf around her neck, pressed a marshmallow with her spoon, pushing it under the chocolate.

"Mom made some for us right before she went for the walk." The marshmallow bobbed to the surface, and she pushed it under again. Tears welled in her eyes, and she wiped at her cheek with the scarf.

Gracie reached for it. "Don't get snot all over it. Mom might get mad."

Lottie's eyes streamed tears. "She won't be mad, 'cause she's not coming back. They're not ever going to find her, are they, Sarah?"

Gracie's mouth fell open, and she stared at her sister. A wail erupted from deep in her chest.

The moment Sarah had been dreading had arrived—one she didn't know how to handle. Greg should have prepared the girls for this. Sarah pushed down the flash of resentment. She had to think about the girls right now, not Greg. Gracie was staring at her with wide eyes.

"I don't know, Lottie. Nobody does until they get through searching. I worry about her, too, and pray she's okay. But that's all we can do." She pulled them into her arms and held them close.

"Sarah?" Lottie looked up at her, wet lashes framing solemn chartreuse-green eyes. "You know, don't you? My mom's not going to come back, is she?"

Sarah led them to the sofa and sank into it, pulling the girls with her.

"I don't know, she whispered, stroking Lottie's back, "I really don't, and I wish I did." Lottie gazed back at her, searching Sarah's face, pleading for honesty, so Sarah conceded, "She's been gone a long time."

Lottie kept her gaze locked on Sarah's eyes. "But she would come back if she could. She wouldn't leave us alone."

Sarah could think of nothing more to say, so she just held them.

"If she doesn't come back, will we get to live with our dad?"

"Well, of course. Who else would you live with?"

They sat still, her arms wrapped around both girls so long Gracie's soft snores told her they'd fallen asleep. She untangled herself, stretched her stiff back, and went to the laundry room for one of the blankets she hadn't yet carried upstairs. She tucked it around the sleeping children, wondering what was keeping Jake.

Her phone rang, displaying an unfamiliar number. Maybe Jake was having a problem with the car. But it was a female voice.

"Hi, Sarah? This is Roberta Adrickson. I don't know if you remember me. I came to help cook."

Sarah pictured the round face, the short, curly hair, and the smile. "Of course, I remember. It's nice to hear from you. It gets pretty lonely out here, especially when I can't get out."

"That's what I'm calling about. I got to thinking of you out there, cooped up with those two kids, and I was wondering—I'm going to Belly's tomorrow for Fiesta Thursday, and it occurred to me that you might like to get out. Greg's there at night to take care of the little girls, isn't he? You could even bring them with you if he's not. Belly's is kind of a gathering place for the locals, especially when the tourists all clear out."

Two invitations in one day, after almost a week of nothing? And to the same event. "Gosh, Roberta, that's really nice of you, but I can't."

There was a moment of silence on the other end. Then, "Is it because of my sexual orientation? Afraid of what people might think? I know it bothers a lot of folks around here, but I thought you coming from the city, you'd be more open-minded. A little more understanding. I'm sorry for bothering you."

"No, Roberta, wait. It's not that. I mean, I didn't even know...nobody told me..." *Nice going, Sarah.* "It has nothing to do with you. It's just that Jake Nichols already asked me to go with him."

Another long silence. "Jake? Are you crazy? You have a death wish or something? If you show up at Belly's with Jake, Julie will kill you!"

Sarah reached for a chair. "I don't understand. Why would Julie—"

"You're an outsider. I guess there's a lot you don't know. Remember, we told you Greg and Julie dated in high school? Julie was nuts about him. I remember once, a few of us girls were going to see a movie. I don't remember the name of it. Just one of those chick-flick things the guys don't like. We asked Julie to go with us, but she said she wanted to hang out with Greg. Didn't matter that he was just tinkering around with his car in the garage. She'd rather do that than go to a movie with her friends."

Roberta paused to take a breath. "Everybody thought they were going to get married. I think Julie was actually planning her wedding before Greg went off to college. He came back married, and Julie about had a cow. She hated Amy. That was the wife's name, Amy. Trash-talked her to anybody who would listen. Then Amy died. Suspicious death, too. Anyway, Julie figured she was going to get Greg back. They dated a few times when he was here on vacations. You can imagine her surprise when Greg came back with another wife. And now that wife is missing. You see a pattern here?"

Was the woman unhinged? "I don't understand," Sarah said. "What does any of this have to do with Jake Nichols?"

"There aren't many eligible men around, so when Greg married Tracy, Julie set her sights on Jake, figuring he's a pretty good catch. She still flirts with Greg every chance she gets, and I think she keeps hoping he and Tracy will break up. But she's pushing thirty and wants to get married. And Jake actually went out with her once or twice."

She paused for breath. "And now, here you are, another pretty little blonde, come to take her man away. Living in the same house with Greg is bad enough. But you're going out with Jake, too? I gotta say, you're a lot braver than I am. She's gonna hate your guts, and bad things happen to women Julie hates."

"Thanks for letting me know, Roberta. I appreciate it. I'll be careful. And I'm sorry we couldn't get together."

Sarah ended the call. *I suppose I've told bigger lies, but I don't know when.* She shuddered. The woman was obviously mentally unbalanced. But images, unbidden, came rushing back: Julie primping before the men came back from the search; Julie taking coffee to both Greg and Jake, ignoring the other searchers; Julie standing between them, chatting; and leaning in to whisper in Jake's ear.

A little shiver of apprehension raised the fine hair on Sarah's arms.

◆◆◆

Gracie had kicked the blanket off, and Sarah went to pull it back over the little girl's feet. The child felt warm. Sarah put a palm on her forehead. Definitely running a temperature.

A search of the kitchen and the downstairs half-bath didn't turn up a thermometer, so Sarah went upstairs, hesitating at the door of the master bedroom. But that bathroom would be the logical place for medications: close at hand for anybody taken ill, and safe from curious children.

Much like the rest of the house, the room had knotty-pine ceilings, walls, and floor; a braided rug, and pine furniture. Dark blue curtains were pulled closed, and the unmade bed was a jumble of blankets and pillows.

In the master bath, twice as large as the one in the guest room, towels hung askew on their rods, and a pile of clothing lay on the floor beside the shower. An open toothpaste tube lay on the counter top.

Sarah found a bottle of Tylenol for Children in the medicine cabinet, behind a prescription for Restoril—whatever that was—for Tracy, but no thermometer. She shoved the Tylenol into her pocket and slid open vanity drawers until she finally found two thermometers, one oral, one rectal. Alongside them was another prescription bottle for Tracy, this one Lunesta. She'd seen commercials for that one: a sleeping pill. A small plastic bag beside it held a vial of clear liquid. On it, written in permanent marker, were the letters GHB. Using her fingertips, she lifted it to the light. *Okay, Sarah, now you're just being nosy.* She put it back in the drawer, picked up the oral thermometer, and dropped it into her pocket alongside the Tylenol.

After checking to be sure the medicine cabinet and drawers were closed, she turned out the light and left the room.

Gracie's temperature was 101.2. Sarah vaguely remembered Laura telling her that children often ran temps a little higher than adults. A quick search on the internet told her Gracie's temperature wasn't anything to worry about if she didn't have other symptoms. Did a reversion to bed wetting qualify?

Sarah put the Tylenol back in her pocket. Apparently, fever in children was not uncommon and was actually believed to help build the child's immune system. She would keep an eye on Gracie and check her temperature again in a few hours.

There were plenty of articles online about bed wetting but nothing on a one-time incident. Did it stem from emotional, rather than physical causes? Was Gracie more troubled by Tracy's absence than she appeared? Sarah would have to do more research. Better yet, she would ask Laura. But right now, she wanted to find out more about the drugs she'd found.

Tracy apparently had trouble sleeping; Restoril, like Lunesta, was a sleeping pill. But what did the GHB on the plastic bag represent?

A light rap on the door told her Jake was back. Finally. Smiling, she hurried to let him in. He'd parked the Highlander in the yard.

"You did it. Thank you."

He nodded, but a frown creased his forehead. "It was no trouble getting it out, but I had a devil of a time before that, trying to figure out why it wouldn't start."

"Dead battery?"

"No. A disconnected coil wire. Sarah, why would anybody do that to your car?"

Somebody had sabotaged her vehicle. She stared at Jake, open-mouthed, unable to think of a response. The only thing that came to mind was the man who'd stood on that road watching the house. Had he been looking for her all along? She shook her head. That wasn't possible; there was no reason. She didn't even know anybody in upstate New York.

Her mind flitted back to Roberta's warning about Julie. But surely, the woman wasn't so jealous of Greg that she'd damage Sarah's car, just because Sarah was staying at the cabin.

She shook her head. "I don't know anybody, except the people who have come out here. I haven't been away from this place since I arrived. Even I can't make enemies that fast."

Jake didn't smile. "This isn't funny. I'm going to call the sheriff and let him know about it. Somebody needs to check it out. You may not be safe out here. Sure you don't want me to pick you up tomorrow night?"

After her conversation with Roberta, she wasn't sure how safe she'd be with Jake, either. If Julie had sabotaged Sarah's car because she was staying at the cabin, what might she do if Sarah went out with Jake?

"No, I'll enjoy driving. Especially now that it's stopped snowing." She wasn't going to let gossip about Julie scare her out of an evening away from the cabin, but it would be best to have control of her transportation. "I'll see you there at seven."

As she stood in the doorway, watching him hike back to his vehicle, she wondered if he was thinking the same thoughts that were churning through her mind. Who, if it wasn't Julie, had a reason to disable her car? She took a quick mental inventory of everybody she'd met, most of them on the day the women had come to the cabin to help with the meals. There was nobody. Even the man who had cast the hateful stare at Greg had no reason to take out his revenge on Sarah—probably didn't even know she existed.

No, it had to be the kidnapper. But why would a kidnapper disconnect the coil wire? It didn't make sense. Nothing she could think of made any sense.

Neither did Greg's frame of mind that evening. He'd been moody and remote before, but now he was even more distant.

"Gracie had a temperature today," Sarah said, at dinner.

He forked a bite of baked potato into his mouth and nodded. "Okay."

Sarah waited, but he said nothing more.

"I just got cold, making snowballs," Gracie said. "Can we go out again tomorrow?"

Greg looked out the window, a vacant expression on his face. "Okay."

Okay? Yesterday, he threw a fit about us being outside, and now it's okay? What is he thinking? He didn't even ask Gracie how she was feeling. *Don't be so judgmental, Sarah. He's under a lot of stress.*

Chapter 15
Thursday Morning

S arah awoke early and lay in bed for a while, thinking about her date with Jake that evening. Much as she was looking forward to getting away from the cabin, she felt a strange reluctance to leave the girls. She was getting far too attached to them.

The house was quiet; the girls must still be sleeping. She got up and went to the window. The ground below glistened almost silver in the bright light of day, and water dripped from the roof.

Careful not to wake anybody, she crept downstairs and made a pot of coffee. Greg's coat no longer hung in the laundry room. He'd left early but had promised to be back by quarter of seven, so she could go into town.

She should check on Gracie, but the little girl had been all right last night, her temperature back to normal. If she still slept, it would be better not to disturb her. Besides, it would give Sarah time to do some online research before the girls got up.

On a hunch, she added "drug" to the "GHB" search string and got several suggestions with "Hydroxybutyrate" in the title. One contained the words "methods of abuse." She clicked on it and found several articles discussing date-rape drugs.

She read GHB comes in powder or liquid form, and a small amount can be slipped into a drink. It is enhanced by alcohol, which may cause the victim to become drunk very quickly. It takes effect in five to twenty minutes, and usually lasts from two to three hours, causing sedation, some degree of compliance, poor judgment, and amnesia about events that happen while under its influence. The victim probably will not realize something happened until later, and her memory of what happened will be absent or incomplete.

Heat crept up Sarah's neck, and she felt a little sick. Had Greg drugged her? Was that why she had no memory of Tuesday night? But why would he do that? She hadn't been sexually assaulted. She'd know; it had been a long time since she'd had sex.

Time to call Dee Callender, Sam's sister, Laura's sister-in-law. Dee had been a cop when Sarah first met her, but she was now a detective on Sacramento's police force.

"Hey, Roomie," Dee said when she answered. "How are things in the big city?"

Dee had stayed with Sarah for a few weeks just before Sarah left for New York. In fact, Dee had come home one night to a nasty, final confrontation between Sarah and her ex-husband, probably saving Sarah from a beating. She smiled, remembering Scott's face when he saw Dee in full police uniform, holding her gun on him, ordering him to back off.

"Not so good, Dee. I'm upstate, at a friend's cabin. She's gone missing and I've been staying to take care of her little girls while her husband is helping with the search. I suspect the husband drugged me Tuesday night with something called GHB. Is there any way for me to be tested for the drug?"

"No, not really. Did you report it? Go to a hospital, so they could do an exam?"

"There wasn't any sex involved. I just can't remember anything from the time I was reading to the girls until I woke up on the sofa, fully dressed and covered with a blanket. And before you ask, no, I didn't drink too much."

Dee's voice was a little muffled, as though she'd turned her head to speak to somebody else, then came back. "I don't understand. He used a date rape drug but didn't follow through? Was he interrupted or something?" She paused. "But you wouldn't know that, would you? You'd be out of it. Sarah, to answer your question, a lab could find GHB in your hair for as long as ninety days, I think, if they knew what they were looking for and tested specifically for that drug. But that's not going to prove he gave it to you. If I were you, I'd just leave. Now. And consider yourself lucky it wasn't any worse."

"I can't. We're snowed in. Well, not literally. We got my rental car dug out. It's just that the airlines are so backed up, I can't get a flight before my scheduled one, on Sunday morning. That is, if we don't have another storm."

"Find a hotel room to hole up in until you can get a flight. Get away from this guy. His wife is missing, and you think he drugged you. That's setting off all kinds of alarm bells with me."

"He couldn't have had anything to do with his wife's disappearance. He was with their little girls when she went missing."

"Now I'm intrigued. You'd better tell me the whole story."

Sarah started at the beginning.

Dee was silent for a few seconds after Sarah finished. "I don't get it. From what you say, the husband has a solid alibi, so has no apparent reason to drug you. If he didn't do it for the more obvious reason, there's got to be something else. Unless that was his intent, and he was interrupted. Maybe by one of the little girls?"

"I don't know. We'd put them to bed already. I was reading to them while they had hot chocolate, and they got tired before I'd finished the chapter. Oh, my God! You don't think...would he have drugged them, too? He gave the older one a sedative one night."

Sarah hadn't found a sedative in Greg's bathroom, though. Just Tracy's sleeping pills, and one of them had been in the drawer alongside the GHB. "He gave her one of Tracy's sleeping pills," she whispered. "Isn't that dangerous?"

"What? I didn't hear you."

"Nothing. At least nothing I'm sure of yet. Wouldn't his fingerprints be on the plastic bag and the vial? And if he didn't wipe them off, wouldn't that at least prove he'd known the drugs were there, that they weren't Tracy's? And couldn't the police—"

"Test for fingerprints? Sure, if they had it. But they don't, and they're not going to search the house without a warrant."

Sarah shifted in the chair. "You're saying I can't prove he drugged me, and even if he did, there was no rape, so there are no grounds for a search warrant? It would end up being my word against his, and my story doesn't sound rational."

"I wish I could be more helpful, but the best advice I can give you is to leave."

"Okay, Dee. You've convinced me. And please don't tell Sam about this, okay? He'll tell Laura, and I don't want her to worry."

"Only if you'll promise to call me back at the first sign you're in real trouble."

"Deal." Sarah ended the call. Despite her promise to Dee, she couldn't leave until she was sure Lottie and Gracie would be all right. Had Greg really drugged them, too? What kind of father would do that? But Gracie's slumber had been so deep that night, she hadn't awakened to use the bathroom; she'd wet her bed.

If Sarah stayed, even for one more night, Greg would have another opportunity to drug her. He could slip it into her coffee, her food—anything.

She went upstairs, slipped into his room and rifled through a desk until she found a clean envelope. Using a pair of tweezers from Tracy's vanity, she lifted the plastic bag containing the vial and dropped it into the envelope. She'd probably smeared Greg's prints the first time she'd examined the bag, but there should still be some on it, along with hers.

After a moment's hesitation, she added the Lunesta and started to close the drawer. The words across a birthday card inside caught her attention: *For my sister...* Sister? Sarah opened the card and read "Tracy, happy, happy birthday. Have a great vacation, and I'll see you on the 22nd. Much love, Cindy."

Greg hadn't mentioned a sister—just the parents. Wouldn't the sister have known where they were, which cruise they were on?

A door opened downstairs. Sarah stood still. Had Greg come back? She dropped the tweezers into her pocket along with the envelope, closed the drawer, and tiptoed toward the bedroom door.

She stood beside it for a few seconds, waiting for the sound of footsteps or a voice. Nothing came. It must have been the girls' bathroom door she'd heard, which meant at least one of the girls was up. Time to get out of the bedroom and back downstairs.

Now that she had the drugs, she wasn't sure what to do with them. If Greg couldn't find them, would he search her room? Her purse? Her car? If she took the bag with her tonight, she still had no place to leave it—nobody she knew well enough to keep it for her. She could imagine the look on Jake's face if she asked him. She'd have to find a hiding place.

Where would a man be least likely to search? She headed for the kitchen and rummaged through the cabinets until she found a likely source—a box of cornstarch. Used primarily as a thickener for pie fillings, puddings. and sauces, it was an item rarely taken from the shelf. She dumped half the contents into a bowl, pressed the sealed envelope into the rest, and refilled it. The carton shouldn't rattle, even if somebody picked it up.

She dusted residue from the outside of the box and set it back onto the shelf, in the same position it had occupied before —behind the box of salt. While she rinsed the bowl and put it in the dishwasher, she did a visual check of the counter and floor. Everything was neat and clean.

Gracie climbed onto one of the stools, holding Rudy, her stuffed dog. "Where's Lottie? I can't find her."

"Isn't she upstairs?"

"She's not in our room or the junk room."

"Maybe she's hiding. Shall we go see if we can find her?"

The search didn't take long. Lottie wasn't in the cabin.

Okay, calm down, Sarah. Think.

She knelt beside Gracie. "I have to go outside to look for her. I'm going to leave you in here, but I won't go so far you can't see me from the windows."

Gracie's chin trembled. "Is Lottie lost, too? Like Mom?"

"I'm going to find Lottie. But I need you to help. Can you stay in here until I get back? Maybe watch *Frozen*?"

"I'll stay by the door so I can see you."

Sarah hugged her. "Good girl. I won't be long." *At least, I hope not.* She pulled on her parka and grabbed the binoculars, locking the door behind her.

Sunlight warmed Sarah's cheeks at the same time cold air touched the back of her neck. Pulling up her collar, she turned to look at Gracie, who stood by the window, peering out. Sarah wiggled her fingers, and Gracie waved back.

Sarah made a complete loop around the house, calling out to Lottie, with no response. The snow on the broad footpath to the bridge lay unbroken. Ignoring the knot growing in her stomach, Sarah called again. Turning, she walked along the back, peering into the woods.

When she called to Lottie again, her voice sounded panicky. She had to stay calm, had to think.

Where would Lottie go? There was no reason for her to be out there, other than an urge to get out of the cabin. The sun was shining, the landscape appealing. Maybe she'd just gone for a walk. But why sneak out to do that? And why wouldn't she answer when Sarah called?

Hands trembling, she inched the binoculars to her right, peering into the trees at the back of the cabin. Something moved and she backtracked. Just a deer. But it stood, ears alert, looking deeper into the forest.

"Lottie!" Sarah squinted but could see nothing. She moved the glasses left again, toward the same area where she'd found the bracelet. Nothing stirred. The knot was twisting in her gut now. She couldn't wait any longer. She had to call for help.

As she turned toward the door, a flash of color made her whirl. Lottie had emerged from behind the shed. She had her head down, looking at the patterns she was drawing in the snow with a small branch. Perhaps sensing Sarah's gaze, she looked up, smiling. "Hi, Sarah. I went for a walk."

"You went for a walk? Without telling me?" Sarah's voice sounded shrill. She drew in a long, deep breath, then let it out. "Lottie, I was scared. I didn't know where you were and I couldn't find you."

The girl frowned. "I'm sorry. I didn't think about that. I just...I needed to get outside, by myself."

Sarah felt tears forming. She couldn't do this. At the moment, she'd like nothing better than to be back in those bustling New York streets she'd been so eager to escape the week before. The snowy landscape she'd found so beautiful a few days before was now just silent and cold and dangerous, and keeping her bound to the cabin.

"Don't tell," Lottie said, grabbing Sarah's hand, her voice barely above a whisper. "Please don't tell."

"Lottie...I can't keep all this from your father. The phone calls, this." Sarah spread her arms to indicate the woods. "If you're not willing to tell him, I have to."

"You can't. You don't understand."

Sarah unlocked the door. "Then tell me why. Help me to understand."

Lottie jerked her hand from Sarah's. "I wish you'd just go away. Leave us alone." She pushed past Sarah, into the cabin and up the stairs. Gracie glanced toward Sarah before following her sister.

Sarah stepped back outside, locked the cabin door again, and trudged toward the center of the path leading to the old road. She needed a walk by herself, too.

Maybe I'll even come back.

Chapter 16
Thursday Afternoon

A car, one she didn't recognize, turned into the lane. Sarah sighed and headed toward the front door. Before she reached it, the vehicle had stopped and two men, wearing long overcoats, got out. They were a contrast in black and white, the African-American very dark-skinned and the Caucasian fair-skinned, with white-blond hair.

He leaned against the car, surveying his surroundings. His companion watched Sarah as she approached. Stepping forward, he held out his hand. He looked to be in his late fifties or early sixties and had a fringe of silvery-white hair surrounding a bare pate. Mild brown eyes peered at her from over a pair of rimless glasses.

"Good morning." He pulled a badge from an inner pocket and showed it to her. "I'm Detective Jasper Ursall, from B.C.I., and this is my partner, Detective Joseph Mason. Is Greg Agerton home?"

"What is B.C.I.?"

"Bureau of Criminal Investigation, the plainclothes detective branch of the New York State Police, " Mason leaned forward to display his own badge before he shook her hand. "We get all the cases requiring extensive investigation or involving felonies."

At least twenty years younger than his partner and several degrees paler, Mason was also an inch or two shorter, but at least twenty pounds heavier. She suspected his weight was more muscle than fat, though; his overcoat settled well on his large frame. He had short-clipped hair and looked at her from eyes that were a startling sky-blue, much like those of Laura's husband, Sam, but not nearly as friendly.

Sarah fumbled in her pocket for the door key. "He's not here. He left sometime early this morning, and I don't know where he is. Probably with the searchers at the lake."

"Do you know when he'll be back?"

She unlocked the front door. "No later than seven."

"May we come in?" Ursall asked, and Sarah stood aside, allowing them to enter, then closed and locked the door behind them.

"I don't know how much I can help. I'm Sarah Wagner, a friend of Tracy Agerton's. She invited me to come up from the city for a week. I've stayed to take care of her little girls while her husband is out with the search parties."

Ursall took off his overcoat, displaying a lean frame with a slight pot belly. "Where are the daughters?"

"Upstairs." Sarah took the coat and waited for the one Mason was removing. No bulge over that belt. His stomach looked flat and taut, like the rest of his body.

"We'd like to ask you a few questions," he said. "Now, while the daughters are upstairs, might be a good time. We'd like to talk to them, too, later. With you here, of course."

Sarah hung their coats in the laundry room. "I have fresh coffee if you would like a cup. Do you want to talk here, or in the living room?" She nodded toward the sofa.

Ursall looked around the room. "No coffee, thanks. What about the dining room table?"

She poured herself a mug of coffee while the detectives settled at the table, taking out notebooks, pens, and a small recorder.

"Do you mind if we record our conversation?" Mason asked. "It's easier than taking notes, and much more accurate. Provides protection for everybody concerned."

She slipped into one of the chairs. "That's fine." She'd been interviewed by detectives before, when Caro had died, and hadn't liked the outcome. *They're here to talk to Greg, not me.* But she had no reason to trust them, even knowing she had nothing to hide.

After filling them in with her name, New York address, telephone number, and the name and address of the design school, she told them about the invitation from Tracy.

"How do you know her?" Mason asked. She'd never imagined eyes that color of blue could look so cold, like an icy lake.

"From the design school. She was taking a class. Not as a full-time student. But we were assigned a class project together, and we got to know each other that way."

"And Greg Agerton? When did you meet him?"

"Not until I got here."

Ursall peered over his glasses. "And when did you arrive here, Ms. Wagner?"

"Friday. Friday afternoon."

Mason looked up from his notes. "Before or after Tracy Agerton disappeared?"

"I...I don't know."

His eyes narrowed. "You don't know?" He shifted in the chair, and it squeaked on the tile. "Ms. Wagner—"

"When I got here, Greg didn't know. Didn't know she was missing. He'd expected her to meet up with me on the road, and she didn't." Sarah looked away from Mason's eyes, toward Ursall, as she told them what had happened: the wrong turn, getting her car stuck, no response to her calls, and finally walking to the cabin. "She might have missed me when I was off the main road."

Mason leaned back in his chair, fiddling with his pen. "Are you sure you didn't see her anywhere?"

"No, I didn't." She had just told him that.

Ursall made notes. "What time did you get your car stuck?"

When had she last checked the time before that? "I was in the car, driving. It was a quarter after one when I first heard about the convict. I looked at the dashboard clock, trying to figure out how far he could have traveled since he escaped."

"Where were you at that time?"

"It was just before I left the turnpike. There were lots of turns after that, but it was only five or ten miles to the cabin. I drove fairly slow, since I didn't know the area, and I'm not used to driving in snow. But I got stuck—oh, wait. I remember now. I looked at my phone when I called Tracy, after my car went off the road. It was about a quarter 'til two. There was no answer. I called several more times, and waited for about half an hour before I got out and started walking."

"You walked to the cabin? How long did that take?"

"I don't know. It seemed like forever. I was scared. The convict could have been out there in the trees, so I was trying to hurry. But I was pulling my suitcase. It kept getting hung up in the snow."

Ursall jotted again in his notebook. "Could you take a guess? Twenty minutes? Thirty? An hour?"

Frowning, Sarah shook her head. "I don't know. Probably closer to a half hour, not counting the time I spent looking at the tire, to see how bad it was, and trying to find some kind of tool to use as a weapon. I don't think the cabin was more than a mile from my car."

Mason nodded toward the window. "That it? The Highlander?"

"Yes. It's a rental. One of Greg's friends just got it out this morning. It was in the ditch for days. Everybody was so busy with the search...and it was strange. The friend, Jake Nichols, said somebody had disconnected the coil wire."

Mason leaned forward. "The coil wire? Why would somebody do that?"

"I have no idea. I don't know anybody here, other than the people who came out to help with the search."

Ursall looked at her over the tops of his glasses. "Tell us what Greg Agerton was doing when you arrived."

"He and his daughters were building a snowman out in front. He was surprised that Tracy wasn't with me. He didn't know about the convict escaping. When I told him, he got us all inside, checked the cabin, locked the doors, and went to look for Tracy."

"How long was he gone?"

Sarah frowned in concentration. She'd changed her clothes, and they were still making cupcakes when Greg got back. "I'd say about three-quarters of an hour."

"So you arrived about three o'clock, give or take a half hour, to find Greg Agerton and his daughters making a snowman?"

"Yes, that's about right."

Ursall was quiet again, flipping through his notebook. With his head bent, sunlight reflected off his bare scalp. He cleared his throat and looked up at her. "What did Mr. Agerton do when he returned?"

Sarah closed her eyes. He'd had coffee, and she'd asked about fixing dinner for the girls. "He was here for maybe a half hour, waiting for some friends to arrive to help him search. He was cold and drank a cup of coffee while he waited."

"You met the friends?"

"Yes, later that night, when it got too dark to search any longer. They came back to the cabin, and I fixed some food. They'd found Tracy's scarf and her phone."

"Where are they? The things they found?"

"I don't know. I never saw them. I just heard the men talking about what they'd found. I suppose Greg has them." But she hadn't seen a scarf or phone in his room. Not that she'd looked. They could be in a drawer.

"Can you give us the names of the friends? And their telephone numbers and addresses, if you have them?"

"I know their names, but that's all. Jake Nichols, Bill Ayers, Paul Jackson, and Tim and Robert Grayson—they're father and son."

Ursall wrote them down. "Can you think of any reason why Tracy Agerton would leave of her own accord?"

Sarah shook her head, glanced at the recorder, and said, "No."

"Can you think of anybody who might have wanted to harm her?"

"No, but I didn't know her well." Should she tell them about Roberta's phone call? No, it was just gossip. Roberta's imagination was on a par with her own—maybe even better.

A noise drew her attention to the stairs. Lottie and Gracie stood on one of the treads, looking down at the strange men in their kitchen.

Mason followed her gaze. "Is it okay if we ask them a few questions?"

"I don't know if I have the authority. I'm not related to them."

"We don't need permission, Ms. Wagner." His eyes assessed her. "They're not suspects in a crime. We just need an adult with them. Somebody they know and trust."

"You have to understand. They don't know me well, and they just realized last night that their mother is probably not coming back. It hit them pretty hard, and I don't want them upset."

She rose and went to the bottom of the stairs. "Lottie, Gracie, these men are detectives—police. They're trying to find your mother, and they want to ask you some questions."

Gracie looked up at Lottie for guidance. Lottie asked Sarah, "Will you stay with us?"

Sarah studied her face. The girl's eyes were pleading. Was she regretting what she'd said to Sarah, trying to make amends?

"Yes. I'll be right there at the table with you." She led the girls toward the detectives, who stood and pulled out chairs for them and introduced themselves.

"Ms. Wagner tells us—" Lottie looked puzzled, so Ursall started over. "Sarah tells me you were helping your dad build a snowman when she arrived."

Gracie smiled. "Dad built most of it. But we built forts with Sarah, out of snow, so we could have a snowball fight."

Mason smiled, his sky-blue eyes now friendlier. "Was that the same day?"

"No." Gracie shook her head. "Not that day. Later, when it wasn't snowing so much."

"Do you remember what time your mother left to go on her walk?"

Gracie's head bobbed up and down. "Sure. She had a headache, and she left while we were drinking our hot chocolate. With marshmallows."

"Not when you were building the snowman?"

Lottie explained. "We were helping Dad with the snowman when Mom called us in for the hot chocolate. After that, she left for her walk, and when we got through, we went back out to work on the snowman some more."

"Did your father stay with you, or did he leave the room to talk to your mother?"

"He stayed with us," Lottie said. "But he drank coffee, not hot chocolate."

"And we went back out, and that's when Sarah came," Gracie added.

Nobody spoke. Gracie swung her legs back and forth in front of her chair, and Lottie scooted a little closer to Sarah, who clasped the little girl's hand.

Ursall's tone was gentle. "Lottie, Ms...Sarah says the searchers found your mother's scarf and phone that first night, when they were searching."

Gracie stopped swinging her legs. "They couldn't have. We put it on the snowman."

"That's the old one," Lottie said. "The one she used to wear all the time. Her new one is still on her dresser."

Mason leaned toward her, his voice still soft. "Do you know where your dad put the scarf he found, and the phone?"

Lottie rose. "Maybe. I'll go look." She ran toward the stairs. "Want to see her new one, too?"

Mason nodded, and Gracie, eager to help, asked, "Want me to get the old one? It's in the laundry room. But Lottie wants to keep it."

"I'd like to see it," Mason said.

Gracie came back with the red scarf a few seconds before Lottie returned with two more, identical except for their color: both plaid, with fringed ends. Lottie held the blue one toward Sarah. "This is yours."

Both detectives looked at Sarah, who shook her head. "No, honey, I never saw that before. Mine is cream-colored, remember? And it's plain, not plaid."

"I know that!" Lottie's voice betrayed her frustration. "But Mom bought this one for you. She was going to give it to you..." Her eyes welled with tears. "She wanted them to be alike, but she said blue was your color and red was hers."

Mason asked, "When did you last see the blue one, Lottie? Before now, I mean."

She sniffled and rubbed a fist across her upper lip. "The night before Sarah came. While Mom was making up the bed in the spare room. She started to leave the scarf there for Sarah, but changed her mind and took it back to her bedroom."

"Do you think she might have taken it with her on the walk? She planned to meet up with Sarah, didn't she?"

"Maybe. I don't know." Lottie pulled the red scarf into her lap, brushing her fingers across the fringe.

"What about her phone? Do you know where it is?" Ursall asked.

Lottie shook her head, and Ursall turned to Sarah. "Do you have your cell phone with you, Ms. Wagner?"

Sarah handed it to him, and he explored its contents. "You were pretty close on the time of your calls. Three of them, between one forty-one and two-eleven, another at two thirty-nine." He jotted the times down and scrolled through her call log. Maybe she shouldn't have given him her phone. *I have nothing to hide, but still...*

"What's the 9-1-6 area code?"

"My cousin in California."

He made more notes before handing the phone back to her. "You don't know what Mr. Agerton did with his wife's phone?"

"No, I never saw it." She'd tried not to think about it ringing in the silent woods, partially buried in the snow—like the bracelet. She pulled it out of her pocket. "I found something else."

Lottie let out a little gasp and reached for it. "That's Mom's."

"I know. I went for a walk yesterday, early in the morning." Facing away from Mason, she spoke directly to Ursall. "I found it snagged on a piece of brush alongside a trail, half-buried in snow. I meant to give it to Greg but didn't get a chance last night, and he was already gone when I woke up this morning."

Lottie scrambled off her chair. "You have to show us. Mom may be there. She was wearing it. She always wore it." She ran to the laundry room, Gracie close behind.

Ursall and Mason exchanged glances and rose to their feet. "I think that may be a very good idea. Lead the way, Ms. Wagner."

Lottie would have pulled Gracie outside without stopping for coats or boots if Sarah hadn't insisted they wait. "Gracie had a temperature yesterday. We don't want her to get sick."

"Don't run ahead of Ms. Wagner, either," Ursall directed. "We don't want to disturb anything."

Lottie, sobered, nodded, and they set off, Sarah in the lead. As she neared the zig-zag path, she slowed, trying to step into the same prints she'd made earlier.

"Wait a minute," Mason said. He turned toward Lottie. "Why don't you girls stay here with Detective Ursall?"

Lottie understood. She nodded, and Ursall led them aside. Sarah moved on, her steps careful now, Mason following, until she located the shrub where she'd found the bracelet.

Mason knelt, examining the broken branches, then rose, taking cautious steps along the edge of the path, much as Sarah had the day before. He motioned for Ursall to inspect the other side.

"Tape it off?" Mason finally asked.

"Yeah. Get your camera, too, so we can take some photos. And get some crime scene techs out here. Snow has probably covered anything useful, but you never know." Ursall turned to Sarah. "Did they have dogs searching out here?"

"I'm not sure. I could hear dogs after the first day or two, but I don't know exactly where."

"Okay, we're going to section this off until we can search it more thoroughly. Try to keep everybody away from here. And, Ms. Wagner, we'd appreciate it if you didn't leave the area for the time being."

"Not leave? For how long? I have to be back in New York Monday for class. My flight leaves Sunday morning."

He shrugged. "I hope we'll have this resolved by then. But in the meantime, it would be helpful if you stayed."

Chapter 17
Thursday Evening

O ther vehicles arrived, and Sarah took occasional glances out the kitchen window as she prepared dinner for the girls. She couldn't see into the depths of the forest—only the flurry of activity as people carried equipment back and forth, around the corner from the vehicles parked in the front yard. She couldn't figure out what they might be doing.

She turned to Lottie and Gracie, sitting at the kitchen counter. "Do you have an Aunt Cindy?"

"Sure," Lottie said. "She lives close to us. We see her all the time."

"What's her last name?"

"Bates."

"Do you know her phone number?"

She had Lottie's attention now. A quizzical expression crossed the child's face. "No, but it's in Mom's phone."

"Did she go on the cruise with your grandparents?"

Lottie giggled. "No, 'course not. She never goes with them. Sometimes she goes on trips with Mom, though."

Ursall tapped on the laundry room door. When Sarah opened it, he handed her two cards. "Our cell phone numbers, just in case you think of anything else you should tell us. We've got a section of the woods taped off and some crime scene technicians working it, so try to keep everybody away from that area."

She stood for a moment or two after he left, looking down at the card. Should she have told them about the drugs? No, it would just be her word against Greg's. What if she was making a mistake? Over-reacting? She couldn't be sure Greg had drugged her. He had no reason to do that, and there might be a perfectly innocent explanation for the GHB. Maybe he and Tracy used it together like kids did at raves. Or maybe it was Tracy's.

Enough! She'd puzzle it all out later. Right now, she needed to get ready for her evening in town.

Lottie was quieter than usual. Gracie, absorbed in *Frozen*, didn't notice. Or maybe she had simply learned to adapt to her big sister's moods. Who knew a child could watch the same favorite movie over and over again?

◆◆◆

She didn't tell Greg about Lottie's walk. Not that she had a chance; he didn't get back to the cabin until seven, a few minutes before the detectives came back. She'd be late for her meeting with Jake.

Lottie probably wouldn't tell him, either, especially after she'd experienced Sarah's reaction to her little adventure. She'd apologized and seemed contrite. Yet, when she appeared to be deep in thought, her mouth curved into that same odd little smile Sarah had noted earlier.

Gracie followed Sarah to the door when she left, clinging to her hand. "Promise you'll come back?"

Sarah kissed her cheek. "Of course, I will. I'm just going to Mountain View to have dinner."

They were getting too attached to her, and Sarah to them. She would miss them when she left, especially knowing she'd probably never see them again, that she couldn't be part of their lives. She blinked away tears. It would be impossible to enjoy her evening if she kept thinking about what was going on at the cabin.

◆◆◆

She eased the Highlander down the lane to the road, a little nervous after sliding it off into the ditch on Friday. All too aware of her inexperience in snow conditions, she was glad Belly's was just over ten miles away.

Once she felt comfortable with the road, she turned on the radio and scrolled for a news station. Apparently, the police department had given a press conference earlier in the day. The absence of a ransom note or any attempted contact with the family had led them to discount the theory of a kidnapper in Tracy Agerton's disappearance. The convict who had been an early suspect swore he had never gone south; his goal had been to reach Canada. All the evidence, including the cabins he broke into, supported his story.

"So," the spokesman had finished, "as of now, it appears somebody else is responsible for Tracy Agerton's disappearance."

Sarah turned off the radio and checked the locks on the doors.

The soft glow of lights ahead told her she'd found Belly's. It had two-stories—one and a half, really—with a peaked roof and a lone window shining light from the upper level.

She circled around and found a well-lit space, parked, and headed for the front door. Jake waited just inside, wearing pressed jeans and a blue-gray sweater that almost matched his eyes. It would be difficult to find a color in exactly that stormy-gray shade.

He took her arm and led her to a table. A coat was draped over one of the chairs. "Have any trouble finding the place?" He held out a chair for her.

"Not once I got past the big traffic jam at the light."

He laughed. "Yeah. It gets crazy during rush hour. Sometimes as many as three cars get stacked up there. And Thursday is one of the busiest nights of the week. Everybody comes in. I hope you like Mexican."

"Love it, as long as it's good and comes with a margarita."

"That can be arranged." He signaled the server. "Is that your drink of choice?"

She laughed. "Only with Mexican. I much prefer wine—merlot. I kind of grew up with it. Wine, I mean. I lived with my aunt, and she had a well-stocked wine cellar."

As soon as she uttered the words, she bit her lip and backtracked. "How about you?"

"Depends. Beer in the summer, mostly, and scotch on the rocks the rest of the time."

The server appeared, and Jake ordered a margarita and a Corona. "Did you have any problems with the car?"

"No, nothing. Thanks again for fixing it. And for getting it out of the ditch. You can't imagine how confining it is, out there in that cabin with no transportation."

He looked over the top of his menu. "How much longer do you think you'll be there?"

"I wish I knew. My flight is scheduled for Sunday morning, but I'm not sure I'm going to be able to take it. Did you hear the news? The detectives have discounted a kidnapper and the convict in Tracy's disappearance. I'm assuming that means they're looking for somebody local."

His eyes narrowed as he lowered the menu. "Why?"

"I guess that's what they're trying to find out."

He shook his head. "Those poor kids. And this has got to be tough for you, too."

Tears tried to flood her eyes again. She pressed her eyelids shut until she'd willed them away. "It looks like I may be here for a while longer than I'd planned. The detectives asked me to stay for the time being. I don't know what that means or why they need me."

"And if you miss the beginning of your next class—"

"How do you know about my class?" She hadn't mentioned it.

He smiled and placed one hand over hers on the table. "Sorry. Tracy told me. Said that's how she met you."

"You and Tracy were friends? I just assumed it was a guy thing. You and Greg, I mean."

The server arrived and placed their drinks on the table, followed a few minutes later by a young man with a pad in hand.

Jake asked Sarah, "Have you decided?"

"The Mexican stir fry sounds intriguing." She took a sip of her margarita. Good.

He nodded. "I'll go with the enchiladas—shredded beef." He handed the menus to the server. "I've known Greg a long time. We went to school together. But after I met Tracy...she and I have a lot of common interests. And she told me all about you. She likes you." His voice was soft.

Sarah ran the tip of her finger around the margarita glass. "What kind of interests?"

Tracy hadn't mentioned Jake to her. Had their conversations about Sarah started after Tracy arrived at the cabin, while she was anticipating Sarah's visit?

"Plays. Books. Movies. And she liked my paintings."

Sarah leaned forward. "What do you do? Oils? Watercolors—"

"Oil, mostly animals. I try to capture them in motion. They're so fluid, so graceful, especially the big cats. And their colors are amazing. Tawny golds, shades of black where the fur ripples ...sorry, I get a little carried away sometimes."

"No, I was enjoying your descriptions. My aunt Caro—she was a painter—used to do the same thing. Made me feel a little homesick for a minute there. I'd love to see some of your work."

"Really? Tracy thought they were good. She was going to try to get me a showing. She knew somebody with a gallery—" He shook his head. "Not that it matters now." He took a long draw from the beer bottle.

Am I that person? The one with the gallery? Laura had set one up in Sacramento for Caro's work, along with some of Laura's own sketches. And because there was a finite supply of Caro's work, the gallery accepted a few other artists.

She wouldn't mention it to Jake. Not until she saw his paintings. If they were good, she might check with Erin Brewster, who managed the gallery. "I'd like to see them. Do you have any displayed—"

A woman passing their table stopped. "Jake. Jake Nichols. And Sarah. It's good to see you again. I've been meaning to call."

Sarah looked up into blue eyes and groped for a name to match the face. Ellen Tisdale, her short hair curling softly around a narrow face. She wore pressed slacks and a white shirt, finished off with a pearl necklace.

"Jake took pity on my raging cabin fever and offered to rescue me," Sarah said.

"Oh, my dear! I should have realized. With poor Greg out searching day and night, you couldn't leave those little girls. So I assume he's home now in the evenings?"

"Well, yes, at least tonight."

"I wonder...I have a little movie get-together on Friday nights. Very informal. Just me and one or two close friends. I have a big screen TV. We make popcorn and pour a little wine. Why don't you join us tomorrow night?"

"I don't know." She wouldn't be there much longer. Or would she? Ellen Tisdale looked like the kind of woman she'd like to know better. "That would be nice. I love movies. Thank you for asking me."

"If you come a little earlier, for dinner, we could get to know each other before my friends arrive for the movie. Around six? Here, I'll give you my address and phone number—draw you a little map."

She dug into her purse while Sarah tried to interpret the look on Jake's face. Alarm? A red spot spread from the center of each cheek, and his mouth twisted in an odd way. He leaned over the table, his face buried in his napkin, coughing. But his eyes, when he looked up at her, danced with mischief. Was he laughing?

Ellen patted him on the back and handed the slip of paper to Sarah. "About six?"

Sarah nodded, still watching Jake. "What's so amusing?" she asked after Ellen walked away. "Is it an inside joke? What's funny about friends hanging out—"

"Hu...hu...hanging out." He bent over, his shoulders shaking.

"I'm glad you're finding this so hilarious, because I don't get it. Maybe you'd like to clue me in."

He sat up straighter, shaking his head. "It's...Sarah, it's—" He buried his face in the napkin again, spasms jerking his body, so she couldn't understand what he was saying. "...movies...big screen...corn..."

"I can't understand. You're saying she has a big screen, they watch movies—"

He nodded.

"And they make popcorn?"

He shook his head, his skin darkening as the blush crept up his face. "Not corn. Porn. They watch racy movies on that big screen." A paroxysm of laugher engulfed him again. "It's probably not that bad, but it's a small town, so everybody thinks it's true porn."

She stared, feeling the heat rushing into her cheeks. "Oh, my God! You're kidding."

"No...not...kidding. Says..." He raised his head and grinned. "She says there are no eligible men around for women her age, so—"

"On a big screen TV? Drinking wine and eating popcorn?" Sarah felt her lips twitch. She grabbed her napkin and buried her face before laughter erupted.

Finally, she raised her head and met Jake's twinkling eyes. "How in hell am I going to get out of that little social engagement?"

"Engagement. That's it! Tell them we're engaged. You don't have need of their services?"

"I'm not <u>that</u> desperate."

He blinked, the smile gone. *Nice going, Sarah. Insult the only person who's cared enough to get your car out of the ditch and you out of the cabin.*

"I...Jake, I didn't mean...you're a nice person, and I like you. I really do. But I just met you and—" She broke off when the lips he'd just been biting down on suddenly pulled into a wide grin.

"Too bad I don't have a stop watch. I'll bet that was the fastest proposal and rejection on record. Good thing I didn't have champagne on ice."

She laughed and took a sip of water. "And here I've been wondering why such a nice, good-looking man was still unmarried. I suspect it has something to do with your technique. You might want to work on that."

"You think? I don't suppose...Do you think a certain somebody might be willing to teach me?"

She tensed, forming words to let him down gently, even before he finished his sentence.

"Somebody like Ellen?" he said.

Water spewed into the palm she'd cupped over her mouth. Laughing, she grabbed the napkin and blotted at the drops on her shirt.

Jake laughed, too. Then his face sobered, and he studied hers. "I like you, Sarah Wagner. I like you a lot. You're caring enough to stay out at that cabin and take care of those kids, but you're fun, too."

"I like you, too, Jake. You're a nice person—"

"Uh-oh. This sounds like the proposal rejection all over again." His lips smiled, but his eyes didn't cooperate. They were serious, thoughtful.

The waiter's appearance with their dinner gave Sarah a few minutes to reflect. She <u>did</u> like Jake. Far too much. He had a depth and a sense of humor that she'd never expected—wouldn't have known existed if she hadn't agreed to have dinner with him. But Scott had been witty and fun, too, in the beginning. *And look where that got me.*

"Jake, I'm still getting over my divorce, and it's been hard. I'm not ready for another relationship, not sure I'll ever be—"

"Who said anything about a relationship?"

Had she misunderstood, or was he joking again? No, his face was serious. She flushed. "I'm sorry. I thought—"

"Sarah, I get it. You don't want a relationship. But don't you have room in your life for one more friend?"

One more? She could count those she had on one hand. She did want friends. But somehow, she'd always thought of them as female. Like the ones she'd met here? Ellen Tisdale with her porn movies? Gossipy Roberta Adrickson? Insecure, jealous Julie Osborne?

She held her hand across the table, and he took it. "Jake, if you really mean it, if it's friendship you want, I'm your girl. No, I mean—"

Grinning again, he took her hand. "Like I said, you're a lot of fun, Sarah Wagner."

"Well, isn't this just so sweet?" Julie Osborne stood beside the table, staring down at their clasped hands. "Cheating on me again, Jake?"

She picked up a glass of water and threw it in his face before turning to Sarah. "Even if you manage to steal him, you'll never keep him. With Jake, there's always another woman." She stalked toward the door.

Chapter 18
Later Thursday Evening

J ake mopped the water off his face. "Just another night at Belly's, where the friendly locals hang out."

Sarah stared at him, at the still damp mustache and beard, glistening in the ambient lighting. "You and Julie?" *Why do I care? We just agreed to be friends. Nothing more.*

It was his turn to stare. "Julie? Are you kidding? We went out once—well, twice, if you count the night we just ran into each other and ended up having a couple of drinks together. Somehow, in her twisted little mind, that made us a couple. Like she always thought she and Greg were a couple. Even after he married two other women. Julie is...well, she's a little strange."

"Jake, this may come as a surprise to you, but almost everyone I've met in this place is a little strange. Julie, Ellen, Lottie sometimes, Greg sometimes, and even Roberta Adrickson. She invited me to Fiesta Thursday after you did and thought I wouldn't go with her because she's gay. She'd never given any indication. How was I supposed to know—"

"Roberta's not gay. She and Roger have been married over twenty years and have three kids. Two girls and a boy."

"But she accused me of turning her down because of her sexual orientation. Why would she do that if she's not gay?"

Jake took another dab at his damp beard, the wet napkin adding more moisture than it absorbed. Sarah handed him hers.

He wiped down his beard and mustache and smoothed them with his fingers. "Roberta is staying in character. She does that."

"Most of us do...most of the time."

"No, it's not that. The theater group is putting on *La Cage aux Folles* this year, and Roberta is playing Albin. Every time she's cast in a role, she drives everybody nuts, especially Roger, by 'staying in character'—even when it's inappropriate."

"But that's a male part. The gay couple in that musical is male."

He raised an eyebrow. "This isn't New York City, Sarah. How many of the men around here do you think would play those parts? And, knowing that, why did they decide on that particular production? Who knows? Like you said, people around here can be a little strange."

Sarah smiled. "I guess I seemed a little strange, too, when I first arrived, pulling a suitcase through the snow and carrying a lug wrench." At his raised eyebrows, she hurried to add "from the Highlander's toolbox...to defend myself against the escaped convict."

"Makes good sense to me."

"Yeah, but I forgot to put it back in the car. I'd better do that tomorrow." She fingered the stem of the margarita glass. "Speaking of strange people, there's somebody I'm curious about, and I don't know who to ask."

"Okay. Let me order another beer first. And some more napkins. Do you want another margarita?"

Sarah put a hand over her glass. "Not for me. I'm driving."

"Me, too. But between all the enchiladas and my cold shower, I think I'm good." He tilted his chair back a little. "Now, who do you want me to gossip about?"

Sarah felt heat creeping into her cheeks. He let the chair down and leaned across the table. "It's okay. That's what friends do, isn't it? Gossip?"

"Maybe your friends." Her laughter trailed off as she envisioned the face of the man who had looked at Greg with so much hatred. She had to ask; Jake might know something about him. She plunged in.

"There was a man at the cabin the day Julie, Roberta and Ellen came to help me cook. You and Greg were at the fireplace with several other men. I recognized some of them, but there was one—he looked at Greg like he hated him."

Jake frowned. "There were a lot of searchers there that night. He was at the fireplace with us?"

"Yes. Julie had taken coffee to you and Greg, and stood between you, talking. This other man looked at Greg like he hated him. It surprised me so much I didn't even notice what he was wearing. The best I can remember, he was about average height and weight, and nothing about his features stood out."

"Brad Denton. Has to be. I couldn't figure out why he was even there, why he would be searching for Tracy. You're right. He hates Greg. But he hates Tracy even more. He's Amy's brother."

"Amy? Greg's first wife?"

"Yeah. She drowned. Not here. Some beach house they owned. The odd thing was—"

"They were having a pool party, with a lot of people there, but she slipped away from them and drowned in the ocean. She wasn't a strong swimmer."

"Greg told you? That surprises me. He's usually pretty close-mouthed about it. He was a suspect for a while, and it was hard on him. He lost a lot of friends, and the Denton family is still convinced he had something to do with her death."

"Encouraged along that line by the police, no doubt. They always suspect family."

"It wasn't just the police. Even the people at the party thought he'd killed her. At least, they did that night. She hadn't been feeling well, and at one point, he went upstairs to check on her. When he came back down, he said she had a headache, had taken something for it, and would rejoin them when it was better. A couple of hours went by, and she still hadn't come down, so he went up to see if she was all right. He was gone so long that time, the guests were getting antsy, until they heard him yelling from the beach. They rushed down there. He was dripping wet. He'd pulled her body to shore."

Sarah rubbed her arms, the image of a dark, lonely beach with cold waves pounding the shoreline flooding her mind.

"The pool where all the people were gathered would have been in the back," she said, "so the beach must have been in the front. That meant the house was probably empty, and it would have been easy for him to take her down the stairs and out the front. So why didn't they prove—"

"He did it?" Jake nodded. "It looked like a slam-dunk. They hadn't been getting along very well, and she was loaded. With money, I mean. The Dentons are probably one of the wealthiest families in the state. Denton Pharmaceuticals."

Jake rolled the beer bottle between his palms. "But the coroner fixed the time of death several hours before Greg found her—not long after she went upstairs."

Sarah sat up straighter and leaned toward Jake. "But he went up to check on her."

"Yeah. But he wasn't gone long enough to take her down to the beach. And it was seawater in her lungs."

Icy prickles crept up Sarah's spine. Greg had an alibi for the time Tracy disappeared, too.

Sarah should have ordered that margarita; she could use a drink. Instead, she signaled the server and asked for a cup of coffee.

"So that's why Brad Denton hates Greg. But why Tracy?"

Jake lifted the Corona bottle to his lips and tilted his chair back again. "Because of the cabin. It originally belonged to the Dentons. They used it when they came up here to go skiing. I guess it was special to Brad and Amy because those vacations were about the only time the family spent together. Pop jetting around the world making business deals, mom busy with social obligations, and both kids off to private schools."

"So you knew them back then?"

He sat up straight in the chair. "Me? Hell no. The vacationers don't mix much with the locals, and the rich don't mix at all. I might have seen them out on the slopes, but that's about it. Most everything I know, I get from Bill."

"Bill Ayers?"

"Yeah. He worked out at the country club, so he got to know quite a bit about them. He liked the old man."

Jake fell silent when the waiter came to fill Sarah's coffee cup and didn't resume his story until they were alone again.

"When Amy found out her new husband—the one she'd met at university—grew up here, she wheedled the cabin out of her old man for a wedding gift. Maybe she figured they'd live in it. If that's what she thought, she didn't know her new husband very well. Greg didn't mind coming back for a few days or even a week or two, but he never wanted to live here."

"So they used the cabin for vacations, just like the Denton family had done."

"Yeah, but now Brad was cut out. The cabin belonged to Amy and Greg, and Greg didn't want anybody else using it. I don't think it mattered to the parents. They just bought a bigger one. But it mattered to Brad."

Sarah ripped a corner off a packet of sweetener and stirred half of it into the coffee before turning back to Jake. "Okay, he's got reason to hate Greg. The cabin, the suspicious death. But why Tracy? What did she have to do with any of it?"

"After Amy died, Brad tried to buy the cabin, and he made an offer so generous, Greg was ready to sell. He didn't care about the cabin, and it looked like a windfall to him. And he needed money."

"But Amy. Didn't he inherit—"

"Nope. Come to find out, her money was set up in a trust. She had plenty to spend, but the old man had tight reins on where it went. There were no kids, so it went back to the Dentons. When Greg married Tracy, all he had was the cabin. And he made the mistake of putting her name on the deed."

"And she didn't want to let Brad Denton have it?"

"I don't think it would have mattered how much Brad offered, Tracy would never have sold that cabin. Not even to a third party, for fear Brad would get it."

"But why?"

"Because Brad had tried so hard to get Greg convicted of Amy's murder. And Tracy had plenty of her own money. She didn't need Brad's."

Sarah looked down at the sweetener packet. She'd folded it into a tiny rectangle and was creasing it between her thumb and finger. "Wow, that's a lot of hate."

"From both sides."

"Enough to kill?"

"I don't know. I can't imagine hating anybody that much. But Tracy is missing, so I can't help thinking about it, wondering. I suspect everybody in town is doing the same thing."

Sarah had finished her coffee. She set the cup on the table "I guess the detectives will figure it out. I'm about ready to go if you are."

He nodded, and she rose from the chair. He held her parka while she slipped her arms inside, then grabbed his coat and shrugged into it on their way out the door. "Where's your car? Never mind, I see it."

Sarah laughed and linked her arm in his as they walked toward the Highlander. "You know it pretty well by now, don't you? Inside and out."

He took a few more steps. "Yeah, but it didn't look like that the last time I saw it."

Sarah stared. A long, uneven scratch ran along both doors on the passenger side. "It's been keyed."

Jake knelt by the back tire. "That's not all, Sarah. Your tire's been slashed."

Sarah moved closer, so she could see the cuts, more like punctures and deep enough to flatten the tire.

Roberta, passing by on her way into the restaurant with her husband, slowed to greet them. She stopped when she saw the tire. "Better check the rest of them, Jake. Julie usually does a pretty good job when she gets started."

Jake rose. "Roberta, Roger." He shook the man's outstretched hand. "Sarah, this is Roger Adrickson, Roberta's husband."

"Oh, really? And does he share your sexual orientation?" Sarah asked, her voice as syrupy-sweet as she could make it.

Jake grinned, and Roger shot a confused look at Roberta. He was small-framed for a man, probably weighing less than his wife, though they were both about five six.

"You've been at it again," he said. "Telling people you're gay."

"Roger, you know I have to stay in character to do justice to the part. We're into final rehearsals now."

Roger held his hand out to Sarah. "I apologize for my wife. People around here know what's going on. They're used to her. And she doesn't mean any harm." He jerked a thumb toward Roberta. "But you're a stranger. She shouldn't have lied to you."

"But that's just it," Roberta said. "I had to see if I could act the part so well somebody who didn't know me would believe—"

Roger sighed and shook his head. "We better take a look on the other side, too, Jake, and see if those tires are okay."

Roberta's voice rose. "I warned you, didn't I, Sarah? I told you Julie would get even if you went out with Jake. You should have listened."

"I believe your exact words were that Julie would kill me."

"Well, she just might. Just like she might have killed Amy, and now Tracy."

Roger rose from examining the tires. "For Pete's sake, woman, will you stop? Amy Agerton died somewhere on the coast, at a beach house, and Julie never left town. And we don't know that Tracy Agerton is dead."

"No, we don't." The voice came from behind Sarah, and she whirled. Ursall and Mason stood in the shadows just outside the circle of light, Ursall's gaze on Roberta, Mason surveying Sarah's car.

"We were told this is a good place to eat," Ursall said, "but it's apparently not such a good place to leave unattended vehicles."

He shook hands with Jake and Roger. "I'm Detective Jasper Ursall, and this is my partner, Joseph Mason." He flashed his identification card. "We're investigating the disappearance of Tracy Agerton." He turned to face Roberta. "It appears you have some information about the case?"

Roger shook his head. "Sir, Roberta—I'm Roger Adrickson, her husband, by the way—my wife tends to exaggerate quite a bit. I don't think—"

"That may well be, Mr. Adrickson, but there's sometimes a basis for that exaggeration, wouldn't you say? And we need to follow up on every possible lead. Why don't you two come on inside, out of the cold, so we can talk about it?" He ushered them toward the front door of the restaurant.

Mason ran one finger along the fresh scrape on the car. "It appears you have enemies you didn't tell us about, Ms. Wagner. Do you know who did this?"

"I...no, not really. There was a woman, Julie Osborne, who was angry with Jake. I guess with me, too. She made a scene in the restaurant. Threw a glass of water in Jake's face on her way out the door."

Mason's lip twitched. "Did she threaten you?"

"No. No, she didn't. I think she was just angry with Jake." *And warned me Jake would cheat on me if I stole him from her.* "Because he asked me out for dinner," she added.

"That true?" Mason asked Jake.

"About sums it up."

"How bad is the tire?"

"Trashed. Two of them. One on each side. And it's too late to find a spare."

Mason glanced down at the tire on his side. "So it was meant to disable?"

Jake shrugged. "Who knows? But it's not the first time."

"The disconnected coil wire. Do you have any reason to think it's the same person?"

Jake straightened and came back around the car, his mouth set in a grim line. "I don't know, but somebody needs to find out."

Mason nodded. "When you finish here, it might be a good idea to check your own vehicle for damage."

Jake's eyes widened, then narrowed. "Good point. I'll do that." He turned to Sarah. "We won't be able to get tires tonight. Why don't I take you back out to the cabin? We can get new tires put on tomorrow, and I'll bring you back in to get your car."

She shivered and pushed her hands deeper into her pockets. "Providing your vehicle is in running condition."

"Yeah, there's that." He gave a slight bow and held out an elbow so she could take his arm. "Shall we check it out?"

She smiled. "We certainly shall."

Mason studied them, a bemused expression on his face, and handed Jake a card. "I'll want to talk to you again. Sometime tomorrow. Call me in the morning, and we'll set up a meeting."

"Okay." Jake put the card in his coat pocket. "Right after I call the tire shop about Sarah's car."

"And Ms. Wagner?"

Sarah looked over her shoulder at Mason. "Yes?"

"I'll probably see you tomorrow, too. And in light of recent events—" He nodded toward her damaged car—"I'd advise you not to take this so lightly. Be careful, and don't forget, there may be a killer in our midst."

Chapter 19
Thursday Night

J ake walked around his vehicle, kneeling by each tire to examine it. "Seems to be okay." He opened the passenger door for Sarah.

She slid inside. "He certainly knows how to take all the fun out of an evening, doesn't he?"

"Detective Mason? Yeah. But he has a point. I don't like the thought of you out there at the cabin without any transportation. Why don't you get a room in town tonight? You could go back out tomorrow after you get the tires."

She glanced up at the mention of a room, trying to read his face, but saw only concern. He closed her door and walked around to the driver's side and got in.

"I promised Gracie I'd be back this evening. And it's safe, Jake. We keep the doors and windows locked, and Greg's there at night."

Unless it was Greg she needed to worry about. He had probably drugged her. But he couldn't have killed Tracy—if Tracy was dead, as Sarah suspected. He'd been with the girls when she disappeared, and the entire area had been searched. If Tracy's body had been anywhere around the cabin, they would have found it.

Jake glanced at her as he turned out of the parking lot. "You're deep in thought."

"Yeah. Just wondering what's happened to Tracy and how this is going to end. I don't have a good feeling about it."

He nodded, and they didn't speak again as he drove back to the cabin. He parked the Silverado near the front door, beside Greg's Tahoe. "I'll call you tomorrow, as soon as I know when the car will be ready." He hesitated. "Sarah, I had more fun tonight than I've had in a long time. I'd like to do it again, but I don't want you to think...I know you just want to be friends."

"I had fun, too. I'd almost forgotten what that was like. Maybe we can get together again before I leave." She grabbed her purse and slid out of the car. "Let me know whom I should call to pay for the tires tomorrow. And thanks, Jake."

He waited until she'd unlocked the front door before he backed up. She waved, went inside, and looked around. The lights were on, but nobody inhabited the big room. The girls should be asleep, but not Greg. Maybe he was roaming around outside again. She draped her parka over a chair by the fireplace, where embers still burned, and went up to her room.

Somebody had been there. The quilt was rumpled. As she dropped her blazer and purse onto the rocking chair, she peered into the shadowed corners. Nothing moved, and the only sound was her own footsteps. Something lay on the bed. A piece of paper from one of the girls' drawing pads, inexpertly folded into a greeting card shape and decorated with colored-pencil flowers.

Sarah smiled as she opened it. The girls would have giggled, their heads close together, as they prepared this surprise for her. Inside was a printed message. "Thank you for taking care of us."

Sarah sat on the bed, her fingers tracing the printed letters on the note. Tears filled her eyes, and she wiped at them with her hand as she rose from the bed and hurried down the hall to the girls' room. Maybe they were still awake, and she could thank them. If they were asleep, she could make sure they were tucked in.

Their door was closed. That was odd. It was always left ajar. She pushed it open and stared at the rumpled quilts. Lottie and Gracie weren't there.

Were they playing a prank on her? Had they heard Jake's car and slipped out of their beds into hiding places, ready to jump out at her?

Greg wouldn't find it funny. Best find them quickly and quietly. Sarah searched the room, then went back to look in her own closet and bathroom. Nothing. Were they downstairs? No, that would have meant hiding earlier, before she got back to the cabin, and they hadn't known when she'd return. Too scary in that big, dark space at their ages.

Even as she swept through the rooms searching, images flitted through Sarah's mind: Lottie running away, twice. The odd little smile later. Standing at her bedroom window, looking out into the night, where Sarah thought she'd seen a flashlight.

Sarah ran back up to Greg's room and pounded on the door. No answer. She edged it open, calling to him. When he didn't respond, she flipped on the light. He wasn't there and a search of the room confirmed that the girls weren't, either. She clattered back down the stairs. None of their coats hung on their hooks, so they were likely together. That didn't settle the unease fluttering in Sarah's stomach. The Tahoe was still there, parked in its usual place.

Why would Greg take the girls out at night? He'd never done that before, even during the day. The only time she'd ever seen them outside together was the day she arrived, when they were building the snowman.

It was well past the girls' bedtime. They'd already been under their covers, asleep, or at least ready for sleep. So why get them up to take them out of the cabin?

Sarah shoved her arms into her parka. She had to find them, be sure they were all right. She grabbed a flashlight and headed out the door, then came to an abrupt stop, staring into the darkness. She would never get used to the black nights in this section of the country, with a moon that rose in the early morning hours of the winter, rather than in the evening, when she needed the light.

Which direction should she go? When Lottie ran away that morning, it was toward the back. At least, that's where Sarah had found her, coming from behind the shed. On Sunday, Sheriff Maynor brought her in through the front door. But that might have been for the benefit of the reporters gathered there.

Lottie was with Greg this time, though. Where did he go when he roamed around the cabin at night?

Keeping her head down, Sarah started toward the shed, casting the light back and forth. The ground was so churned up, tracking would be impossible. The detectives and crime scene technicians had made multiple trips back and forth between their vehicles in the front yard and the woods in back. They had left broad swaths of broken snow around both sides of the cabin and into the back woods.

Once beyond the shed, she angled to the left until she found unbroken snow beside the trampled path. If she walked on that undisturbed snow, she could study the tracks beside her without smudging them and possibly find one of the girls' smaller boot prints imprinted on top of the others.

She trudged from the woods into the deeper, more forested area, keeping her focus on the footprints beside her.

A noise, a little to her left, brought Sarah to a halt. "Greg, is that you? Lottie?" Breaking brush crackled deeper in the woods. A deer. Unless it was the moose Greg had mentioned.

Icy air pushed around the edges of her parka hood. With fingers made clumsy from both the cold and the thickness of the mittens, she pulled it tighter around her face. Were the girls dressed for this? Maybe, if Greg had taken them out. More likely, Lottie had run away again, taking Gracie with her, and Greg was trying to find them, just as she was. And if that were the case, she couldn't be sure either of the girls were adequately dressed. Sarah started looking closer at dark shapes in and under the brush.

Something moved. She aimed the light at the fluttering crime scene tape left by the technicians. How far did it stretch? She couldn't cross it. She'd have to go around. But the girls might have ducked under the tape and gone inside. Sarah would have to look into it as far as she could as she walked alongside the tape.

But which side? She could already be on the wrong path. She'd found no footsteps.

She needed help. Fumbling through the opening of the parka, she searched her pants pocket for the phone. It wasn't there. She'd left it in her purse, on the rocking chair in her bedroom.

Sarah stood still. *Calm down and think.* Go back and make some calls? It was too far. It would take too long. Keep going? She'd seen nothing to indicate Lottie and Gracie had come this way.

If she moved left and followed the tape to the end, it would put her beyond the broken paths. If the girls had gone on from there, she would see their footprints. If not, she'd cross along the end of the tape, casting for prints, and if she didn't find any, she'd come back along the other side, to the cabin and her phone.

She tried to pick up her pace. The trees crept in closer, darker and more ominous. The vegetation had thickened, and she stumbled over a root, dropping the flashlight. She groped for the lighted end and pulled it from under the snow-laden shrub where it had rolled. Something moved in the trees to her left, and she swung the light in that direction.

"Greg! Lottie! Gracie! Where are you?"

Nothing but silence answered, then a few cracks of brush and a glimpse of an animal tail. Another deer?

The deep thickets forced her to slow, working her away around and between them, farther away from the tape. She kept the light focused on the ground and where she placed her own feet as she looked for footprints.

There! Coming out of the brush just ahead on her left were two sets of prints. The large one, undoubtedly a man's, sank into the snow deeper than the smaller one, which belonged to a child or a small woman. Lottie's? And if it was, where was Gracie's? Maybe the deeper prints of the man weren't just from more weight; maybe he was carrying Gracie. But if she was so tired Greg was carrying her, why was he headed away from the cabin, rather than toward it?

The footprints might be hours old. Some deep, primordial sense told Sarah otherwise. Somebody was close, within range of her voice. Why hadn't he—or they—answered?

Instinct kept her quiet. Whatever Greg was doing, it was strange behavior, and she needed to find out what was going on. Memories flitted back to her: Lottie's erratic behavior; the strange drawing she had made with the looming figure behind the woman and girls; begging Sarah "not to tell" when Sarah caught her with the phone, and again when Gracie wet the bed: Lottie running away.

Another memory came, full-blown, of Lottie bolting from the sofa where Sarah was trying to comfort her. Sarah had thought at the time it was her own inept handling that had sent the girl running up the stairs, but she was wrong. It had been Greg, suddenly standing in the doorway, watching and listening.

She must be past the taped-off area now. Hooding the flashlight as much as possible with her mittened hand, she crept forward, following the tracks. She had to avoid every twig that might break, every shrub that might make a sound as she brushed past it.

The trail was easy to follow now. Nobody else had been in the area recently. The search parties had moved on to the lake by the time the snow quit falling on Wednesday morning, leaving a clean landscape. A wolf, or perhaps one of the dogs, had been here, as well as some rabbits. *I don't even know what kinds of animals inhabit this forest.*

A deer had crossed, stepping onto the edge of one of the man's footprints. That told her his tracks probably had been there for a while—unless it was the deer she'd heard earlier. She bent over for a closer look. The small track was uneven, its owner perhaps getting tired, lagging a little.

A rabbit darted from the brush just ahead, startling her, and she took a step back before she realized it was harmless. *Get a backbone, Sarah. You can't jump at every bunny rabbit.* But her thumping heart didn't listen.

Her nerves screamed at her to go back, to get help. She had no weapon, no way to defend herself. But it would take too long. The girls could be gone by then. What could she tell the police or the sheriff, anyway? That a father was walking in the woods with his daughters? She couldn't be sure the girls had run away.

Holding the flashlight low, she cast it a few feet ahead until she picked up the tracks again. She'd caught a glimpse of something else—an opening in the trees, winding back toward the west: the two-track road the men had talked about, and toward the end, something solid. A vehicle of some kind? It was too dark for her to be certain. If she edged to her left and worked her way through the brush, she could probably get nearer without being seen.

Brush crashed behind her on the left. She whirled. A hand clamped across her nose and mouth, smothering her gasp. She couldn't breathe.

"Don't make a sound, and you won't get hurt." He pulled the flashlight from her hand and shoved it into his own pocket. She turned her head, trying to loosen his grip on her face. The parka hood blocked her vision. He pulled her back, against his chest.

Was this what Tracy had felt? A shudder rippled through Sarah's body. She struggled to suck in oxygen, to twist free of the fingers digging into her cheek. He was suffocating her. Bunching her shoulder muscles, she jerked, pulling away enough to draw in a deep, ragged breath.

He placed the hand across her mouth again but left her nose free this time, so she could breathe. Standing rigid, he held her against him. More brush crackled yards away, on their right. Greg and the girls. She had to draw their attention. Letting herself go limp, she tried to slide toward the ground, free the hand from her mouth, so she could yell. The man clasped his other arm around her waist, pulling her upright.

They stood still, her captor barely breathing, as the sounds moved farther away—not that she could have heard them over the pounding of her own heartbeat. Still her captor waited, the minutes ticking by until silence finally settled over the woods again.

He released his hold on Sarah's numb face. "Give me your phone."

She shook her head, the words heavy in her numb mouth. "I don't have it."

He searched her pockets. "Okay, so much the better." He pushed the parka hood down, shoved something cold and slick into her mouth, and tied the ends at the back of her head, so she couldn't speak.

Her rubbery legs didn't resist when he pushed her to a sitting position against a small tree. He looped something around it, and her waist and arms, knotting it behind the tree. Another loop of the slick material went around her wrists, tying her hands together.

He turned away into the darkness, leaving her there, on the snow. How long would it take for her to freeze to death?

"Dad!" Lottie called, from the direction of the road, and tears blurred Sarah's vision. Greg had gone the other direction. He must have gotten separated from the girls, and now he was too far away to help. He wouldn't hear his daughter's cry.

The man moved toward the sound. Sarah caught a glimpse of his dark shape as he moved through the trees. Beyond him was a flash of red, and a smaller figure. Lottie or Gracie.

"Get in the car," the man said, and Sarah jerked her head, pushing her tongue against the gag, trying to free it so she could yell at Lottie to run.

A car door slammed, followed by another. The engine started, and headlights swept the trees as the vehicle turned. Then it was gone, the sound of the motor fading along with the last faint glow of its lights.

The flashlight lay beside the tree. It must have fallen from her attacker's pocket. Not that it would help; she couldn't reach it. But it at least lifted the darkness around her. Until the batteries died. *Or will I go first?*

Pulling her wrists in opposite directions, she tested the tightness of the knot. The material stretched a little. She pulled again, harder. More stretch. Whatever the stuff was, it didn't spring back to retain its shape. Maybe the knots didn't matter. Pulling again, she widened the loop enough to slip one hand through, releasing the other. Could she stretch the strip around her face enough to get the gag out?

It was deep in her mouth, too tight to pull down. Her fingers were clumsy, so she removed the mittens. Working cold fingers under the edges, she finally got her hands under the gag, palms against cheekbones, and pulled outward. It gave a little. Again, harder.

The material reminded her of something. She closed her eyes, concentrating on its texture. It was like the plastic bags used for mailing soft goods. When scissors weren't handy, she had often torn those parcels with her fingernails.

Turning her palms outward, she dug her nails into the material and pulled. It ripped. She tore it away from her face.

Damp cold seeped into her hips and legs, and her hands were freezing. She dug her nails into the loop around her waist until it parted.

Shivering with cold, she fumbled the mittens back on, then used the tree for support as she pushed her numb body upward. *Hurry.* She had to hurry.

She grabbed the flashlight and aimed it toward the road, despite knowing there was nothing there. They were gone, and the only help would come through her phone, back at the cabin.

She started off, slogging through the snow, every nerve screaming at her to hurry. With every passing minute, the car—and the girls—were getting farther away. But she had to go slow enough to backtrack her footprints, to avoid losing her way. Casting the light back and forth, she forged ahead, her calves aching.

A piece of deadwood buried in the snow tripped her, sending her sprawling. The flashlight flew from her hand into some low brush, out of reach. Sharp twigs tore at exposed skin as she wriggled inside, pushing against the branches to get closer. Finally, her fingertips touched it. Shoving forward a few more inches, she grasped the end. Holding it tight, she lowered her head and pushed backward until she was clear.

Cursing her clumsiness, she lurched to her feet and staggered on. The woods were thinning; she was near the cabin. A few more minutes, and the edges of the shed took shape beyond the trees. *Just a few more yards, Sarah. You can do this.*

She cleared the woods and passed the shed, into the back yard. She had to stop. Her breathing was so ragged she couldn't go on. Bending, she placed her hands on her knees, gasping for air. *There's no time, Sarah. Hurry!*

She straightened and made one last sprint, bursting through the door on her way to the stairs and her phone.

A hand grabbed her arm, bringing her to an off-balance stop, and she almost fell. Raising a fist, she swung blindly.

Chapter 20
Later Thursday Night

Greg grabbed her wrist. "Where the hell are the girls? What have you done with them?"

Sarah lowered her arm, and with it, her entire body threatened to sag. "Man took them...in car...getting away...call 9-1-1."

He stared at her, his mouth open. She pulled her arm from his grasp. "Call...Now!"

Finally, comprehension dawned, and he punched at his phone.

"On the old two-track. Had a car." She stopped to gasp for breath. "Got them inside and drove away. Couldn't stop them."

Only when he had relayed that information to the dispatcher did Sarah's legs give way. She sank to the floor. Greg pulled her to her feet and led her to a chair.

"When I got back, your car wasn't here," he said. "The girls were gone, so I thought you took them somewhere, and I couldn't figure it out."

"The Highlander's still in town. Somebody punctured my tires, so Jake brought me home. Nobody was here. Why did you leave them alone?"

"I...they were asleep. I couldn't...I needed some air—thought they'd be all right if I locked the door." He sank onto the chair beside her. "Oh, God, not the girls, too."

Anger surged through her, a current so strong she almost slapped him. All the hours she'd been confined to this cabin to keep the girls safe, and he couldn't stay with them for a few hours while she went out for dinner.

He raised his head, looked into her face, and flinched. Without speaking, he rose and walked away.

Sarah sat at one end of the big table, repeating her story for the third time. Greg had heard it first, gasped out in short, jumbled bursts. She'd had more time to organize her thoughts before Maynor arrived, so he got a more coherent version. His questions had clarified details she incorporated into her narration for Mason and Ursall.

The detectives sat in the side chairs closest to her, Mason on her right, and Ursall on the left. Greg sat beside Ursall, facing the window, staring into the night. He didn't look at Sarah, hadn't met her gaze since their confrontation.

Ursall's brown eyes peered at her over the rimless glasses pushed down his nose. "From what you're telling us, it appears the kidnapper didn't intend to harm you. He didn't knock you out, didn't even tie you securely. If he had, you might have frozen to death before anybody found you." His gaze lowered, to the strip of yellow material she still held in her hands—hacked from the crime scene tape the detectives had placed in the woods. Sarah had pulled it from around her neck after she reached the cabin.

She shook her head. "I doubt he knew it would stretch and tear. If it hadn't, I don't think I could ever have untied the knots." She pulled at the scrap of material. It felt thin, like paper lightly coated with plastic.

"Or maybe he did know, and he just wanted to delay you long enough to get away. You said he checked you for a phone, and you didn't have one. So he knew you couldn't call for help until you got back here. You weren't harmed."

Mason's sky-blue gaze bored into hers. "Don't you find that a little strange, Ms. Wagner? A gentle kidnapper?"

"Gentle?" She glared at Mason. "I guess you had to be there. I thought I was going to freeze before I could get myself loose. My fingers were numb. And when he grabbed me, he held me so hard I thought he'd crack my ribs. The hand clamped over my mouth was so tight, I couldn't breathe—"

"That's when you heard the other person nearby?" Ursall asked. "The one you thought was Mr. Agerton?" He inclined his head toward Greg.

"Yes, that's right," Sarah said. "Lottie heard him, too. She called out to him."

Ursall turned to Greg, his mild eyes assessing. "You said you had to get out of the cabin. Your daughters were asleep, so you went out for a walk. Exactly where did you go, Mr. Agerton?"

Greg flushed. "I know. It was stupid. But they were sound asleep, and I locked the doors..." He focused on the window. "I went a little way into the woods, then angled back toward the old road—the one with the bridge out."

"That's northeast of the cabin. You weren't near the northwest two-track, where Ms. Wagner encountered the man?"

"No. I went what was probably due north for a bit, then angled off."

Mason studied him from across the table. "That would be approximately where the cordoned-off area is."

"Yes, I saw it. That's when I veered off."

"And you didn't see or hear anything out of the ordinary?"

"Not until I got back to the cabin and went up to check on the girls."

Ursall ran a finger down his jotted notes. "But you didn't call to report them missing until Ms. Wagner came back. Why is that?"

"I thought Sarah had them. Her car wasn't here."

Mason's eyes narrowed. "But she'd gone out to dinner with Jake Nichols. Why would you assume she'd returned?"

"I had to pass her room on my way down the hall. The door was open, and I saw her purse and blazer on a chair."

"How did you know they were the same ones she'd left the cabin with? Most women have several of both."

Greg shook his head. "She only brought one small suitcase for the entire week." He paused, then added, "And she was wearing the blazer when she left for dinner and was carrying that purse."

"You're more observant than most men, Mr. Agerton. You're telling us her blazer and purse—probably the only ones she had available, and the ones she took with her when she left the cabin—were on the chair, and you assumed she'd gone back out. Wouldn't she have taken them with her?"

"I..."

Mason kept his gaze riveted on Greg's face. "Where did you think she'd gone with your daughters? I understand she doesn't know many people in the area."

"I don't know. It sounds stupid now, but it seemed to make sense at the time. They were all gone, and so was the car."

"Did you try to call her?" Ursall asked. "To find out where she'd gone?"

"I was trying to call her when she came back." He paused, looking into the near distance, then continued, speaking slowly. "I...there was no answer. I finally realized it was ringing upstairs. That was right before she came back and..." His voice trailed off. He put a hand over his mouth, as though he might get sick.

The detectives shuffled through their notes. Sarah's hands clenched under the table. They should be out looking for the girls, not asking stupid questions. That could come later. No, she was being irrational. Before the detectives arrived, the sheriff had issued a BOLO, as well as an AMBER alert. She could do nothing now but wait—always hard.

"So, who was the other person in the woods?" Mason muttered, his voice so low he appeared to be thinking out loud. "Let's back up a little. Julie Osborne left Belly's before you did, Ms. Wagner. At least, she wasn't on the premises after you found your car with the slashed tires."

"Julie?" Greg said. "You think Julie slashed the tires?"

"That surprises you, Mr. Agerton?"

"Yes. No. Well, maybe." He ran a hand through his hair. "I don't know. Julie can be a little nuts sometimes. She's done some weird stuff, so I suppose she might, if she was mad enough. But she wouldn't have any reason to take the girls."

"Can you think of anybody who would?"

Greg shook his head. "I don't know. Sarah had seen a man sneaking around, watching the cabin. We thought he was a kidnapper, that he'd taken Tracy and was trying to make contact, but that hasn't happened. Maybe he took Lottie and Gracie, too."

Mason swivelled toward Sarah, then looked again at Greg. "And neither of you thought this man was important enough to mention to us or Sheriff Maynor."

Sarah felt warmth spreading upward from under her jaws. It had seemed so logical at the time, not telling Maynor or the detectives. Now, she squirmed a little in her chair. "I didn't know...I couldn't be sure. I only saw him once."

"What did he look like? Can you describe him?"

"Not really. I didn't see much of him. Dark hair, maybe six feet tall. He was getting into a car. It was just patches of gray, through the trees."

"Did you see the man or the vehicle again?"

"No, and I was watching for him. We thought at the time he was the kidnapper, trying to make contact, and were hoping to catch him when he came closer to the cabin."

"Don't you think that might better have been left to law enforcement?"

"Maynor would have swooped in here with another press conference," Greg said, "instead of setting up a stake-out. We had a plan—"

Mason studied both of them, making no attempt to hide his disgust. "You had a plan. How nice. How did that turn out for you? I doubt we're dealing with a kidnapper, since he never tried to make contact with you or anybody else. We don't even know if the same person took your daughters."

Frowning, he leaned in closer to Greg. "That said, it doesn't seem likely we'd be dealing with two different abductors. So, is it possible your wife went willingly, then came back for your daughters? Or paid somebody to come back for them?"

Anger flashed in Greg's eyes, and he half-rose from the chair. "What are you suggesting? Why would she do that?"

Mason gazed at him, his expression mild, and Greg lowered himself back into the chair. "That's ridiculous. There would be no reason. We were getting along fine. And she was expecting Sarah at the time she disappeared."

Sarah bit her lip. Despite Greg's protestations, something strange had been going on in that cabin.

Ursall's attention was now on her hands, clenched together in a tight, prayer-like grip on the table-top. He rose from his chair. "It might be helpful if we could see the girls' rooms."

Greg stood. "Of course. There's only one. They like to be together."

Sarah got to her feet, too. "While you're doing that, I'll try to find a hotel, before it gets too late." She couldn't stay in the cabin, with the girls gone.

Mason nodded. "If you want to pack your things, we can give you a ride into town."

They climbed the stairs, Mason in the lead. Sarah flicked on the light at the top and almost bumped into the detective when, without warning, he bent in front of her open door to pick up a folded scrap of paper. Smoothing it out, he asked, "Did one of the girls leave this?"

Sarah looked at the paper, then at the blazer she'd tossed on the chair when she got back from Belly's. The creepy man on the plane had pushed it into her pocket just as they landed. She hadn't worn the blazer again until tonight and had forgotten all about the note. "No, that's mine."

She reached for it. Mason glanced at it again before handing it to her.

"The girls' room. It's down there?" he nodded toward the end of the hall.

"Yes, on the left."

"All right. We'll leave you to your packing." He turned away, and Sarah pulled her suitcase from the closet. It didn't take long; she hadn't brought much. There was no way she'd be able to retrieve the bag of drugs she'd stashed in the cornstarch container.

When she pulled out her phone to look for hotels, it showed several missed calls. Probably Laura. No time to check the messages now. She'd do it from the hotel.

Sarah still stood there, working her phone, when Ursall came back down the hall. "Problem?"

Her frustration must be showing. "I can't find anything in Owl's Head or Mountain View."

He nodded. "We had the same problem. They're both part of Belmont. We found rooms there. In fact, if you like—" He pulled a card from his pocket. "Here's the place where we're staying."

Did she want to stay at the same hotel? Why not? It was unlikely she would get a room close to them. She dialed the number and made a reservation.

"How long?" the clerk asked.

"Um...I'm not sure. How about just one night for now, and I'll let you know if I need to extend it."

The clerk agreed, and she took one last look around the room before she called Jake. His phone rang several times before he picked up, his voice groggy. It was well after midnight. He had been asleep, meaning Greg hadn't called him about Lottie and Gracie.

"Sarah?" His voice sharpened. "What's wrong?"

"The girls—Lottie and Gracie—somebody has taken them. They were gone when I got back to the cabin."

"What?" He was fully awake now, and she told him the entire story, the fourth time she'd related it. With each telling, it became more complete, more polished, but also more removed from her, almost as though she was telling it about somebody else.

"Are you all right? No, of course you're not. I'll be right there, just as soon as I get dressed."

"No, I'm not going to be here. I can't stay in the cabin with Greg. There's no reason for me to be here, with the girls gone. I've reserved a hotel room, and the detectives are giving me a ride. But I think Greg could use a friend right now."

"Okay. I'm on my way. I'll call you as soon as the car's ready. And if you need anything, anything at all, you let me know."

A small lump formed in her throat, making it difficult to speak. Jake Nichols was a kind, sweet man. *And I'm exhausted, both physically and mentally, or it wouldn't be affecting me this way.*

"I have to go, Jake. I can hear the detectives going down the stairs."

She walked down the hall to Lottie's and Gracie's room and stood in the open doorway, trying to imprint the memory. Rudy, Gracie's stuffed dog, lay on the floor. The little girl would have trouble going to sleep without him. *I don't see Lucy, though. Maybe she has the doll.*

She picked up the dog. It had a zipper along the stomach. Was it a pajama bag? No, it was too small. Sarah unzipped it a little way and smiled. Stuffed inside were Barbie doll clothes, including a pair of boots; a pink ribbon; the recorder; and a butterfly hair clip.

"Ms. Wagner? Are you about ready?" Ursall's voice floated up the stairs.

Sarah dropped the dog on the bed. Glancing around the room one last time, she turned to retrieve her suitcase and carry it downstairs.

Greg looked up as she descended the last few steps. "Sarah...thank you. I'm sorry your visit turned out to be so...so traumatic, and I can never thank you enough. I wish...well, never mind. Just stay in touch. No matter what happens. You have my number. If I don't see you again after all this, call me. The girls—" His voice broke then. "Lottie and Gracie. They'll want to hear from you."

The lump was back in her throat. He took a step in her direction, but before he could put an arm around her, she grasped his. "Please keep me in the loop about what's going on. I have to know. And if—when you find them—give them my number so they can call me."

"I'll do that."

He wouldn't. He might keep her updated about the search for the girls, but he would never give them her number. Lottie wasn't allowed to use the phone.

Her own phone rang just a few minutes after she'd checked into her hotel room.

"Sarah?" It was Greg. They must have found the girls; there would be no other reason for him to call so soon.

Before he could say another word, barely able to contain her excitement, she asked, "They're safe? They're all right?"

"What?" His voice was all wrong, without a trace of joy. Dread crowded out her elation, and she tried to brace herself for his next words.

"What did you do with the drugs, Sarah?" The slight tremor in his voice hinted at a touch of panic.

"Drugs? I don't—" *The plastic bag I hid in the kitchen.* He was talking about the GHB and sleeping pills. "I don't know what you're talking about," she lied. "What drugs?"

Silence, then he spoke again, his voice hurried. "Never mind. It's not important. I'm not thinking straight. Sorry I bothered you."

He ended the call before she could respond. Sarah stared at the phone, replaying the conversation. There had been something undefinable in the tone of his voice. Worry or despair? She wasn't sure.

Why were the drugs so important?

Chapter 21
Friday Morning

Sarah grabbed her ringing phone and glanced at the time. Six thirty-three. She didn't go to bed until after two, and it had taken her a long time to fall asleep in the hotel room.

"Sarah? Why the hell didn't you call me back?" Laura's voice was fast and high-pitched. Sarah, still groggy from a lack of sleep, took a few seconds, not only to orient herself but to pinpoint the heavy darkness that had invaded every cell of her body. Images from the night before crashed into her, filling her with despair.

"Lottie and Gracie are gone, kidnapped, and I—"

"What?" Laura didn't wait for an answer. "It was real, then. Somebody grabbed you, held you. Tied you up. You couldn't get loose—"

"Oh, God! You had another one of your scary dreams."

Laura's voice dropped almost to a whisper. "I knew you were in trouble. I knew. I could see it, and I couldn't do anything. I kept calling, but you didn't answer. I thought...I remembered what you said about Tracy, and I pictured your phone lying in a snowbank. Then I saw you, struggling...Why didn't you return my calls? I've been up all night."

Her phone had been ringing in the cabin, then. Was that during the time Greg was in the woods?

"I'm sorry, Laura. I saw the missed calls, but there was so much going on, I thought I'd wait to call you. I should have known you'd dream...that you always know when somebody you love is in trouble. I was just so tired—"

"Are you all right?"

"I'm okay. Just a little sore and bruised, and heartsick over the girls."

"Tell me what happened."

Sarah told her about the preceding night's events. "Then, after I checked into the hotel, Greg called and asked what I'd done with the drugs. He sounded strange. Maybe a little panicky. I lied—told him I didn't know what he was talking about."

After a moment's silence, Laura asked, "Why would it be so important to him? You can't even prove he used them."

Sarah had asked herself the same question. She'd sat for a long time after Greg's call, staring at the phone at first, then pacing the room. Finally, unable to come up with a rational answer, she'd decided to leave it until morning, after she'd had a good night's sleep. But the few hours she'd slept hadn't helped.

"I don't know. None of this makes any sense, and I'm so worried about Lottie and Gracie, it's hard to think about anything else. How about I call you back later, when my brain is back in gear and I know more?"

"Okay, but answer my calls. And, Sarah, be careful."

How could she be careful when she didn't even know what was going on? The only thing she could be sure of at this point was that Lottie and Gracie were gone, taken by the man in the woods, Tracy was still missing, and there was something strange about Greg. It was impossible to unravel the puzzle when her uncooperative brain insisted on asking the same questions over and over again, in an endless loop. Where was Tracy? Was she still alive? Where were Lottie and Gracie? Who had them and why? Was it the same person who had taken their mother?

She needed a way to organize her thoughts. A computer. A printer wouldn't hurt, either. She picked up the phone. It was time to spend some of Caro's money.

The front desk promised to order what she wanted as soon as the stores opened. In the meantime, they would send up a supply of writing pads and pens.

After showering and dressing, she ordered breakfast, along with an extra carafe of coffee. While she waited for it, the writing supplies arrived, and she started making notes. It was a slow process; she was out of practice writing by hand.

After breakfast, room service came to collect the dishes and leave another carafe of coffee. Sarah barely looked up from her notes.

"Want me to get that?" The man gestured at an overflowing wastebasket, connected to the desk by a trail of wadded paper.

"Yes, please." She dug in her wallet for a tip and had just turned back to the notes when the phone rang. She didn't recognize the number but instantly knew the voice.

"Jake. Have you heard anything? Is there any news—"

"Nothing. There are BOLOS and AMBER alerts out, but so far, there's no trace of the girls. They seem to have vanished, just like Tracy."

They could be anywhere, and the police might be looking for the wrong vehicle. She couldn't be sure it was gray. The man who had taken the girls might not be the one she'd watched with her binoculars.

"If I'd been able to get free sooner, get close enough to see the vehicle better..."

"It was dark. You did everything you could. You're lucky he didn't kill you."

Cold prickles crept up her spine, almost as icy as the snow she'd sat on the night before, tied to the tree.

"I just called to see if you're okay and if there's anything I can do. The Highlander is ready. If you want, I can pick you up and take you to the tire shop."

"That's thoughtful of you. Could we do it a little later?"

"Sure. How about meeting for lunch in the dining room, sometime around one?"

"That sounds good. Thanks, Jake."

"It's what friends are for."

She could almost hear the smile in his voice. She should ask how Greg was doing. *But I don't want to go there.* Not with Jake, one of his best friends. But maybe he knew something about Cindy.

"Do you know Tracy's sister?" she asked.

"Sister? Oh, yeah, Tracy did mention a sister. I got the sense that they were close. Why do you ask?"

"I just wondered why she's not here. Do you know where she lives? I got the impression from the girls that it's close to them in the city, but I don't even know what part of New York they live in."

"I don't think Tracy ever said. But it is strange that the sister hasn't shown up. I'll ask Greg about it."

"No! You can't—" Sarah gripped the phone. There had to be a reason why Greg hadn't called Tracy's sister. "No," she said again, in a calmer voice, searching for an explanation for her outburst. "I...Greg is a little annoyed with me, and I don't want him thinking I'm poking my nose in where it doesn't belong."

"How can he be annoyed with you, after all you've done? And it's natural you'd be concerned enough about the girls to ask questions."

"Maybe so, but I'd just as soon not upset him any more. He's...Jake, he's my only connection to Lottie and Gracie. If I don't stay on good terms with him—"

"Okay. I won't mention you. But I might ask him, just to satisfy my curiosity. Seems a little strange that none of Tracy's family is here. I'll let you know what I find out."

"Okay. Thanks. I have to go. There's somebody at the door."

It was a man from the computer store. "It's all ready to go," he said, as he lifted the laptop from a box. "The software you wanted is installed, and the discs are here."

Sarah motioned toward the desk. "Put it over there."

After he left, she sat and stared at the computer screen, trying to bring some order to the thoughts whirling around in her mind, tangling together like a clothes dryer set on high spin.

Where to begin? Chain of events? Yes, she'd start a log of everything that had happened since her arrival. Then she'd go over it with Laura, who might remember enough from their phone calls to fill in the blanks.

But one day at the cabin had been much like another, so keeping the time line straight proved to be more difficult than she'd expected. The days had blended into one long, mostly unbroken, week. It might be more productive to list every event she could remember, then fit them into the proper sequence.

That didn't work well, either. Questions popped into her mind as she worked, leading to other questions, all of them a distraction. Finally, she opened another file: one for events, another for questions.

If there had been no convict in the area and no kidnapper, either somebody else had taken Tracy or she'd gone willingly. Sarah shook her head. Tracy wouldn't have left Lottie and Gracie behind. Not unless she'd planned to come back for them. Had she lured Sarah to the cabin knowing her friend would watch over the girls until then? Was she in the car with the man last night, an accomplice? Had he been watching the house, waiting for an opportunity to grab them?

Sarah stood, rubbing the small of her back. It was a complicated plan, complete with the dropped scarf and phone. Why not just take the girls and leave? Greg had been suspected of killing his first wife, but if Tracy were afraid of him, she wouldn't have left the girls at the cabin—unless she feared for her own life, but knew he wouldn't harm his daughters. But Lottie had a strained relationship with him. Something was going on there.

An image came back, of Lottie standing at the window, looking out at the back woods where Sarah thought she'd seen a flashlight. Had Lottie been watching for somebody? Known he was coming? It was well past time to find out who was on the other end of Lottie's phone calls.

When Sarah punched it in, all she got was a recorded message. The number had been changed or disconnected. *If I'd called it earlier*—Now, she'd have to locate a reverse telephone directory. But that, too, proved futile; she couldn't find the number listed.

Sarah went back to the call log. Lottie had made the first call Saturday afternoon when Sarah had left her phone on the counter. Later that same day, Sarah saw the man for the first time, watching the house with binoculars. Had Lottie given him the address and planned to slip away to meet him the next day? That might be why she'd been so desperate she sneaked into Sarah's room to use her phone Sunday night—to explain that she had been caught by Sheriff Maynor, and possibly to set up a new meeting.

But that was the last call, despite the unsuccessful approach on Monday night, and Lottie's failed runaway Wednesday morning. How had she arranged the final meeting on Thursday night?

Something didn't fit. Sarah walked to the window and stared out onto the snow-lined street below. It reminded her of the forts the girls had built, the day they had the snowball fight.

Lottie wouldn't run away without Gracie. So what was she really doing Sunday afternoon, and again on Wednesday morning when she left the cabin? Meeting somebody? Or going to a pre-arranged spot to leave or get messages? She didn't have a phone, and Tracy knew that.

Sarah stopped, mid-stride. Yes. That explained Lottie's satisfaction when she saw the tracks the next morning. The watcher hadn't tried to approach the house; he'd left either a message or a phone in a place she could get to fairly easily—arranged in that Sunday night phone call. Lottie had that same little self-satisfied smile on her face Wednesday morning, when Sarah finally found her, coming from behind the shed.

Sarah would bet she'd picked up a phone, because she hadn't used Sarah's again, after she promised she wouldn't. Wanting to trust the girl, Sarah had never put a password on it.

Later that same day, the girls had been in the room when Sarah agreed to meet Jake for dinner the next night. It would be their best chance to get away. So Lottie had made the call that set the plan in motion. Tracy and her accomplice would pick the girls up in the woods, and be gone before Sarah got back to the cabin.

Sarah plopped down on the bed, almost smiling with relief. Clever, brave little girl. All of them—Tracy, Lottie, Gracie—were safe, and Tracy would make contact with Sarah later, probably back in the city.

The smile faded. If Tracy had planned this with Lottie, she would have made sure the girl had a phone stashed away. And Lottie was smart and resourceful, but no ten-year-old could act that well. Not for a week. Lottie had believed her mother was missing. Could Tracy have left without telling the girls, then hired somebody to get them, knowing how much anguish the girls would suffer in the meantime? No. It was unthinkable, cruel. Especially for a mother.

Sarah stood and paced the room again. Lottie had plotted with somebody other than Tracy, and it had to be a person she trusted. Who? Tracy's sister, Cindy? Is that why the woman had never shown up? If so, the girls were safe. But if not—

Sarah called Dee Callender.

"Is there any way to trace a phone number? I've tried to call it and get a recording that it's been disconnected or changed. I've tried reverse directories, with no success."

"It's probably a burner or a burner app. So unless you have more information, I'd say no. Why do you need it?"

After Sarah explained, Dee said, "You should turn all this over to the detectives, pack your bags and get on a plane."

"I'd love to, but they've asked me not to leave."

Dee was silent for a few seconds. "Do you know why? Have they indicated they're suspicious of you in any way?"

"No, not really, but since my last experience, I'm paranoid about detectives, so I'm no judge."

"Probably just doing their jobs. You were there all the time this was going on, so they may be keeping you around in case they think of more questions to ask. Like you said, you don't have much reason to trust detectives—present contact excepted, of course. But if you have any reason to believe they're actually honing in on you, call me. Or Dave. I'm deep in a complicated murder case right now, but I can at least answer questions."

"Thanks. I'll keep that in mind." Sarah ended the call and plopped onto her back on the bed, staring at the ceiling. Everybody she loved and trusted, anybody she could go to for help, was three thousand miles away, across the country. She no longer even had Lottie and Gracie.

Stop sniveling, Sarah. You got what you wanted. You're out of the cabin. An unexpected memory of her mother surfaced, telling her, "Be careful what you wish for. Things can always be worse."

Her phone rang. She stared at the display for a moment before answering. "Hello, Greg. Is there any news?"

He was silent for so long her breath caught in her throat. His voice, when he spoke, was low, almost a growl. "What did you do with the drugs?"

Caught off guard, she tried to think of what to say.

"You know what I'm talking about," he said. "I've searched the girls' room—the entire cabin. They're not here. You're the only one who could have taken them. I finally figured it out. You found them when you got the thermometer, the day Gracie was sick. What else did you take?"

Surprised he'd even remembered that, she hesitated. Maybe Greg hadn't been as detached as she'd thought. Had he been alert, watching and listening the entire time she'd been at the cabin?

"I don't know what you're talking about. And I certainly can't see what it has to do with finding your missing daughters. Maybe you'd like to enlighten me?" She sucked in her breath, waiting for his response.

"You don't know what you're doing. This isn't a game, Sarah. You're going to regret it if you don't bring the stuff back."

Chapter 22
Friday Mid-day

Sarah sat still after he disconnected, waiting for her breathing to steady. A sudden memory of Greg came back to her, hurrying toward the door, patting the bulge in his coat pocket, telling her, "I have a gun, and I'll use it if I have to."

Why were the drugs so important to him? Sarah couldn't prove he'd used them; he must know that. The real question was why he had drugged her and the girls. He'd done nothing to Sarah, other than drug her. Had Lottie been his target? Is that what Greg feared coming to light? It would explain Lottie's behavior, and her need to get away from him.

Sarah had to find Tracy's sister. If the girls weren't with Cindy, she'd at least be able to answer some of Sarah's questions. *Too bad I didn't snoop more in the cabin when I had the chance.* The number was probably there.

Back at the computer, Sarah accessed one of the "find people" sites. She entered *Cindy Bates* and, as she expected, got a long list. It was a common name, especially with *Cynthia Bates* included. But each listing showed approximate age and vicinity, along with relatives. Sarah chose two, one showing "Tracy," the other showing "Theresa" as a relative.

Once she had the numbers, she composed a message: "I'm Sarah Wagner, a friend of Tracy Agerton, trying to contact her family about something that has happened at the cabin. It's important, so if I have the right person, please call me right away."

Satisfied it was the best she could do to stress the urgency, while not imparting bad news over the phone or divulging too much information to a potential stranger, she called both numbers and left the message.

It was time to meet Jake for lunch.

She spotted him as soon as she got off the elevator, sitting on a sofa in the lobby, leafing through a magazine. A smile creased his face when he saw her: a nice smile, in a nice face. In that moment, her world didn't feel quite so lonely.

Once seated at a window table, she almost ordered a glass of merlot with her soup and sandwich combo, ready to relax and enjoy his company. Better not. She would have to be on guard, filter every word she uttered. Greg and Jake had a lifelong friendship. He would look at her in disbelief if she told him about the drugs and Greg's threat. She couldn't even discuss her theory about the girls' disappearance without explaining why Lottie would want to get away from Greg.

She chose her words with so much care, the spontaneity and fun of Friday night disappeared, replaced by a strained, stilted exchange.

"Are you all right?" he finally asked. "Last night...that had to be scary. I can't imagine how that felt, having him grab you, being tied up..." His words trailed off when she folded her arms around her waist.

"I'm sorry," he said. "That was stupid of me, to bring it up. And I know you're worried about the girls. If there's anything I can do—"

She let her arms drop into her lap. "Do you know if the detectives questioned Julie about damaging the Highlander?"

"From what I'm hearing, they took her in. She may still be there, for all I know. Not just for the damage to the car, but the threats."

"Did she actually make any? Or was that just Roberta's gossip?"

"That glass of water in my face wasn't gossip." Smiling, he stroked the beard Julie had soaked with water. "Neither were your tires."

"We don't even know if she did that. We just assumed, after everything Roberta said—and after your water bath—that it was Julie."

"Good point. I can't see her harming anybody. A little kooky, and she goes off the deep end sometimes, but that's about it."

"What about the ex-brother-in-law? Amy's brother? Seems to me he's a more likely candidate."

"Brad Denton? Not sure. He may not have stuck around. I haven't seen him since Sunday at the cabin. But we don't run in the same circles. You're right, though. The detectives are probably interested in talking to him."

A waiter came to refill their water glasses. Sarah waited for him to move on.

"I think you're right. Julie is a little strange, but I can't see any reason for her to harm the girls. That wouldn't endear her to Greg. I should think Brad's the prime suspect, as soon as they find out how much he hated both Greg and Tracy. What better way to get even than to kill Tracy and have Greg convicted of it? But does he hate them enough to have the girls kidnapped?"

Jake studied her face. "You've put a lot of thought into this. I suppose we're all assuming at this point that Tracy is dead. Who do you suspect?"

"That's what's so frustrating. I don't know."

She couldn't think of anything more to say—at least, nothing safe, but Jake veered onto a subject she'd just as soon avoid.

"I've been thinking about Tracy's sister ever since we talked. Tracy said they were close. I'd think Cindy would be on the next plane as soon as she heard."

"Maybe she doesn't know—" Sarah bit her lip.

Jake's hand stopped, the fork several inches from his lip. "Doesn't know? It's all over the news. Everybody in the country knows. Besides, Greg would have called her...." His gaze locked onto hers, his mouth still open. As though realizing that, he closed it and put the fork down. "You think he steered her away?"

"I don't know. It's just...Tracy's been missing for a week and her sister—one she's supposed to be close to—hasn't shown up. That strikes me as really odd."

"Maybe Greg told her to wait, that there's nothing she can do here."

And leave me, a stranger, taking care of the girls? She didn't say it—didn't have to. His eyes widened as realization struck, then he looked away, not meeting her gaze.

"There's got to be a good reason. Maybe she's out of the country, and he hasn't been able to contact her. Or it's impossible for her to come right now. Or—"

Sarah looked down at her plate, avoiding his eyes, but the silence went on too long. When she raised her head, his gaze held hers again, his eyes narrowed.

"What is it? There's something you're not saying, and it seems to be about Greg...like you think he's hiding something. What, for God's sake?"

She had stumbled into exactly the conversation she'd wanted to avoid. How to get it back to safe ground?

"I didn't say that. I was going to suggest it might be personality clashes or some past disagreement that's caused friction between them. Enough that he couldn't cope with her at the same time he was trying to find Tracy."

It sounded weak, even to her own ears. If it were Laura missing, nothing could keep her away. She grasped for something more, but he spoke first.

"No, that's not what you meant. So why don't you just spit it out? What's your problem with Greg? I'll admit he's moody, not himself, but I'd think you could cut him some slack, considering his wife is missing and now the girls—"

Cut him some slack? Easy for Jake to say. He hadn't been the one cooped up in that cabin, trying to take care of two children—one of them troubled—cooking, cleaning, and dealing with those dark moods.

"You think I don't know that? In case you've forgotten, I was there. In that cabin with them. And since you brought it up, don't you think he's acting a little strange sometimes, even considering the circumstances? Roaming around outside the cabin at night, doing God only knows what. He's secretive, hiding something." *That came out wrong. I should have worded it better.*

Jake didn't look at her now. "Are you somehow implying that he's involved in Tracy's disappearance? How? He was outside with the girls when Tracy took her walk. He didn't leave again until after you got there. If I remember right, he called the sheriff before he even went out to look for her. And he wasn't gone long enough—"

"I know all that. Like I said, I was there."

The woman at the next table turned to look at them, and Sarah lowered her voice. "There are things you don't know. Greg—"

But it was too late.

"Greg what? His wife and daughters are missing. He doesn't know who has them, whether they're dead or alive. I was out there this morning. He's a basket case, so jumpy he can't sit still for more than five minutes. And you're suggesting he's hiding something? That's odd, Sarah, because he claims you took things—"

"Yeah? Well, he's lying. I didn't take anything. Maybe his nerves aren't just about his missing family. He's worried about some drugs he thinks I took. He threatened—"

Jake signaled the waiter for their check. "If you're through, I think I'd better take you to pick up your car."

Dump me, he means. She'd blown it and lost the only friend within three thousand miles. She put her napkin on the table.

Jake's attention had shifted to something behind her. She turned to look just as Detective Ursall spoke.

"Mind if I join you? The dining room is a little crowded, and I can't seem to find a table."

"Of course." Jake gestured to a chair, and the detective sank into it. His suit had a slept-in look, his tie was loose around his neck, and his eyes were a little bloodshot.

"You look tired, Detective," she said, as the drink server arrived, coffee carafe in hand.

"Long night." Ursall put his hand on the server's arm. "Leave the coffee."

"Is there any news about the girls?" Jake asked.

Ursall shook his head. "Nobody matching their captor's description has bought a plane ticket or chartered a flight. At least not in person, and we're running down all on-line purchases made in the last week for three tickets. We've checked the trains and buses, so we're assuming they're still in the car."

"But the BOLO and the AMBER Alert," Jake said. "Wouldn't somebody—"

"It was late, Mr. Nichols. Dark. The car would be easy to miss, especially if he's familiar with the back roads in the area. And we don't know what we're looking for, other than the descriptions of the girls. We don't have the make of the car or a license number."

"I can't even be sure it's the one I saw at the end of the road," Sarah said. "If I'd been able to get loose a little sooner, I could have got a better look at it."

"He might not even be in the same car," Jake said. "He might have rented something else, or stolen one."

"The owner would report a stolen car. You'd know about that, wouldn't you?" Sarah asked Ursall.

He shrugged. "Probably, unless it was stolen from some place like long term parking at the airport. Then it might take weeks, if somebody is on an extended vacation." He sighed and topped off his cup of coffee.

"There are a lot of uninhabited cabins around," Jake said, "If he knows the area, he could be holed up somewhere, the car under cover until he thinks it's safe to drive again."

Ursall nodded. "Rented weeks ago, to have it ready. Without a name or description, we have no way of checking."

He shifted, leaning a little toward Sarah. "Chances are, he's the man you saw watching the house. What can you remember about him?"

"I don't...it was dark, but the build might have been about the same as the one who grabbed me. I never got a good look at either of them. From what I could see in the binoculars, the guy watching the house was at least six feet tall, with dark hair. So, yes, I suppose it could be the same man."

"Last night was traumatic. You were frightened and worried, and high on adrenaline. Now that you've had a chance to settle down a little, is there anything else you can tell me about the encounter in the woods? Anything at all? Even faint impressions?"

Sarah took a quick gulp of water. "No, and I've gone over it so many times, it's like a movie playing in my head. Every step, every rustle in the brush."

Ursall persisted. "You've told us what you saw and heard, even what you felt. What about your other senses? Taste or smell?"

Sarah grabbed the water glass again, the taste of the slick yellow tape back in her mouth. There was something else, too, so fleeting, when the woman at the next table laughed, it drifted away.

"I have a suggestion if you're willing," Ursall said, his voice gentle. "I've seen some amazing recall under hypnosis. If—"

"Yes. Of course. Anything I can do. How soon can you arrange it?"

Ursall took his cell phone from an inside jacket pocket and scrolled through numbers. "Here it is." He scribbled on the back of a business card and handed it to her. "See how soon you can set up an appointment. We've used this woman before, with good results. I'll contact her, too, and see if I can speed up the process."

"Thanks. I'll call her right away." Sarah slipped the card into her purse just as Ursall's phone rang.

He glanced at the display before answering. "Yeah? What've you got?...okay." He rose, turning his face away from them. "Sorry. I have to go. Don't forget to make that appointment." He strolled toward the lobby, the phone to his ear.

Jake rose. "Ready?" And without waiting for her response, he threw some bills on the table and strode toward the door.

He didn't speak to her on the way to pick up her car. The friendship was over, ended before it even got started. Greg stood between them. If it were true that you could judge a man by the company he kept, she shouldn't trust Jake any more than she trusted Greg.

She kept her focus on the landscape outside her window, seeing nothing until Jake turned into the lot for the tire shop. She'd have to pull herself together, concentrate better on the way back.

The instant Jake stopped the car, Sarah grabbed her purse and slid out.

"Thanks." She closed the door and headed for the office to pay her bill and get the keys for the Highlander. No door opened or closed behind her, and she didn't look back. From the counter inside, she faced the big window fronting the lot. Jake hunched over the steering wheel of his gray Chevy Silverado.

He didn't start his motor until she drove to the lot's exit into the street. When she stopped to check traffic, he drove away in the opposite direction.

You got yourself into this by letting him get too close. She should never have gone out with him—not when she knew Lottie was troubled and there was something off about her relationship with her father. She should have done lots of things: made sure Lottie didn't get close to her phone, kept a closer eye on them, instead of whining to herself about being bored.

Her Grandmother Nan used to say "Should haves never fixed anything, missy. Stick to 'will nots' if you want to stay out of trouble." Sarah might have smiled at the memory, if not for the desolation that left her so hollow.

Chapter 23
Friday, Early Afternoon

The drive back to the hotel was short, which was fortunate because she paid little attention to her surroundings. The only business she noticed was the store where she stopped to buy two bottles of merlot and some plastic cups.

Once she got back to her room, the only question was whether she poured a drink before she called Laura or after. Before, definitely, giving her the internal warmth of the wine and the external warmth of a familiar voice.

"I've been waiting for you to call me back." Laura's tone was not nearly as warm as Sarah had envisioned.

Sarah gulped, rather than sipped, a swallow of wine. "I'm sorry. I haven't had a chance. I was at lunch with Jake, then Detective Ursall joined us. After that, Jake took me to get the car, and I just got back."

"What about Lottie and Gracie? What's happening?"

"I don't know. I haven't heard anything. I'm waiting, just like you are." Pain jabbed Sarah's left temple. She pulled the phone away from her ear and took another large sip of wine. *I know you care, but they're just children to you, not the little girls I've grown to love.* Sarah shook her head. *What is wrong with me?*

"Sarah, I'm so sorry. I know how hard this waiting must be for you. I wish I could do something to help."

"Maybe you can. I'm trying to work up a time line for the days I spent in the cabin, but I'm having a tough time with it. One day kind of blends in with another. Do you think—would you mind jotting down what you remember from our phone calls? Maybe I can piece it all together."

"Of course. But why?"

"I'm not sure. There are so many loose ends, things I can't remember well enough, and I have a feeling some of them may be important. And that reminds me. I've got to call a hypnotist and set up an appointment—see if she can help me remember more about the kidnapper. I'll call you if there's anything new."

The hypnotist was gone for the day. No, gone for the weekend; it was Friday. She called Ursall to let him know.

"Not much we can do about that," he said. "I'll leave a message with her answering service to try to fit you in as early as she can next week. There are a couple of others we work with, but they'll be gone, too."

Next week? What was she going to do all weekend? *Stop whining. You've done enough of that. Get to work figuring this out. And put the wine away.*

"Yes, ma'am." She stood up, resisting the urge to salute her image in the mirror. Definitely put the wine away.

After she ordered fresh coffee from room service, she booted up the computer and tried more search sites for Cindy, in the suburbs surrounding New York City. She found only three, and none of them listed "Tracy" or "Theresa" as a relative. They were in the same age range, though, so she paid for the information, called the numbers, and left messages.

A search for Julie Osborne turned up little. Born in Malone, she'd lived in the area her entire life, even attending the local community college in Malone for her Associates degree, while Greg went away to university. That couldn't have been by choice. Probably a money issue. *I wonder why she stayed after Greg came back married? Especially twice.*

Time to explore the Denton family and Denton Pharmaceuticals.

Other than articles on the business and social events the family attended, Sarah found little, other than the news coverage of

Amy's death. Apparently, the detectives working the case had suspected foul play, and for a while, Greg seemed to be their prime suspect. But nothing happened for weeks. News coverage dwindled, then stopped entirely. Amy's death was eventually ruled an accidental drowning.

Laura texted a message: *Talked to Dee. Hypnotist not a good idea. Something you say while you're under could implicate you. Talk to an attorney first.*

Sarah rubbed the back of her neck, trying to relax knotted muscles. She had to get away from the computer. Maybe a massage would help. She called the front desk.

◆◆◆

"Try to relax," the masseuse said, her fingers digging into Sarah's back muscles. "Maybe a glass of wine would help?"

"No. No wine." She'd had enough for now. There was little point in leaving an alcoholic husband if she became one herself.

As her muscles relaxed, she drifted toward drowsiness. *Think about the woods, the man, the feel and smell of him.* Instead, the slickness of the yellow tape came back, so strong she could taste it. Why did she keep remembering the tape, and not the man?

It fluttered in the breeze, not at night, but during the day. She was there, in the woods, after she found the bracelet. Lottie had said her mom always wore it, so Tracy had been wearing it on this vacation. But that wasn't what was bothering Sarah. There was something else tucked away in her subconscious, so deep she couldn't dig it out. The shed? Yes, she'd overlooked something there. Something important. But her thoughts drifted back to the woods, hovering over them like a police helicopter searching for a lost hiker.

What am I missing? And why can't I dredge it out of my memory?

She had been on high alert every time she entered those woods, aware of every sound, every movement. Could there be others underlying them that she'd picked up but not recognized?

There was only one way to find out. She'd have to go back. But how could she, with Greg there? She had no way of knowing when he'd be at the cabin.

Yes, I do. The blue Chevy Tahoe. It would be easy to spot. She could drive by on the main road, find the two-track where the kidnapper had parked, and work her way back to whatever she needed to see. Not the shed, of course. That would be dangerous.

Too excited to lie still any longer, she paid the masseuse and went back to her room. She'd have to wear warm clothing—her parka and boots. And it was too late to go today. Greg would be coming back to the cabin for the evening, and she didn't want to be in the woods then. Best wait until tomorrow morning. If she got there early enough to see him leave, she'd know she had at least an hour or so. Plenty of time to check out the woods.

He might see her on the road. No problem. She could turn the Highlander in and get something else. It was just a short drive back to Saranac Lake. While she was at it, she could shop for a different parka. The dark blue would stand out too much in the snow-covered trees and be too recognizable.

She grabbed a pen and paper from the desk and scribbled a list, adding binoculars. Shop first, before the stores closed, then head to Saranac Lake, exchange cars, and get back in time for dinner and a good night's sleep.

She smiled and grabbed her purse.

❖❖❖

Shopping took longer than the drive, largely because of the diversity of her list and her unfamiliarity with the town. Under different circumstances, she might have enjoyed the adventure of exploring a new place, but not today. She had too much to do and not enough time, but the weather was much more agreeable for the drive than it had been the week before. Had it only been a week? It seemed more like a month.

With the key scratches, she'd known the car exchange wouldn't go quickly, but it was even slower than she expected. She'd forgotten about the lug wrench, still on the closet shelf in the cabin.

"The mechanic probably didn't replace it when he put on the new tires," she said, not wanting to explain why she'd removed it from the tool box.

"New tires? The tires were good. They didn't need replacing."

"They did after somebody slashed them. Don't worry. I paid for them, and I'll pay for the missing wrench. The scratches, too, if my insurance doesn't cover it.""

The clerk raised his eyebrows, but called somebody over to examine the Highlander, then went to talk to his boss. He came back with a receipt and the keys to a white Ford Explorer.

"No, not that. Find me something else."

"It's all we've got. It's that or the Highlander."

She took the keys and shoved them into her pocket. This wasn't going to turn out well.

When she dug them out to start the car, another key came with them: the key to the cabin. She'd forgotten to give it back to Greg.

Despite her misgivings about the Explorer, an old familiarity with the model, born of the hours she'd driven one around Sacramento, made the trip back to the hotel effortless. Still, an inner voice whispered that it was an ill omen, considering what she planned to do. With the key to the cabin still in her possession, she could even go inside long enough to grab the drugs. No, not a good idea. Forget the drugs.

She parked behind the hotel, left part of her purchases locked in the back of the vehicle, and hauled the rest up to her room.

Now for an early dinner, a good night's sleep, and she'd be ready for her fact-finding mission.

She didn't like eating in restaurants alone, and briefly considered room service. But after the week in the cabin, the walls of the hotel room closed in on her. She'd go back to the dining room and find a table by the window, so she could look out.

The dinner hour hadn't arrived, so the room wasn't crowded. A few people who had probably knocked off work early for the weekend filtered into the bar for a quick drink before heading home. A foursome at a nearby table held an animated conversation, and a young couple held hands and whispered to each other. Maybe room service would have been a better option.

Her phone buzzed, and she glanced at the display. A 9-1-6 area code. Maybe Dee.

It was her father. "Sarah, don't hang up on me—"

"What do you want?" she said, her voice almost a snarl.

"I...Sarah, I just called to tell you I'm sorry. I know you can't forgive me. But, your grandmother...Nan is so hurt over this. She can't understand the rift. So I...I told her. The whole sorry story. Now, maybe things will be all right between the two of you. And I won't call you again."

He ended the call before Sarah could think of anything to say. She stared at the phone, a slow ache starting at the back of her head.

With a trembling hand, she reached for a glass of water, and glancing around the room, glimpsed a familiar figure. Jake? No, it was Bill Ayers, angling his tall, wiry body toward an empty table on the other side of the room. He settled into a chair and picked up the menu. How long before his all-encompassing gaze found her? He never missed anything. At the moment, he'd raised his head, his attention on two men who stood in the doorway, looking in her direction. Mason and Ursall, and they had spotted her. Did they have news about the girls?

She half-rose from her chair as they approached, then sat back as she noted their expressions. They didn't come bearing good news.

Ursall placed both hands on the other side of the table. His tone was almost apologetic as he leaned in toward her.

"You can forget about that appointment with the hypnotist, at least for now. We need to talk to you."

"All right. If you haven't had dinner, maybe you'd like to join me?"

"Not here."

"I don't understand. Why not?"

Ursall didn't answer.

"This isn't a social call," Mason said, reaching for her arm. In one sickening lurch of her stomach, she knew she was in trouble. Visions of handcuffs flashing through her brain as she scrambled to her feet and took a step back, brushing his arm away.

"All right. But I don't need help." She couldn't let him drag her through the restaurant and the lobby, with people staring —especially Bill Ayers. "I'm capable of walking without assistance, Detective. Let's go and get this cleared up."

Does my voice sound as shaky as I feel? Why am I in trouble? Greg. It had to be Greg. What had he told them?

Chapter 24
Friday - Late Afternoon

The room was not that different from the one where Sarah had been "interviewed" in Sacramento, after Caro's death. It held the same well-worn industrial table, the same three chairs, and the same mirror that probably hid an observation window. Only the brown plastic tray with coffee carafe and Styrofoam cups was missing. There would be no pretense of a friendly meeting this time.

Both detectives had remained silent, treating her with a cool reserve during the drive, and spoken few words as they led her to the room, where she'd waited for over half an hour.

What could she possibly have done to warrant this? Nothing. But that didn't matter. They wanted to solve the case, and Greg wanted to incriminate her. He was following through on his threat, and anything he told the detectives would be his word against hers. He had the advantage. All the people who had visited the cabin were his friends, not hers. Only Gracie and Lottie could refute his claims, and they weren't here. Even if they were, Sarah doubted they'd be much help. They'd paid little attention to anything other than their movies and video games.

What could he possibly have told Mason and Ursall that would harm her? Tracy had disappeared before she got there, so it had to be something to do with Lottie's and Gracie's disappearance.

The detectives hadn't taken her phone, but the room was not a good place for a private conversation. Sarah tapped out a brief text message to Laura instead: *Don't call. Been taken in for questioning. Might be a good time to find that lawyer. Call Dee and let her know.*

The door opened while she was pushing the phone back into her pocket, and the detectives entered. Ursall set up the recorder with the same lie Sarah had heard before: it was for her protection, as well as theirs. Yeah, right.

"How did you meet Tracy Agerton?" Mason asked as he took one of the chairs across the table from her.

"I told you earlier. At the design school. She was taking a class—"

"No, what I mean is, what was the initial contact? Didn't you approach her first?"

"I don't know. How can I possibly remember something like that? We were in the same class, and everybody said 'hi,' or 'good morning,' or 'see you tomorrow.' That sort of thing. Real conversation? Probably when we were assigned to the same project. There were four of us, and we got to know each other pretty well."

"Did you ask for that assignment?"

"It didn't work that way. The instructor would just start pointing. 'You, you, you and you are design team one.' Then he'd point at the next four people for design team two."

"So you sat next to her."

"Not that I remember, until after we collaborated on the project. Then the four of us usually sat together. But that didn't mean we'd all be chosen for the next project. The idea was to force you to work with different people, so there was no way of knowing how the groups would be selected."

"So the people on your team all became good friends?"

"Friends? No. We got to know each other pretty well. It was a big project, a corporate logo design, and everybody had their strengths and weaknesses. But we learned from each other, too, and I respected all of them. I'd already been in classes with some of them, but never on the same project before."

Mason drummed his fingers on the tabletop, his nails clicking against the metal. "Okay, let's back up. Why did you come all the way across the country to that particular school?"

To get away from too many memories. To start over after her divorce. Possibly to distance herself from a too-strong attraction to Dave Wheeler. To wean herself off her dependence on others. But she couldn't tell them any of that.

"It was the best design school in the country."

"When did you first hear of Tracy Agerton? Hear her name spoken?"

"Probably at roll call the first day of class."

Mason leaned in closer. "And you expect us to believe that, on the basis of one class, a woman you'd just met invited you to spend a week with her and her family at their vacation cabin?"

"Yes, because that's exactly what happened. I hadn't just met her. We'd worked together for weeks, and we clicked, the way people sometimes do. I don't know why. Maybe because we had things in common. We're both blonde and petite, we like good books and old movies, we were both interested in design, and she was warm, intelligent and fun to be with. Who knows why people connect?"

"But a week—"

"It was open-ended. That's why I rented a car—so I could leave early if things didn't work out."

"You called her from the airport for directions to the cabin."

"No, I didn't. She told me how to get there earlier, before she left."

That was a mistake, and Mason pounced on it. "If she gave you directions, she certainly would have warned you about the wrong road and the washed-out bridge. Yet, you took that road and ran your car off into the ditch."

"I didn't remember...I'd forgotten—" How could she explain her distraction, that she was paying scant attention to Tracy's directions, puzzling over the behavior of the man she'd met on the plane?

Ursall leaned in now. *Smelling blood?*

"I was distracted," she said, "not used to driving in the snow, in an unfamiliar car. I wasn't paying enough attention. Then, when I heard about the convict—"

"Exactly," Mason said. "You're in an unfamiliar area, in a rental car, setting out in bad weather to find a remote cabin, and there's a convict loose. You would have been paying very close attention to where you were going, Ms. Wagner, to ensure you got there safely." He settled back in his chair. "And you were. You knew exactly where you were going, didn't you? Probably from a hand-drawn map, with every landmark noted so you couldn't go wrong. And your destination was that abandoned road."

"What? Are you—" She bit down on her tongue. She'd almost said 'crazy,' and that wouldn't help. But this was insane. "What are you talking about?"

"You had an accomplice, the man who helped you abduct Tracy Agerton, and later, her daughters. He drew a map and gave you instructions."

Sarah stared at them, disjointed thoughts swirling through her mind. He really was crazy. "That's the most ridiculous thing I've ever heard. Why would I do that?"

Neither of them responded. *They don't have an answer.* This was all conjecture, built on some hypothesis fueled by Greg. That's why they hadn't arrested her. They couldn't figure out her motive. Given time, they would invent one, and the arrest would come then.

"If Greg Agerton has been feeding you this line of crap, you're on the wrong track. He's doing this to intimidate me. He called this morning and threatened me."

"Threatened you? How?" Ursall asked.

"He warned me that if I didn't return some drugs to him, I'd be sorry."

"What drugs?" He exchanged a glance with Mason.

Now they'll add drug trafficking to their bogus charges.

"GHB and sleeping pills. He used them to drug me—and the girls—Tuesday night."

"You're claiming he raped you?" Mason asked.

"No, I said he drugged me. I don't know why. I just know he did, and I found the drugs in his room. He's so desperate to get them back, he's threatening me, and I don't know why they're so important to him."

Ursall and Mason exchanged another glance. "Can you think of any other reason why he'd drug you, Ms. Wagner?" Ursall asked, his voice soft.

"No. I've been trying to figure it out, but it doesn't make any sense."

"And you have the drugs?"

"No. After I found them, I didn't want him to be able to use them again, and I couldn't get away from the cabin so I hid them."

"In the cabin?" Mason's tone bordered on the incredulous.

"Yes, where he would never look. In a cornstarch container in the kitchen."

Ursall's lip twitched, but before he could speak, Mason cleared his throat.

"Okay, let's go back to Tracy Agerton and your accomplice."

"I don't know what you're talking about. I have no accomplice. Tracy is a friend. I would have no reason to harm her—or to kidnap her—and I don't know who did."

"But you know who took her daughters, don't you?"

"No. When I thought about it later—after I saw him in the woods—I wondered if somebody was with him, if Tracy had run away, then came back for them. But she wouldn't do that to her girls—leave them thinking she was dead. So I thought maybe it was her sister Cindy. It's somebody Lottie knows. She was in contact..."

"No, you were the one in contact. And it wasn't with the girls' aunt. You called the man at least twice after you got here, to set up the kidnapping. The number's the same as the one on that piece of paper I found outside your bedroom door—the one you admitted was yours."

"What?" It took Sarah a few seconds to make the connection. "It's the same number the creep gave me?" She shook her head. "No. That can't be. It would mean—"

As she struggled to her feet, the room tilted. Grabbing the arm of the chair, she steadied herself against the wave of nausea that threatened to erupt.

Ursall's voice sounded distant. "Are you all right?" He guided her back into the chair. "You look pale. Are you going to be sick?"

She stared up at him, willing her numb lips to move. "I...I think I might. I know who has Lottie and Gracie. The creepy guy on the plane. The pedophile. He was ogling a little girl."

Sarah's words tumbled out, unedited, as they came to her. "Lottie...Greg and Tracy wouldn't let her use a phone. He asked me to keep mine away from her. He said they'd caught her visiting some questionable sites—that she was too young to understand the danger. She must have made contact with the man on one of those sites, and she's been calling him ever since."

Ursall handed her a tissue. She stared at it, then the back of her wet hand. *Pull it together. This is no time for tears.*

"I caught her using my phone Saturday. And she sneaked into my room to use it Sunday night, after she tried to run away and got caught. I didn't know...I tried to get her to talk to me...and all that time, she was trying to get to him. That's why he was on that plane. To meet up with his next victim."

Lottie.

Chapter 25
Friday Evening

U rsall, his voice urgent now, asked "Who is he? What's his name?"

"I...Oh, God, I don't know. I tried to push it out of my mind—didn't want to have anything to do with him. But"—she lifted her head—"He asked me out for dinner, mentioned Belly's, so he must be local."

Mason flipped through his notes. "I think I've got it here, somewhere."

He probably did. After he picked up the paper from the floor outside her bedroom that night, he'd studied it for a moment before handing it to Sarah. He'd probably jotted it down as the two detectives walked away from her, down the hall toward the girls' room.

That was at least eighteen hours and pages of notes ago, so it took a while to find it.

"Here it is. Just Pete, and the number." He looked at Sarah. "That's all I have. Does the name jar your memory?"

"No, I'm sorry. I—"

"A description then. What did he look like?"

Sarah closed her eyes, trying to transport herself back to the plane and the man who had sat beside her. "Tall, with a wiry build. Dark hair, kind of curly. He had a beard and eyebrows so thick they reminded me of caterpillars. Dark eyes—brown, I think. Big hands. Oh, and he had a crooked front tooth."

Something was nagging at her, something important. What was it? His words—something about his words. No, it was his voice, the same one she'd heard later.

Sarah gasped. "It was him. In the woods. It was the same deep bass voice."

Mason clicked the recorder off. "Stay here," he ordered, as both he and Ursall hurried from the room.

Sarah, left elbow planted on the table, held her trembling chin in that palm, fingers covering her mouth. What was his name? She had to remember. The girls' lives might depend on it. It was a common name, one syllable, or maybe two.

She dredged up memories from that short flight. She'd ignored him for most of it, after she'd seen the look on his face as he studied the little girl. The conversation before that—what had he talked about?

With a sharp intake of breath, she sat up straighter. Had she said anything to lead him to Lottie? How had their conversation gone? He'd asked her what brought her to Saranac Lake and she'd said—what? *I remember thinking I'd told him too much.* Not their surname, though, and not the girls' names. She'd told him Greg Wheeler was Tracy's husband. What else? That there were children. Had she mentioned daughters? No.

He'd wanted to stay in touch with her; shoved the paper with his phone number into her pocket. And he had stayed close to her from the time they got off the plane until she left the rental car lot. Why? To find out what kind of car she was driving? Even after he knew that, he'd stood there, watching, until she left the lot.

Maybe Lottie had told him the family was going to be at the cabin that week, It might have been the best place to make contact, but she'd probably paid little attention to road signs, and couldn't give him directions. She likely would have told him her last name, so he was looking for Lottie Agerton. But the child's name wouldn't be listed anywhere. It was a vacation cabin, and she didn't go to school in the area. If he knew Greg's and Tracy's names, the conversation with Sarah might have alerted him.

Everything fit except the last name. Had she hesitated before she said 'Wheeler'?

Mason strode back into the room and closed the door behind him. Sarah's thoughts kept coming, tumbling out now, in an unbroken stream.

"I had an eerie feeling on the drive, that he might be following me. But I would have noticed, once I got off the turnpike. No, maybe not, I was watching the road so closely. Visibility was low. If he stayed back far enough—did I lead him to the cabin? To Lottie? No, I couldn't have. I only got as far as the old back road. But that was where I first saw him with the binoculars, watching the cabin. Oh, God." She dropped her face into her hands. "I led him to her."

Mason pulled out the chair across the table from her, and the recorder clicked as he turned it on.

"Detective Ursall is searching the sex offender databases, but it's not likely he'll turn up anything with just one name. Have you remembered anything more?"

Numb, Sarah looked up at him, shaking her head.

"Frankly," Mason said, "I don't think we'll find him there."

"You don't think he's ever been charged?"

"No. I don't believe he's a child molester. At this point, I'm not sure what he is, but we suspect he took Tracy Agerton, too. With your help."

Again, Sarah was on the verge of telling him he was insane. How did they come up with these off-the-wall scenarios? Were they so desperate to solve a crime, close the case, that they didn't care about the truth?

"We believe you purposely came to New York," he continued, "to make contact with Tracy Agerton. You had done your background work, and knew she'd enrolled in a class at the design school, so you registered, too."

"I didn't—I told you. I never knew Tracy before I met her in class. I'd never even heard of her. And exactly how would I get information that she'd registered? I doubt the school gives that out."

"You wormed your way into her confidence and wrangled an invitation to the cabin. Once you had the date, you notified your partner. The one you so conveniently don't have a last name for, despite a full description—which is probably bogus. You would take the plane from the city. To avoid the appearance of traveling together, he picked up the flight in Boston."

"I never met the man before he got on the plane."

Mason's gaze was on her hands now, as they twisted the balled tissue she held in her palm. If he thought his questions were making her nervous, he was wrong. It was fear, knowing Lottie and Gracie were in the hands of a pedophile. Where had he taken them?

"You had adjoining seats," Mason said, relentless as a wild animal gnawing at the last shreds of meat on a bone. "You stayed together through baggage pickup and the car rental so you would know each other's vehicles. Before you left the lot, you called Tracy Agerton and lured her into a meeting at the intersection of that abandoned road. You parked there and waited for her. Your partner showed up then, threw her in his car and left, while you picked up the bracelet she'd dropped and drove on down that abandoned road and off into the rut."

"So I could walk a mile through a snowstorm to the cabin, and spend a week cooped up inside, babysitting, cooking, and cleaning? That sounds like such a great plan, I'm surprised more people haven't considered it."

"It put you inside, so you could provide your partner with information, keep him informed about the search, and plot the kidnapping of the little girls. You had his number in your pocket. You called him at least twice."

"He shoved the phone number in my pocket because I'm a woman and he's a pervert. And I didn't call him. Lottie did. Now she and Gracie are in his hands, and you're wasting time with this crazy idea that I'm mixed up in it somehow. Without one plausible explanation of a motive."

He frowned, his blue eyes icy. "If you wanted them found, you'd tell us where to find Pete whatever-his-name-is."

Sarah clenched her teeth to keep from screaming that he was an idiot, a moron who didn't know the truth when it slapped him in the face.

"How many times do I have to tell you I don't know? The first time I saw the man was when he took the seat beside me at Boston. The last time I saw him, he was standing in the rental car parking lot...That is, until I saw him watching the house, if it's the same man, and it looks like it is, since he's the one who took Lottie and Gracie."

Mason sat back, studying her face. "Okay, say we believe you. It was a coincidence that you and Tracy Agerton took the same class in the city and hit it off so well, she invited you to the cabin. It was a coincidence that you were sitting beside the man who took the girls and probably took Tracy. It was a coincidence that you got stranded during the exact time Tracy Agerton disappeared. It was a coincidence that you took that abandoned road, even though she would have warned you about it. And it's a coincidence that you were in the woods with the girls the night they were taken, but were tied so loosely, you had no trouble getting free, unharmed. That's a hell of a bunch of coincidences, Ms. Wagner, and I'm not buying it."

A young man opened the door and motioned to Mason, who got up and went to join him. After a whispered conversation, the detective came back.

"Your attorney is here. He'd like to speak to you. You're free to go, for now."

That was quick. How did Laura pull that off from three thousand miles away? She must be in panic mode.

But the man who entered the room was neither a lawyer nor a stranger. His gaze locked onto hers and he gave a slight nod. Interpreting it as a signal to say nothing, Sarah hesitated. He wasn't a friend. Why was he here, and what did he want?

But Mason was watching, and it was a way out of the interrogation, so she grabbed her purse and walked out with Bill Ayers.

Chapter 26
Later Friday Evening

They didn't speak until they were in Bill's black Jeep.

"Why are you helping me?" Sarah asked.

Bill shrugged and looked out the rear view mirror as he started the motor. "Why wouldn't I? And, to be honest, it seemed off. Wrong, somehow. That made me curious."

It took a few moments for her to get past the musical cadence of his syllables to their content.

"What do you mean, it seemed off?"

"The way they took you in. They had to have something. I sat there, mulling it over all the time I ate, wondering if they'd found something I'd missed. I didn't think so. They're probably off on the wrong track, like I was to begin with."

"You've lost me. They think they have something, or they're trying to convince me they do—a house of premises built on a wobbly foundation. What track were you on, and why?"

"I'd rather talk about that a little later. Someplace where we can have a conversation. In fact, that's why I came to the hotel for dinner. I was hoping I'd run into you."

Bill Ayers talked so little, it was hard to imagine a conversation. "So, let's go there and talk."

"Not now that they're watching you. We need someplace quieter, where we won't be interrupted." He glanced behind him before changing lanes, and Sarah studied his face. Why should she trust him? He was Greg's friend, not hers. He might be taking her to Greg right now. Her legs tensed, toes pressing against the floor, and her hand moved to the door handle. But she couldn't jump out into the traffic.

"Where, then?" she asked. Could he hear the tremor in her voice?

"My office."

"What kind of office?" She knew little about him, or any of the men who had spent so many evenings at the cabin. She'd been absorbed with worry over Tracy, and taking care of Lottie and Gracie. The only thing she knew about Bill Ayers was his beautiful voice, a penetrating gaze, and his long friendship with Greg Agerton. Yet she was alone with him in a vehicle headed for an unknown destination, plucked from the security of a police station. And, she had to admit, an unwelcome interrogation. "What do you do?"

He cast a quick glance in her direction, one eyebrow raised, before he turned his attention back to the street. "I thought we'd already established that. I'm an attorney."

"A real one? I mean—"

"Unless the state of New York issued my license in error, yes, a real one."

With that voice, he should be able to mesmerize juries. But why would one of Greg's friends go out of his way to help her?

"Don't worry," he said. "You're safe." Was he a mind reader, too?

Slowing, he turned into an alley and eased the Jeep down to an empty parking lot. The backs of the buildings surrounding them formed something resembling a courtyard, but a gloomy one, the age-darkened walls blending into the snow-damp concrete. *Easy for him to say I'm safe.*

He opened the door into a dimly-lit hallway, flipped on a light, and stopped long enough to fiddle with the thermostat. She hesitated, then followed him.

"It'll warm up in a few minutes."

They walked past restrooms and something that might have been a supply closet, toward the street entrance. Just before they reached it, he unlocked a door with gold lettering on the window "William J. Ayers, Attorney at Law." *So he wasn't lying.*

The decor of his suite—office, waiting room, and conference room—was designed to portray the image of a successful attorney. Creamy walls served as a background for several shades of brown furnishings: shelved legal volumes, desk, tables, and leather chairs. Only the framed prints on the walls offered a touch of color, most of them the greens and whites of snow-capped mountain landscapes, and the blues and whites of water rushing over rocky stream beds.

"You want something to drink?"

"No. Why are you helping me? You and Greg are good friends, and he—"

Bill motioned her to a chair on the visitors' side of the desk, went around to the other side, and settled into his own chair. "He's not yours?"

"No. Not anymore, if he ever was. I didn't even know him until I came to visit Tracy. Then I just stayed to help."

"Why don't you think he's a friend? You took care of his daughters—"

"You wouldn't believe me if I told you."

Again, that quirk of one eyebrow. "You might be surprised. And if I'm going to help you, I have to know what's going on."

Why should she trust him? Greg might have put him up to this. She was already a suspect. She didn't need an attorney who would be working against her.

"Okay," he said. "I'll try to make it easier, clarify things a little. Greg and I were classmates, nothing more. He was Jake's friend, and Jake was mine, so we spent some time together, but that's all. And it's been a long time since high school, and he hasn't been around a lot. I consider Greg Agerton a long-time acquaintance, not a close friend."

"But that first night, when he couldn't get the sheriff to come out, you showed up with Jake and the Graysons, and Paul. And you stayed."

"Yes. Jake called and told me Tracy was missing, so, of course, I came. But it wasn't just to help. I also had another objective, a favor for a man who is a friend. Edward Denton."

"Amy and Brad Denton's father? How did you get to know them? Jake said they didn't mix with the locals."

"They don't. But not because they're snobs. I used to work out at the country club when I was in high school, and they spent a lot of time there. And Ed...he's a great guy. I don't know why he got interested in me, but he helped me get into a good college—one my folks couldn't afford."

"So he's a philanthropist? Spreading some of his wealth around?"

A smile tugged at Bill's lips, the kind that comes with fond memories. "I suppose, although I never thought of him that way. He told me I could work it off, then made sure I did, several times over, in legal hours. But I hadn't heard from him for a while." He shifted in his chair, the smile disappearing. "Until now, that is."

"You're investigating Amy's death?"

"Not really. Well...maybe a little. As soon as Ed heard Tracy was missing, he asked me to stick to Greg and the search, to find out as much as I could. He knew Brad would be a prime suspect if she weren't found."

That explained his quiet observation of people, that penetrating gaze. *Often directed at me.*

"You thought I was involved."

"I wasn't sure. It seemed strange that you showed up just as Tracy went missing."

"Yeah, so I hear. The detectives think so, too. They believe—"

"Hold on." Bill held up a hand. "Just so I don't forget anything, do you mind if I turn the recorder on?"

"Yes, I mind." *Everybody wants to record me. Just like a rock star. But I don't feel like a celebrity.*

"Okay, no problem. Go on. What do the detectives believe?"

"That the guy watching the house is my accomplice, that we'd hatched a scheme to grab Tracy. What they didn't know is that he was here to get Lottie. Apparently, she'd connected with him on some website for pedophiles. That's why she ran away Sunday—to meet up with him."

"My God!" The legs of Bill's chair scraped as he pushed to his feet. "Have they caught him?"

"No. They don't know who he is. All they have is the description I gave them, and his first name. I can't remember the last one."

Bill's eyes narrowed. "So you do know him."

"No." Sarah described their meeting, from the time the man had dropped into the seat beside her on the plane until she'd last seen him, standing in the parking lot.

"And from that, they think you were in collusion with him?"

"There's more." Sarah told him about the telephone calls and the slip of paper the man had pushed into her pocket, that Mason later found outside her bedroom door. "He also thinks that man was gentle"—Sarah did air quotes with her fingers —"with me in the woods."

She stopped, giving her pulse time to stop racing, then went on. "He's right in one respect. I was tied so I'd be able to get free fairly quickly. Probably so I didn't freeze out there in the woods. The man didn't mean me any harm, which makes me doubt he did anything to Tracy. I think he just wanted me restrained long enough to get away with Lottie and Gracie."

Bill's voice was soft. "So you think he's non-violent? That he's not a killer, and that gives you a little comfort?"

"Damned little, considering that I'm the one who may have led him to Lottie. But yes, I think it does."

"Sometimes we have to hang onto whatever thin rope we can grab." He fiddled with a pen. "So I take it the detectives don't believe your story?"

"Hard to say. They're trying to find a pedophile, yet they tell me they think I'm making it up, that I helped him kidnap both Tracy and the girls. I asked them what possible motive I could have, and they didn't have an answer. I figure that's why they didn't arrest me."

"You're right. They may have concocted opportunity, but they have no motive. And what Mason is calling a series of coincidences, I see as a chain of events—one logically leading to another. Except meeting the guy on the plane. That was a coincidence. Anyway, I think you should tell me everything you can remember about that interrogation."

"Then you'd better make a pot of coffee because it will take some time."

While he worked at a side console, making the coffee, she pulled out her phone and scrolled through messages. Nothing from either detective. What was happening with Lottie and Gracie? She had to get to a quiet place so she could concentrate on the kidnapper's last name. Maybe if she went through the alphabet, letter by letter? Aa? No. Ab? No.

Bill set the cup of coffee on the table in front of her and carried another back to his own seat. Sarah put the phone away and told him about the meeting with the detectives.

"So they're trying to tie you to both Tracy's disappearance and the girls' kidnapping. Makes a nice, neat package for them."

"Yes, but I have no motive. They're settling on me simply because I'm the only one who had contact with the man who took the girls."

"So it appears I'm working for the two primary suspects, Brad Denton and you."

"Why me?"

Bill shrugged. "One, because you're also a suspect and need an attorney. Two, I don't believe you did it. Three, you were in that cabin all week, and I think by working together we can help each other."

"I'm getting my own attorney. I don't like the idea of sharing one with Brad Denton. But I'm willing to work with you, up to a point."

He sat for a few minutes, not speaking, then nodded. "Okay, that'll work, too. Now would you mind telling me why you no longer consider Greg Agerton a friend?"

Sarah told him about the night Greg had drugged her and the girls, about finding the GHB and sleeping pills and hiding them in the kitchen.

"He called after I left, threatening me if I didn't give them back to him. He thinks I took them, and I can't figure out why it's so important to him to get them back. I can't prove he used them. And he didn't...do anything to me, so I thought maybe Lottie... she's troubled, and she ran away from him."

Bill leaned forward, with the same intent gaze he'd focused on her in the past. "What night was it? Do you remember?"

"Yes. It was Tuesday night, and I've been trying to remember what else happened that day, or the next, with no success. One day was just like another in that cabin. I even started a sort of time line, with the few things I can recall, but I'm not getting very far with it."

Bill rose, beckoning to her. "I have something to show you." He led her into the conference room, equipped with a ten-foot long table of heavy, light-colored wood; eight matching cushioned chairs with rollers; and walls adorned with cork boards and whiteboards. On one of the cork boards, a sheet of white paper held Greg's name at the top, with arrows pointing down to Amy, on one side, and Tracy, on the other. Under each woman's name, he'd scrawled a list.

"Those are similarities," Bill said. "Both wealthy women, both missing from Greg's house at a time when other people were present, giving him a rock-solid alibi, and both cases unsolved thus far."

"You think Greg murdered Amy? And possibly Tracy?" Sarah shook her head. "From what I understand, Amy drowned in the ocean, and Greg couldn't have put her there at the time of death."

"No, but a person doesn't have to be in the ocean to drown in sea water. A bucket will work just as well. And he had time to do that, then carry both her and the bucket down to the ocean well after the time of death. But nobody could prove it."

"But the bucket? Wouldn't they search—"

"Oh, they did. And they eventually found a bucket. It didn't have any fingerprints on it."

"None? Would the water wash them away?"

"Maybe. More likely, it was wiped clean."

"So you think he got away with Amy's murder. But there's no way he could have killed Tracy. Both Lottie and Gracie say he was with them from the time their mother called them in for hot chocolate until she went for her walk. By the time I showed up, she'd already been gone longer than expected."

"But he went out again after that, supposedly to look for her."

"Yes, but...you're saying he killed her then? That she was taking a longer walk than he said, and he knew where to find her?" Sarah shook her head. "She knew I was coming. I can't see her taking a long walk and not being there when I arrived. I'd never even met Greg or the girls. But even aside from that, what would he have done with her body? He wasn't gone that long. Maybe forty-five minutes at most. How could he have killed her and hidden her body where none of you could find it?"

Bill nodded. "And I don't think there's an inch we didn't search. So...he paid somebody else to do it—to grab her somewhere along that walk."

"How would that person know when to find her and where? Greg couldn't have known ahead of time that she'd decide to meet me."

"No, but he could have arranged it so he'd call when the opportunity presented itself."

"That would mean the killer had to be close by, waiting. Greg would have planned for it to happen sometime this week, while they were at the cabin, just because it's somewhat remote. I suppose it's possible. But much as I dislike him, I don't see a motive."

Bill used a laser to point at the second item in each woman's list. *Wealthy.* "I think he finds wealthy women, marries them, then makes sure they have an accident so he inherits. For a while, I thought you were the next candidate."

"Me? You checked me out—knew I had inherited money?" That helped to explain his scrutiny while she was at the cabin. "You thought we had a thing going, that I was part of—"

"Not necessarily. Just that, knowing you were Tracy's friend, he might have assumed you had money, checked it out, and decided you might do nicely for the next round."

"Good God!" Sarah buried her face in her hands. "This just gets creepier and creepier."

"Here."

She looked up as a stapled sheaf of papers slid across the table toward her. "Maybe this will help."

She leafed through the pages, his own time line of events at the cabin and the search sites—much more detailed than hers. Just a glance jarred some of her own recollections into place.

"Bill, this is...it's so detailed. How did you remember—"

"I didn't. I'm an attorney, and I was working a case. I carried a recorder in my pocket. I went home every night and wrote up my reports, using the recordings and notes I'd jotted down during the day, and those evenings at the cabin—reports I sent off to Ed Denton. But I had no way of knowing what was happening when I wasn't around. You were, so maybe—"

Her phone finally rang, and she grabbed for it. The display showed an unfamiliar number. One of the detectives, maybe, with news of Lottie and Gracie. "Sarah Wagner."

"You're Tracy's friend? The one she invited to the cabin?"

"Yes. Who is this?"

"I'm Cindy Bates. I have a message that you called me? Something about my family. Have they found my sister?"

So she knew about Tracy. Why wasn't she here?

"I'm sorry. They haven't located her yet. I'm calling about Lottie and Gracie."

"Are they all right? This has got to be hell for them, and Lottie already—"

"No, I'm afraid they're not. I thought you might have heard by now. There's a BOLO out, and an AMBER Alert."

"AMBER—Oh. I've been out of the country. Just got back last night. I just found out about Tracy." Her voice fell several octaves, followed by several seconds of silence. "Do they know who has the girls?"

Why did the woman sound so calm? So thoughtful? Was she in shock? Maybe that's why Greg had kept her away, knowing she couldn't handle the stress and worrying about the effect that would have on the girls.

"We think she's been in contact with a pedophile, and he may have them. There's not much information about him. Just a description and his first name, and maybe the color of the car he was driving. And he has a deep, bass voice."

"Pete? It was Pete?"

"You know him?"

"Yeah, I know him. Pete Bennett. He's no pedophile. He's Tracy's ex-husband. Lottie's and Gracie's biological father, and those girls are his life. I tried to warn Tracy—I knew he'd go berserk if she and Greg did this—took the girls away. He'd hunt them to the ends of the earth, and God only knew what he'd do when he finally found them. Whatever—" Her voice cracked. "Whatever he did to Tracy, he'll do worse to Greg, and Greg knows it. He must be scared shitless."

Chapter 27
Friday Night

Sarah punched the speaker button so Bill could hear. "What did Greg and Tracy do?"

"I don't...look, I know you're Tracy's friend, but I'm not sure I should tell you—"

Bill said, "Cindy, this is Bill Ayers. I'm an attorney and a good friend of Tracy's. We're trying to find out what happened to Tracy and the girls, and the sheriff and police department aren't being very helpful."

"The painter? You're that friend?"

"No, that's Jake. He and I are friends, too. We need to know anything you can tell us."

There was perhaps a full minute of silence before Cindy spoke.

"They took his kids away. I think it was Greg's idea because Tracy and Pete were getting along pretty well, sharing custody. Then, after she met Greg, everything changed. He didn't like Tracy or the girls having any contact with Pete."

"But he was their father," Bill said. "He could have fought that."

"Not the way they did it. They started finding excuses why the girls couldn't spend time with him. They were sick, or it was the day of a friend's birthday party, or a recital, or some other bull-shit."

Still, if it went on too long, and he could prove he wasn't seeing them—

"Pete was persistent. He'd threatened to go back to court. That really grated on Greg. Finally, he came up with this scheme. They would move without letting Pete know. Greg and Tracy would get married, so she and the girls would have a new name. Tracy would home school the girls."

"How long ago was this?" Bill asked.

"Two years. I didn't even know they were going to do it until Tracy called to give me her new cell phone number. I warned her—"

Two years ago Lottie would have been eight, Gracie four. The longing look on Pete Bennett's face when he'd studied the little girl on the plane took on new meaning. And the child had looked a lot like Gracie. No wonder he was watching the little girls. He was trying to find his daughters, and they would have changed in two years. Especially Gracie.

Images flooded Sarah's mind. Lottie's strained relationship with Greg, saying he "always lied," telling Sarah "you don't know anything."

You were so right, Lottie. I didn't know anything. Sarah had tried to be patient, realizing the girl was troubled, but had sometimes thought Lottie was petulant and sulky. *I owe you an apology, honey. I thought my father was a sleazeball, but Greg Agerton wins that contest.*

"Was Lottie close to her father?" Sarah asked Cindy. "To Pete Bennett?"

"Oh, yeah. Big time. She tried to call him, and Greg took her phone away. I think, by that time, Tracy was having second thoughts. She hadn't realized what it would do to the kids, especially Lottie. Gracie—she was younger, and began to forget, to accept Greg. But not Lottie."

"Do you think Pete Bennett killed your sister?" Bill asked Cindy.

"I...I don't know. He was probably furious, desperate, and thought he had good reason. But it's hard to imagine. Greg, though, yeah. I think Pete would kill Greg Agerton in a heartbeat."

"What about Greg? Do you think he's capable of harming Tracy?"

A quick intake of breath, then nothing but silence on the other end of the call.

Just as Sarah started to speak, Cindy said, "Yes. I worried about it, with the uncertainty over his first wife's death. And there was something about him...always scheming—"

Sarah hesitated. It was a tough question to ask. "Do you think he would have paid somebody to kill your sister?"

"Paid? No. He's capable of it, but he couldn't have. They had a prenup, and Tracy had him on a short leash. After a while, she started worrying that he'd married her for money, so she kept everything in her name, except a small account she set up for him. She put money into it every month. He was pretty bitter about it—called it his allowance. But she made sure he didn't have access to anything else."

"Do you have any idea who might have taken her?" Bill asked.

"Brad Denton. Unless Pete was even angrier than I thought."

"Is there any chance they could have planned this together? That Tracy is with Pete, and they both took the girls?"

Cindy was silent again, so long Sarah thought she wasn't going to answer. Then she said, "I can't see it. There was too much bitterness between them. And Tracy wouldn't have left the girls with Greg."

"Even knowing I was arriving?" Sarah asked.

"No, I don't think so."

"Okay, Cindy. Thanks for all this. I'm so sorry about Tracy. I wish I'd arrived a little earlier, before she went missing." Sarah hesitated. "Do you think...would Pete Bennett mind if I called the girls once in a while?"

"I don't know. I'll ask, tell him how much Tracy liked you. I'm going to call him as soon as we hang up, and tell him he needs to turn himself in. I'm packing right now, getting ready to head up there, so I can take care of Lottie and Gracie—just in case."

"Thank you. That means a lot. I'd like to have a chance to say goodbye." Sarah ended the call and looked up at Bill.

"This puts me a little higher on the suspect list, doesn't it? Greg is out. He didn't kill her himself, and according to Cindy, he didn't have the money to hire somebody. The only thing left is a 'Stranger on the Train' scenario."

"Made for a good movie, but a little hard to accomplish in real life—opening up a conversation with a stranger about committing a murder for each other."

"Yeah, and now we know Bennett had good reason to kill Tracy. And they've tied me to Bennett."

"Don't forget, Brad Denton is still right up there with you."

"Which may give me a little time. Do we have to tell the detectives about Bennett?"

"Yes, and I think it would be to your advantage if you were the one who made the call. Maybe Bennett will turn himself in sometime tonight."

"I hope he can convince them we're not in cahoots." She punched in Ursall's number. He didn't answer, so she left a message.

"It's late. They're not going to do anything tonight. That gives me a little more time." She flipped through the sheaf of papers Bill had given her. "It's getting late. Is it all right if I take this, work with it some tonight, and maybe get back together with you tomorrow?"

"Sure. I'll do the same, and we can touch bases in the morning."

◆◆◆

They spoke little on the drive back to the hotel but it was a comfortable silence now, and fragments of memory started coalescing around the new information.

Somehow, Lottie had managed to maintain enough contact with her father to let him know they'd be at the cabin that week. He might have waited months for the girls to be in that remote location. She probably couldn't give him directions, so he came up ahead of time to check it out. That would explain his knowledge of the area and his familiarity with that back road.

Lottie had known he was coming, was watching for him, but had no access to a phone. Somehow, in the calls she'd managed, they had agreed on a place where Pete would leave one for her, probably somewhere behind the shed. She'd been watching for him the night he left it, been afraid Greg would catch him. That first night, right after Sarah had spotted the watcher, the men had gathered in the kitchen to devise a way to capture him. Lottie had taken Gracie upstairs, and Sarah thought she'd heard a noise later. Lottie, listening, scared they would catch her father before he could rescue her. Poor, frightened little girl.

Had Greg suspected Pete was out there? Possibly. He'd lied, said a lost hiker was in the woods that night, but he might have suspected Pete had found them. That explained why he was so agitated, why he roamed the property at night, and why he insisted the girls stay inside.

I told her she could go live with Pete Bennett. The girl had asked if they would live with their father if their mother didn't come back. *I didn't understand what she was really asking when I said "yes."*

"Sarah? We're here." Bill tilted his head toward the hotel entrance. "You've been immersed in thought."

"Yeah. Tell me. Why would Greg want to keep Tracy's daughters, once she was gone? Why not let their father know where they were, rather than hiding them away in that cabin?"

"I don't know, but it's a good question. I suspect, based on what Cindy said, that they inherit from Tracy. If he has them, he has access to their money. I'll give it some thought, see what I can find out. Get some sleep, and we'll talk about it tomorrow."

"Okay. Can we do it in the afternoon?" At his quizzical look, she added, "so I have more time to go over the time line?"

His gaze was just as penetrating as it had been when it settled on her in the cabin. "I thought we were going to work on that together."

She looked away from him. "I just...I'm too tired to think straight right now. It's been a long day, and I don't know how long I can stay awake to work." She opened the door and slid out of the Jeep. "I'll call you in the morning." She closed the door before he could respond and made a dash for the hotel.

Standing just inside the entrance, Sarah waited until Bill left. She was starving; Mason and Ursall had interrupted her dinner. The dining room might still be open, but she needed a few other items she'd overlooked on her shopping trip. She hurried to the Explorer, trying to remember the exact location of the convenience store she'd seen earlier, on the edge of town.

The store, almost deserted at this late hour, had what she wanted: a small Maglite, some protein bars, and bottled water, in case her mission took longer than expected; and a ham and cheese sandwich for dinner.

She ate the sandwich on the way back to the hotel and eyed the protein bars. No, those were for tomorrow. If she still felt hungry after she got back to her room, she'd get something from the mini-bar.

Nobody was in the elevator or in the hallway leading to her room, and she'd just pulled the key card out of the slot when her phone rang. Laura. Sarah pushed the door open and went inside as she answered.

"Hi, Cuz. I was going to call you. I just got back to my room. It's been a long day." She filled Laura in on the day's events.

"Did the lawyer get in contact with you?" her cousin asked.

"Lawyer? You mean Bill Ayers? I just told you—"

"No, the one I called. He's supposed to be good. He said he'd get in touch with you right away, maybe send a text message since he wasn't sure what your situation was, if you were being questioned—"

"I don't think so, but I'll check my messages. It's too late to call him now, anyway. I'll try in the morning if I'm not arrested first."

Laura's voice rose. "It's that bad?"

"I don't know. You remember how it goes. They suspect you, and you have to disprove all their assumptions. I have a lot to do. How's the work on the time line going?"

"Kind of slow. I think it would be better if we could go through it together."

Sarah told her about Bill's notes. "I'll put those together with mine tonight, and then get back to you, to fill in the missing pieces. It'll take a while, so how about I call you tomorrow afternoon?"

Laura agreed, and after they ended the conversation, Sarah checked her text messages. It was there. Leland Carrington, Esq. Did parents give their kids those lawyerly names, hoping they would become attorneys? Or did the name drive the choice of occupation?

Enough procrastinating. She had to settle down to work, then try to get some sleep so she would be alert tomorrow morning.

The phone rang again. Jake. That was a surprise. "Sarah, I...look, I'm sorry. I should have listened. Bill called and filled me in on a bunch of stuff. I still find some of it hard to believe, but...well, I'm sorry."

Why was Bill Ayers talking to Jake about their conversation? Who else was he talking to? Edward Denton, for sure, and maybe Brad. If it ever came to a choice between defending her or Brad, she had no doubt which client he'd dump. She needed to call the other lawyer.

"Sarah? Look, if you don't want to talk to me, I understand. I just wanted to tell you I'm sorry."

"No, it's fine. I'm just curious about what Bill told you."

"Could we talk about it over breakfast or lunch tomorrow?"

"I'd better take a rain check. I've got all kinds of things coming down on me and a lot to do."

"No problem. If you decide you want to talk, call me, okay?"

"Maybe sometime late tomorrow." *If I'm not in jail by then.* "I'll see how it goes." How many people had she promised to call the next day? Jake, Bill, Laura, and she had to contact the new attorney.

"Okay, I'll wait until I hear from you, then. Oh...something else. Those detectives took that lug wrench you left at the cabin. Greg said it was something about DNA evidence."

Sarah gripped the phone, much like she'd gripped that wrench when she'd made the long, fearful trek through the snow to the cabin. She could almost feel its solidity, its heft. How hard would it be for Greg to add a touch of Tracy's DNA? Running her hairbrush down the end would undoubtedly leave at least a few strands of hair.

"Did he say when they did that?"

"Sometime this afternoon."

After she'd left their office then. Mason and Ursall thought they had new evidence. How long would it take them to test for DNA? Could they tell if it was planted?

That wouldn't even occur to them. They would be coming for her sooner than she'd expected.

Chapter 28
Saturday Morning

She dreamed she was diving from the edge of the pool into the deep end, focused on the red flower at the bottom. Her instructor had thrown it there, and Sarah had to retrieve it.

When she surfaced, splashing water, she twisted her head toward the rows of metal bleachers and her father, his face flushed from the mid-summer sun. Holding her arm aloft, she brandished the flower, showing him she had it.

The straw hat shaded his eyes, but she knew they watched her, and she waved before she sank beneath the water again.

She awoke with the memory back in her head—not of the flower—she wasn't sure what she'd dived for—but of her father that hot summer when she was four or five years old, learning to swim. Either he or her mother had sat there every Saturday, in the baking sun, while she fought her fear of the water.

"Why do I have to do it, Daddy?" she'd asked.

"Because Uncle David is putting in a pool, and you're going to be over there a lot, playing with Laura. So you need to know how to swim."

"But I won't go in, Daddy. I'm scared of the water."

"I know you are, sweetheart. But you might fall in, and we have to keep you safe. Besides, you might learn to like it."

He'd been right. She'd come to love that pool, and she and Laura, along with their friends, had still been hanging around it when they were teenagers. When had they stopped? Not until after her mother had died and her dad married Anna, so probably when Sarah was sixteen and went to live with Caro in Sacramento.

Sarah crawled out of bed and looked out the window. The sun was no more than an orange-pink smudge, its faint glow lifting the blackness of night to a gauzy gray dawn.

She had to go now, had to find whatever bothered her about those woods before Ursall and Mason came to arrest her. She no longer had a choice.

If she left now, she would be at the cabin well before Greg left—assuming he did leave. Would he still be going out every day, joining the search party, or had they given up on finding Tracy? Right now, they were probably searching for Lottie and Gracie, on the chance that the girls and the man who had taken them were still in the area, perhaps in a remote cabin. But they wouldn't be in the woods close to the house.

Even that search would end today, when word got out that the girls were with their biological father. What would Greg do then? Return to the cabin? She had to get moving—be in and out early.

Twenty minutes later, she was on the road, passing a big billboard: Vote for Maynor for Sheriff. She wasn't eligible to vote in a local election but, for an instant, wished she could. She'd cast her ballot for Deputy Jody Martin, even though she'd never met him.

When she reached the road leading to the washed-out bridge, she slowed, peering through the trees toward the cabin. The Tahoe wasn't there; he'd left early this morning.

Increasing to a normal speed, she drove past the lane, not slowing again until she reached the unfamiliar terrain beyond it. The two-track road couldn't be far; it cut into the forest behind the cabin. Hunching over the steering wheel, she scanned the shoulder on her right.

A wide spot loomed and beside it, a narrow space through the trees. The two-track? Yes, some vehicles had been in and out recently, breaking slushy ruts in the snow. Sarah eased off the gas and gripped the steering wheel. She didn't want to go off the road again. But if other cars had made it in and out, the Explorer would, too. She inched forward until a flutter of yellow in the distance told her she'd almost reached her destination. She could walk the rest of the way.

The copse of trees to her right should shield the Explorer from view of the road. There wasn't enough room to get off the track, but that didn't matter. She parked, clambered out of the vehicle and shrugged into her parka, then slung the binoculars around her neck, stuffed the Maglite into one pocket and the phone into the other, beside the house key. The water and protein bars could stay in the vehicle for now.

She trudged through the snow toward the fluttering yellow and black tape. A small loop of it marked the tree where she'd been tied. A churned path led from it into the woods, in the general direction of the cabin—some of it made by her, the rest by the detectives and whatever crime scene technicians had visited the scene.

She cut across the broad swath of broken and partially melted snow and ducked under the tape still strung among the trees. The cops had probably finished their investigation; there wasn't much to find.

Working her way through the vegetation, she finally reached the zig-zag pattern through the trees where she'd found Tracy's bracelet. Lowering herself onto her haunches, she searched the edges. *This is insane. I don't even know what I'm looking for.* But something about this scene was nagging at her, something she needed to find. Rising, she moved a little farther, bending to examine the terrain. *What am I missing?*

Then, like one of those pictures hidden within a larger image, she saw it—a pattern within the larger jagged course, snaking between the trees. It was faint and uneven, but it was there: broken twigs and branches marking each side, about the same distance apart. She'd seen a few of them before and thought they'd been made by animals. Snow had been heavy on the ground then, covering most of the vegetation. Now, with so much of the snow melted, the evenly-spaced pattern emerged. No wild creature had made this. What, then? Snowshoes?

That would make sense. A person wearing them would choose the course that wove around the trees and bushes. The path was probably well known to those who traversed these woods. It would explain the bracelet if Tracy had snowshoed here recently.

The discovery might stop the nagging, but it wasn't going to help her find out what had happened to Tracy. There was something else. And it was in the shed.

No. It's too dangerous.

Maybe not if she could get close enough to see if the Tahoe was still gone. It would take only a few minutes to duck in and take a look, and she'd hear Greg's Tahoe long before it turned down the lane to the cabin. She'd have plenty of time to get out, run behind the building and into the woods. And it might be the place where she found the answers.

The cabin, still obscured by trees, lay ahead, slightly to her left. If she angled right, she should come out behind the shed.

Edging from tree to tree, maintaining cover, she sneaked closer to the cabin. A glimpse of the shed's rough siding told her she'd gone too far left; she'd have to backtrack a little and make her approach again.

The next time she came out of the woods, the back of the shed was directly ahead. Standing behind the last screen of trees, she tried to gauge the distance, then shook her head. She'd be out in the open, exposed to any car coming along the road. But the Tahoe wasn't anywhere around, and if she didn't make any sudden movements, nobody should notice her. Edging from behind the trees, she walked, maintaining a steady pace, keeping her gaze centered on the back of the shed.

Once she reached it, she hugged the wall, waiting for her heart to stop pounding so she could hear again. Nothing stirred around the cabin. The only sound came from the woods far to her left, probably close to the washed-out bridge: a heavy animal crashing through the brush. A moose? She stood still, straining to hear, but no further sound came, other than the normal rustling of small creatures scurrying through the brush. Time to move.

She sidled along the right edge of the shed. Her pulse quickened as she hurried to the door, and her fingers fumbled with the iron latch.

Finally, with it securely in the loop, she pulled the door open, forgetting its loud squeak. She darted in and closed the door. Even if Greg came back—or anybody else, for that matter—he wouldn't notice the displaced latch or the glow cast by the small Maglite. Not unless they came to the shed, and there was little reason to assume they would.

Standing still, she waited a few minutes, allowing her eyes to adjust to the darkness, breathing in the musty dampness. Her vision was better than she'd expected. Maybe she wouldn't have to use the Maglite.

Several sets of snowshoes hung on the side walls. They were about eight to ten inches wide, and their edges could certainly break small branches. How wide a path would they make through the snow? How far apart would they be, when worn?

She turned, assessing the dust-covered contents of the shed. She'd stood here the first time she'd come inside. What had her subconscious picked up then, that still bugged her?

Sunlight slashed across the wall, along with the creak of the door.

She jerked and turned, squinting to put details on the dark form in the doorway, aware, even before he spoke, that it was Greg.

"What are you doing here? Is this where you put the drugs?"

She could see his face now, and the faint smile lifting the corners of his lips.

If she told him where the drugs were hidden, would he let her go? Or would she be safer if she lied?

"Give me your phone," he said, taking a step toward her.

"My phone? Why?"

He took two more quick steps. She pulled the phone from her pocket and held it out, to keep him at bay. "I don't know what you want to see. There's nothing—"

"It's too bad, you know." He cocked his head to one side, smiling again. "It might have worked out all right between us, in time. But you had to snoop."

His steps toward her had left a clear path to the door, which still hung open. If he moved a little more to the right, she might get past him, dodge out the door, and slam the bar down into the slot.

"They're over there," she nodded toward the tarp in the right front corner. "I didn't want to leave them where anybody might find them. I was going to leave a note on the door...one only you would understand."

He glanced at the corner, then back at her, took a step to his right, then looked at her again. "You'd better not be lying."

"Why would I lie, after I came all the way out here?"

He nodded and turned toward the corner.

She waited until he took a few more steps, then ran. He whirled and reached out, his fingers brushing her arm. She was past him, the door only feet away. Straining to force more speed from her body, she gasped when his hand closed around her upper arm.

He backhanded her across the face and shoved her toward the darker end of the building, sparks of anger flashing in his eyes. "Where are the drugs?"

He raised his fist, then hesitated, studying her face. "No, we can't have you all beat up, can we? Somebody might question that." He smiled. "It's not going to matter now, anyway. You won't be able to tell anybody about them. Take off the parka."

She obeyed, then shuddered as his hands ran down her body. They stopped at her pockets, and she stood still. *He's just patting you down to see if you're armed. If you don't move, maybe that's all he'll do.*

He stepped away from her, picked up the parka, and pulled out the Maglite and keys. Nodding, he shoved them back into the pocket. "I'll let you keep the binoculars and keys. Not that they'll do you much good in here, but we want you to look natural. The light, too. You would have brought one with you to do your snooping. And it might make your nights a little easier. Or maybe just one night, 'til the batteries run out."

"What are you talking about?"

He shoved her phone in his jacket pocket. "Your nights here in the shed. As long as you last. Probably not long, without water."

"You're leaving me in here? You can't. Somebody will miss me, come looking. They'll find my car—"

"No. They'll find that white Ford Explorer I saw on the two-track."

That's why she hadn't known he was there; he hadn't come back in the Tahoe, but through the woods, on foot. Had he been there all the while, watching her?

"Nobody's going to connect that car to you. At least, not for a while. They'll just think it's some hiker, somebody exploring the woods. And when they do get around to checking it out, they'll think the same guy grabbed you that got Tracy. They'll be combing the forest, checking out abandoned cabins, the mines—"

He stopped, looking into the near distance, his gaze unseeing. Then he nodded, and focused on her face again.

"Nobody's going to think to look here. At least, not for a while. And by the time they get around to opening this shed, it'll be too late."

"You can't—"

"After they find your body, they'll figure it all out. You parked in the woods, sneaked into the shed, and somehow didn't get the iron bar fastened far enough into the loop. It fell, locking you in. Too bad you dropped your phone outside, maybe while you were opening the door. You couldn't call for help."

"I told my cousin I was coming out here. She'll know where I am."

"And who will she call? She doesn't know anybody here. Maybe Sheriff Maynor?" He laughed. "Good luck with that old fool. He won't even consider you missing for two days."

"They'll wonder why I'm in here. What reason would I have?"

"Who knows?" He backed toward the door. "I'll leave that for somebody else to figure out. Maybe it'll be another one of those unsolved mysteries."

Before she could move, he stepped out the door and slammed it shut. Then the iron bar fell into place, with a solid thunk.

Chapter 29
Saturday

The only light came from a small window at the end opposite the door, near the roof. It faced the open area at the edge of the forest, with no trees to block the early-morning sunlight. But it was a pale winter sun, and the window was small, facing north.

Sarah looked up at it, her throat dry. She should have brought one of the water bottles. But he would have taken it. What did he mean, the drugs didn't matter?

Oh, God! Because I'll be dead, and even if somebody finds them, they won't connect them to me—or him.

Bill Ayers would, but that wasn't going to help her.

She had to find a way out.

The shed was old; maybe some of the boards were loose, or at least weak enough to break if she pounded on them hard enough. But if he was still close by, waiting and listening, the noise would bring him back, and he'd do something to ensure she couldn't get out. Tie her up? No, he wouldn't be able to explain that as an accident. He'd probably knock her out, not drug her. That would show up in an autopsy. She shuddered.

There was no way to know if he was nearby. Unless...where was the Tahoe? Had he left it out in the woods somewhere, near the Explorer? If he had, he'd want to get it away from there, stay far from that area until after her vehicle was found. Odds were, he'd gone to get it, and she didn't have much time. The sound of the motor would alert her when he came back. She'd have to stop every few minutes to listen for it.

A tool would help—ideally, a sledge hammer. But that would be asking too much. There was no time to search for one right now, anyway. She had to test for weak spots first.

The boards were rough, but she had no choice but to remove her mittens. Splinters were the least of her worries, and she needed to feel any cracks in the wood, no matter how small.

Starting with the shelving at the back, she thrust her hands in and out, shoving cans and bottles aside, groping her way along the wall. Even if she found a weak spot, the shelves would be a hindrance unless she could get them loose, too, but the back was her only option. The front and sides were visible from the house. She'd leave them as a last resort, for a possible way out after dark.

She had worked her way about halfway around the back wall when the sound of the motor alerted her. A car door slammed. She held her breath, waiting. A slight, shuffling noise. Footsteps? His coat brushing against the wall? She couldn't tell.

"Sarah?"

If she didn't answer, he might come in to see what she was doing. The shelves behind her held dozens of projectiles. She would wait until he was inside, then start throwing cans and bottles. In that short distance, with luck, one of them might do enough damage to let her get past him.

Edging along the shelving, she chose a can small enough to fit in her palm, a good throwing weight. Her other hand closed around the neck of a heavy bottle. Then she waited, watching the door.

It didn't open. The sound, when it finally came, was of the cabin door opening. He'd gone inside. Would he go upstairs, so he could monitor the front and sides of the shed from her old bedroom window? Doubtful, but it didn't matter; he couldn't see the back.

Would the sound of breaking wood carry to the interior of the cabin? Maybe, but she'd worry about that later. First, she had to find a place to break through. Starting where she'd left off, Sarah went to work, pushing at the boards.

There were no weak spots; the wall and shelving were solid. She would have to try one of the sides, the west-facing one first, less visible from the house.

The light coming through the window had diminished. The sun must be directly overhead, the window shaded by the roof. Past the time she should have called Bill Ayers and the new attorney. What time had she told Laura and Jake she'd call them? People would be wondering where she was, but not alarmed yet.

Would light from the overhead bulb glow through that small window? It probably wasn't visible from the house, but it would be from the woods, especially after the sun went down. There was little chance anybody would be out there, this close to the cabin, and she had nothing to lose. If it alerted Greg enough to come in, she could still pelt him with bottles and cans. She flipped the switch.

The light didn't come on.

Turning on the Maglite, she approached the tarp-covered mound Greg had started to search earlier for the drugs. Time to look for a tool. It was slow going, holding the Maglite in one hand while shifting the contents of the pile with the other. All she found were a small pair of rusted gardening shears and a couple of tent stakes—poor tools for the job at hand, but if she could find something to pound with, the tips of the tent stakes might slip between the boards so she could pry them apart. Maybe there'd be something in the other pile.

A car started. Sarah stood still, listening. The Tahoe. He was leaving.

The interior of the shed was dimmer. How much longer until dark? She shuddered at the thought of spending the night in the shed. The temperature would drop, and she had nothing but her parka and the tarps to keep her warm.

She glanced again at the overhead bulb, then farther up, to the beam running the length of the shed. It ended about a foot below the window, and there was a space of four or five feet between it and the center of the steep roof. If she could get up there, she could drop through the window, even if she had to break it...and it wouldn't be the first time she got out of a tight spot by using her old gymnastics skills.

She shook her head. That was the problem; they were old. She hadn't even done the flips and back flips she'd shown Eric and Jamie, once she left California nine months ago. But, considering the alternative, it wasn't much of a choice; if she fell to her death, it would at least be quick. She pushed away the thought that she probably wouldn't die from that height—just break several bones, making her lingering death even more agonizing.

The beam ran the length of the shed. The rowboat hung from lengths of chain bolted to the beam. Under it was the wooden boat cradle. Getting into the cradle would be no problem, but there was nothing but open space between it and the boat, and no way to jump into it from the cradle. Even if she could, she would still have to shimmy up one of those chains to the beam and hope the bolt held. *And I'm a little out of practice at chain shimmying.*

The shelving might provide a better path up, providing it was securely fastened. The bottom seemed strong enough, but that didn't mean the top would be as sturdy. And it hadn't been designed for climbing.

If she were going to attempt this, it had to be now—while he was gone, and she still had enough light from the window.

She couldn't hold the Maglite while she was climbing, nor could she wear the bulky parka. She eyed the mittens. No, she needed a firm grip on those shelves. Maybe the exertion would keep her warm.

The discarded parka looked a little like a body, arms outflung on the rough floor. If the mittens were a little closer to the sleeves...She pulled both to the corner and rearranged them, then stood to survey the result. Not bad, especially in the dark corner. The parka, draped over a bunched-up edge of the tarp, resembled a person lying on her stomach, arm stretched out, mitten covering the hand. It might satisfy Greg if he peeked in.

The soft cotton rope hanging on the side wall was too long, but the gardening shears finally hacked though one of them. She twisted it into a coil, looped it over her head and under one arm, leaving her hands free while she carried the rope. Time to climb.

The close spacing of the shelves made it awkward. They were about a foot deep and eighteen inches apart, forcing her to bend her body around those between her feet and her hands. It was also noisy. Some of the cans and bottles she pushed aside teetered on the shelf, then plummeted to the floor. If Greg was on the property, he'd soon be jerking the door open and pulling her down. *Or shooting me down.*

Propelled by fear of discovery, she clambered higher, putting a foot on the next shelf. It moved. She stopped, caught her breath, and took another cautious step up. Nothing happened. Another step. A screech of nails and the shelving pulled a quarter-inch away from the wall.

The wooden beam was still a couple of yards above her. She clung to the shelving, not daring to move. But she had to; she couldn't hang there forever, and her weight was pulling against the nails. Hand trembling, she reached for another shelf. It felt stable. She put more weight on it. No movement. Maybe it was just one weak place. She hoisted her feet to the next level. It held, and she raised an arm for the next hand grip. With the shift of weight, the nails screeched again, all the way out of the wall.

She grabbed, trying to close her palms around another shelf, anything solid. All she found was air, and her feet were slipping. Twisting, she flailed her arms. As she pitched sideways, one hand caught at the chain but missed. The heavy metal swayed, slapping into her right leg.

Crying out in pain, she grabbed with the other hand and caught the chain, but her body was slipping downward, toward the boat. She got the other hand around the metal, then her thighs, and hung there, between the beam and the boat.

The chain, too short for much sway and weighted down by the boat, soon steadied.

Up or down? No choice. She had to go up. If she went down, she would be trapped, the climb back down to the floor her only option. Wrapping her legs around the chain, she gripped with both feet, then let go of the chain with one hand. Her body started slipping downward, and she slapped the hand back around the chain, a little higher than it had been before, and pulled herself up. Only an inch or two, but higher. More than she'd slipped downward?

She tried again, pushing with her feet. Her weight still pulled her down, but not as much. Reaching high for the next handhold, she pulled herself up and paused for a minute. Both arms ached now. The beam was less than a yard above her, but a yard was a long way when her pace was measured in inches. There was no way to rest—not while gripping a chain. She had to go on.

By the time she got to the top, she was drenched in sweat, and her arms and legs were leaden. But if she could just get them limbered up, the rest was going to be easy. She'd get out the window, retrieve the phone from wherever Greg had dropped it, and call for help.

Had she not been so tired, she'd have walked the beam to the window; she'd traversed narrower ones than this. But, not trusting her legs, she opted to straddle it and scoot, trying to ignore the spider webs.

The one-paned window had no latch; it hadn't been designed to open. Breaking it would come with a lot of noise and probably some cuts. Best get to it before Greg came back.

Wrapping her legs around the beam, she lifted the cotton rope from around her neck and shoulder and used one end to tie a loop around the beam.

Sitting with both hands behind her, gripping the beam, she raised one foot. Careful to maintain her precarious balance, she kicked at the center of the pane. Most of the glass flew outward, but a fine shower of shards coated her lap. She kicked again at the sharp edges of glass framing the gap. There was no way to get them all. If she took off her heavy sweater, wrapped it around her arm...No. She'd have to put the sweater back on or leave bare skin exposed, and she couldn't shake all the glass out of it. It would slice into her flesh every time she moved. *The glass that keeps on giving.*

She'd hang onto the rope and go out feet first, trying to stay in the middle, away from the broken glass, and say her prayers. All the way down.

She tied the loose end of the rope around her waist as insurance, in case she lost her grip. Then she turned on the narrow beam, edged backward to the window frame, and worked her legs through the opening. Dangling, she let go of the frame and grasped the rope, first with one hand, then the other. It burned through her bare hands before she could grip it tight enough to stop her free fall.

Her right foot hit the ground first, absorbing the shock. Pain shot through the ankle and the calf, where the chain had hit. The leg crumpled beneath her. Gritting her teeth to keep from screaming, she lay still. Had she broken it? She had to move, had to find out. Drawing in a deep breath, she sat up. The calf still hurt, but there was no intense jab. She stood, favoring the other leg. Still no jab. She took a step and winced, but the ankle didn't appear to be broken. It was probably a bad sprain. Her left arm was wet, her sweater sleeve torn and soaked in blood.

I'm screwed. There's no way I can get to the Explorer, and this little adventure has accomplished nothing. She sat down, her back against the wall, one hand holding the wet edges of the sweater together against her arm.

Greg had just tried to murder her, but nobody was going to believe that. The parka and mittens were there, inside the locked shed, but he would claim he'd found them, along with the pulled-down shelves and the broken window. Any explanation he came up with would be more believable than the truth—her climb to that beam. Nobody was going to believe that. At least nobody but Laura and Sam, and probably Dee and Dave. All of them were aware of her gymnastics background.

But this climb had been dicey. Sarah shivered. *If I get out of this one, I'm going to start working out again.*

But first, she had to get out of this one.

Her only chance was to find the phone and call for help. Greg might be back any time, and she'd be out in the open, unable to move very fast. She'd better get started.

It was slow going, but every time she tried to speed up, the pain in her ankle jolted her to a stop. *Slow and steady, Sarah. Get the phone, call for help, then get under cover. And hope Greg doesn't open the shed to check on me.* The path between the shed and the cabin was so churned up, she wouldn't have to worry about tracks, if she drug her feet a little. No problem in her current condition.

What would he do if he saw one? Go into the shed and shoot her parka?

She should go back inside—get it and her mittens, before she froze. *No.* She couldn't go back in there. A wave of nausea washed over her at the thought. She'd rather freeze than take the chance of being locked in there again, with no way out. Once those shelves had fallen, there was no way to climb.

She'd made it to the front corner of the shed. The yard, all the way to the cabin door, was empty. She'd have to move out a little farther to find the phone.

Greg had pushed it into a drift of snow alongside the path, so deep only the top edge was visible. She wiped the wet screen with the sleeve of her sweater. Nothing happened. Had the snow damaged it? *Now I'm really screwed.*

She'd have to try for the Explorer.

Her sleeve was soaked, and perspiration dampened the back of her sweater. When she stopped moving, it would turn icy. But how long could she keep going? She needed that parka.

No, I don't. I just need a coat, and one of Tracy's will fit me. She had the key. Her only chance of surviving would be to go inside, stop the bleeding and get some warm clothes. With luck, she could be out of the cabin and under cover before Greg got back. She probably couldn't make it to the Explorer, but she might get to the road, and somebody should be looking for her soon. Would they think about the cabin?

It's not like I have a lot of options. She limped to the laundry room door, turning every few feet to brush out the edges of any tracks. Once inside, she rested on the bench for a moment, absorbing the dying warmth of the fireplace. Parkas and coats hung on the pegs above her, but she didn't need one right now, and Greg might notice it missing. She'd find something upstairs.

The kitchen beckoned, but there was no time for food; she had to get out of sight, and the big room had never loomed as cavernous.

The stairs were a challenge, but with the help of the hand rail, she pulled herself up, hobbled into the master bedroom, and dug through the drawers until she found one of Tracy's sweatshirts. After she'd unfolded it and spread it on the bed, she went in search of medical supplies, piling them into the center of the sweatshirt: a tube of antiseptic cream, gauze, adhesive tape, sterile pads, an Ace bandage, Tylenol.

It was time to get out of Greg's room, find a safer place. She folded the sweatshirt around her collection and carried it down the hall, to Lottie's and Gracie's bathroom.

First, a glass of water. Then more with some Tylenol.

Dried blood washed from her hands, pink water swirling toward the drain. Her fingernails were torn and jagged, one torn away from its bed, and she ached in so many places, she couldn't count all of them. Her palms were rope-burned, scratched, cut, and imbedded with splinters. A nail had torn away a flap of skin on her thumb. The most serious wound, the one she had to take care of, was the gash in her arm. It was still bleeding. How much blood had she lost?

She glanced at the shower, the fastest way to scrub her skin clean before using the antibiotic. No, if he came back while she was in there, she wouldn't hear him. But he'd hear the shower. The sink would have to do. First, she had to close the bathroom door and cover the window with a towel. It faced the back, but she couldn't be sure how far the glow would spread.

Once the window was covered, she stripped off the sweater and went to work with soap and water as hot as she could stand it. She'd have to try to tape the edges of the cut, which would be difficult with one hand. Even more difficult without scissors to cut the lengths of tape. *Why didn't I think to look for some?*

Gracie had a pair: blunt nosed, with dull blades, but they might saw through the tape.

They did, with a lot of work, and Sarah cut a dozen lengths, laying them out along the edge of the vanity. With one hand, she fumbled to hold the cut closed while taping across it. Blood still oozed from the wound.

With a little more work, she got one end of the Ace bandage taped just above one edge of the cut, wrapped it around the arm, holding it with her teeth while she tightened it over the tape, and fastened the bottom with another piece of tape. It wasn't tight enough, and she now had nothing to support the ankle, but it had diminished the bleeding, at least for now.

While she was pulling the sweatshirt over her head, a glow flashed across the bedroom window, and she flipped off the light. A car was coming down the lane, into the yard. Probably Greg's Tahoe.

Chapter 30
Saturday Evening

_____

Sarah tried the phone again, almost whimpering in frustration, willing the display to light up. Maybe the battery was dead. The charger was in the Explorer, but there might be one, maybe two, in the master bedroom.

It was too late to search. Greg would be in the house any moment.

What other choices do you have, Sarah? You've got to risk it.

Maybe not. The phone might just be damp inside. She wrapped it in a towel, then pushed it under Lottie's pillow. *God, how I'd like to crawl under that quilt and get warm. Wake up and discover this has all been a bad dream.*

She'd wait a few minutes, give the phone time to warm up, if it was going to, and for Greg to settle into whatever he was going to do. Then, if she had to, she'd try for a charger in his bedroom.

He rarely came upstairs before bedtime. At least he hadn't while she'd been there, taking care of Lottie and Gracie. Now that he was alone, his patterns might have changed. She'd have to wait and see.

The girls' room looked the same as it had when Sarah had left the cabin: beds unmade, discarded clothing on the floor, a book, open face down, on the foot of Gracie's bed. Beside it were several stuffed animals, including Rudy, the stuffed dog Sarah had picked up from the floor the night the girls had run away. Gracie had taken Lucy. *I wonder what Lottie took to comfort her?* Probably nothing; being reunited with her father would be enough. Sarah felt a little stab of envy.

She picked up Lottie's sketch pad and flipped through it, stopping at the troubling drawing: the woman and two girls with the ominous, undefined shape looming behind them, and the man running in their direction. Tracy, Lottie, and Gracie. Greg ominous, Pete Bennett trying to find them. *I wonder why Tracy is not holding Lottie's and Gracie's hands?* Did Lottie feel that alone, disconnected even from her mother? Poor little girl; she'd been carrying a heavy secret.

Memories flooded back as Sarah sat on Gracie's bed, gazing at the room: Lottie and Gracie bending over their drawing pads; sitting on the rug, pulling on their socks; curled up in bed while she read to them. Their voices reverberated. Gracie: "Can we go outside? Can we have pancakes for breakfast? You have pretty hair. Yuk, no gray cake. I didn't get to throw even one snowball."

Lottie: "Is Mom lost? You don't know anything! Mom always makes us hot chocolate. He always lies. Please don't tell."

Downstairs, playing their racing game, watching *Frozen*, interviewing each other with the recorder, voices low, so Sarah couldn't hear.

She sat up straighter, searching her memory, making connections. She should have paid more attention to the girls. They all should have, especially Mason and Ursall. They were the detectives.

She put the drawing pad down. Even with the doors open, no sounds came from the floor below. What was Greg doing? Eating take-out? Having a beer? Climbing the stairs?

He hadn't gone out to check the shed; she would have heard the outside door open. Would he do it from up here, where he could see the perimeter of the entire property? She was staking her life on the premise that he'd skip Lottie's and Gracie's room because he couldn't see much of the shed from there. Sarah's old room would serve better for that.

The phone still didn't work. She had to go, before he came upstairs—find the charger and get back, so she could charge the phone.

No. It was too risky; she couldn't do it. *I'm not that brave.* There was no way to avoid making noise. The floors on this level were wood; they would creak in places she'd never before noticed—and she was limping.

But if I don't call for help, I'm going to die in here.

She had taken only two steps when a faint beep stopped her. The phone. It was working, and she'd neglected to turn it off. Had Greg heard? Bandaged fingers fumbling under the pillow, she found the phone and turned it off. Finally, a little luck. *Thank you, God.*

But she'd made two mistakes: leaving the phone on, and bandaging the fingers. She'd need dexterity to text, and there was no room for mistakes—not if she wanted to live. *So, slow down and think. You have to get this right.*

If she called 9-1-1, help would come. But what could she tell them? She was injured, but Greg could disclaim any involvement. As far as he was concerned, she must have broken into the shed, accidentally locked herself in, and injured herself getting out. He hadn't even been home.

How long would she remain safe? He couldn't let her live; she knew too much. And he'd never be brought to justice for Amy's and Tracy's murders.

Sarah sat still, thinking again about the shed, her parka, the way she'd left it arranged. What if somebody saw Greg try to kill her? Mason or Ursall or even Sheriff Maynor? Would it matter if he'd only shot a parka, if his intent had been murder? It was worth a try if she could set it up: call 9-1-1, then lure him into the shed with the gun...but whom could she trust to help her?

Nobody here, on this side of the country. Bill had divulged privileged information to Jake and would drop Sarah in a minute if her case threatened Brad Denton's. Jake? He was Greg's friend, and even though he'd apologized after Bill talked to him, those ties were still deep. Would he betray Greg?

She had to put her life in the hands of somebody. Who would be the better option? Probably Bill, because he would have another motive for helping her; it might also get Brad Denton off the hook. And he might have more credibility with law enforcement.

"No time for full story," she texted him. "Need help. Greg locked me in his shed. Intends to leave me there until I die. Has a story concocted that I accidentally locked myself in. Doesn't know yet I got out. When he does, he'll track me down. I'm injured, but I have a plan."

His message came back within two minutes. "Where are you?"

Would he tell Greg? She had no choice but to trust him.

"Hiding inside the cabin and he's downstairs. Can you bring somebody to arrest him? If you sneak in through the woods, you might catch him attempting murder."

"Too dangerous. I'm on my way. Call 9-1-1."

"No. Wait."

"Okay. But not a good idea. Too dangerous."

"Wasting time. He's going to find me. I'm hurt. Can't move fast. If he believes somebody is coming to look for me, he'll go out there to kill me."

Sarah wiped blood off the phone and waited. Her fingers ached. She'd medicate them again when she finished texting.

Bill's message came back. "I'll call Maynor, call the cops, get out there as fast as I can."

"Come quietly. Text when in place."

"Okay. How long?"

"Soon after you text, so be ready. Have to go now."

"On my way."

While she waited for Bill to text back, she set the phone to vibrate and drafted a message to Laura, the one person Sarah knew she could trust. "No time to explain. Urgent you do exactly what I ask. Call Greg Agerton right away." Sarah checked the number, then filled it in. "Tell him you're worried about me. I told you I was going to the cabin to check something out in his shed. I should have been back hours ago. Has he seen me or the Ford Explorer I was driving, or heard from me? You're really, really worried."

Now she had to wait before she sent it—give Bill time to do his part and get into position, then send the text.

Blood stained the sleeve of the sweatshirt now, but she could do nothing about it. She couldn't even wash her hands; Greg might hear water running through the pipes. She crept back into the small bathroom where she'd left the medical supplies laid out on a thick towel, and cleaned her hands and fingers as best she could with tissue. The ointment and Band-Aids were trickier, using one injured hand.

I can't even swear—not out loud, at least.

On the plus side, she had plenty of time, as long as she didn't make any noise, and Greg didn't come upstairs.

When she finished dressing her wounds, she rolled the medical supplies up in the towel. There was no place to hide them, so she left them at the end of the counter, near the wall. If Greg came upstairs, she'd step into the bathtub, behind the shower curtain.

No sound came, not even the voices of the TV journalists, reporting the evening news. If things went well, they'd have a riveting story for tomorrow night's broadcast. On second thought, they'd have a story, even if things didn't go well, the only difference being, she wouldn't be around to hear it.

Finally, the phone vibrated with Bill's text. "At the back of the cabin, just west of the shed, behind some shrubs. Ready when you are."

Sarah sent the text to Laura. Her cousin would be on top of her phone, waiting for Sarah to call her.

Laura texted "Okay, but please tell me what's going on."

"No time. Call him now. No more texts."

She waited, counting off the seconds. Finally, a sound came from downstairs: Greg's phone. Sarah strained to hear, but couldn't make out his words. *I hope he's talking to Laura, that he didn't get a call from somebody else.* Like Roberta, who could probably gossip for an hour.

The voices stopped, and he was moving. She sent the text to Bill. "Any time now."

There was a creak. He was coming up the stairs. The call had come from Bill, not Laura. He'd betrayed her.

She stepped into the tub as silently as she could and pulled the shower curtain. The hooks clicked against the bar. Another mistake; she should have pulled it into position earlier.

With clumsy fingers, she pulled the phone from her pocket and dialed 9-1-1: "I'm at Greg Agerton's cabin and he's trying to kill me," she whispered. What was the address? All she knew was the name of the road, so she gave the dispatcher that and ended the call.

Pressing her spine against the end of the tub enclosure and taking shallow breaths, she stood still and waited.

The footsteps stopped. Where was he? The master bedroom. He went inside, then came out again, walking faster, receding.

He came to get the gun. He's going out to kill me. Or, at least, my parka. Bill didn't tip him off.

Sarah crawled out of the tub and hurried to the window. *I wish I could see Greg's face when he realizes he's been set up.*

The back door opened, sending a shaft of light into the darkness. He strode across the yard, fumbled with the bar over the shed door, and opened it. When he flicked on the flashlight, Sarah caught a glimpse of something in his other hand. A gun? She couldn't be sure until he fired two shots in rapid succession.

Figures emerged from the shadows then, from both directions, converging on Greg, still standing in the open doorway, gun in hand.

Sarah sank to her knees, a sob escaping as she lowered her face into her hands. The tension ebbed away as she cried, leaving her as limp and empty as a collapsed balloon.

It had been close, so close, but she was safe. She rose to her feet. She wanted to see Greg in his defeat—wanted him to see her and know she had beat him.

She limped down the hall, hobbled down the stairs, and out into the night. By the time she got there, Greg was already hand-cuffed. And in the distance, far down the main road, a car hurtled toward them, lights flashing and siren wailing. 9-1-1 to the rescue.

Sarah hurried to get closer, so she could watch Greg Agerton being led away in handcuffs. *For murdering my parka.* A giggle started deep in her throat, threatening to erupt. *It's exhaustion, Sarah, you always do that when you're tired.*

"No, it's just funny," she said aloud as Bill, a deep frown etching his forehead, picked her up.

The car with the flashing lights had pulled into the yard, and the woman driving it had turned off the siren. Bill put Sarah into the back seat and climbed in beside her. Warmth crept through her body. It had been a long day, and she was so tired, so sleepy. If she could rest, just for a little while, she'd be able to understand what they were asking her.

"Sarah, are you all right?" Bill Ayers's musical voice.

She tried to open her eyes, but they weren't communicating with her brain.

"It's partly the sedative," a man said. "Along with her injuries, blood loss, exposure. Right now, she needs rest more than anything else."

Pain shot up Sarah's ankle, and she let out a yelp. A man in scrubs was pressing his fingers into the flesh around her ankle. Sarah sat up. She was on a bed in a small, open cubicle.

"Sorry," the man said. "I couldn't see any fractures in the X-ray. It looks like a bad sprain. You'll need to stay off it for a while. I'm more concerned about the arm. It's a nasty cut, but the doctor who will be operating is a good plastic surgeon, so the scars shouldn't be too bad."

"Operating?" Sarah sat up straighter. "I need to call my cousin, tell her—"

"It's minor surgery, and it won't take long. But give me the number. I'll call."

"Just be sure to tell her I'm okay."

"Doctor," a woman said, from the chair beside the bed. "I need to talk to her."

She had dark, curly hair and honey-gold skin, almost the color of her khaki uniform. Patches adorned the shoulders, and a holstered gun hung on her belt.

The doctor shrugged. "Okay with me, if she's up to it. But they'll be taking her to the O.R. any minute, and she's a little groggy from the sedatives."

Bill Ayers leaned one shoulder against the wall, watching the doctor. "You okay?" he asked.

Sarah nodded. "I'll live. A few hours ago, I wasn't so sure."

"Yeah, but you got your killer," he said.

"Not necessarily." The woman's hazel eyes assessed Sarah. "I'm Deputy Jody Martin, and if you're up to it, I have a few questions for you."

"Oh." Jody Martin was a woman. "Deputy?" Sarah asked. "What happened to Mason and Ursall? And Maynor? And what do you mean, not necessarily?"

Bill grinned. "They declined my invitation to the party. One of them said something about entrapment, and another questioned my source of information. I seem to recall one asking if I'd been drinking. I can't remember which was which, and I didn't have time to sort it all out. Fortunately, Deputy Martin here was willing to dance. She's running against Maynor in the upcoming election."

Jody Martin flushed. "That's not why I—"

Bill smiled and in a voice almost like a lullaby, he said, "I know it's not. I was just trying to point out to Sarah that you're smarter than Maynor. But then, most everybody is." His gaze lingered on her face for a moment, and she flushed.

"What do you mean not necessarily," Sarah asked again.

"We don't have any proof he's a killer," Deputy Martin said. "Firing bullets into an empty shed isn't against the law, and Greg Agerton has a solid alibi for the time his wife disappeared."

"No, he doesn't. It's been there all along. It's just that nobody asked the right questions. Or asked the right people."

Two young men in scrubs pushed a gurney to the door.

"Sorry to interrupt," one of them said. "But we're taking her to surgery now. There's a waiting room up there. Somebody will come and get you when she's out of recovery. It shouldn't take more than—"

Sarah talked faster. "Lottie and Gracie. We never asked them if they actually saw Tracy the day she disappeared. Gracie said her mother had a headache. Both girls said she went for a walk while they were drinking their hot chocolate."

Bill stepped out of the cubicle to make room for the gurney. Deputy Martin stared at Sarah. "We know all that. Agerton was with them—"

Sarah kept talking while the men positioned the gurney next to the bed and helped her shift onto it.

"Greg Agerton did not normally spend much time with his step-daughters. He was setting up his alibi. One of the girls—I can't remember which one now—said Tracy always called them in for hot chocolate after they'd been playing in the snow. The key word is always."

The men rolled the gurney out the door, and Sarah craned her head toward Bill.

"The girls found a recorder in the bookshelves. It's in the cabin, zipped into a stuffed dog on Gracie's bed. Find it. Tracy's voice is going to be on that recorder, calling the girls in for hot chocolate, and probably saying something about going for a walk. She did both often enough to give Greg plenty of opportunity to record her."

Chapter 31
Late Saturday Night and Sunday Morning

Her eyes closed, Sarah smiled.

"We've got to stop meeting like this," Dave Wheeler had just said. Those were the same words he'd uttered the second time she'd walked down Caro's stairs to find him waiting at the bottom. And, just like this, he'd visited her in the hospital in Sacramento, bringing her yellow Shasta Daisies and a book. She murmured, "Did you bring me a Michener?"

He bent forward, his sensual lips brushing her cheek and, just to see what they felt like, she turned her head so her lips touched his. They weren't as soft as she'd expected. Probably because they were pressing against hers.

Oh my God! What did I just do? She pulled away, opening her eyes to the bright lights of the recovery room and Jake's face, smiling down at her. She'd been dreaming—dreaming of Dave.

How the hell am I going to explain that kiss? She closed her eyes again and went back to sleep.

❖❖❖

Jake was still there when she woke the next time. This room had a window, and she looked out into darkness. "What time is it?"

"Almost two a.m."

"How long have you been here?"

"Bill called me when you went into surgery and told me what happened. I came and sat with him for a while until you were in recovery, and we knew you were okay. Then he went home to get some sleep. I decided to stick around for a while, to see if you need anything."

"I'm surprised they didn't kick you out. Don't they have visiting hours?"

"Yeah, but family can stay."

"Family?"

"Yeah. We're engaged, remember?"

Sarah laughed, then remembered her dream and felt heat spread ing upward from under her jaw. "I...Lottie and Gracie... have you heard anything? Are they okay?"

"They're fine. Bennett had leased a cabin weeks ago under a fictitious name, up in that area close to the Canadian border, north of Malone. He and the girls were holed up there, waiting for the search to die down enough to leave. He contacted the police department as soon as Cindy called and told him he was a suspect in Tracy's disappearance."

"So where are they now?"

"Cindy got in last night. She's out at the cabin with the girls. Last I heard, Bennett was still being questioned by Mason and Ursall."

"Do you have any idea how long they're going to keep me? I need to get back to New York. My classes start tomorrow."

He shook his head. "I don't think that's going to happen."

"But I thought...the snowstorm is over. My flight should go out."

"It's not that. They've got long lines at the airport, and even if they release you today, I don't see how you can get back to New York, much less your classes, when you're supposed to stay off that ankle."

"I'll figure something out."

He smiled. "I suspect you will. And I'll help, any way I can. Maybe if I drove you back—"

"You're a good friend, Jake."

"No. No, I'm not. If I'd believed you when you tried to tell me about Greg, helped you, maybe none of this would have happened."

"The two of you had been friends for a long time. And you're loyal. I like that. Now let's see how soon I can get out of here, and we can get on the road."

"Okay." He squeezed her hand and rose from the chair. "Call me when they're ready to release you. In the meantime, I'd better grab a little sleep so I can drive tonight."

But Bill Ayers had other ideas. He came to see Sarah later that morning, after Jake left.

"They may have to cut Greg Agerton loose."

"You're kidding! After everything I went through? After he tried to kill me?"

"No proof. He says he was shooting at a rat."

Sarah sat up straighter, wincing when the pressure of her arm against the mattress sent a jolt of pain up her shoulder. "A rat! That no-good, lying—"

Bill dropped into the chair beside the bed. "He no longer has a solid alibi for Tracy's disappearance, but that's a long way from proof of murder. He had no motive. He wasn't going to inherit. Despite all the searching, we didn't find a body. So, no motive, no weapon, no body, no case."

"But he tried to kill me! He shot my parka. Isn't that evidence?" She fell back onto the pillow. "The Case of the Murdered Parka. Has a nice ring to it."

He gave her a sharp glance. "You okay?"

"Yeah. Just tired and frustrated. And mad, too, I guess. A rat!" She stared up at the ceiling.

"One piece of news—Bennett has an alibi. He was in a grocery store up near the Canadian border, stocking up on groceries, when Tracy disappeared. Looks like he drove straight up there from the airport. He has a receipt and witnesses who saw him.

That puts a big hole in the detectives' theory that the two of you were colluding to grab Tracy."

"Bill, they're not stupid. They've got to know it was Greg."

"Maybe so, but they don't have any way to prove it, so they're taking a harder look at Brad Denton, and they still have you in their sights. They say they have some evidence."

Sarah pulled herself erect again. The lug wrench with the phony DNA. She'd forgotten about it. That put her in the same category as Greg. Maybe worse: no alibi, no body, but what they thought was a weapon. She wasn't going back to New York with Jake; she'd be lucky if they didn't arrest her.

"I have an idea I want to run by you," Bill said.

"Okay. I'm listening."

"I gather you don't have much affection for detectives Ursall and Mason."

"No. But to be fair, I suppose they're just doing their jobs. It's me—I don't have any use for detectives, don't trust them."

"What about Maynor?"

"I don't know. He didn't impress me if that's what you're asking. Where are you going with this?"

"I think we can figure this whole thing out if we put our heads together—me, you, and Jake. We were out there every day, either in the cabin or with Greg, searching."

Sarah shook her head. "Ursall and Mason aren't going to believe anything we come up with. They're not interested in anything I have to say."

"What about Jody...Deputy Martin? I suspect she'd cooperate with us, especially since she's running against Maynor."

Sarah smiled. "I can just see it. She solves a case, pulls it out from under him right before the election."

"So you're in?"

"I'm in. Where do we start?"

"I'll talk to Jake and Jody Martin to see if they're willing. If they are, we can meet in my conference room later this afternoon. I'll let you know."

◆◆◆

Jake picked Sarah up as soon as she was released from the hospital and took her to Bill's office. They took chairs next to Jody Martin, who sat at one end of the long table.

"You were right about the recorder," Jody said, "and I talked to the little girls this morning. They never saw their mother that day. Greg Agerton no longer has an alibi for the time of his wife's disappearance, and since she hasn't turned up, it's reasonable to assume she's dead—and that he probably killed her."

Jake's face had gone pale. "You mean Tracy was already dead, and he played that recording so they would think she was still alive?"

"Probably ran in to get a scarf for the snowman, or to go to the bathroom—whatever—then did the same thing to shut it off. Then the same scenario for the walk. Or just hurried into the cabin before the girls got inside. It wouldn't have taken much to fool them since it was pretty routine."

"But before that. When did he...?"

Sarah frowned. "I think, from what Gracie said about Tracy having a headache, that Greg told them their mother was lying down that morning and would come downstairs later. So he might have killed her the night before."

Deputy Martin looked up from the recorder she'd set up on the table. "That's what Ayers and I figured. We think Agerton had been planning it for a while. He had to do it while they were up here at the cabin, where it's more remote. Your visit was the catalyst for doing it on this trip—a reliable adult witness during the critical time between the disappearance and the body being found. The news bulletin about the escaped convict was just an unexpected bonus."

She stopped, staring into space. "I wonder, if it had been just the girls there, if they'd been the only witnesses, if the detectives would have questioned them more? Dug deeper?" She sighed. "Anyway, we have a more pressing problem. To convict Agerton, we have to find the body. Where did he hide it? The entire property was searched, and everything for miles around. They even brought in dogs."

Bill nodded. "I would swear her body isn't out there anywhere. We searched every day, sometimes going over the same area we'd covered the day before."

"Did you look in the shed?" Sarah asked. "That first night?"

Jake and Bill exchanged a glance. "No, not the shed. There was no reason. Greg said she'd taken a walk to meet you on that abandoned road."

"She wasn't there—in the shed," Jake said. "Some other searchers looked in there. I saw them."

"When was that? Was it before Tuesday?" Sarah asked. She shook her head. "Never mind. It had to be, because all those searchers were here on Sunday, all over the place."

"Why did you ask about the shed?" Deputy Martin asked, "and what is significant about Tuesday?"

Sarah bit her lip. "I...Greg drugged me—and the girls—Tuesday night. I couldn't figure out why because he...he didn't do anything. I found the drugs and hid them so he couldn't use them again. But he was so desperate to get them back, he threatened me."

Jake's hand settled on her shoulder, and his voice was gentle. "Why?"

"I don't know. I thought..." His hand tightened a little. *He's trying to support me, help me.* "I thought he might be molesting Lottie. She was troubled, and they had a strange relationship. I couldn't think of any other reason. The girls and I were confined to the cabin, so we wouldn't have been aware of anything he was doing outside, even if we weren't drugged."

Jody Martin's face looked a little paler. She closed her eyes for a moment before she looked back at Sarah. "What does that have to do with the shed?"

"Oh!" Sarah sat up straight. "I never would have put the two together—Tuesday night and the shed. The next morning, I woke up early and went for a walk to try to clear my head. That's when I found Tracy's bracelet out by that strange, zig-zag path."

Jody nodded. "But our CSI people didn't find anything out there."

"No, I didn't either, but something was bothering me about it. Yesterday, the snow had melted, and I could see a pattern of broken branches within the zig-zag path. I thought maybe it was snowshoes, that Tracy had lost her bracelet along a well-known snowshoe path. But when I was locked in the shed, I realized something else that had been bugging me. I went in there Wednesday morning, too. Everything was covered with dust, except something that didn't register at the time. The sled—that bright blue sled. And the runners on it would have been about the same width as that pattern. I think Greg moved Tracy's body the night he drugged us. He strapped her to that sled and took her somewhere, and her bracelet fell off along the way."

She paused. "Oh, I just realized. That's why he was so desperate to get the drugs; he was afraid somebody would believe me and make the connection. And that's why he was in the woods the night the girls were taken. He was afraid there might be something else out there that would incriminate him. So he left Lottie and Gracie alone and went to search the area."

"If he were smart," Jody said, "he would have taken the body to a place that had already been searched, so she wouldn't be found for a while."

"The mine!" Jake and Bill said, almost at the same time.

"He waited until after the mine had been searched," Jake said. "That was when? Monday. I remember now, because we knocked off a little early when we finished." He frowned. "So why did he wait until Tuesday night to move her?"

Nobody said anything. Bill got up and went to the console. Sarah recognized the sheaf of papers he picked up: his time line.

"The snow," he said, looking up from his notes. "All that snow we had. It quit snowing Monday evening. He had to have snow after he moved her, to hide the sled tracks. It stopped snowing."

"Oh." The expression on Greg's face that night, when he looked out the window, came back to Sarah. "I couldn't figure out why he changed so much that evening. He brought several bottles of wine back to the cabin, said they'd finished at the mine. He had dinner with me and the girls—the first time he'd ever done that. Then, after they went to bed, we drank a glass of wine—"

She folded her arms across her stomach. "He glanced out and saw it had stopped snowing. His voice sounded odd. It was almost like he was disappointed. And then he poured the rest of the wine into our glasses. He planned to drug us that night, didn't he?"

Jody had her phone out. "I'll get a search started."

"If you can, do it without Maynor knowing," Bill said. "He'll go out there with a bunch of reporters and hold a press conference—take credit for solving the entire case."

Jody grinned. "He's out of town. Why do you think I chose today for this?"

Bill put his time line back on the console. "Even if we're right, if Tracy is there, we still haven't tied it to Greg. Where was the body between the time he killed her—probably Thursday night or Friday morning—and Tuesday night, when he moved her?"

Sarah leaned back and closed her eyes. Something was there, just under the surface, something Lottie had said. Or had it been Gracie?

"All that time we were out there, cold and tired, looking for her," Jake said, his voice bitter. "He knew she was dead. Everything he put us through, and Sarah, and those little girls—"

"That first night, when we went out to search," Bill said, his voice slow and measured, "we found Tracy's phone and scarf. We know now Greg must have planted them to bolster the premise that somebody had kidnapped her."

Sarah nodded. "That's what he had in his pocket, under his coat, that night. Not a gun."

"He put them close to that old two-track road, to make it look like somebody had put her in a vehicle. But he must have known it would raise questions because that's not the direction Tracy would have taken if she'd really gone to meet Sarah. Was he trying to keep us away from the bridge?"

Jake shook his head. "There would be no reason. We searched out there the next day. And later, with the dogs, using her scarf."

Sarah's head jerked up. "The blue scarf? That's the one you used for scent? But that wasn't Tracy's. Lottie said it was one she'd bought as a gift for me. It would have little scent on it. According to the girls, Tracy bought a matching one for herself, only it was red."

The room fell silent as the implication sunk in. The dog searches had been fruitless, just as Greg had known they would be.

"Then where was Tracy's real scarf? The one she wore before she bought the new ones?" Bill asked.

"On the snowman." Images were surging through Sarah's mind again: the red scarf Sarah had found by the snow forts after the moose had destroyed them. Lottie holding it, crying. Greg yelling, yanking Gracie's arm, pulling her from behind the snowman, angry because they were outside. Then, the next day, he paid little attention when they made plans to have a snowball fight.

"Oh, my God!" She struggled, trying to rise to her feet. She had to get to the bathroom; she was going to be sick. She ran, hand over her mouth.

Jake stood outside the door when Sarah came out. "Are you all right?"

"I'll never be all right." She looked at the others. "He hid her in plain sight. She was right in front of us all the time. In front of me when I arrived. In the snowman."

Somebody gasped. Sarah took a moment to gather her thoughts. "Gracie said 'Daddy did most of it.' He'd started it the night before, while the girls slept. He couldn't do the entire thing. Snowmen don't magically appear, and he needed an alibi. So he tied her around that bird feeder...he tied her to it and covered her enough to start a snowman. Probably in the bottom.

Jake nodded. "She's...she was small, like Sarah. It wouldn't have taken much snow to cover her."

"The bottom was too big for the rest," Sarah said. "And it was the biggest snowman I've ever seen."

"So, when the girls woke up," Jody said, "he went through the charade of Tracy having a headache. Then they went out to...to build a snowman. Around their mother...to hide her dead body."

Sarah's voice was strangled, almost a sob. "We played out there, having fun around that snowman. Until Wednesday morning, when it was torn apart."

"But the dogs," Jody said. "They would have found her."

"No," Bill said. "The dogs were never close to the cabin. Just out in the woods. They didn't figure there was any need, the area had been so thoroughly searched before Maynor ever got out there."

Jake slumped in a chair, staring at Sarah. "It makes so much sense now," he said. "Cooping you and the girls up inside the cabin all the time, keeping everybody else away."

"And all those nights, when he was out there prowling around, when I thought he was grieving, he was probably packing more snow around that snowman."

Jake rose, walked the half-dozen or so steps separating them, and put an arm around her. "Sarah, I'm so sorry. None of us saw this. I should have seen—when he disabled your car—he was so paranoid about keeping you and the girls inside the cabin. Wouldn't even let you out long enough to go to the grocery store."

"That, and he needed to keep her here for an alibi until that body was gone," Jody said.

Sarah put a palm on Jake's cheek, against the silkiness of his beard. "You tried to help. You fixed my car. The day we had the snowball fight. Gracie hid behind the snowman. Greg came home and jerked her out, so angry he hurt her arm. Tracy was in there, Jake."

"I know, Sarah. I know." Tears glistened in his own eyes as he folded his arms around her. She leaned against him and cried.

Chapter 32
Monday

S arah stood at the open door of her apartment building, her gaze on Jake Nichols's back as he walked down the steps. He had never mentioned the kiss in the recovery room. *And he never will, unless I bring it up.*

He would have a long drive home and she had to be in class Tuesday, already a day late. She'd called to let them know and to tell them Tracy wouldn't be coming back. They already knew, of course. The press had descended early that morning, digging for every morsel of news. Reporters had thronged the street outside Sarah's hotel. Some waited in the parking lot, too, ambushing them when she, Jake, and Bill tried to sneak out the back door. Jake led her to his Silverado, suitcase in hand, with Bill on the other side, shielding her as best he could.

Then the reporters had focused on Sarah and her escape from the shed. But as the hours ticked by, the ugly details of Tracy's murder leaked out, splashed across every newspaper in the country: *The Snowman Murder*. Lottie and Gracie would see it, hear it. Nobody could protect them from that. It would haunt them for the rest of their lives. Greg hadn't just killed a woman—probably two; he had shattered countless other lives. *And almost took mine.*

They'd found Tracy's body in the mine and traces of her DNA on the bird feeder.

"Greg Agerton won't be killing any more women," Jody Martin had said when she called.

Sarah shuddered; she might have been next. "What I can't figure out is why. Why did he kill her? If she didn't trust him enough to give him access to her money, it's not likely he was going to inherit."

"No, the girls do. But he was hoping to hang onto them. They were also beneficiaries of some hefty insurance policies. I guess he figured, even if he couldn't keep the girls long enough to get his hands on the inheritance, he'd be able to get that insurance money."

"It must be a lot."

Jody laughed. "Just a few million."

Another reason not to let people know about my inheritance. "From what I'm hearing on the news, I suspect you're going to be the next sheriff."

"Maybe, thanks to you and Bill. I won't forget it. If you ever need anything, just let me know. And if you want a job in law enforcement, give me a call."

"Thanks, but no thanks. And it was Bill who got me on the right track, so give him a hug. One from me, too."

Jody laughed again. "I might just do that."

Bill had already given Sarah a hug—a tight one—when they said goodbye. "Promise you'll come back," he said, "so we can show you what it's really like up here."

"You mean when I'm not snowbound in a cabin with two little girls? I'll consider it if you promise to sing to me," she had teased.

"Get your request list ready. We'll make a party of it. Singing, drinking wine, skiing." He held her away from him for a moment so he could look into her eyes. "I mean it, Sarah. Come back and we'll erase all the bad memories with new ones. Good ones."

"Are you going to invite Deputy Martin to that party?"

He smiled. "You don't miss much, do you? I'd like to. The question is whether she'd come."

"Oh, I think she might. Ask her."

Bill and Jake had both proven to be good friends, and she'd promised to return. But not to the cabin, and not for a while.

On the drive, she had talked to Pete Bennett, a brief telephone conversation, and he'd passed the phone to both Lottie and Gracie so she could say goodbye.

"Can you come and see us when we get to our new house?" Gracie had asked.

"I don't know, Gracie. Where is it?"

"Massachusetts. That's where we're going to live now. And Aunt Cindy is in the city. That's close. She's going to come to visit. Maybe you can come with her."

"Maybe." Sarah smiled and said, "Give Lucy a hug for me. Did you find Rudy in your room? He kept me company for a while last night."

"Yeah, but I can't find the recorder. Did you see it?"

"Um...yes, I did. I think Deputy Martin has it now."

"That's okay," Gracie said. "It's not important."

Sarah smiled. Ah, if the girl only knew. Then the smile faded. She would know, eventually. They would know everything. *Damn you, Greg.* "I've got to go, honey. I love you. Tell Lottie I love her, too."

"Wait. My...my dad—my real one—wants to talk to you again."

Pete Bennett hesitated, then said, "I was going to call, to thank you for looking after Lottie and Gracie so well. They talk about you all the time. But, more than that, I want to thank you for helping to put that...that bastard away. And please, stay in contact with the girls. Come and visit them if you can."

Sarah swallowed hard. "Thanks, I appreciate that. I've missed them, and I've always wanted to see Massachusetts."

"Do it soon. I mean it. While the girls have fond memories of you. If you wait, someday they're going to start associating you with all the rest of it."

"You're right, and I'll really try. Maybe someday you can all make a trip to California, and we can take the girls to Disneyland. That would be a nice association."

He laughed. "I'm glad you didn't mention that to them, or I'd never hear the last of it. But I'll certainly keep it in mind. Thanks again."

She ended the call and, turning her head to the window so Jake wouldn't see the tears, she groped for a tissue. He handed her his handkerchief.

"You'll see them again. Massachusetts isn't that far away. You can rent a car and drive over there some weekend."

"I know. It's just—Lottie is already troubled. This is going to be traumatic for her, and I don't want to stir up bad memories."

He nodded. "But you may be the only good memory they have of the past week. Keep that in mind."

She smiled. "Jake, I never did see your paintings, and I wanted to. Do you have any on exhibit in the city?"

"I do. It's a little gallery, and the woman who owns it has been kind enough to take a couple. I'll give you the address."

"Yes, I'd like that." She would go, and if they were good, she'd talk to Erin Brewster about putting some in the Sacramento gallery.

Maybe one way to create new memories for her and Lottie and Gracie would be to meet in a different setting—carry through on the Disneyland idea. They could do it during spring break if Pete approved. Make it a group trip with Eric and Jamie. What a great way to spend some of Caro's money.

She had to find a gym, too, and start working on her gymnastics. *Too bad I can't find a place to hone my bullshit meter, too.* Greg Agerton really had her convinced he was a grieving husband. At least for a few days.

She and Jake had talked little as they drew closer to the city, and he'd stayed only long enough to carry her bags inside.

"I better get on the road. It's a long haul back." He folded his arms around her again, and she leaned in a little. Those arms were strong, supportive. Just like the man. She put a palm on his cheek, stroking his beard, then stepped away. "Call me when you get there."

"Sure thing. Take care of that leg. Don't push it. Okay?" He turned then and walked down the steps.

She had to call Laura, let her know she was home. *No, Not home.* A wave of homesickness washed over her at the thought of those she loved—family and friends—so far away. *My other friends. I have friends in this part of the world now, too, close enough to visit on a weekend.*

She smiled and closed the door, a memory coming back to her—words Dee had spoken when Sarah told her she'd lost too many people—that she didn't have many left in her life: *You manage loss by finding more people to care about you.*

She would call Dee tomorrow right after class and tell her all about the ones she'd found. Dee would like them.

Haunted by the Innocent - Chapter 1

For the first few hours of that Saturday morning in October, Garrison Webb was having a great game at Emerald Creek Golf Course.

He lined up his putt, allowing for the fast green and the slight break to the left, and tapped the ball. It ran a little to the right of his visual line, then straight for the middle of the cup, slowing just enough to drop inside. A perfect putt. Maybe his best ever. That gave him three strokes on a par four, and his first birdie.

The flagpole fell across the ball's path with a soft thump.

"Damn it, Joe, that's not funny." Webb scowled at Joseph Dimitrio, who had dropped the flag. Joe could be a real ass —especially when they were playing for money. But this was going too far.

Dimitrio, crumpling to the ground, didn't respond.

"What the hell!" Was the man having a heart attack?

Something slammed into Webb's right shoulder, and he dropped the putter. Pain drove his attention to the red stain on his polo shirt. He stared at it. A gunshot? He hadn't heard anything, still didn't hear anything, other than the hammering and pounding from the construction site across the slope. Then the closer sound of metal hitting metal shook him from his stupor. He ran, holding his bleeding shoulder with one hand, stumbling over his own feet in his haste to get off the green, away from those open spaces he'd so savored a few minutes earlier.

The rough, with its brush and trees, seemed to recede, so distant he knew he wasn't going to make it. They would provide sparse cover, but he had no place else to go, so he ran. His back muscles tensed, waiting for the next shot.

He tripped and fell. His bladder gave way. He hugged the ground, trying a one-armed crawl, sucking in his breath against the grinding pain in his shoulder. But he was too exposed; he had to get to cover. He pushed to his feet and ran, cradling his injured arm. He sprinted the last few yards and plunged into the sparse brush, rolling behind a small oak tree just as a sliver of bark peeled away from its trunk.

Webb hunkered there, the pain intensifying as he applied pressure to his wounded shoulder, trying to stop the bleeding. The tree trunk offered little protection unless he stood. Holding onto the rough bark, he pulled himself erect with his left arm.

What happened to the others? Had there been more shots? He didn't know; he hadn't heard the first ones. But another *thunk* came as something hit a nearby tree. An unfamiliar, coppery scent filled his nostrils. It took a few minutes to recognize it as his own blood, possibly because of the stronger odor wafting upward from his urine-soaked slacks.

He dug into a pocket for his cell phone. It slipped from his blood-soaked fingers and skittered into the brush.

Gritting his teeth against the pain, he finally summoned enough courage to peer around the tree trunk. Joseph Dimitrio sprawled on the green, looking like he might have dressed for the Fourth of July: blue pants and white polo shirt decorated with a wide red splotch.

Roberto Perez, a slender, wiry man, crawled toward the sand trap between Webb and the green, ten or twelve yards to Webb's right. Perez pulled himself by his arms, dragging one leg. Red streaks smudged his white golf slacks. He needed help, but Webb couldn't will his legs to move.

Jim. Where was Jim Keyes? He had been on the far side of the green, and beyond him was a grove of trees—the only place the shots could be coming from. *Where are you, buddy?*

Keyes would have to cross most of the open green to get to the rough where Webb hid. Maybe he was down, like Dimitrio. Webb squinted, visually searching for his friend.

A flutter of motion by the golf cart, parked on Webb's side of the fairway, caught his attention. Jim Keyes. How had he made it to this side of the green? Was he trying to hide behind the cart? Or get in it and leave?

Keyes jerked. Had he been shot? No, the sound was metal against metal again, probably the golf cart, and Keyes was running hard toward Webb. He slid down the last few feet of the slope, into the brush.

A solid *thunk* sounded near Webb's ear. He drew his head back. Pressing his body against the trunk, he closed his eyes and whispered the words to prayers he hadn't uttered since childhood. He suspected God would probably hear him about as well as Webb remembered them.

Anchored by fear, he stood on tiptoe, trying to elongate his body to fit behind the slender tree trunk. He waited there for the next shot to finish Keyes. It didn't come. Webb edged his head out from the oak for a better view. Perez had rolled into the sand trap and wedged his small frame under the three-foot-high lip. Was he out of the shooter's view? And where was Keyes now?

Webb spotted his phone, just under the edge of a bush, about four feet away. Too far. He'd never be able to reach it.

A piece of wood splintered from a tree limb in front of him. He jerked his head back and heard a grunt from the brushy area to his right. Had the killer moved? Was he close to them now, letting out an involuntary noise when a tree branch unexpectedly hit him in the face? He might be stalking them, coming to finish them off, his footsteps as silent as his shots.

The oak wouldn't protect Webb from a side attack. He pressed his body closer to it, anyway, the bark making indentations in his skin. He had nowhere else to go, and he couldn't be sure the shooter had moved.

Minutes ticked away. Nothing—not even the birds or small animals—emitted a sound. The pain in Webb's shoulder screamed at him to get help. His polo shirt, sticky with blood, stuck to his chest, and the wet golf slacks clung to his thighs. He applied more pressure to the wound as he waited and listened. Silence settled over the area surrounding the green. Where was the shooter?

Distant voices came to Webb—golfers on other greens and fairways. The only other sound was his own rasping breath. He concentrated on drawing air deep into his lungs, then letting it out.

"Jim?" Webb finally called, his voice soft, when he could no longer endure the silence. "Where are you?"

There was no response. Maybe Keyes had made it deeper into the rough, out of the range of Webb's low voice. Or he was afraid to answer.

A golf ball made a soft *thump* as it landed in the sand trap beside Perez, who let out a startled yelp. The next group of golfers had teed off on the sixteenth and were coming up the fairway. Was the killer still in position, waiting for them, too?

The voices were louder now, and the next ball dropped at the end of the green. The golfers were somewhere in the middle of the fairway, past the dogleg. Perez shouted at them to stay back; there was a shooter waiting to ambush them. Did they hear him, or understand what he was saying? Their voices got louder. Maybe they'd glimpsed Perez, his leg resting on a red patch of sand in the trap, or looked toward the green and seen the red-white-and-blue mound of Joseph Dimitrio.

"What the hell is going on?" one of the golfers asked, as he pulled out his cell phone. Webb didn't answer; his thoughts else-where. Where was the killer? Gone, or taking aim at one of the new arrivals?

Webb stayed behind the tree.

Haunted by the Innocent - Chapter 2

Dee Callender didn't know about the shooting at Emerald Creek. Her cell phone was off, and her sole objective that Saturday morning was to beat Dave Wheeler at racquetball. Pushing off her long legs, she lunged, stretching low for the ball. She connected, already turning the racquet as she calculated the spin needed to ricochet the ball off the side wall.

Dave, his body relaxing into a premature victory, grunted in surprise and charged across the court, reaching for the ball. He missed by inches.

"Game!" Dee grinned. "No power drink this morning, Detective Wheeler?"

"That was a sneaky move."

"Not sneaky. Smart. And you showed me how to do it."

"Okay. I'll give you this one. Good game. Meet you out front?" He touched his racquet to hers as he wiped beads of sweat from his forehead.

Dee headed for the showers. It was going to be a great day: Racquetball with her best friend, then an afternoon with her brother Sam and his family, followed by a few hours out at the firing range with her Sig Sauer.

She didn't spend much time in the locker room. After years in the military and law enforcement, she could shower, dress, and be out the door in fifteen minutes. She kept her chocolate-brown hair short, and the style suited her. It was easy to manage, though she was due for a trim.

Dave joined her at a bench near the door, his dark hair still damp from the shower. He smiled as she approached, filling her with a warm surge of affection. They'd been friends even before she'd become a cop, and he'd never let her down. She trusted him more than anybody she knew, maybe even more than her brother. Not that she couldn't trust Sam; they'd just drifted apart during his drinking years, and, while she loved him, he hadn't been sober long enough to rekindle the closeness of their childhood.

But he, his wife, Laura, and their two young sons, Eric and Jamie, were the only family she had in Sacramento. Last year, she'd formed a close attachment to Sarah Wagner, Laura's cousin, but Sarah was in New York now, going to a design school, and Dee didn't know when she'd be back.

Dave opened the front door, and they walked out into the bright October morning, a typical day for Sacramento. The temperature had stayed in the low to mid-seventies, and the beginning of the rainy season—if they had one this year—was weeks away. The state was in a drought, and the fire season had been—and continued to be—a bad one. A dark smudge against the eastern sky and a faint whiff of smoke told her the latest blaze wasn't out.

"Your cousin's coming tonight?" Dee asked Dave.

"This morning. Eleven twenty-three flight."

He slowed a little, and Dee glanced at his face. "You don't seem very happy about it."

"It's just—I don't know him very well. He says he's here on business and came a few days early, so we could spend some time together, reconnecting."

"What kind of business?"

"I don't know. I didn't ask. Monkey business, if he's anything like I remember. Would you mind coming over tomorrow? I tried to get it across to him, in a nice way, that—"

"Of course you did. You're so good at that sort of thing." Dee took a swig from her water bottle.

"Hey, I can bullshit with the best of them when I have to. I'm a detective, after all. Anyway, I suggested that a weekend is a long time to spend with somebody you don't know, you never felt connected to in the first place, and didn't like, so—"

Dee's laugh spewed water onto the front of her shirt, and she swiped at it with one hand. "I see what you mean. Very smooth,

Detective Wheeler. Maybe you'd better sign up for some more of those bullshit classes."

"What I actually said to him was that we wouldn't have much to talk about for an entire weekend. Then he suggested we get together with some of my friends—"

"Oh, that's where the B.S. came in. You told him you had friends."

He grinned, his eyes sparkling. "No, I told him I didn't have any because my insecure, needy fellow detective keeps driving them off. Do you think you can come over tomorrow? I'll order pizza."

Their shoes crunched red maple leaves. The tree still had most of its foliage, as did the birch trees just beyond it. But those, too, had dropped a few leaves, part of the yellow-gold mounds around the concrete benches.

"How can I resist," she asked, "now that you've dangled a mysterious cousin in front of me? And I'm always good for pizza, as long as you have some cabernet."

"Cabernet? With pizza?" He gave a slow head shake, as though he couldn't quite believe what he'd just heard. "Cold beer, that's all you get. It's just wrong to have wine with—"

"Well, there's a sight for sore eyes." The middle-aged woman, short with curly, iron-gray hair, waddled to a stop in front of them, her head cocked to one side. "A brother and sister spending time together. You don't see much of that these days." She smelled faintly of lavender.

Dave grinned, a mischievous glint in his eyes. They both had lean frames, long legs, dark hair and eyes, and had often been mistaken for siblings. But Dave's hair was curlier, with a reddish tint in sunlight—though you couldn't see it now, with his hair damp. Their eyes were a different shade of brown. Dave always described Dee's as "the color of old copper."

"No, ma'am, you surely don't," he said, reverting to his childhood Texas drawl. "And it's hard to squeeze in the time. But I make an extra effort to give Sis here a few hours once in a while." He winked at the woman and leaned toward her ear, lowering his voice. "She doesn't get many dates, you know, and this gets her out of the house for a while. Kind of makes up for the fact that Mom always liked me best."

Dee smiled, brushing a damp strand of hair away from his eye. "That's just 'cause you're so purty, big brother. She always thought you were a girl. Remember how she used to fasten a bow into those curls?" She turned to the woman. "But it's okay. It kind of evens out 'cause Daddy likes me best. He appreciates brains more than looks."

Dave couldn't keep a straight face, and Dee burst out laughing. The befuddled woman stared at them, a puzzled frown wrinkling her forehead. They ducked their heads and moved on.

"Sis?" Dee said. "Sis? If you were my brother, I'd have strangled you with your diaper. Or bludgeoned you with your baby bottle. Or..." He didn't respond. She waved a hand in front of his eyes. "Come in, Dave, from wherever you are."

"Huh? Oh, sorry, Dee. I was wondering how I'm going to manage a weekend with Frank. He has no sense of humor."

"Are you sure he's related?"

"Pretty sure. I can't imagine Aunt Lynn fooling around, and Frank looks an awful lot like Uncle Bob. Come to think of it, Uncle Bob never got a joke, either."

Her steps slowed. "Want to stop somewhere for coffee?"

He hesitated, then shook his head. "I'd better head out to the airport. I'll order the pizza around six tomorrow. No, make that five. I can't do it any earlier, can I? You're on your way to Sam's place?"

"No, I'm meeting him and Laura at Emerald Creek. They're at the clubhouse, having an early lunch before we take the kids to a pumpkin patch out that way. One of those places with a maze. Laura thought it would be a good idea to get some food in the boys first."

"Sounds better than my plans. Running around a cornfield with Eric and Jamie would be fun. I've never done that. Tell them I said Hi."

"Bob Walters and I are planning to get together at the firing range later this afternoon. Want to tag along?"

"Not with my cousin, unless I can figure out some way to ditch him. Or maybe use him for target practice. But won't Bob mind?"

Dee shot a glance at him. "Why should he care?"

He lifted his shoulders a little, a kind of half-shrug. "I just figured there must be a reason you two are going out there so often."

Dee stopped so abruptly, Dave had taken a step ahead of her. He turned. "Did I say something wrong?"

"You think because Bob and I go out to the firing range, we have something going? I spend a lot of time with you, too, but you don't think anything of it. I'm just trying to improve my shooting. So is Bob. And if he has a thing for somebody, it's probably Mandy, in Dispatch."

"He's in C.S.I. He doesn't even have to shoot."

"He does it for fun. He likes trying to beat me."

"Never going to happen. You're already the best shot in the unit. Probably on the force. What are you trying to prove?"

"With a rifle, maybe, but I need to work more with my Sig."

She didn't try to answer the other part of his question, about what she was trying to prove. They'd had that discussion too many times, and he still didn't get it. Unlike her, he'd been a detective for a long time. He'd proven himself. The other men accepted him. They still had misgivings about her. She'd risen too quickly, and she'd heard rumors circulating that she'd slept her way into the job. Dave never noticed the smirks, the knowing glances, the whispered comments. And the only way she knew to change the perceptions was to work longer, harder, and smarter.

At the corner, Dee turned toward the parking garage.

"I'm down the other way," Dave said. "Snagged a space at the curb. Give Sam and Laura my regards."

Her gaze followed him to the intersection, but he didn't look back. His body language alone would have told her he was troubled, even if he hadn't confided in her. She'd definitely be there for pizza the next afternoon. After she stopped to buy a bottle of cabernet.

She walked to the parking garage, got into her department-issued white Chevy Caprice, and headed south on Highway 99, toward Emerald Creek Golf Course and a fun-filled afternoon with her family.

◆◆◆

Snowbound is the second book in the Wagner-Callender mystery series. The first book is *Love, Murder and a Good Bottle of Wine.* The third is *Haunted by The Innocent.* All are available on Amazon. To find them, go to Amazon books, type in *Chris Phipps*, and click on the book.

Word-of-mouth is crucial for any author to be successful. If you enjoyed this book, please consider leaving a review on Amazon. Even a line or two would be a tremendous help.

My website has more information about my books, a little about my life, and a few short stories. The best way to contact me is by email at chris@chrisphipps.com.

Are you reading *Snowbound* in your book club, or planning to? If so, the next pages offer some questions to help you get started.

Suggested book club questions:

1. Sarah went from California to New York partially to get away from her family and her dependence on them. She wanted to learn to "stand on her own two feet." Do you think she succeeded?

2. Sarah's past has left her with a deep distrust of men. Will her experiences in *Snowbound* deepen that distrust or alleviate it somewhat? Why?

3. How realistic was the characterization? Would you want to meet any of the characters? Did you like them? Hate them?

4. Did your opinions of any of the characters change through the course of the book?

5. Did Sarah's actions seem plausible? Did they surprise you?

6. In the past, Sarah's strongest relationships have been with women and her two young nephews. How has that changed in *Snowbound*?

7. At what point did you suspect that Greg was not Lottie's father? What did you think about their relationship at that point?

8. Can you "see" the setting? The cabin itself? The snowy woods? The shed?

9. Did you read *Love, Murder and a Good Bottle of Wine*? If so, did the author carry the threads of that story into this one in a satisfactory manner? If you didn't read the first book, did you get a good sense of Sarah's back story in *Snowbound*?

10. What themes did the book touch on? Did they give you deeper insight into the subject? Were they necessary to the story?

11. Does Sarah change over the course of the book? If so, in what ways?

12. Which character did you empathize with most? Which did you find the most interesting? The most amusing? The most surprising?

13. What do you think is happening between Sarah and her father?

14. In both *Love, Murder and a Good Bottle of Wine* and *Snowbound*, Sarah feels compelled to protect small children. Do you think that instinct is related to the death of her little brother, Richie, when Sarah was herself a small child?

15. Were there any points where you would have taken a different course of action than that taken by Sarah?

16. At what point did you begin to unravel the mystery of Tracy's disappearance? If not until the end, was it satisfying? Did it make sense? Fit all the clues?

17. What surprised you the most about the book?

18. Do you think Sarah will visit Lottie and Gracie in the future? Will she go back to upstate New York?

19. If you could pick a character to date, who would it be?

20. What passages did you most enjoy? Perhaps there's a some dialog that's funny or poignant or that encapsulates a

character? Perhaps there's the action of a specific character, or a satisfying bit of description?

Do you have a question for the author?
Email chris@chrisphipps.com

Made in the USA
San Bernardino, CA
29 October 2018